M.L Augee

Proceedings of the Linnean Society of New South Wales

Volume 137

M.L Augee

Proceedings of the Linnean Society of New South Wales
Volume 137

ISBN/EAN: 9783741168703

Manufactured in Europe, USA, Canada, Australia, Japa

Cover: Foto ©Andreas Hilbeck / pixelio.de

Manufactured and distributed by brebook publishing software
(www.brebook.com)

M.L Augee

Proceedings of the Linnean Society of New South Wales

THE LINNEAN SOCIETY OF
NEW SOUTH WALES
ISSN 1839-7263

Founded 1874
Incorporated 1884

The society exists to promote the cultivation and study of the science of natural history in all branches. The Society awards research grants each year in the fields of Life Sciences (the Joyce Vickery fund) and Earth Sciences (the Betty Mayne fund), offers annually a Linnean Macleay Fellowship for research, and publishes the *Proceedings*. It holds field excursions and scientific meetings including the biennial Sir William Macleay Memorial Lecture delivered by a person eminent in some branch of natural science.

mbership enquiries should be addressed in the first instance to the Secretary. Candidates for ction to the Society must be recommended by two members. The present annual membership is \$45 per annum.

pers are published at http://escholarship.library.usyd.edu.au/journals/index.php/LIN and access ree of charge. All papers published in a calendar year comprise a volume. Annual volumes are ilable to any institution on CD free of charge. Please notify the Secretary to receive one. "Print demand" hardcopies are available from eScholarship.

ck issues from Volume 1 are available free of charge at www.biodiversitylibrary.org/title/6525.

OFFICERS and COUNCIL 2015

esident: R.J. King
ce-presidents: M. Gray, D. Keith, D.R. Murray
easurer: I.G. Percival
cretary: J-C. Herremans
uncil: M.L. Augee, J.P. Barkas, M. Cotton, E. Gorrod, M.R. Gray, J-C. Herremans, D. Keith, J. King, H.A. Martin, D.R. Murray, P.J. Myerscough, I.G. Percival, J. Pickett, H.M. Smith, B. elch and K.L. Wilson
litor: M.L. Augee
sistant Editor: B. Welch
ditors: Phil Williams Carbonara

e postal address of the Society is P.O. Box 82, Kingsford, N.S.W. 2032, Australia.
lephone and Fax   +61 2 9662 6196.
nail: linnsoc@iinet.net.au
ome page: www.linneansocietynsw.org.au/

Linnean Society of New South Wales

ver motif: Illustration of Science House from original 1932 booklet.

PROCEEDINGS
of the

LINNEAN SOCIETY

of
NEW SOUTH WALES

For information about the Linnean Society of New South Wales. its publications and
activities, see the Society's homepage
www.linneansocietynsw.org.au

VOLUME 137
December 2015

Spawning of Threatened Barred Galaxias, *Galaxias fuscus* (Teleostei: Galaxiidae)

DANIEL J. STOESSEL, TARMO A. RAADIK AND RENAE M. AYRES

Department of Environment, Land, Water and Planning, Arthur Rylah Institute for Environmental Research, 123 Brown Street, Heidelberg, Victoria, 3084 Australia

Published on 27 April 2015 at http://escholarship.library.usyd.edu.au/journals/index.php/LIN

Stoessel, D.J., Raadik, T.A. and Ayres, R.M. (2015). Spawning of threatened barred galaxias, *Galaxias fuscus* (Teleostei: Galaxiidae). *Proceedings of the Linnean Society of New South Wales* **137**, 1-6.

Barred galaxias *Galaxias fuscus* is an endangered freshwater fish endemic to south-eastern Australia. Little is known of the species' ecology. We investigated spawning biology of *G. fuscus* in three headwater streams and found spawning to occur mid-August to late September when photoperiod was 10 h 39 min – 12 h 25 min. Spawning sites were in fresh (range 35.3 – 56.6 EC, mean 44.7 EC), slightly acidic (range 5.7 – 7.1 pH, mean 5.9 pH), moderate to fast flowing (range 0.4 – 2.0 m/s, mean 1.0 m/s), shallow (range 70 – 310 mm, mean 174 mm), well oxygenated (range 10.8 – 12.4 mg/l, mean 11.3mg/l), clear (range 1.2 – 6.3 NTU, mean 3.8 NTU), cool waters (range 8.4 – 10 °C, mean 9.1°C) immediately upstream of pools. Multi-layered clusters of up to 218 eggs were generally adhered close to the stream bed on the downstream side of cobbles greater than 180 mm diameter.

Manuscript received 14 September 2014, accepted for publication 22 April 2015.

Keywords: Freshwater, life history, nest site, reproduction

INTRODUCTION

The barred galaxias, *Galaxias fuscus* is a small (maximum 160 mm TL, 40 g), endemic, scaleless, non-migratory fish (Raadik et al. 1996). Remnant populations are restricted to 12 geographically isolated headwater streams above 400 m in elevation in the Goulburn River system in south-eastern Australia (Raadik et al. 1996; Koehn and Raadik 1995; Allen et al. 2003). This range is likely to represent fragmentation of a much wider and continuous historic distribution within the catchment (Raadik et al. 2010). Predation by alien rainbow trout (*Oncorhynchus mykiss*) and brown trout (*Salmo trutta*) (Salmonidae) is the primary cause of the decline (Raadik et al. 1996; Raadik et al. 2010). Changed water regimes, genetic isolation and deleterious stochastic events including wildfire and drought also represent significant long-term threats to *G. fuscus* (Raadik et al. 2010). The species is listed as Endangered under the Commonwealth Environment Protection and Biodiversity Conservation Act 1999 (EPBC Act) and the Australian and New Zealand Environment Conservation Council (ANZECC),

and as Critically Endangered Internationally (Wager 1996).

Knowledge of *G. fuscus* biology is limited. Preliminary observations suggest that spawning occurs in late winter-early spring, and is likely to be triggered by increasing day length and water temperature (Raadik 1993, Shirley and Raadik 1997). Fecundity is low (~500 ova), and eggs are adhesive and large (~2.2 mm; Raadik 1993). Limited observations of two nest sites, suggest multi-layered clusters of eggs are laid underneath and on the downstream side of large rocks in fast-flowing, shallow, cold (1 – 5 °C) water (Raadik et al. 2010), and incubation time of eggs is approximately 30 days in water at 7 °C in an aquaria (Raadik, T. unpublished data).

This paper further investigates the spawning of *G. fuscus*, and includes data on habitat, spawning season and site, egg description, incubation period, and description of larvae. The biological information obtained is vital for the preparation of management strategies to maintain, enhance or restore processes fundamental to survival, reproduction and viability of remnant populations.

MATERIALS AND METHOD

Study area and sites

The study was conducted in three geographically closely associated headwater streams (S Creek, Kalatha Creek and Luke Creek) of the Goulburn River in south-eastern Australia (37° 28′ S, 145° 28′ E) (Fig. 1). Considerable bushfires in the region in February 2009, had resulted in varying loss of riparian cover. At the S Creek reach riparian vegetation and tree canopy cover was non-existent, while at Luke Creek approximately 50 % of tree canopy cover remained, and at Kalatha Creek the area remained unburnt. Coarse sand within the stream channel was most prevalent in the S Creek study reach and least noticeable at Kalatha Creek.

G. fuscus was the only fish species present in the study reaches (Raadik et al. 2010), which were at elevations above 400 m (Australian Height Datum) and located 1 – 2 km upstream of large natural instream barriers which had prevented the headwater colonisation by other native fish and, importantly, by alien salmonids. The freshwater streams were

clear, well-oxygenated, cool, narrow (1 – 4 m wide), had moderate to fast flow and alternating sequences of pools and riffles. The substrate was typically composed of boulder, pebble, gravel and sand (Raadik et al. 1996).

Within each reach, a 100 m long monitoring site was established and surveyed repeatedly during the study to assess for the presence of reproductively ripe females. A second site, 200 m in length, and located immediately upstream was later searched for newly laid eggs.

Monitoring of fish spawning condition

G. fuscus were surveyed weekly from July to September 2010 (mid austral winter to early austral spring) at the monitoring site in each study reach, using a Smith Root® model LR20B portable electrofishing backpack unit operated at settings of 70 Hz and 500 to 1000 V. Fish caudal fork lengths (mm) and weights (g) were recorded. Females were determined as ripe, when ovaries filled >90 % of the body cavity, eggs were large, body cavity clearly distended, and eggs could be extruded by gentle pressure on the body wall. Spawning vent in males and females in addition was enlarged and extended (see Pollard 1972). All fish collected were released once processed.

Spawning habitat search

Once ripe females were no longer observed at all monitoring sites, searches to locate eggs were conducted. All instream structures, including timber debris, undercut banks, and closely associated riparian habitat, were examined for the presence of eggs. Where eggs were found, they were left instream and their location marked with flagging tape so the site could be avoided during kick sampling (see below).

A drift net (500 mm mouth opening, 150 µm mesh) was deployed downstream of each site within each stream during the search period to capture drifting eggs or newly hatched larvae. The contents of the drift net were sorted at the completion of the search period. In addition, substrate kick sampling was undertaken over multiple, randomly chosen stream sections (1 x 1 m) at each site to search for eggs potentially deposited on sand or gravel beds. This involved gently disturbing an area of stream bed immediately upstream of a dip-net (250 x 300 x 20 mm with a 400 mm long x 1 mm multifilament mesh bag attached) for approximately 10 seconds.

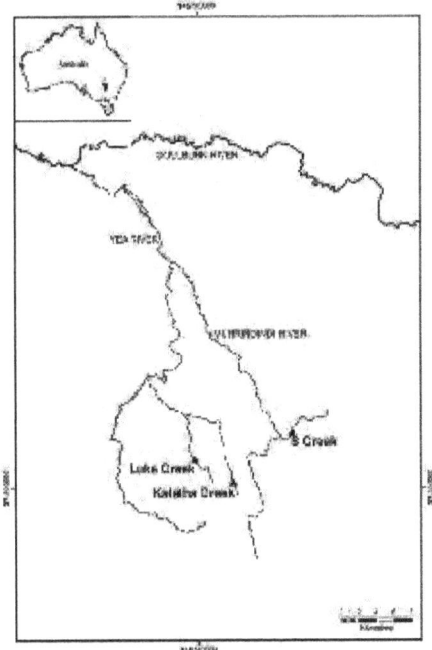

Figure 1. Location of barred galaxias study sites in Ka-laltha, Luke and S creeks in south-eastern Australia.

2

Proc. Linn. Soc. N.S.W., 137, 2015

Where eggs were located, water depth, flow (Hydrological Services Current Meter Counter Model CMC-20), the type and dimensions of the spawning structure, and the characteristics of the placement of eggs on the structure, were recorded. In addition, water electrical conductivity (EC standardized to 25°C μS.cm^{-1}), pH, dissolved oxygen (mg/L and % saturation), turbidity (NTU) and temperature (°C) were measured in situ at a maximum depth of 0.2 m below the water surface during each spawning condition monitoring event, and immediately adjacent to egg nest sites using a TPS 90FL-T Field Lab Analyser.

Egg Incubation

On completion of recording habitat attributes at nest sites, eggs were transferred to aquarium facilities and placed into indoor 20 l aquaria. Each aquarium contained a Perspex holder housing eight egg hatching baskets (see Bacher and O'Brien 1989), into each of which was placed a single batch of eggs. Aquarium water was aerated, recirculated and kept chilled to between 9.5 – 10.5 °C. Hatching baskets were removed each day from aquaria, placed under a microscope and eggs inspected for fungus. Any found to be infected or killed by fungus were removed using sterilised tweezers. The presence and degree of embryo development was visually inspected and the time and date of any hatching recorded. Following inspection all hatching baskets (along with eggs) were placed into a salt solution (10 g/l) for 20 min to minimise the possibility of fungus infection, before being returned to the aquarium.

RESULTS

Spent female *G. fuscus* were present at all sites in surveys conducted 21 Sept 2010. Subsequent egg searches undertaken 28 – 30 Sept 2010, located 13 egg clusters: four in Kalatha Creek (the least sediment and fire affected site); eight in Luke Creek (the moderately sediment and fire affected site); and one in S Creek (the most severely sediment and fire affected site). Individual clusters were adhered to the downstream side of cobbles (115 – 280 mm, mean 180 mm) close to the stream bed, in riffles immediately upstream of pools, in moderately to fast flowing (0.4 – 1.9 m/s, mean 1.0 m/s, shallow (20 – 310 mm, mean 174 mm), cool (8.4 – 10.0 °C, mean 9.1 °C), fresh (35.3 – 56.6 EC, mean 44.7 EC), slightly acidic (5.7 – 7.1 pH, mean 5.9 pH), well oxygenated clear water (10.8 – 12.4 mg/l, mean 11.3 mg/l). Clusters were composed of up to 218 (mean = 78) eggs, were

multi-layered (up to three layers), and coated with sand and fine gravel particles. Eggs were not found attached to timber debris, aquatic plants, or moss. No eggs or larvae were collected in kick samples or larval drift nets.

Water-hardened, fertilised eggs were spherical, approximately 3 – 4 mm in diameter, adhesive, demersal, and transparent to relatively opaque. Embryos in approximately half of the egg clusters from Kalatha Creek, and the majority from Luke Creek, were sufficiently developed to clearly distinguish their eyes when visually inspected in the field. Embryos in the egg cluster from S Creek were fully developed and hatched within 30 minutes of being located and removed from the creek 29 Sept 2010.

Eggs from Luke Creek placed into the aquarium facility hatched 6 Oct 2010 –11 Nov 2010, those from Kalatha Creek 1 – 17 Nov 2010, and those from S Creek 29 Sept 2010 – 5 Oct 2010. Ninety percent of eggs hatched within 44 days of being brought into captivity, with the last eggs hatching by day 48.

Newly hatched larvae were transparent, 8.4 – 9.7 mm in length (mean 9.0 mm, n = 10) and were active swimmers which utilised the entire water column excluding times when they were seen to periodically lay motionless on the bottom of aquaria in the days immediately after hatching. Yolk sac (1.5 – 2.0 mm in diameter) absorption was generally complete within 3 days of hatching, and feeding commenced within 24 – 48 hours of hatching. Larvae appeared to use the entire water column for feeding, were only limited by gape size as to what they were feeding, and readily switched from one feed to another.

DISCUSSION

This study confirms that *G. fuscus* are a demersal egg layer, preferring to use nest sites on cobble substrates located in moderate to fast flowing water. Eggs are relatively large and generally laid in a tight multi-layered cluster, spawning occurs during late austral winter to early spring, and the time of larval development is relatively long. As the only other nest sites located (*n*=2) prior to this study were found attached to boulders (Raadik, T. unpublished; Raadik 1993; Raadik et al. 1996; Raadik et al. 2010), a substrate size that was lacking in our study streams, the combined findings suggest that *G. fuscus* prefer to lay eggs on larger in stream rock substrates, and to avoid pebbles and gravels.

Despite the average fecundity of mature females suggested as being ~500 (Raadik et al. 1996), individual nest sites found in this study had an average of ~80 eggs present. This suggests that females may spawn at multiple sites, laying many, small clusters of eggs, thereby reducing the risk of potential loss of all eggs deposited if laid in a single cluster. This strategy is uncommon in the Galaxiidae, having only been documented in the flat-headed galaxias (*Galaxias rostratus*) (Llewellyn 1971), which is comparatively highly fecund, and lays batches of eggs over an extended spawning period of up to a month (Llewellyn 1971). The spawning period of *G. fuscus* is alternatively likely to be relatively short, as we found the proportion of mature/ripe females declined rapidly once spawning began at individual reaches. Therefore if *G. fuscus* undertake spawning at multiple nest-sites, it is likely that this occurs over a period of days, rather than weeks.

Eggs collected from the wild took a maximum of 48 days to hatch in captivity. Assuming eggs which hatched last were spawned just prior to collection, this finding extends the suggested incubation period by at least 18 days (Raadik 1993; Raadik et al. 1996; Raadik et al. 2010). However, a strong relationship between development of larvae and ambient water temperature exists for many fish species (Pauly and Pullin 1988; Pepin 1991; Pepin et al. 1997), and therefore annual differences in stream temperatures would likely alter the incubation period of eggs of the species. Back-calculating by the egg incubation period of 30 – 48 days suggests a spawning period for *G. fuscus* lasting from about mid-August to the end of September (late austral winter to early spring).

Differences in the stage of maturation, and in the subsequent date of hatching, of eggs between the three study streams indicates spawning was not synchronous across the populations within a small geographic area (~10 km²). The S Creek population probably spawned several weeks prior to the Luke Creek population, which in turn spawned one to two weeks earlier than the population in Kalatha Creek. Similar variation in the time of breeding in other galaxiid species has been attributed to water temperature (O'Connor and Koehn 1991; Allibone and Townsend 1997) and changes in stream levels (Moore et al. 1999). However, environmental cues that initiate spawning were not obvious in this study and could not be directly associated with changes in water flow or water temperature, although spawning did occur at a time when water temperature was increasing. Photoperiod may also be influential (Shirley and Raadik 1997). However, the lack of synchronicity across the populations in the current study suggests additional stimuli could be responsible. As fire had recently removed much of the riparian vegetation

and over-storey canopy cover at S Creek, and to a lesser extent at Luke Creek, it is possible that such differences may be attributed to increases in light intensity, and resident fish perception of photoperiod at these sites. Similar changes in the time of spawning as a consequence of photoperiod alterations, often independent of temperature, have also been shown in other fish species (see Björrnsson et al. 1998; Davies and Bromage 2002; Elliot et al. 2003; Howell et al. 2003).

Nest-site characteristics of *G. fuscus* are similar to that described for the ornate mountain galaxias (*G. ornatus*; see Raadik 2014). Both lay a small number of relatively large, adhesive eggs in a protected site, usually on rock (O'Connor and Koehn 1991). In addition, both barred and ornate mountain galaxias lay their eggs predominantly in riffles, where the surrounding water is relatively fast-flowing and well-oxygenated (O'Connor and Koehn 1991). Adhering eggs to large stone substrates can be advantageous as the substrate is relatively stable and thus eggs remain within the area chosen by the parent. However, demersal egg-laying may result in eggs being susceptible to environmental disturbances to streambeds, such as siltation (Growns 2004). In addition, reduced water levels during the breeding season may expose spawning habitat or eggs at nest sites, thereby limiting spawning habitat availability and reducing egg survival and overall spawning success (Moore et al. 1999). Similarly, post-fire sedimentation can reduce the availability of spawning habitat thus limiting spawning potential, or smother eggs at nest sites causing egg mortality and decline in spawning success (O'Connor and Koehn 1991).

The study reconfirms the importance of larger loose rock substrates for *G. fuscus* reproduction (spawning), and highlights that the loss of such habitat could result in the decline of remnant populations of the species. Similar loss of habitat has been implicated in the decline of a number of fish species worldwide (see Scott and Helfman 2001; Pillar et al. 2004; Wyatt et al. 2010). Much of this habitat has been lost due to anthropogenic degradation of riverine habitats, primarily through siltation. Rehabilitation of streams is today common, however, the strategy is often tailored towards improving habitat of larger, auspicious, recreational fish species. To date, little augmentation of suitable substrates for smaller bodied, demersal egg laying freshwater fish has occurred. The introduction of rock substrates to streams affected by siltation may be of particularly value where threatened demersal egg laying fish exist, and where remediation works (such as fencing and replanting of the riparian zone) has occurred.

4

ACKNOWLEDGEMENTS

Funding for this study was received from the 'Rebuilding Together' program of the Victorian and Commonwealth governments Statewide Bushfire Recovery Plan, (October 2009). We thank Mike Nicol, Lauren Dodd, Dean Hartwell, Joanne Kearns, Tony Cable and Scott Raymond from the Arthur Rylah Institute (ARI) of the Department of Environment and Primary Industries Victoria, for assistance with field and laboratory work, Graeme Seppings (a volunteer) for providing field and laboratory assistance, and John Koehn (ARI) and three anonymous reviewers for comments on earlier versions of the manuscript. This study was conducted under Fisheries Victoria Research Permit RP827, Victorian Flora and Fauna Guarantee Act research permit 10005451 and animal ethics permit 10/20 (ARI Animal Ethics Committee).

REFERENCES

Allen, G.R., Midgley, S.H. and Allen, M. (2003). 'Field guide to the freshwater fishes of Australia, revised edition'. (CSIRO Publishing: Collingwood).

Allibone, R.M. and Townsend, C.R. (1997). Reproductive biology, species status and taxonomic relationships of four recently discovered galaxiid fishes in a New Zealand river. *Journal of Fish Biology* **51**, 1247–1261.

Bacher, G.J. and O'Brien, T.A. (1989). Salinity tolerance of the eggs and larvae of the Australian grayling *Prototroctes maraena* Günther (Salmoniforms: Prototroctidae). *Australian Journal of Marine and Freshwater Research* **40**, 227–230.

Björrnsson, B.T., Halldórsson, Ó., Haux, C., Norberg, B. and Brown, C.L. (1998). Photoperiod control of sexual maturation of the Atlantic halibut (*Hippoglossus hippoglossus*): plasma thyroid hormone and calcium levels. *Aquaculture* **166**, 117–140.

Davies, B. and Bromage, N. (2002). The effects of fluctuating seasonal and constant water temperatures on the photoperiodic advancement of reproduction in female rainbow trout, *Oncorhynchus mykiss*. *Aquaculture* **205**, 183–200.

Elliot, J.A.K., Bromage, N.R. and Springate, J.R.C. (2003). Changes in reproductive function of three strains of rainbow trout exposed to constant and seasonally-changing light cycles. *Aquaculture* **43**, 23–34.

Growns, I. (2004). A numerical classification of reproductive guilds of the freshwater fishes of south-eastern Australia and their application to river management. *Fisheries Management and Ecology* **11**, 369–377.

Howell, R.A., Berlinsky, D.L. and Bradley, T.M. (2003). The effects of photoperiod manipulation on the reproduction of black sea bass, *Centropristis striata*. *Aquaculture* **218**, 651–669.

Koehn, J. and Raadik, T. (1995). 'Flora and Fauna Guarantee, barred galaxias *Galaxias olidus var. fuscus*. Action Statement No. 65'. (Department of Conservation and Natural Resources: Melbourne).

Llewellyn, L.C. (1971). Breeding studies on the freshwater forage fish of the Murray-Darling River system. *The Fisherman* **3**, 1–12.

Moore, S.J., Allibone, R.M. and Townsend, C.R. (1999). Spawning site selection by two galaxiid fishes, *Galaxias anomalus* and *G. depressiceps* in tributaries of the Taieri River, south island, New Zealand. *New Zealand Journal of Marine and Freshwater Research* **33**, 129–139.

O'Connor, W.G. and Koehn, J.D. (1991). Spawning of the mountain galaxias, *Galaxias olidus* Günther, in Bruces Creek, Victoria. *Proceedings of the Royal Society of Victoria* **103**, 113–123.

Pauly, D. and Pullin, R.S.V. (1988). Hatching time in spherical, pelagic, marine fish eggs in response to temperature and egg size. *Environmental Biology of Fishes* **22**, 261–271.

Pepin, P. (1991). Effect of temperature and size on development, mortality, and survival rates of the pelagic early life history stages of marine fish. *Canadian Journal of Fisheries and Aquatic Sciences* **48**, 503–518.

Pepin, P., Orr, O.C. and Anderson J.T. (1997). Time to hatch and larval size in relation to temperature and egg size in Atlantic cod (*Gadus morhua*). *Canadian Journal of Fisheries and Aquatic Sciences* **54**, 2–10.

Pillar, K.R., Bart H.L. and Tipton, J.A. (2004). Decline of the frecklebelly madtom in the Pearl River based on contemporary and historical surveys. *Transactions of the American Fisheries Society* **133**, 1004–1013.

Pollard, D.A. (1972). The biology of the landlocked form of the normally catadromous salmoniform fish *Galaxias maculatus* Jenyns 3. Structure of the gonads. *Australian Journal of Marine and Freshwater Research* **23**, 17–38.

Raadik, T.A. (1993). 'A research recovery plan for the barred galaxias, *Galaxias fuscus* Mack, in south-eastern Australia'. (Department of Conservation and Natural Resources: Melbourne).

Raadik, T.A. (2014). Fifteen from one: a revision of the *Galaxias olidus* Günther, 1866 complex (Teleostei, Galaxiidae) in south-eastern Australia recognises three previously described taxa and describes 12 new species. *Zootaxa* **3898** (1), 1-198.

Raadik, T.A., Saddlier, S.R. and Koehn, J.D. (1996). Threatened fishes of the world: *Galaxias fuscus* Mack, 1936 (Galaxiidae). *Environmental Biology of Fishes* **47**, 108.

Raadik, T.A., Fairbrother, P.S. and Smith, S.J. (2010). 'National recovery plan for the barred galaxias *Galaxias fuscus*'. (Department of Sustainability and Environment, Melbourne).

Scott, M.C. and Helfman, G.S. (2001). Native invasions, homogenization, and the mismeasure of integrity of fish assemblages. *Fisheries* **26**, 6–15.

Shirley, M.J. and Raadik, T.A. (1997). Aspects of the ecology and breeding biology of *Galaxias fuscus* Mack, in the Goulburn River system, Victoria. *Proceedings of the Royal Society of Victoria* **109**, 157–166.

Wager, R. (1996). *Galaxias fuscus*. In: IUCN 2012. IUCN Red List of Threatened Species. Version 2012.2. www.iucnredlist.org. Downloaded on 12 April 2013.

Wyatt, L.H., Baker, A.L. and Berlinsky, D.L. (2010). Effects of sedimentation and periphyton communities on embryonic rainbow smelt, *Osmerus mordax*. *Aquatic Sciences* **72**, 361–369.

A Preliminary Investigation of the Reproductive Biology of the Blind Shark, *Brachaelurus waddi* (Orectolobiformes: Brachaeluridae)

ANNE FOGED[1] AND DAVID MARK POWTER[2, 3]

[1]Department of Bioscience, Aarhus University, Denmark (annefogedpedersen@hotmail.com);
[2]English Language and Foundation Studies Centre, University of Newcastle, Ourimbah 2258, Australia; and
[3]School of Environmental and Life Sciences, University of Newcastle, Australia.

Published on 29 April 2015 at http://escholarship.library.usyd.edu.au/journals/index.php/LIN

Foged, A. and Powter, D.M. (2015). A preliminary investigation of the reproductive biology of the blind shark, *Brachaelurus waddi* (Orectolobiformes: Brachaeluridae). *Proceedings of the Linnean Society of New South Wales* **137**, 7-12.

Although the focus on shark conservation has increased in recent years, small, economically unimportant species are often overlooked. The blind shark, *Brachaelurus waddi*, is endemic to eastern Australia and is commonly encountered in commercial fisheries. However, this is the first study of the species' reproductive biology. Males were sexually mature at 520-540 mm total length (TL) and all females ≥ 563 mm TL were sexually mature. Only the right ovary was functional and two distinct groupings in follicle size indicated that the reproductive cycle is at least biennial. Reproductive output may be smaller than previously suggested, with an average of four pups per gravid female in this study.

Manuscript received 15 June 2014, accepted for publication 22 April 2015.

Keywords: bycatch, conservation, elasmobranch, IUCN Red List, reproduction, sexual maturity

INTRODUCTION

The focus on elasmobranch (sharks, rays and skates) conservation and management is increasing as populations decrease worldwide mainly due to overfishing and other anthropogenic impacts (Peres and Vooren 1991; Stevens et al. 2000; Kyne et al. 2011). Many sharks adopt a K-selected life history strategy and consequently have low rebound potentials (Cortés 2000; Stevens et al. 2000). As predators at or near the highest trophic levels, their removal may have cascading effects on marine ecosystems (Cortés 1999; Stevens et al. 2000). Hence, knowledge of their biology and ecology, especially reproductive strategies, is crucial to elasmobranch conservation and management.

Most studies focus on large species (e.g. Pratt 1979; Mollet et al. 2000; Lucifora et al. 2005), whilst smaller, rare or non-targeted species are often overlooked, although they may be equally important ecologically, and knowledge gaps may hamper effective conservation and fisheries management (Kyne et al. 2011). The blind shark, *Brachaelurus waddi*, is a small (max. 1200 mm TL), cryptic and economically unimportant coastal shark endemic to eastern Australia (Jervis Bay to Moreton Bay; 0-137 m) (Compagno 2002; Last and Stevens 2009; Fig. 1). There are no specific fishing regulations, and catch records are not maintained for blind sharks. However anecdotal reports indicate that they are commonly encountered as bycatch in trap fisheries within their range and, although often released alive, post capture mortality is not known. No previous scientific studies are known and existing knowledge is limited and anecdotal. Despite being listed as "Least Concern" on the IUCN Red List, based mainly on the assumption that the species is common and on the absence of commercial exploitation, the need for research is acknowledged (Kyne and Bennett 2003). This is the first investigation of the reproductive biology of *B. waddi*, and provides important biological data and the foundation for further research.

MATERIALS AND METHODS

Samples were obtained from the bycatch of a commercial trap fishery operating between Killcare (33°32'S, 151°21'E) and Lion Island (33°33'S, 151°19'E), New South Wales, Australia (Fig. 1). A total of 66 sharks (38 males, 28 females) were collected between January and May 2011. Total length (TL) (Compagno 2002) was measured to the nearest 1 mm.

Male size at sexual maturity was estimated utilising three common indices (e.g. Pratt 1979; Peres and Vooren 1991; Walker 2005; Huveneers et al. 2007; Kyne et al. 2011). Inner clasper length (Compagno 2002) was measured to the nearest 1 mm. Clasper calcification status was categorised as uncalcified (soft and flexible), partially calcified (partially hardened) and calcified (fully hardened). The testis index was determined visually and assigned as immature (testes not differentiated from epigonal gland); maturing (partially differentiated); and mature (enlarged and dominating the epigonal gland). The proportion of mature males was determined by logistic regression using maximum likelihood probit analysis (Walker 2005) and the total length at which 50% (TL_{50}) were mature was calculated for each index.

Ovary index and oviducal gland index, both determined visually, were used to determine sexual maturity in females (Walker 2005). Ovaries were categorised as immature (undifferentiated from epigonal gland); maturing (differentiated but lacking vitellogenic follicles); and mature (contained vitellogenic follicles ≥ 2 mm diameter). The oviducal gland was categorised as immature (undifferentiated from the oviduct); maturing (differentiated but lacked visible zonation); or mature (differentiated with visible zonation). However, no immature females were captured.

To assess female ovarian fecundity, the number of vitellogenic ovarian follicles (≥ 2 mm diameter) were recorded and measured to the nearest 1 mm diameter. The temporal size distribution of maturing follicles was tested using a non-parametric Kruskal-Wallis one-way analysis of variance by rank. From the size distribution of maturing follicles, ovarian fecundity was estimated. Uteri were examined for the presence of embryos (measured to the nearest 1 mm), with intact yolk sacs measured to the nearest 1 mm. Uterine fecundity was defined as the total number of uterine eggs or embryos (Peres and Vooren 1991). A non-parametric Spearman's rank correlation was used to investigate whether fecundity was correlated with TL.

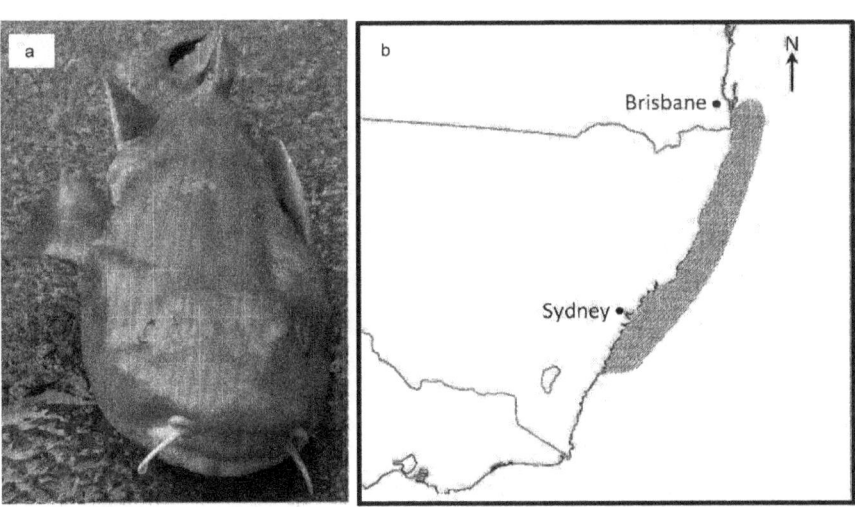

Figure 1. (a) Photograph of *Brachaelurus waddi* and (b) map of distribution (map modified from Geoscience Australia (http://www.ga.gov.au/corporate_data/61755/61755.pdf)).

RESULTS

Males reached sexual maturity (TL_{50}) between 519.9 mm and 542.1 mm TL based on the three indices ($n = 38$, Fig. 2). All females (563 to 720 mm TL; $n = 28$) were mature using both indices. Consequently, size at maturity and at maternity was ≤ 563 mm, as

Of the seven embryos caught in May, three (43%) were male. The uteri of gravid females were fully extended.

There was no significant correlation between the number of follicles ≥ 7 mm diameter and TL in non-gravid females (ovarian fecundity; Spearman's rho = 0.41, $p = 0.05$, $n=24$). Follicle diameter

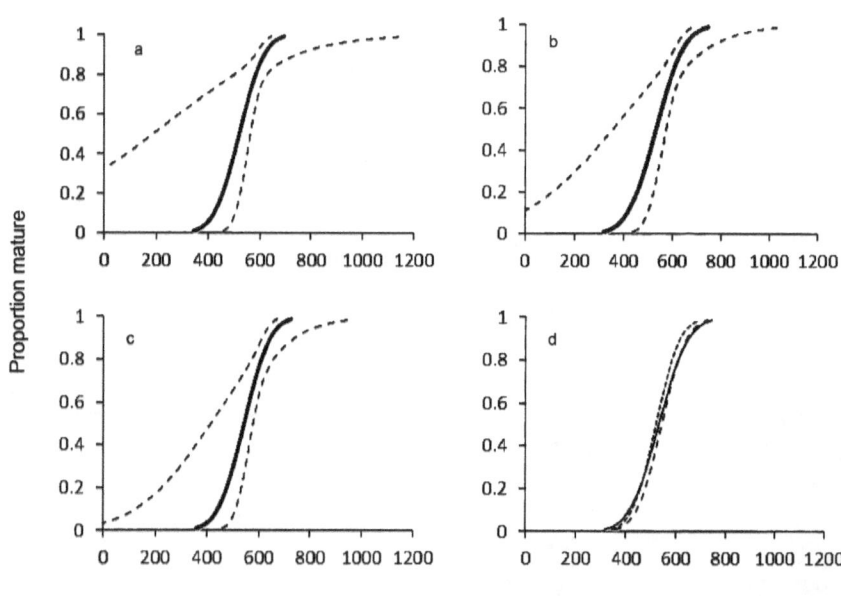

Total length (mm)

Figure 2. Proportion of mature male *Brachaelurus waddi*, given as (a) clasper length, (b) clasper calcification, (c) testes index (± 95% confidence interval; dashed line) and (d) combined (clasper length=dotted line; clasper calcification=solid line; testes index=dashed line).

the smallest female was also gravid. Only the right ovary was functional in mature females.

Two gravid females, 610 and 583 mm TL, were captured on January 13, carrying four and five embryos, respectively (20.5 mm ± 2.6 mm TL; mean ± s.d.), with one intact yolk sac (42 mm diameter). Two females, 587 and 563 mm TL, captured on May 13, had three and four embryos, respectively (143.9 mm ± 2.9 mm TL) with a mean yolk sac diameter of 24.8 mm (± 1.0 mm, n = 7). It was not possible to determine gender in embryos caught in January.

increased significantly over time in non-gravid females (Kruskal-Wallis| = 92.9, $p < 0.001$, df = 3; Fig.3). Only small (≤ 7 mm) ovarian follicles were present in gravid females. These small follicles were also present in all non-gravid females, but they also possessed larger, maturing follicles which increased in size and number over time to a maximum diameter of 31 mm by May (Fig. 3). Hence two distinct follicle size distributions occurred in gravid and non-gravid females, respectively.

Proc. Linn. Soc. N.S.W., 137, 2015

9

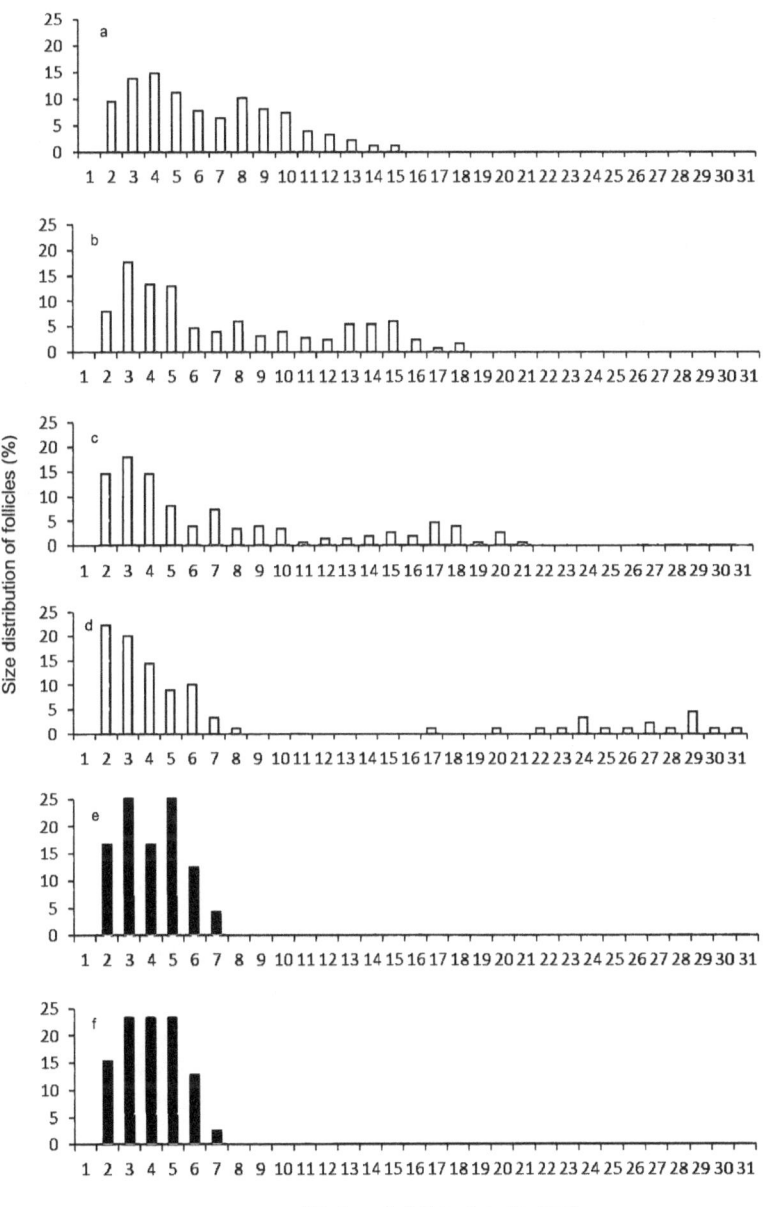

Figure 3. Size distribution of vitellogenic ovarian follicles in non-gravid female *Brachaelurus waddi* (open bars) captured in 2011 on (a) 13 January; (b) 8 February; (c) 15 February; and (d) 13 May; and gravid females (solid bars) captured on (e) 13 January; and (f) 13 May.

DISCUSSION

Although these results are preliminary and further study is required, the previously reported reproductive parameters for *B. waddi* appear questionable. Size at maturity was smaller than previously reported in both sexes. Males reached sexual maturity at approximately 520-540 mm TL, as opposed to the 600 mm (Last and Stevens 2009) and 620 mm (Compagno 2002) previously reported. The size at maturity and maternity of females in this study was ≤ 563 mm, compared with the previously reported 660 mm (Compagno 2002; Last and Stevens 2009), and, given that the uteri of all gravid females were fully distended, uterine fecundity is likely to equal maximum potential litter size (Compagno 2002; Last and Stevens 2009). However, the small sample size warrants caution.

Two distinct distributions in follicle size in combination with the low proportion of gravid females (12.5%) indicates at least a biennial reproductive cycle and not an annual cycle as previously assumed (Kyne and Bennett 2003). This is further supported by maturing follicles reaching a maximum diameter of 31 mm by May, well before the November mating season (Compagno 2002), and a 42 mm yolk-sac in a gravid female in January. In benthic elasmobranchs, follicles > 40 mm are generally associated with biennial or triennial ovarian cycles, while follicles < 30 mm are typically associated with annual ovarian cycles (Huveneers et al. 2007). However, the small proportion of gravid females (12.5%) may suggest a triennial cycle, but further data is required to establish this. Based on a biennial cycle and estimated fecundity, the reproductive potential of *B. waddi* may be as little as four pups every two years, or 25% of previous estimates (Compagno 2002; Last and Stevens 2009).

Although not targeted by commercial or recreational fishers, *B. waddi* is commonly caught by both, with most presumed to be released alive (Kyne & Bennett 2003). However unconfirmed reports from commercial fishers suggest some may be killed, as a nuisance which occupies traps and consumes target fish/bait, while others are released at sites remote from the trapping areas (D. Powter, field obs.). Post-capture survival is thought to be high, but not known definitively (Kyne & Bennett 2003). These factors and the more conservative life history found in this study, suggest the need for more research and new considerations for future fisheries management actions and conservation evaluations, such as those by the IUCN.

ACKNOWLEDGEMENTS

Financial help was awarded by Fakultetstipendiet (Aarhus University), the Hanne and Torkel Weis-Fogh fund and Oticon Fonden, making the study possible. Thanks to Tomas Cedhagen (writing assistance/support), to Jens Tang Christensen (statistics) and to NSW commercial fishers Dave Lindfield and Dean Pinsak for the sharks.

REFERENCES

Compagno, L.J.V. (2002). 'Sharks of the world. An annoted and illustrated catalogue of shark species known to date. Volume 2: Bullhead, mackerel and carpet sharks (Heterodontiformes, Lamniformes and Orectolobiformes)'. Food and Agriculture Organization of the United Nations. FOA Species Catalogue for Fisheries Purposes No. 1

Cortés, E. (1999). Standardized diet compositions and trophic levels of sharks. *ICES Journal of Marine Science*, **56**, 707-717.

Cortés, E. (2000). Life history patterns and correlations in sharks. *Reviews in Fisheries Science* **8**, 299-344.

Huveneers, C., Walker, T.I., Otway, N.M. and Harcourt, R.G. (2007). Reproductive synchrony of three sympatric species of wobbegong shark (genus *Orectolobus*) in New South Wales, Australia: reproductive parameter estimates necessary for population modelling. *Marine and Freshwater Research* **58**, 765-777.

Kyne, P.M. and Bennett, M.B. (2003). *Brachaelurus waddi*. In: IUCN 2013. IUCN Red List of Threatened Species. Version 2013.2. SSG Australia & Oceania Regional Workshop, March 2003. Retrieved from www.iucnredlist.org on 05 January 2013.

Kyne, P.M., Compagno, L.J.V., Stead, J., Jackson, M.V. and Bennett, M.B. (2011). Distribution, habitat and biology of a rare and threatened eastern Australian endemic shark: Colclough's shark, *Brachaelurus colcloughi* Ogilby, 1908. *Marine and Freshwater Research* **62**, 540-547.

Last, P.R. and Stevens, J.D. (2009). 'Sharks and rays of Australia. Second edition.' (CSIRO Publishing, Australia).

Lucifora, L.O., Menni, R.C. and Escalante, A.H. (2005). Reproduction and seasonal occurrence of the copper shark, *Carcharhinus brachyurus*, from Patagonia, Argentina. *ICES Journal of Marine Science*, **62**, 107-115.

Mollet, H.F., Cliff, G., Pratt, H.L. and Stevens, J.D. (2000). Reproductive biology of the female shortfin mako, *Isurus oxyrinchus* Rafinesque, 1810, with comments on the embryonic development of lamnoids. *Fisheries Bulletin* **98**, 299-318.

Peres, M.B. and Vooren, C.M. (1991). Sexual development, reproductive cycle, and fecundity of the school shark *Galeorhinus galeus* off Southern Brazil. *Fishery Bulletin* **89**, 655-667.

Pratt, H.L. (1979). Reproduction in the blue shark, *Prionace glauca. Fishery Bulletin* **77**, 445-470.

Stevens, J.D., Bonfil, R., Dulvy, N.K. and Walker, P.A. (2000). The effects of fishing on sharks, rays, and chimaeras (Chondrichthyans), and the implications for marine ecosystems. *ICES Journal of Marine Science* **57**, 476-494.

Walker, T.I. (2005). Reproduction in fisheries science. In: '*Reproductive biology and phylogeny of Chondrichthyes: Sharks, batoids and chimaeras*'. (Ed W. C. Hamlett.) pp. 81-127. (Enfield, USA: Science Publishers).

12

Proc. Linn. Soc. N.S.W., 137, 2015

Translation to English of Speeches Given in French to Honour William Macleay at a Picnic of the Linnean Society, 1st May 1875

GRAHAM R. FULTON[1] AND PETER BIALEK[2]

[1]School of Veterinary and Life Sciences, Murdoch University, South Street, Murdoch, WA, Australia
(grahamf2001@yahoo.com.au), [2]339 Rue de Belleville, 75019 Paris, France

Published on 8 July 2015 at http://escholarship.library.usyd.edu.au/journals/index.php/LIN

Fulton, G.R. and Bialek, P. (2015). Translation to English of a Speech Made in French to Honour William Macleay at a Picnic of the Linnaean Society, 1st May 1875. *Proceedings of the Linnean Society of New South Wales* **137**, 13-16.

A translation of the French speeches given at the Linnean Society's picnic to congratulate William Macleay on his upcoming expedition to New Guinea, in 1875, is presented. The speeches, in French, were made by Professor Badham, the French Consul, Mr. Simon and Lieutenant Villemot. The speeches show the cordial nature present between a young Australia and France at the time.

Manuscript received 30 April 2015, accepted for publication 20 May 2015.

Keywords: Chevert, Linnean Society of New South Wales, Sir William Macleay, Charles Badham, Eugène Simon, Henri Villemot

INTRODUCTION

On May 18, 1875, William (later Sir William) Macleay departed Sydney on board the *Chevert* bound for New Guinea. He headed and fully funded a team of biologists and explorers on the first expedition to leave Australia for foreign shores (Fulton 2012). The expedition was enormously successful adding approximately 1,000 birds, 800 fish, and many reptiles, mammals, insects, spiders, marine molluscs and ethnographic objects to Macleay Museum's collections (Macleay 1875; Fletcher 1893; Fulton 2012).

On the lead up to this historic event a picnic was held (on the first of May, 1875) by the fledgling Linnean Society of New South Wales to complement William Macleay on his fast approaching expedition (Anonymous 1875). The picnic was attended by a litany of senior dignitaries and luminaries from politics and the academia of Sydney including: the Premier, Hon. Mr. John Robertson; the Attorney General, Hon. William Dalley; Professor, Charles Badham of The University of Sydney "and other Gentlemen" (Anonymous 1875). Also in attendance were the Consul of France, Mons. Eugène Simon and Lieutenant Henri Villemot, Commandant of the *Cher*

(Anonymous 1875). A toast with speech was given by the Premier and responded to by William Macleay. These were reported verbatim in the *Sydney Morning Herald* newspaper. The only other speeches were by Professor Badham who welcomed the French guests in French and subsequently the guests (Mons. Simon and Henri Villemot) responded in their native tongue (Anonymous 1875; Fletcher 1929). These speeches were published, verbatim, in French, in the same newspaper article. To the best of my knowledge they have never been translated into English—until now.

The translation was fraught with difficulty: initially because the surviving scanned, newspaper-article was difficult to read with some words heavily smudged or otherwise distorted; then subsequently, because the French language used by the speakers was rich with metaphors that are not straightforwardly translated across languages. Not all words or phrases are directly translatable across time, cultures and languages: "translating from one language into another is like viewing Flemish tapestries from the wrong side, when, although one can make out the figures, they are covered by threads that obscure them, and one cannot appreciate the smooth finish of the right side" (Cervantes 1615). All speeches at the Linnean picnic were presented in the argots associated with their time, place and culture. We have tried to retain in our translation the meanings and emotions rather than present it mechanically, in the belief that readers will gain deeper insights if the sense/feelings of the times, as well as the facts, are retained. All diacritical marks are retained where appropriate to facilitate correct pronunciation and meaning (following Fulton 2011). Spelling and grammatical mistakes present in the original newspaper article have been retained to avoid any distortion of what was given to the readers of the day.

NEWSPAPER ARTICLE IN FRENCH

Loud calls were made for Dr. Badham, who proposed in French the following toast:—

Dr. BADHAM said: Monsieur le Ministre, — Vous voyez mon hésitation et sans doute vous en devinez la cause, si j'avais seulement voulu donner libre cours à ces sentiments d'amitié personnelle qui me sont communs avec toute la compagnie qui nous entoure, j'aurais fait ce que la discrétion et la modestie exigeaient; je me serais servi de ma langue maternelle pour remplir le devoir qui m'est imposé. Mais la présence de ces deux Messieurs qui ont bien voulu assister à cette fête, et qui portent le plus vif intérêt au grand projet de notre cher Président me force d'entreprendre une tâche bien autrement difficile. Je ne prétends pas représenter la nation Française; mais, si M. le Consul de France et M. le Capitaine du Cher me le permettent, j'oserai devant eux et en parlant leur langue, vous rappeler un fait incontestable: c'est que dans tous nos projets, qui ont été dictés par le sentiment de l'humanité, dans tous ces travaux, dont le but a été la civilisation des peuples, l'Angleterre a toujours pu conter sur la sympathie de la France. Je propose donc que, le verre en main, nous témoignions à nos convives, combien nous apprécions l'honneur qu'ils nous ont faits, en partageant les vœux que nous exprimons aujourd'hui pour la prospérité de notre excellent ami, et pour le triomphe de ses nobles aspirations. Et comment me puis-je armer de ce symbole de la cordialité sans réfléchir que c'est à la France que nous devons cette âme enchanteresse de nos festins, ce fidèle interprète de nos cœurs, cette fée pétillante qui offre même au plus faible orateur et les trésors de la pensée et le riche vestiaire de la parole. Je porte un toast à l'honneur de tous les français vivants, morts et à venir, en y joignant le nom d'un homme qui a parfaitement compris la mission de son pays, et l'a rendue la sienne. A la santé de M. Eugène Simon, Consul de France!

Mons. Simon, who was much applauded, responded to this toast: Messieurs, —du moment où Mr. le Dr. Badham s'est levé, je venais de lui dire combien je regrettais de ne pas posséder la langue Anglaise comme on voudrait la posséder quand il s'agit de parler devant une compagnie aussi nombreuse et aussi choisie. Je regrettais de ne pouvoir vous exprimer les sentiments que me suggèrent l'entreprise de Mr. Macleay, lorsque le Dr. Badham, se fit en excellent Français, l'interprète de ma pensée; et il l'a si fidèlement traduite que je ne trouve rien à ajouter à ce qui vient de dire. Je profiterai toutefois l'autorisation qu'il m'a donnée, si délicatement donnée de votre part pour vous dire encore à quel point je trouve remarquable ce voyage qui se prépare. Et en vérité je ne saurais trop le répéter: jamais efforts plus grands n'ont été faits pour le progrès et pour le bien de l'humanité que ceux qui ont été faits par la nation Anglaise, jamais plus grands résultats n'ont été atteints. Et non contente d'agir elle-même, voilà qu'elle agit par ces enfants et que son dernier né se montre déjà jalous de continuer sa mission. Voilà que, du sein de sa plus récente colonie, du sein d'un pays parfaitement inconnu il y a cent ans, se dispose à partir une expédition qui, s'élevant au-dessus des intérêts matériels immédiats, se propose le but le plus noble et le plus désintéressé: la science et les découvertes scientifiques. Ce n'était, jusqu'né du moins, ce n'était ordinairement qui une époque aliez avancie de leur existence que les nations pensaient à agrandir le domaine abstrait des connaissances scientifiques. Les Argonautes, en Colchide, ne pensaient qu'a la Toison d'Or; l'Espagne en Amérique ne voulait qu'étendre sa domination sur un monde nouveau et sur les richesses qu'il pouvait renfermer; ce n'est qu'incidemment et comme par surcroit que l'Angleterre elle-même a ajouté à ces plus belles conquêtes territoriales les plus conquêtes intellectuelles. Vous, Monsieur, en consacrant votre fortune et vos loisirs aux recherches et aux explorations que vous méditez, vous avez élevez votre pays au niveau des pays les plus anciens et les plus distingués. Ceux de ses représentants officiels qui vous entourent en ce moment, l'honorent eux-mêmes en montrant la haute importance qu'ils attachent à votre voyage. Vous ajoutez un titre puissant à l'intérêt que l'Australie, et la Nouvelle Galles du Sud en particulier, avaient déjà su s'attirer de la part des autres parties du monde un titre que les amis de la science n'oublieront pas. Je suis heureux, Monsieur, à me trouver associé à la manifestation dont vous êtes l'objet et je vous prie de me permettre d'ajouter mes souhaits et mes félicitations à ceux qui viennent de vous être offerts.

Captain Villemot, Le Lieutenant de Vaisseau, Commandant le Cher, who was much cheered, said:—Messieurs, permettez-moi d'ajouter quelques mots, pour la Marine Française, aux sentiments si bien exprimés par le Consul de France. Je regrette bien vivement, messieurs, que mon peu de connaissance de l'Anglais, m'empêche de vous remercier, dans votre langue, de votre cordial accueil, ainsi que du gracieux toast que vient de nous porter le savant et aimable Docteur Badham; mais je me console, en pensant que, lorsqu'on parle avec le cœur, on est toujours compris. Je suis sûr que la France, et la Marine Française en particulier, applaudiront à la nouvelle de l'expédition scientifique que va entreprendre en Nouvelle-Guinée, la brave nation Anglaise, représentée par Monsieur Macleay et ses compagnons. Je suis moi-même, vraiment charmé qu'un heureux hasard fasse que ce soit un ancien bâtiment de guerre de notre marine qui ait l'honneur de porter la commission dans ces parages encore peu connus; j'ai fait, comme officier, sur ce navire, un voyage de quarante jours (de Tahiti à San Francisco), et je puis vous assurer, Messieurs, que le Chevert, remplit toutes les conditions désirables, pour mener à bonne fin l'expédition, et ramener au milieu de vous, sains et saufs, ces nouveaux et hardis pionniers de la science. Je ne puis m'empêcher, en terminant, Messieurs, d'exprimer le regret de ne pouvoir m'associer à vos savants compatriotes, moi qui ai eu le bonheur de combattre plusieurs fois à côté de vos braves marins et soldats.

FRENCH TO ENGLISH TRANSLATION

Dr BADHAM said: Sir Minister — You see my hesitation and with no doubt you may guess the cause, if I only wanted to give vent to the feelings of personal friendship, that are commonly shared with the whole company, I would have done what discretion and modesty require; I would have used my mother tongue to fulfil my duty. But the presence of these two Gentlemen who have agreed to attend this party, and who share the greatest interest to the great project of our dear President, obliged me to undertake a much more difficult task. I do not claim to represent the French nation; but if, Mr The Consul of France and Mr The Commandant of the *Cher* allow me, I would venture before them and speaking their tongue, remind you of an indisputable fact: It is that in all our projects, which were driven by the sense of humanity, in all of these works whose goal was the civilisation of nations, England could always rely on the sympathy of France. I offer therefore, that glasses in hands, we reflect to our guests, how

much we appreciate the honour done, by sharing our wishes that we express today for the prosperity of our excellent friend, and for the triumph of his noble aspirations. And how can I arm myself of this symbol of warmth without thinking that it is due to France that we have this enchanting soul at our feast, this faithful interpreter of our heart, this sparkling fairy offering even the weakest orator the riches of our language. I propose a toast to the honour of all French, living, dead and to come, inviting the name of a man who perfectly understood the mission of his country, and made it his own. To the health of M. Eugène Simon, Consul of France!

Mons. Simon, who was much applauded, responded to this toast: Gentlemen, from the moment when the Dr Badham stood up, I was just telling him how sorry I felt not to have the knowledge of the English language as we would like too, when we have to speak in front of such a numerous and chosen group. I regret not to be able to express my feelings of the enterprise led by Mr. Macleay, when Dr. Badham made himself such an excellent Frenchman, such a good interpreter of my thoughts. And he has been so faithful to my thoughts that I do not find anything to add to what he has just said. I will however take advantage of the authorization he gave me so gently, to tell you how remarkable I find this journey that prepares. And in truth, I cannot repeat too often: never, such efforts have been put into progress and in the interest of humanity, than such made by the English nation, and never such great results achieved. And as if it was not enough, she is acting through her children and the latest, is already eager to carrying on his mission. And now, coming from the heart of its most recent colony, from a country completely unknown hundred years ago, an expedition is getting ready, which considering its immediate material interests, proposes the most noble and selfless purpose: science and scientific discoveries There wasn't a time, in history, when progress wasn't typically allied with advancing the existence of a nation's thought by enlarging the domain of abstract scientific knowledge. The Argonauts, in Colchis were only thinking of the Golden Fleece; Spain in the Americas only wanted to expand their domination on the new world and its treasures: and incidentally, it is only England itself that has added intellectual conquests to its beautiful territorial conquests. You, Sir, by devoting your fortune and your hobbies, to the research and explorations that you meditate, you raise your country to the level of the most ancient and distinguished countries. The official representatives that are around you at this moment, honour it themselves by showing you the high importance that they attach to your voyage. You add a powerful significance to the title of Australia, and to New South Wales in particular, whose title had already noticed by other parts of the world, as the friends of science will not forget. I am delighted, Sir, to be associated to this event, which honour you, and if I may, I would add my best wishes and congratulations to the others made to you today.

Captain Villemot, Navy Lieutenant Commander *le Cher*, who was much cheered, said:– Gentlemen, if I may, I would add a couple of words, in the name of the French Navy, to the feelings here so well expressed by the Consul of France. Gentlemen, I deeply regret that my little knowledge of English prevents me from thanking you, in your language, for your cordial welcome and the gracious toast just cheered by the savant and amiable Doctor Badham; but I console myself, thinking that when speaking from the heart we will always be understood. I am sure that France and the French Navy, in particular, will applaud the news of the scientific expedition that the brave English nation, here, represented by Mr. Macleay and his companions, will be undertaking to New Guinea. I am myself, really charmed that serendipity has given this veteran warship of our Navy the honour of taking this commission into these parts still unknown; I did, as an officer of this vessel, a forty day trip (from Tahiti to San Francisco), and I can assure you, gentlemen, that the Chevert, fulfils all the desirable conditions, to carry out a successful expedition, and bring back, safe and sound, these new and bold pioneers of science. In conclusion, gentlemen, I cannot help but to express my regret at not being able to join your learned compatriots, I who have had the pleasure to fight several times alongside your brave sailors and soldiers.

ACKNOWLEDGEMENTS

We thank Mike Augee and Jean-Claude Herremans for reviewing this manuscript. I thank Cheung Yee Wan for support and encouragement. I acknowledge the traditional owners the land upon which the Linnaean picnic was held and the speeches given: The Gadigal people of the Eora Nation.

REFERENCES

Anonymous (1875). The Picnic of the Linnæan Society. *Sydney Morning Herald*, **LXXI** , p 5. (Monday, May 3, 1875).

Cervantes Saavedra, M. (1615). 'Second part of the Ingenious Knight Don Quixote de la Mancha.' (Madrid: Juan de la Cuesta).

Fletcher, J.J. (1893). 'The Macleay Memorial Volume.' (Sydney: Linnean Society of New South Wales).

Fletcher, J.J. (1929). The Society's Heritage from the Macleays. Part ii. *Proceedings of the Linnean Society of New South Wales*, **54**, 185-272.

Fulton, G.R. (2011). Diacritics — to be or not to be: nomenclature, pronunciation and early history of Faure Island, Shark Bay, Australia. *Records of the Western Australian Museum*, **26**, 94-97.

Fulton, G.R. (2012). Alexander, William Sharp, and William John Macleay: Their Ornithology and Museum. In: 'Contributions to the History of Australasian Ornithology Vol. 2.' (Eds. W. E. Davis, Jr., H. F. Recher, W. E. Boles and J. A. Jackson.) pp. 327-393. (Cambridge, Massachusetts: Nuttall Ornithological Club).

Macleay, W. (1875). Notes on the zoological collections made in Torres Straits and New Guinea during the cruise of the Chevert. *Proceedings of the Linnean Society of New South Wales*, **1**, 36-40.

16

Proc. Linn. Soc. N.S.W., 137, 2015

Fruiting Phenologies of Rainforest Plants in the Illawarra Region, New South Wales, 1988-1992

Matthew Mo[1] and David R. Waterhouse[2]

[1]NSW Department of Primary Industries, Elizabeth Macarthur Agricultural Institute, Woodbridge Road, Menangle NSW 2568 (matthew.mo@dpi.nsw.gov.au); [2]4/1-5 Ada Street, Oatley NSW 2223

Published on 20 August 2015 at http://escholarship.library.usyd.edu.au/journals/index.php/LIN

Mo, M. and Waterhouse, D.R. (2015). Fruiting phenologies of rainforest plants in the Illawarra region, New South Wales, 1988-1992. *Proceedings of the Linnean Society of New South Wales* **137**, 17-27.

Phenological patterns of fruit production have an important influence on the ecology of frugivores, and vice versa. A longitudinal study of fruiting cycles in rainforest plants was carried out in the Illawarra region between 1988 and 1992 as part of an investigation on food resources for frugivorous birds. A total of 82 species of fruit-producing plants were recorded, and seasonal availability of fruiting plants was examined by the mean number of species in crop production per month. Fruiting plants were available year round, with peaks occurring in autumn and early winter. The crop periods of most species were subject to substantial variability from year to year. There were no positive correlations between the monthly numbers of trees, and vines and climbers in fruit and climatic variables such as rainfall and temperature. Rainforests in southeastern Australia have lower botanical diversity than those of lower latitudes, attributing to substantial geographical variation in frugivore-plant relationships. Core crop periods were determined in 23 species of trees, three species of shrubs, six species of vines and climbers. Fruiting patterns in the remaining species were sporadic. Data presented in this paper provide baseline data for further studies, with important implications for natural resource and conservation management.

Manuscript received 8 February 2015, accepted for publication 22 July 2015.

KEYWORDS: ecology, fruit, Illawarra region, phenology, rainforest plants, seasonal patterns

INTRODUCTION

Phenological patterns of fruit production in rainforest plants have an important influence on the ecology of frugivorous fauna. Typically, a large number of species exhibit irregular fruiting cycles (Frankie et al. 1974; Crome 1975; Foster 1982; Heideman 1989; Waterhouse 2001), forcing fruvigores to orientate their movements and dietary patterns in accordance to food availability. Seasonal abundance of fruit pigeons have been correlated with fruiting phenologies (Crome 1975; Innis 1989). In tropical regions at least, the breeding seasons of some birds coincide with peaks in fruit abundance (Snow and Snow 1964; Crome 1975, 1976; Innis and McEvoy 1992). Other frugivores such as bowerbirds broaden their diet to include other plant and animal materials in order to remain sedentary during seasonal declines in fruit availability (Donaghey 1996; Frith and Frith 2004).

The relationship between frugivores and fruiting plants has value for the latter as well. In tropical and subtropical regions, frugivores are considered 'keystone species' for their role in seed dispersal (Green 1993). For example, Webb and Tracey (1981) reported that fauna play a significant role in the reproductive cycles of more than 80 percent of flora in subtropical rainforests. In temperate climates, there is a shift toward rainforest flora relying more heavily on wind and hydrology as vehicles of seed dispersal, which is observed in a reduction in fruit-producing species (Blakers et al. 1984). Mills (1986) found that rainforests of the Illawarra region, south of Sydney, effectively lie in a transition zone between these two elements; a disproportionately high number of tree, shrub and climber species remained dependent on fauna, however herbs largely relied on abiotic strategies of seed dispersal.

Most of the rainforest areas of southeastern Australia have been severely depleted in size, which introduces an additional dimension of variability for frugivore-plant interactions. Ecological studies of rainforests at higher latitudes have important implications for natural resource and conservation

(a)

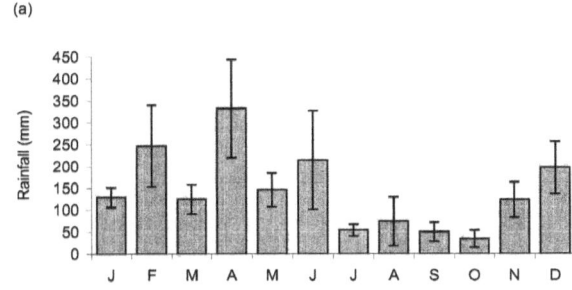

(b)

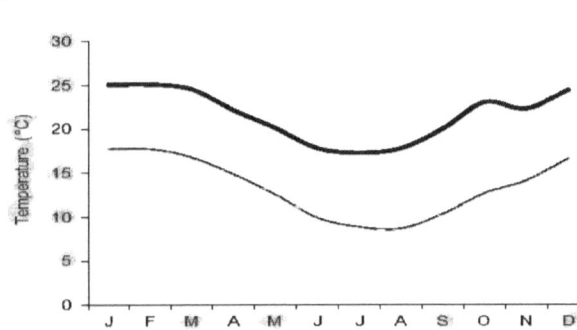

Figure 1. Climate statistics for the Wollongong University weather station between 1988 and 1992. Mean monthly rainfall (a) and mean maximum and minimum temperatures (b).

management. This paper reports on a five-year study of the fruiting phenologies of rainforest plants in the Illawarra region.

RAINFORESTS OF THE ILLAWARRA REGION

The Illawarra escarpment stretches approximately 50 km from the Royal National Park in the north to the Minnamurra Rainforest in the south (Macquarie 2013). This geographical area boasts a complex mosaic of different vegetation communities, including eucalypt forests, sparse woodlands and rainforests, especially on the higher altitudes (Ashcroft 2006). Rainforest sections to the east of the escarpment are supported by the slopes providing shelter from drying westerly winds, high rainfall generated by orographic precipitation (Bywater 1978; Reinfields and Nanson 2001, 2004; Macquarie 2013; Croke et al. 2014), perennial humidity (Fuller 1995; Ashcroft 2006) and low light penetration, especially in the cooler months (NSW NPWS 2011). The cliff line

forms the approximate watershed between two catchments (Switzer et al. 2005; Thornton et al. 2007), feeding the creeks that pass through rainforests and wet sclerophyll forests to the east (Mills 1998).

Many subtropical plants reach their southern limit in the Illawarra rainforests (Mills 1986). The unique vegetation communities in the Illawarra district have been attributed to the close proximity of the escarpment to the coast (Schulz and Magarey 2012), a warm temperate climate and fertile soils below the escarpment (French and Westoby 1992; NSW NPWS 2000). In general, subtropical rainforest occur on the lower slopes, and temperate rainforest on the upper slopes and gullies.

During the study period, the Illawarra region received a mean annual rainfall of 1726 mm (Australian Bureau of Meteorology, Wollongong University station, 1988-1992). Peaks in rainfall occurred in February, April and June, although the amount varied considerably from year to year (Fig. 1a). Mean day temperatures ranged from 8°C (minimum; August) and 25°C (maximum; January) (Fig. 1b), similar to those reported by Ashcroft (2006).

METHODS

Study sites

The majority of this study was conducted at two sections of the Illawarra Escarpment State Conservation Area (Fig. 2). Mount Keira (34°24'S, 150°51'E, ~600ha area) was routinely surveyed via Robertson's Lookout, Byarong Park, the Mount Keira Ring Track (~5.5 km) and the Dave Walsh's Track (~800 m). The summit is 464 m above sea level. The foothills contain small isolated pockets of Illawarra Subtropical Rainforest, an endangered ecological community. Bulli Mountain (34°20'S, 150°54'E, ~100ha area) was routinely surveyed via Bulli Lookout and a walking track that extends to Sublime Point (~2.5 km). The plateau contains an isolated section

18

Proc. Linn. Soc. N.S.W., 137, 2015

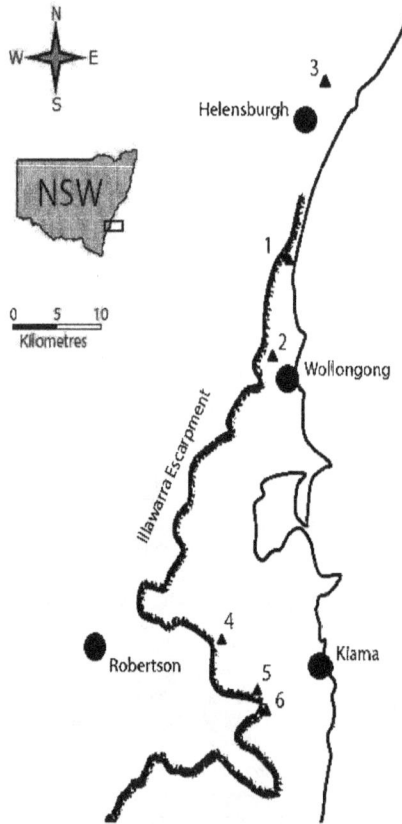

Figure 2. Locations of the main study sites, Bulli Mountain (1) and Mount Keira (2), and four additional sites, Bola Creek (3), Minnamurra Falls (4), Saddleback Mountain (5) and Foxground (6).

of Southern Sydney Sheltered Forest, an endangered ecological community that occurs on sandstone-shale transitional soils. Rare plant communities have been identified at both Bulli Mountain and Mount Keira (NSW NPWS 2011).

Occasional visits were also made to four additional sites containing remnant Illawarra rainforest: Bola Creek in the Royal National Park (34°9'S, 151°1'E, ~100ha area), Minnamurra Falls in Budderoo National Park (34°38'S, 150°43'E, ~90ha area), Foxground (34°43'S, 150°46'E, ~60ha area) and Saddleback Mountain (34°41'S, 150°47'E, ~70ha area) (Fig. 2). The former two were accessed via walking tracks maintained by the NSW National Parks and Wildlife Service. The rainforest remnant at

Foxground is mainly situated on private holdings and was surveyed by making observation while driving slowly along the road. Surveying of Saddleback Mountain was also carried out from a vehicle, with some sporadic explorations on foot, especially near the summit.

Data collection and analysis

The study design involved both routine surveys of the main sites (Mount Keira and Bulli Mountain) and sporadic surveying of the additional sites. The main sites were surveyed on a fortnightly basis between January 1988 and December 1992, hence providing a total of 132 field days. This involved traversing the established walking tracks and recording the presence of plants that produce fruits that could provide food resources for frugivorous birds, and whether fruiting was occurring. Additional trips to Bola Creek, Minnamurra Falls, Foxground and Saddleback Mountain broadened the area coverage of the study, and were undertaken monthly.

Plant species recorded were grouped into four broad categories: trees, shrubs, vines and climbers, and herbs. The fruiting periods for each species were determined at a monthly scale by pooling data from the five years of study. Core crop periods (CCP) for each species were determined based on fruit production occurring in the same months for at least three years.

The seasonal availability of fruiting plants was studied by examining the mean number of species in fruit per month. Linear regression analyses were applied to patterns in the number of fruiting species available (all plants, trees, and vines and climbers) and climatic variables (rainfall, maximum mean temperature, minimum mean temperature, and mean temperature). The limited numbers of shrub and herb species recorded were not sufficient for this analysis. Climatic data was sourced from the Australian Bureau of Meteorology (Wollongong University station). For trees, monthly means were also compared to the number of species fruiting reliably per month over the study period. In this context, reliability refers to fruit production occurring in a species in a month for three or more years.

RESULTS

This study recorded a total of 82 species of fruit-producing plants. Approximately half of these were trees (42 species). Shrubs, vines and climbers, and herbs comprised 15, 22 and three species respectively. The timing of fruiting in each species was generally simultaneous across all sites.

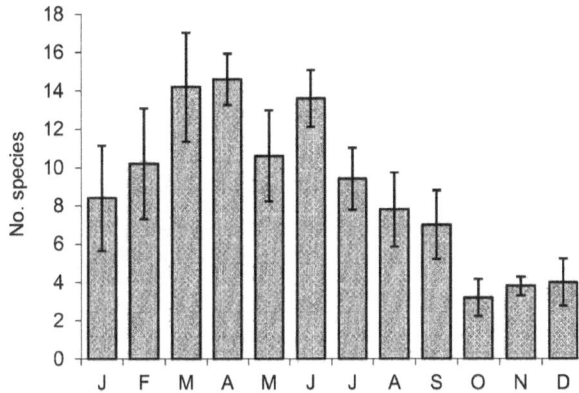

Figure 3. Mean number of fruiting species in the Illawarra rainforests between 1988 and 1992.

Trees comprised approximately half of species recorded (42 species), and their seasonal pattern followed these trends (Fig. 4). The mean number of shrub species in fruit was greatest from mid summer to early autumn (January, 2.2 ± 0.7; February, 2.2 ± 1.1; March, 3.0 ± 0.8). In other times of the year, less than two species were fruiting in any one month. The mean number of vine and climber species in fruit was relatively consistent (~2.5 species per month), although troughs in fruiting species occurred in some of the warmer months (February, 1.2 ± 1.0; October, 0.4 ± 0.2; November, 0.4 ± 0.3; December, 0.6 ± 0.4).

Seasonal patterns in fruiting periods

The fruiting periods of most species were extremely variable from year to year (Fig. 3). Overall, peaks in the mean number of species producing fruit occurred in autumn and early winter (March, 15.6 ± 2.8; April, 15.0 ± 1.3; June, 14 ± 1.5). The diversity of fruiting species available appeared to build up over the second half of summer (February, 11.2 ± 2.9) and decline over the winter months, reaching depression in spring (October, 3.2 ± 1.0; November, 3.8 ± 0.5).

Regression analyses did not detect any positive relationship between monthly availability of fruiting species (all plants, trees, and vines and climbers) and four climatic variables (rainfall, maximum mean temperature, minimum mean temperature and mean temperature) (Table 1). However, from a comparison between Figures 1 and 3, it appears that lowest overall fruit production occurs three months following the coolest and driest months.

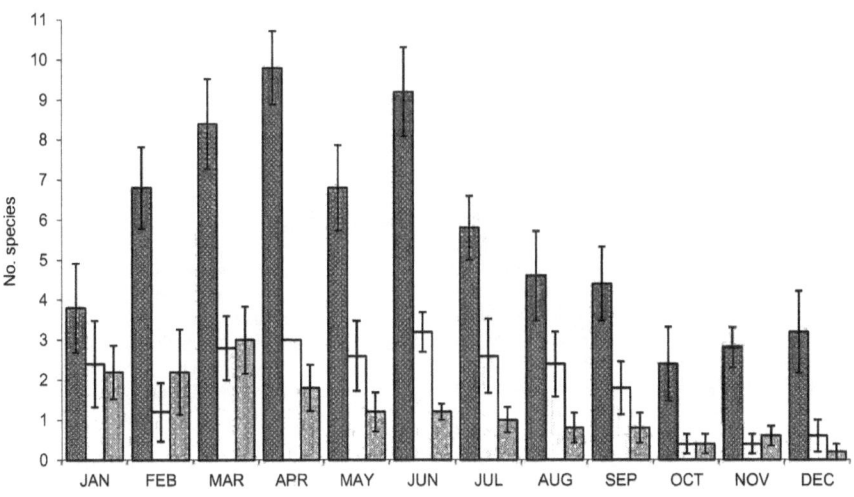

Figure 4. Mean number of fruiting species of trees (dark grey), vines and climbers (white) and shrubs (light grey) in the Illawarra rainforests between 1988 and 1992.

20

Proc. Linn. Soc. N.S.W., 137, 2015

Table 1. R2 values resulted from regression analyses comparing the number of species in fruit with four climatic variables.

	R^2	$F_{1,59}$	P
ALL PLANTS			
Rainfall	0.05030	3.07186	0.00000
Max Mean Temperature	0.00492	0.28650	0.02818
Min Mean Temperature	0.00539	0.31452	0.01679
Mean Temperature	0.00003	0.00168	0.03672
TREES			
Rainfall	0.09163	5.85089	0.00000
Max Mean Temperature	0.01172	0.68805	0.00812
Min Mean Temperature	0.00028	0.01643	0.00216
Mean Temperature	0.00188	0.10916	0.00794
VINES AND CLIMBERS			
Rainfall	0.01176	0.69021	0.00000
Max Mean Temperature	0.10492	6.79881	0.00028
Min Mean Temperature	0.03289	1.97233	0.00083
Mean Temperature	0.06428	3.98452	0.00074

Fruiting periods of trees

Twenty-two species produced fruit on a reliable basis, that is fruiting occurred at a certain time of year for more than three years (50% of species recorded in the study) (Table 2). Monthly trends in the total number of species fruiting and the number of species fruiting reliably followed a similar pattern, except for reductions in the latter in May and December that did not correspond with the former (Fig. 5).

Of four species of figs recorded, only two had reliable fruiting periods. These were the Sandpaper Fig *Ficus coronata* and Moreton Bay Fig *F. macrophylla*, which both produced fruit reliably from summer to autumn. Koda *Ehretia acuminata*, Crabapple *Schizomeria ovata* and Brush Cherry *Syzygium australe* followed a similar seasonal pattern. Churnwood *Citronella moorei* mostly fruited in the latter half of summer. Yellow Ash *Emmenosperma alphitonioides* had a wide-ranging fruiting period, from late summer to early spring, but was only considered reliable in February and June.

The CCP of Jackwood *Cryptocarya glaucescens*, Sassafras *Doryphora sassafras* and Maiden's Blush *Sloanea australis* were apparently restricted to autumn. For species like Red Olive Plum *Cassine australe*, Sweet Pittosporum *Pittosporum undulatum* and Pencil Cedar *Polyscias murrayi*, reliable fruiting continued from autumn into winter. The CCP of Featherwood *Polyosma cunninghamii* continued until early spring. Species like Lillypilly *Syzygium smithii* and Bolwarra *Eupomatia laurina* only fruited reliably in winter, and Yellow Pittosporum *Pittosporum revolutum*, Giant Stinging Tree *Dendrocnide excelsa* and Black Plum *Diospyros australis* were further restricted to early winter. In spite of this, some species with restricted CCP did sporadically produce fruit over a wider range, for example fruiting in Black Plum was observed from March to September.

Wild Quince *Alectryon subcinereus* and Cabbage Tree Palm *Livistona australis* also fruited reliably in winter, with their CCP extending to spring and early summer respectively. Fruiting in Brown Beech *Pennantia cunninghamii* was observed between September and February, but reliable fruiting was restricted to late spring and early summer.

Nine tree species only produced fruit in a single month throughout the entire study period; three in autumn (Corkwood *Endiandra sieberi*, Deciduous Fig *Ficus superba* and White Beech *Gmelina leichhardtii*), one in winter (Illawarra Flame Tree *Brachychiton acerifolius*), two in spring (Red Ash *Alphitonia excelsa* and Murrogun *Cryptocarya microneura*) and three in summer (Native Carsacarilla *Croton verreauxii*, Flintwood *Scolopia braunii* and Whalebone Tree *Streblus brunonianus*). A further 11 species only fruited for a few months in one or two years.

Fruiting periods of shrubs

Fifteen species of fruit-producing shrubs were recorded in this study, three of which were invasive weeds (Table 3). Only 20 percent of species fruited reliably, while two species (Grey Myrtle *Backhousia myrtifolia* and Brittlewood *Claoxylon australe*) did not fruit during the study period. Orange Thorn *Citriobatus multiflorum* was the only native species that produced fruit reliably, with a CCP from winter to early spring. Indian Strawberry *Duchesnea indica* fruited sporadically in different months, but was only considered reliable in early autumn. The CCP of Jerusalem Cherry *Solanum pseudocapsicum* was from mid-summer to autumn, though some fruit also occurred in early spring.

Fruiting periods of vines and climbers

A total of 22 species of fruit-producing vines and

Proc. Linn. Soc. N.S.W., 137, 2015

21

Table 2. Fruiting periods of tree species in the Illawarra rainforests. Numeric values represent the number of years fruiting occurred per month, and shading on values ≥3 years.

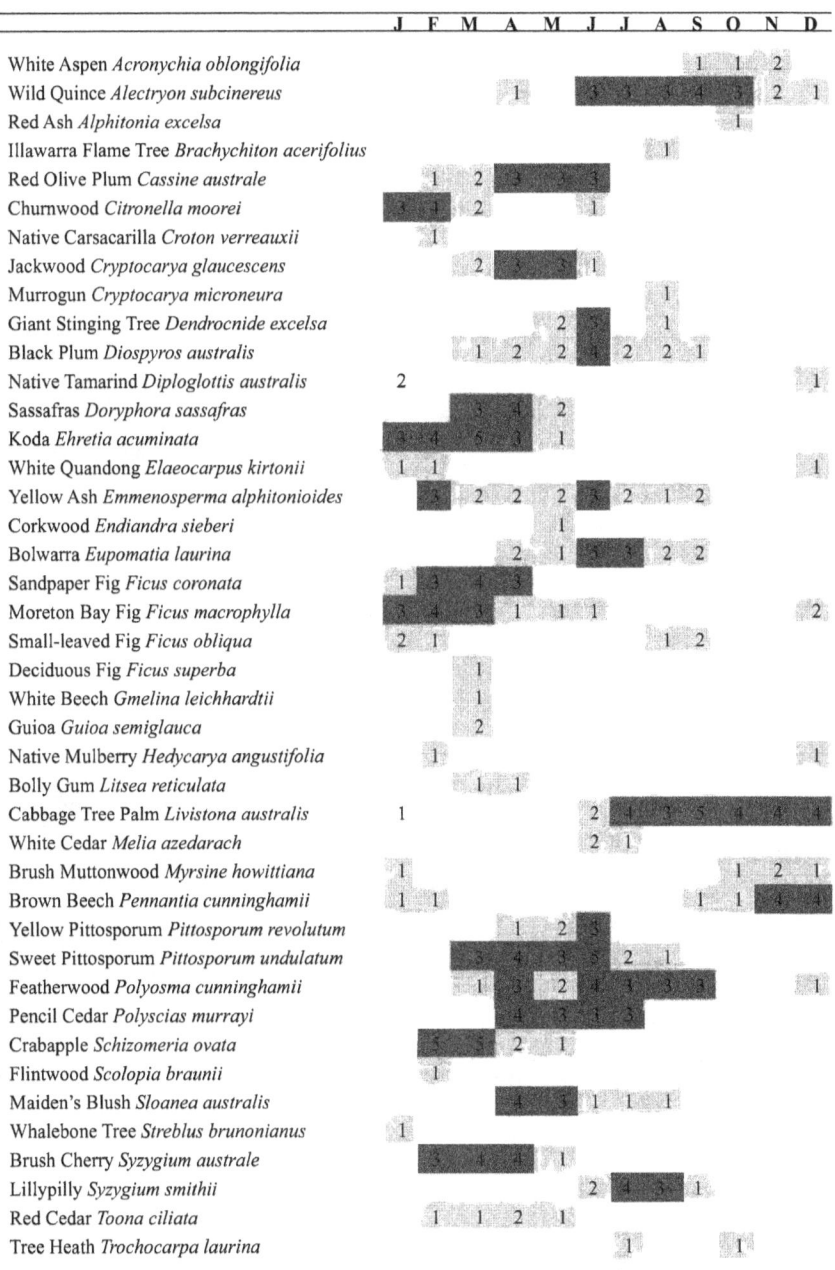

Species	J	F	M	A	M	J	J	A	S	O	N	D
White Aspen *Acronychia oblongifolia*								1	1	2		
Wild Quince *Alectryon subcinereus*					1	3	3		4	3	2	1
Red Ash *Alphitonia excelsa*								1				
Illawarra Flame Tree *Brachychiton acerifolius*							1					
Red Olive Plum *Cassine australe*			1	2	3	3	3					
Churnwood *Citronella moorei*	3	1	2				1					
Native Carsacarilla *Croton verreauxii*	1											
Jackwood *Cryptocarya glaucescens*				2	3	3	1					
Murrogun *Cryptocarya microneura*								1				
Giant Stinging Tree *Dendrocnide excelsa*						2	3	1				
Black Plum *Diospyros australis*			1	2	2	4	2	2	1			
Native Tamarind *Diploglottis australis*	2											1
Sassafras *Doryphora sassafras*					3	4	2					
Koda *Ehretia acuminata*	3	4	6	3	1							
White Quandong *Elaeocarpus kirtonii*	1	1										1
Yellow Ash *Emmenosperma alphitonioides*				3	2	2	2	3	2	1	2	
Corkwood *Endiandra sieberi*						1						
Bolwarra *Eupomatia laurina*					2	1	3	3	2	2		
Sandpaper Fig *Ficus coronata*			1	3	4	3						
Moreton Bay Fig *Ficus macrophylla*	3	4	3	1	1	1						2
Small-leaved Fig *Ficus obliqua*	2	1							1	2		
Deciduous Fig *Ficus superba*					1							
White Beech *Gmelina leichhardtii*					1							
Guioa *Guioa semiglauca*					2							
Native Mulberry *Hedycarya angustifolia*	1											1
Bolly Gum *Litsea reticulata*			1	1								
Cabbage Tree Palm *Livistona australis*	1						2	3	5	4	4	4
White Cedar *Melia azedarach*							2	1				
Brush Muttonwood *Myrsine howittiana*	1									1	2	1
Brown Beech *Pennantia cunninghamii*	1	1								1	1	4
Yellow Pittosporum *Pittosporum revolutum*				1	2	3						
Sweet Pittosporum *Pittosporum undulatum*				3	4	3	5	2	1			
Featherwood *Polyosma cunninghamii*			1	3	2	4	3	3	3			1
Pencil Cedar *Polyscias murrayi*				4	3	3	3					
Crabapple *Schizomeria ovata*			3	3	2	1						
Flintwood *Scolopia braunii*			1									
Maiden's Blush *Sloanea australis*				4	3	1	1	1				
Whalebone Tree *Streblus brunonianus*	1											
Brush Cherry *Syzygium australe*			3	4	3	1						
Lillypilly *Syzygium smithii*							2	4	3	1		
Red Cedar *Toona ciliata*	1	1	2	1								
Tree Heath *Trochocarpa laurina*							1			1		

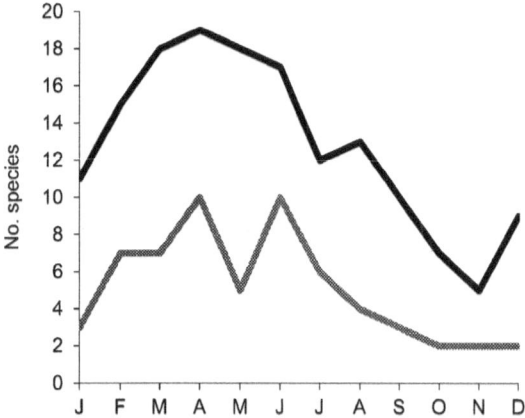

Figure 5. A comparison of monthly trends in the total number of tree species fruiting and the number of tree species fruiting reliably (≥3 years).

reliability was recorded in 27 percent of species. Wombat Berry *Eustrephus latifolius* had the most extensive fruiting period, covering 10 months of the year, though the CCP was between autumn and early spring. The CCP for Staff Vine *Celastrus subspicatus*, Water Vine *Cissus hypoglauca* and Jasmine Morinda *Morinda jasminoides* encompassed autumn and early winter, with each species producing fruit reliably in three months of the year. Native Grape *Cissus antarctica* was recorded fruiting from late autumn to spring, with a CCP between June and September. Pepper Vine *Piper novaehollandiae* produced fruit in the summer months, but was only reliable in January. There were five species recorded that were not observed fruiting at any time during the study period. These were Toothed Clematis *Clematis aristata*, Round-

climbers were recorded (Table 4), two of which were invasive weeds (White Moth Vine *Araujia sericifera* and Elmleaf Blackberry *Rubus ulmifolius*). Monthly leaf Vine *Legnephora moorei*, Milk Vine *Marsdenia rostrata*, Wonga-wonga Vine *Pandorea pandorana* and False Sarsaparilla *Smilax australis*.

Table 3. Fruiting periods of shrub species of the Illawarra rainforests.
Numeric values represent the number of years fruiting occurred per month, and shading on values ≥3 years. *indicates an invasive weed species; +did not produce during study period

	J	F	M	A	M	J	J	A	S	O	N	D
Grey Myrtle *Backhousia myrtifolia*+												
Coffee Bush *Breynia oblongifolia*	2	1	2									
Orange Thorn *Citriobatus multiflorum*	1					1	3	3	3	3	2	2
Brittlewood *Claoxylon australe*+												
Prickly Currant Bush *Coprosma quadrifida*		1										
Indian Strawberry *Duchesnea indica**	2	2	3				1					1
Small-leaved Privett *Ligustrum sinense**		1				1	1	1				
Cockspur Thorn *Maclura cochinchinensis*	1											
Mock Olive *Notelaea longifolia*	1											1
Bleeding Heart *Omalanthus populifolius*					1	1						
Hairy Psychotria *Psychotria loniceroides*						1						
Native Elderberry *Sambucus australasica*				1	2	2						
Native Grape *Solanum aviculare*	1	2	2	2								
Jerusalem Cherry *Solanum pseudocapsicum**	3	3	4	4	3	2	1					
Common Wilkiea *Wilkiea heugeliana*							1	1				

Proc. Linn. Soc. N.S.W., 137, 2015

23

Table 4. Fruiting periods of vine and climber species of the Illawarra rainforests. Numeric values represent the number of years fruiting occurred per month, and shading on values ≥3 years. *indicates an invasive weed species; +did not produce during study period

Species	J	F	M	A	M	J	J	A	S	O	N	D
White Moth Vine *Araujia sericifera**	1											
Staff Vine *Celastrus subspicatus*			3	3	2	3	1					
Native Grape *Cissus antarctica*				1	1	5	4	3			1	1
Water Vine *Cissus hypoglauca*		2	3	4	3	1	2	1				
Toothed Clematis *Clematis aristata+*												
Wombat Berry *Eustrephus latifolius*			4	5	3	5	3	4	4	1	1	1
Scrambling Lily *Geitonoplesium cymosum*	2											
Round-leaf Vine *Legnephora moorei+*												
Milk Vine *Marsdenia rostrata+*												
Southern Melodinus *Melodinus australis*								1	1			
Jasmine Morinda *Morinda jasminoides*			1	2	4	4	4	1	1	1		
Anchor Vine *Palmeria scandens*			1									
Wonga-wonga Vine *Pandorea pandorana+*												
Common Silkpod *Parsonsia straminea*	2	2										
Pepper Vine *Piper novaehollandiae*	4	1										1
Broad-leaved Bramble *Rubus moluccanus*							1					
Bush Lawyer *Rubus nebulosus*	1	1										
Native Raspberry *Rubus parvifolius*	1											1
Elmleaf Blackberry *Rubus ulmifolius**	1	1										
False Sarsaparilla *Smilax australis+*												
Snake Vine *Stephania japonica*		1										

Fruiting periods of herbs

Three species of fruit-producing herbs were recorded (Table 5). Settlers Flax *Gymnostachys anceps* exhibited a CCP from January to March, with fruiting also occurring through to June in 1992. Inkweed, an invasive weed, was only reliable in March, but also fruited until June in 1990. No CCP was determined for Black-fruit Saw-sedge *Gahnia melanocarpa*. This species only fruited in two months over the entire study period, which were February and March 1989.

DISCUSSION

The Illawarra region contains the most extensive area of rainforest in the Sydney Basin Bioregion (Erskine 1984; NSW NPWS 2002), but has not been unaffected by extensive clearing (Mills 1998). The Illawarra rainforests are regionally significant as one of six major concentrations of rainforest in New South Wales (Floyd 1990), as well as the southern limit of the subtropical, warm temperate and littoral rainforest groups (Keith 2004; Schulz and Magarey 2012). This longitudinal study is unique in its focus on fruiting reliability, providing baseline information for further ecological study in the region, such as exploration of the carrying capacity of local frugivorous species.

In some tropical rainforests, strong correlations between peak fruiting periods and climatic factors, such as temperature and rainfall, have been demonstrated (Smythe 1970; Frankie et al. 1974; Humphrey and Bonaccorso 1979; Raemaekers et al. 1980; Foster 1982, 1985). In more temperate climates, this relationship is less evident (Yap 1982;

24

Proc. Linn. Soc. N.S.W., 137, 2015

Table 5. Fruiting periods of herb species of the Illawarra rainforests.
Numeric values represent the number of years fruiting occurred per month, and shading on values ≥3 years. *indicates an invasive weed species.

	J	F	M	A	M	J	J	A	S	O	N	D
Black-fruit Saw-sedge *Gahnia melanocarpa*	1	1										
Settlers Flax *Gymnostachys anceps*	3	4					1	2	1			
Inkweed *Phytolacca octandra**			3	1	1	1						

Heideman 1989). The results of this study reflect the latter, in which the number of fruiting plants available did not directly correlate with seasonal variations in rainfall and temperature. Peaks in the mean monthly availability of fruiting plants occurred in autumn and early winter, apparently following on from warmest and wettest parts of the year by periods of lag of up to three months. Fruiting plants were available in all months despite obvious fluctuations in seasonal diversity.

The number of fruit-producing plants is dramatically reduced in the Illawarra rainforests compared with the species assemblages observed in tropical regions (Blakers et al. 1984). This raises the need to understand fruiting phenologies in view of the ecology of frugivores (Waterhouse 2001). The Illawarra rainforests are a significant area for frugivores listed under the NSW Threatened Species Conservation Act, such as the Grey-headed Flying Fox *Pteropus poliocephalus* (Parker et al. 2008), as well as three species of fruit doves *Ptilinopus* sp. that have been recorded as vagrants (Wood and Simcock 1993; Schulz and Ransom 2010). The region has also been identified as core habitat for such species as the Green Catbird *Ailuroedus crassirostris* (NSW NPWS 2011; Schulz and Magarey 2012).

Many of the major food items of fruit pigeons recorded in southeastern Queensland (Innis 1989) were not available in the Illawarra region. Consequently, the diet of Topknot Pigeons *Lopholaimus antarcticus* in the Illawarra rainforests differed from other parts of their distribution (Crome 1975; Innis 1989), with a focus toward fruiting plants that produced at least one good crop season in five years (Waterhouse 2001). Similarly, at least two-thirds of the diet of the Green Catbird *Ailuroedus crassirostris*, a regionally important species, comprised of species that produced fruit with reliable seasonality (Mo and Waterhouse, unpub. data; cf. Innis and McEvoy 1992). The identification of important feed species and knowledge of its phenology provides a more informative basis for rainforest restoration, which is currently underway in many private landholdings.

Anthropogenic factors present further implications for the ecology of fruiting plants and frugivores. Like many of the rainforest areas of southeastern Australia, the Illawarra region has experienced extensive clearing of natural vegetation. European settlement began around 1815, during which time the rainforests were believed to cover a total area of at least 22 850 ha (Mills 1986). The plentiful supply of Red Cedar *Toona ciliata* attracted private timber getters, which in turn opened up the region for pastoral and agricultural land uses (MacDonald 1966; Hunter 1974; Bywater 1978; Dunstan and Fox 1996; Adams 2005). In areas of mild topography, the fertile soils were exploited for growing crops (Mitchell 1997). Today, less than 6000 ha of rainforest remain, a mere quarter of its original area (Mills 1986; Stork et al. 2008; Riviere and Rowlatt 2013; Mo and Waterhouse 2015). Its dramatic reduction has heightened the need for thorough studies (e.g. Bywater 1978; Floyd 1982; Erskine 1984; Mills 1998), in particular those focusing on biodiversity and geographical significance.

ACKNOWLEDGMENTS

We thank Maurizio Rossetto and one anonymous reviewer for helpful comments that improved the manuscript.

REFERENCES

Adams, M. (2005). 'Little Bulli: the Pioneering of Stanwell Park and Northern Illawarra Till the 1860s'. (Cultural Exchange International: Russell Lea, NSW).

Ashcroft, M.B. (2006). A method for improving landscape scale temperature predictions and the implications for vegetation modelling. *Ecological Modelling* **197**, 394-404.

Blakers, M., Davies, S.J.J.F.and Reilly, P. (1984). 'The Atlas of Australian Birds'. (Royal Australasian Ornithologists Union/Melbourne University Press: Melbourne).

Proc. Linn. Soc. N.S.W., 137, 2015

25

Bywater, J.F. (1978). Distribution and ecology of rainforest flora and fauna in the Illawarra district. Honours thesis, University of Wollongong.

Croke, J., Reinfelds, I., Thompson, C. and Roper, E. (2014). Macrochannels and their significance for flood-risk minimisation: examples from southeast Queensland and New South Wales, Australia. *Stochastic Environmental Research and Risk Assessment* 28, 99-112.

Crome, F.H.J. (1975). The ecology of fruit pigeons in tropical northern Queensland. *Australian Wildlife Research* 2, 155-185.

Crome, F.H.J. (1976). Some observations on the biology of the cassowary in northern Queensland. *Emu* 76, 8-14.

Donaghey, R. (1996). Bowerbirds. In 'Finches, Bowerbirds and Other Passerines' (Ed. R. Strahan) pp. 138-187. (Angus and Robertson: Sydney).

Dunstan, C.E. and Fox, B.J. (1996). The effects of fragmentation and disturbance of rainforest on ground-dwelling small mammals on the Robertson Plateau, New South Wales, Australia. *Journal of Biogeography* 23, 187-201.

Erskine, J. (1984). The distributional ecology of rainforest in the Illawarra in relation to fire. Honours thesis, University of Wollongong.

Floyd, A.G. (1982). Rainforests of Northern Illawarra. Unpublished report to NSW National Parks and Wildlife Service, Sydney.

Floyd, A.G. (1990). 'Australian Rainforests in New South Wales.' (Surrey Beatty and Sons: Sydney).

Foster, R.B. (1982). The seasonal rhythm of fruitfall on Barro Colorado Island. In 'The Ecology of a Tropical Forest' (Eds E.G. Leigh, A.S. Rand and D.M. Windsor) pp. 151-172. (Smithsonian Institution Press: Washington, DC).

Foster, R.B. (1985). Plant seasonality in the forests of Panama. *Monographs in Systematic Botany* 10, 255-262.

Frankie, G.W., Baker, H.G. and Opler, P.A. (1974). Comparative phenological studies of trees in tropical lowland wet and dry forest sites in Costa Rica. *Journal of Ecology* 62, 881-919.

French, K. and Westoby, M. (1992). Removal of vertebrate-dispersed fruits in vegetation on fertile and infertile soils. *Oecologia* 91, 447-454.

Frith, C.B. and Frith, D.W. (2004). 'The Bowerbirds'. (Oxford University Press: Melbourne).

Fuller, L. (1995). 'Wollongong's Native Trees'. (Kingsclear Books: Alexandria, NSW).

Green, R.J. (1993). Avian seed dispersal in and near subtropical rainforests. *Wildlife Research* 20, 535-557.

Heideman, P.D. (1989). Temporal and spatial variation in the phenology of flowering and fruiting in a tropical rainforest. *Journal of Ecology* 77, 1059-1079.

Humphrey, S.R. and Bonaccorso, F.J. (1979). Population and community ecology. In 'Biology of Bats of the New World Family Phyllostomatidae. Part III'. (Eds

R.J. Baker, J.K. Jones and D.C. Carter) pp. 406-441. (Texas Tech University Press: Lubbock, Texas).

Hunter, S. (1974). From rainforest to grassland: a study of man's impact on vegetation in the Jamberoo area, N.S.W. Honours thesis, University of Sydney.

Innis, G.J. (1989). Feeding ecology of fruit pigeons in subtropical rainforests of south-eastern Queensland. *Australian Wildlife Research* 16, 365-394.

Innis, G.J. and McEvoy, J. (1992). Feeding ecology of green catbirds (*Ailuroedus crassirostris*) in subtropical rainforests of south-eastern Queensland. *Wildlife Research* 19, 317-329.

Keith, D.A. (2004). Ocean shores to desert dunes: the native vegetation of New South Wales and the ACT. NSW Department of Environment and Conservation, Hurstville, NSW.

MacDonald, W. (Ed) (1966). 'Earliest Illawarra'. (Illawarra Historical Society: Wollongong, NSW).

Macquarie, P.C. (2013). Valuing landscape, performing landscape: a case study of the Illawarra Escarpment. PhD thesis, University of Wollongong.

Mills, K. (1998). The clearing of the Illawarra rainforests: problems in reconstructing pre-European vegetation patterns. *Australian Geographer* 19, 230-240.

Mills, K.G. (1986). The Illawarra rainforests: a historical, floristic and environmental study of their distribution and ecology. PhD thesis, University of Wollongong.

Mitchell, G. (1997). The garden of the Illawarra. In 'A History of Wollongong'. (Eds J. Hagan and A. Wells) (University of Wollongong Press, Wollongong, NSW).

Mo, M. and Waterhouse, D.R. (2015). Historical insight on the Topknot Pigeon *Lopholaimus antarcticus* in the Illawarra rainforests through the 20th Century. *Australian Zoologist* 37, 337-342.

NSW NPWS. (2000). Royal National Park, Heathcote National Park and Garawarra State Recreation Area: plan of management. NSW National Parks and Wildlife Service, Sydney.

NSW NPWS. (2002). Wollongong LGA bioregional assessment (part I): native vegetation of the Illawarra Escarpment and coastal plain. NSW National Parks and Wildlife Service, Sydney.

NSW NPWS. (2011). Illawarra Escarpment State Conservation Area: draft plan of management. NSW National Parks and Wildlife Service, Sydney South.

Parker, K., Head, L., Chisholm, L.A. and Feneley, N. (2008). A conceptual model of ecological connectivity in the Shellharbour Local Government Area, New South Wales, Australia. *Landscape and Urban Planning* 86, 47-59.

Raemaekers, J.J., Aldrich-Blake, F.P.G. and Payne, J.B. (1980). The forest. In 'Malayan Forest Primates: Ten Year's Study in Tropical Rain Forest'. (Ed D.J. Chivers) pp. 29-61. (Plenum Press: New York).

Reinfields, I. and Nanson, G.C. (2001). 'Torrents of terror': the August 1998 storm and the magnitude, frequency and impact of major floods in the Illawarra region of New South Wales. *Australian Geographical Studies* **39**, 335-352.

Reinfields, I. and Nanson, G.C. (2004). Aspects of the hydro-geomorphology of Illawarra streams: implications for planning and design of urbanising landscapes. *Wetlands (Australia)* **21**, 238-237.

Riviere, R. and Rowlatt, M. (2013). Community driven conservation: Illawarra woodland and rainforest project. *Nature New South Wales* **57**(3), 21-23.

Schulz, M. and Magarey, E. (2012). Vertebrate fauna: a survey of Australia's oldest national park and adjoining reserves. *Proceedings of the Linnean Society of New South Wales* **134**, B215-B247.

Schulz, M. and Ransom, L. (2010). Rapid fauna habitat assessment of the Sydney metropolitan catchment area. In 'The Natural History of Sydney' (Eds D. Lunney, P. Hutchings and D. Hochuli) pp. 371-401. (Royal Zoological Society of New South Wales: Mosman, NSW).

Smythe, N. (1970). Relationships between fruiting seasons and seed dispersal methods in a neotropical forest. *American Naturalist* **104**, 25-35.

Snow, D.W. and Snow, B.K. (1964). Breeding seasons and annual cycles of Trinidad land birds. *Zoologica (N.Y.)* **49**, 1-40.

Stork, N.E., Goosem, S. and Turton, S.M. (2008). Australian rainforests in a global context. In 'Living in a Dynamic Tropical Forest Landscape' (Eds N.E. Stork and S.M. Turton) pp. 4-20. (Blackwell Publishing: Carlton, Vic).

Strom, A. (1977). On the Illawarra. In 'Parks and Wildlife Vol. 2 No. 1 – Rain Forests'. (Eds W. Goldstein and A. Fox) pp. 13-17. (NSW National Parks and Wildlife Service: Sydney).

Switzer, A.D., Pucillo, K., Haredy, R.A., Jones, B.G. and Bryant, E.A. (2005). Sea level, storm or tsunami: enigmatic sand sheet deposits in a sheltered coastal embayment from southeastern New South Wales, Australia. *Journal of Coastal Research* **21**, 655-663.

Thornton, E., Neave, M. and Rayburg, S. (2007). Hydraulic geometry in river channel networks as a method for the assessment of river condition. In 'Proceedings of the 5th Australian Stream Management Conference: Australian Rivers, Making a Difference.' (Eds A.L. Wilson, R.L. Dehaan, K.J. Page, K.H. Bowmer and A. Curtis) pp. 401-406. (Charles Sturt University, Thurgoona, NSW).

Waterhouse, D.R. (2001). Observations on the diet of the Topknot Pigeon *Lopholaimus antarcticus* in the Illawarra rainforest, New South Wales. *Corella* **25**: 32-28.

Webb, L.J. and Tracey, J.G. (1981). Australian rainforests: patterns and change. In 'Ecological Biogeography of Australia'. (Eds A. Keast and W. Junk) pp. 606-694. (The Hague, Sydney).

Wood, K.A. and Simcock, R.A. (1993). Birds of the Illawarra district, 1982-87. *Emu* **93**, 137-144.

Yap, S.K. (1982). The phenology of some fruit tree species in a lowland dipterocarp forest. *Tree Physiology* **45**, 21-35.

28

The History and Status of Apostlebirds (*Struthidea cinerea*) in the Sydney Region

Matthew Mo

NSW Department of Primary Industries, Elizabeth Macarthur Agricultural Institute, Woodbridge Road, Menangle NSW 2568 (matthew.mo@dpi.nsw.gov.au)

Published on 28 August 2015 at http://escholarship.library.usyd.edu.au/journals/index.php/LIN

Mo, M. (2015). The history and status of apostlebirds (*Struthidea cinerea*) in the Sydney region. *Proceedings of the Linnean Society of New South Wales* **137**, 29-35.

The avifauna of the Sydney region has undergone substantial change since 1900. The apostlebird (*Struthidea cinerea*) is a passerine predominately of inland areas of eastern Australia that does not naturally occur east of the Great Dividing Range in New South Wales. Database records showed that apostlebird sightings have been sporadically reported in the Sydney region as early as 1895. In at least four cases, individuals persisted for periods of seven months to 12 years. Since 1998, three populations have established in Nurragingy Reserve in Doonside, the Pinegrove Lawn Cemetery, Minchinbury and Plumpton. Breeding has been recorded in these three populations, as well as in Lane Cove and the Megalong Valley in the 1960's.

Manuscript received 20 March 2015, accepted for publication 22 July 2015.

KEYWORDS: apostlebird, breeding attempts, citizen science, database records, naturalisation, population establishment, *Struthidea cinerea*, Sydney region, urban ecology

INTRODUCTION

Many authors have documented substantial change in the Sydney region's avifauna. Recently, evidence was presented that most of the 15 extant parrot species were rare in the region prior to 1900 (Burgin and Saunders 2007). Some became widespread after escapes from aviaries, whereas others expanded their distribution naturally (Hoskin et al. 1991). Another example, the Australian white ibis (*Threskiornis molucca*) was considered a vagrant prior to 1950, only seen in any numbers in Botany Bay and the Hawkesbury Swamps (Morris 1983; Corben and Munro 2008). Now, it has become widespread in the region.

The apostlebird (*Struthidea cinerea*) (Fig. 1), a conspicuous gregarious passerine, is abundant in the inland areas of eastern Australia, with an isolated population in the Top End, Northern Territory (Fig. 2). Changes in the distribution in last century were well-documented, showing that at least half its current range was penetrated in the last 100 years (McAllan and O'Brien 2001; Barrett et al. 2003). Habitation of some localities apparently occurs in response to climatic conditions, receding in times of drought (Mack 1967).

Figure 1. An apostlebird *Struthidea cinerea* at the Pinegrove Lawn Cemetery, Minchinbury. Photo, M. Mo.

Apostlebirds do not naturally occur east of the Great Dividing Range in New South Wales (NSW). Individuals located in the metropolitan areas of Sydney and Newcastle are believed to be aviary escapees or deliberate releases (Hoskin et al. 1991). Likewise, individuals had sporadically turned up in Brisbane in the 1960's (Stenhouse 1964). Occurrences of apostlebirds in coastal areas have historically

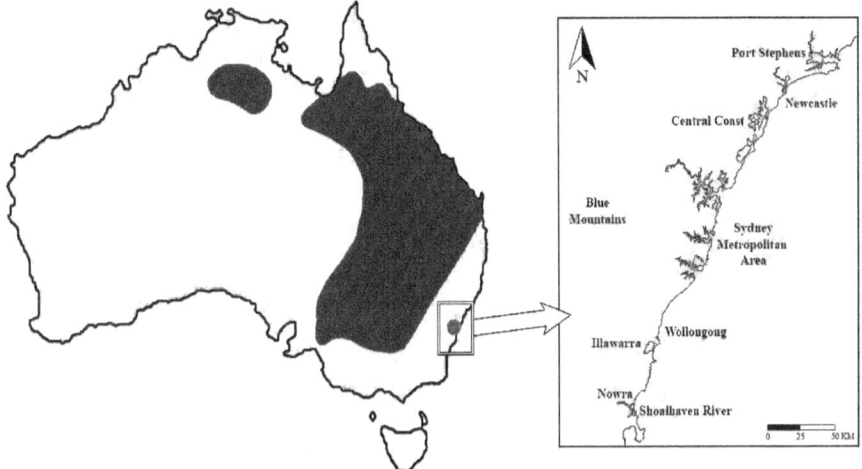

Figure 2. Map showing the natural distribution of the apostlebird *Struthidea cinerea*. Inset map shows the study area in an Australian context.

been short-lived, with freed individuals presumably not surviving as indicated by the absence of many subsequent sightings. More recently, apostlebirds have become a frequent sight in three locations in western Sydney.

This paper synthesises information on the history of apostlebird sightings in the Sydney region, and examines the regional status of this species.

METHODS

In this paper, the Sydney region is defined as the area bound by Port Stephens in the north and the Shoalhaven River in the south, west to the Blue Mountains and Great Dividing Range (Fig. 2). Sightings of apostlebirds were extracted from the Atlas of NSW Wildlife (OEH 2015) and Atlas of Living Australia (ALA 2015), which also includes preserved specimens lodged at the Australian Museum, South Australian Museum and Tasmanian Museum and Art Gallery. Sighting records were also obtained from three organisations: NSW Bird Atlassers (NSWBA), Cumberland Bird Observers' Club (CBOC) and Birdlife Australia.

NSWBA was established in 1982 with the aim of monitoring bird distributions. Its database comprises of records contributed by members and other bird-watching groups, as well as locations inferred from literature.

The CBOC database has been maintained since 1986. In addition to sighting locations, members

also provide an indication of flock size (1-5, 6-20, 21-50, 51-100, >100) and breeding information.

Birdlife Australia collects records from its members through the web portal Birdata. To date, the organisation has conducted two nation-wide atlas surveys, the first during 1977-1981 (Blakers et al. 1984) and most recently during 1998-2001 (Barrett et al. 2003). In addition, Birdlife Australia (then Birds Australia) compiled the Historical Bird Atlas (HBA), which is a collection of records derived from museum collections, personal notebooks, published and unpublished literature between 1629 and 1976.

Records presented in this paper were current in February 2015. Duplicate records were identified and removed. Some interpretations were made based on the number of records available, such as recurring records from the same location within a short time period (<6 months) possibly representing the same individuals persisting. It should also be noted that in some cases, a submitter may observe apostlebirds over consecutive days and only lodge one record; hence the subsequent observations are not represented in the data. Additional data were gathered from published literature and personal observations.

RESULTS

The database search retrieved 291 records, 76 percent of which were from localities in western Sydney (Blacktown, Hawkesbury, Hills, Penrith and Macarthur districts; Tables 1, 2). The earliest known

30

Proc. Linn. Soc. N.S.W., 137, 2015

Table 1. Records of the apostlebird *Struthidea cinerea* **in the Sydney region prior to 1950.**
Source: NSWBA = New South Wales Bird Atlassers, HBA = Historical Bird Atlas (Birdlife Australia), ALA = Atlas of Living Australia

Location	Date	Source
Hyde Park	Jun 1895	NSWBA, ALA
Mosman	1920	NSWBA, ALA
Upper Colo	Oct 1923	HBA, NSWBA, ALA
Doonside	1925	NSWBA, ALA

records occurred in Hyde Park in the central business district over two days in June 1895, presumed the same individual (Table 1). A further three sightings occurred in the 1920's with no consistency in their locations.

Reports from the majority of locations since 1950 were also transient individuals (Table 2). There was no clear geographical pattern to these data, except for a series of sightings in the Sutherland district in 1972 and the early 1980's (Fig. 3). There have been two records from the Royal National Park (NSWBA, in litt.; Anyon-Smith 2006), however other comprehensive fauna surveys did not detect the species (Andrew 2001; DECCW 2011; Schulz and Magarey 2012). Two breeding events recorded pre-date the establishment of populations in western Sydney (Smith and Smith 1990; Higgins et al. 2006; Table 2). Whether these breeding attempts were successful is not known.

Persisting individuals

Although much of the data relate to sporadic records, there were some series of records identified that were common in location and time (Fig. 3; Table 2). These series suggests that some apostlebirds persisted over a short period of time, for example, records in Chatswood West between 1961 and 1962, and Annangrove in 1974.

The earliest known records of apostlebirds in southern Sydney occurred in the Kurnell and Cronulla area in the mid-1950's (Fig. 3; Table 2). Some apparently persisted for at least 15 years (Morris in Higgins et al. 2006), which possibly explains resurgence in records from various locations in the Sutherland district in 1972. In 1961, 12 sightings were recorded in Holsworthy, with subsequent records nearby at Deadmans Creek in 1962.

Established populations

Records for three established populations (Fig. 3) constituted 55% of the data; Nurragingy Reserve,

Doonside (n = 12), Plumpton (n = 65) and Pinegrove Lawn Cemetery, Minchinbury (n = 83).

There were records in Nurragingy Reserve in 1998, which discontinued until 2010 (Table 2), however Roberts (2009) considered apostlebirds a common sight within this period (Fig. 4). The largest flock size to date numbered six individuals (CBOC, in litt.). At least three breeding events were recorded; one fledgling was located on 28 November 2010 and nest building was observed on 21 October 2013 and 26 October 2014 (CBOC, in litt.).

There were two records at the Pinegrove Lawn Cemetery in 1988, but it was only until 1998 that regular sightings began to occur (Table 2). Initially, the rate of reported sightings was low, with intervals of up to six months between records from 1998 to 2001. From 2002 to the present day, the number of database records per year ranged from two to 12. Several more sightings have occurred without formal lodgment in databases (A. Katon, B. Way, A. Lumnitzer and G. Turner, pers. comm; pers. obs). The earliest known breeding event at this site was recorded on 21 February 2002, although the observer did not specify any further details (CBOC, in litt.). Additional accounts of breeding include a nestling seen on 14 November 2008 and nests with eggs reported on 17 October 2011 (CBOC, in litt.). The largest flock size recorded here was six apostlebirds. Individuals had also been seen in the adjoining Wonderland Sydney site prior to its closure in April 2004 (B. Way, pers. comm).

Since January 2007, 65 database records have concentrated on two parkland reserves in Plumpton, Alroy Park and Plumpton Park (Table 2). A nestling was located on January 2007; hence these individuals had occupied the area as early as 2006. Breeding events have been recorded each year since 2007 (CBOC, in litt.). Nest building was observed in the months of March, April, June, August and September to December. Nests with eggs were located in September 2007, September 2011 and October 2012, and fledglings were located in January 2009 and November 2010.

DISCUSSION

Records of apostlebirds in Sydney could be categorically placed into three sitings: transient individuals, persistent individuals and established populations. The sporadic appearance of transient individuals suggests that several separate introduction and/or dispersal events have occurred, either by deliberate releases, aviary escapes or movements

Proc. Linn. Soc. N.S.W., 137, 2015

31

APOSTLEBIRDS IN THE SYDNEY REGION

ble 2. Summary of apostlebird *Struthidea cinerea* records in the Sydney region post-1950.
cords have been grouped into general time periods based on author discretion. Abundance has been
:orded as a range by some databases. Source: NSWBA = New South Wales Bird Atlassers, CBOC =
imberland Bird Observers' Club, BLA = Birdlife Australia, HBA = Historical Bird Atlas (Birdlife
istralia), AS = 1977-81 atlas survey (Birdlife Australia), ALA = Atlas of Living Australia, OEH = Atlas
NSW Wildlife (Office of Environment and Heritage)

ocation	Date	Abundance	Source
ity and surrounds			
Randwick	Feb 1966		NSWBA, ALA
Surry Hills	1989		AM, ALA
Erskine Park	Sep 2008	21-50	CBOC
orthern Sydney			
Dee Why	Jun 1959		CBOC, NSWBA
	Dec 1984-Jan 1985		NSWBA
Chatswood West	Nov 1961-Jun 1962[SR]		NSWBA, HBA
Lane Cove	1962[B]		Higgins *et al.* 2006
Marsfield	Mar 1970		NSWBA
lacktown district			
Blacktown	1974		NSWBA, ALA
	Jul 1990-Dec 1991		NSWBA, ALA
	Jun 1993		NSWBA, ALA
	Sep 2003	1-5	CBOC
	Jul 2004		CBOC
	Aug 2005-Apr 2006[SR]	1-5	CBOC
Northmead	1974		NSWBA, ALA
Minchinbury	May, Nov 1988		NSWBA, ALA
	Dec 1998-present[EST, B]	51-100	CBOC, BLA, NSWBA, ALA, pers. obs.
Mount Druitt	Jan 1989		OEH, ALA
	Jun 1999-May 2000		NSWBA, ALA
	Sep 2007	6-20	CBOC
	Mar 2011		OEH
Nurragingy Reserve, Doonside	Aug, Dec 1998	1	NSWBA, CBOC, BLA
	Oct 2010-present[EST, B]		CBOC, ALA
Featherdale Wildlife Park, Doonside	May 2005		ALA
Plumpton	Mar 2002	6	OEH, ALA
	Jan 2007-present[EST, B]	6-20	CBOC
Westmead	No date		Roberts 2009
awkesbury			
Scheyville	Feb-Jun 1974		HBA, NSWBA, ALA
Marsden Park	Nov 1977		NSWBA, ALA
	Oct 2006	1-5	CBOC
Cattai	Apr 2000		NSWBA, ALA
	Aug 2008		NSWBA, ALA
Wilberforce	Jan 2006		NSWBA, ALA
Pitt Town	Aug 2008		ALA
Ebeneezer	Aug 2008		NSWBA, ALA
ills district			
Annangrove	Apr-Oct 1974[SR]		NSWBA, ALA
enrith district			
Penrith	Mar-Jun 1998		NSWBA, ALA
Emerton	Apr 2000		NSWBA, ALA
Bidwill	Jul 2000		NSWBA, ALA
Emu Plains	Aug 2004		ALA
Ropes Crossing	Apr 2010		BLA, CBOC, ALA
Bringelly	Feb 2013	1	CBOC
Luddenham	Dec 2013	6-20	CBOC

Location	Date	Abundance	Source
Table 2 continued			
Sutherland district			
Kurnell	Dec 1954		NSWBA, ALA
Cronulla	Mar 1955		NSWBA, ALA
	Jan 1972		HBA, ALA
	Apr-Jul 1981		NSWBA, ALA
Caringbah	Nov 1972		NSWBA, ALA
Sutherland	Jan 1972		HBA, ALA
	Jan 1981	9	OEH, ALA
Taren Point	Nov 1972		HBA, ALA
Menai	Nov 1972		HBA, ALA
Barden Ridge	Nov 1972		NSWBA, ALA
Heathcote	May-Jun 1981[SR]	1-5	OEH, CBOC, NSWBA, ALA
	Oct 1982	1-5	CBOC, NSWBA, ALA
	Jun 1983	9	CBOC, NSWBA, OEH, ALA
Royal National Park	May 1983		NSWBA, ALA
	No date		Anyon-Smith 2006
Bankstown district			
Holsworthy	Apr-Sep 1961[SR]		NSWBA, ALA
Sandy Point	May-Aug 1962		NSWBA, ALA
Milperra	Oct-Nov 1985	2	CBOC, OEH, ALA
Macarthur district			
Narellan	Sep 1956		NSWBA, ALA
	Jun 2012		ALA
Camden	Dec 1989		NSWBA, ALA
Blue Mountains			
Megalong Valley	1968[B]	2	Smith and Smith 1990
Newnes State Forest	May 1998		NSWBA, ALA
Katoomba	Jul 2000		ALA
Hunter Region			
Lake Macquarie area	3 records ~1977-81		AS
Raymond Terrace	Dec 1978		AS
Seaham	Dec 1978		NSWBA, ALA
Shortland	Feb 1996		NSWBA, ALA

[SR]SR = Subsequent records (≥5) in short uccession (<6 months)
[EST]EST = Established population
[B]B = Evidence of breeding

from established populations.

Previous studies on apostlebird movements suggest that it is sedentary (Britton and Britton 2000; Griffioen and Clarke 2002), though may move widely over large home ranges (Chapman 1998; Robinson 2000). This suggests that apostlebirds present in an area should be easily detectable, especially in the metropolitan region; however no information on movement patterns in urban environments is available. The volume and consistency of records from Doonside, Minchinbury and Plumpton give a clear indication that populations have naturalised at these locations. Less frequent records at nearby suburbs such as Mount Druitt and Blacktown suggest that apostlebirds periodically disperse into these areas. Despite established populations, apostlebirds have so far remained localised, unlike parrots, ibis and exotic avifauna (Barrett et al. 2003; Burgin and Saunders 2007).

The apostlebird frequently exploits parks and gardens in settled areas (Stenhouse 1964; Longmore 1978; Britton and Britton 2000). The occurrence of apostlebirds near Cronulla from the 1950's to 1970's represent the first coastal population in NSW, although these individuals did not remain extant. Records of breeding in Brisbane in the 1960's (Stenhouse

Proc. Linn. Soc. N.S.W., 137, 2015

33

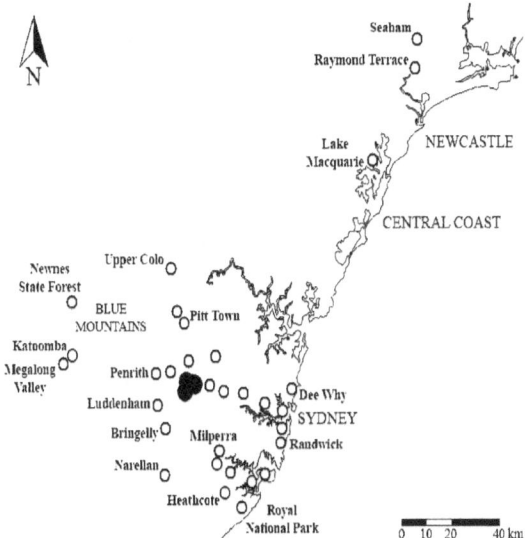

Figure 3. Locations of sporadic records (white circles) and established populations (black circles) of the apostlebird *Struthidea cinerea* in the Sydney region.

cats are a major threat to avifauna (Barratt 1998), the powerful mobbing defence seen in apostlebird flocks (Woxvold and Magarth 2004) may reduce their vulnerability.

An important consideration in this study is the possibility that apostlebirds present in an area may either not be detected or not be recorded in databases, hence an absence of records does not necessary reflect an absence of the species. The Cumberland Plain has historically supported a number of inland woodland species (Schulz and Ransom 2010), such that the possibility that an unrecorded population of apostlebirds have always been present should also be considered. In particular, movements of inland species into the Sydney region have often been attributed to drought conditions in central and western New South Wales (Keast 1995; Bayly 1999; Major and Parsons 2010).

1964) demonstrate the possibility of coastal urban populations forming in Sydney. Being a mudnester, the climate of the eastern seaboard may perhaps facilitate its breeding by the continuous availability of damp soil and reliable rainfall. In addition, urban environments present fewer natural predators such as birds of prey and monitor lizards. Although domestic

ACKNOWLEDGEMENTS

Several observers have lodged database records over the years, including Ákos Lumnitzer, Mark Young, Alex Zografos, John Cresswell, Rob Child, Max Breckenridge, Jenny Stiles, Ashwin Rudder, Peter Booth, Edwin Vella, Anthony Katon and Bob Way. Their labours, while at the time may have felt monotonous, has been instrumental to understanding occurrence patterns of apostlebirds and other species in the Sydney region. I especially appreciate the Cumberland Birds Observers' Club for their involvement in the preparation of this paper.

Figure 4. A flock of five apostlebirds *Struthidea cinerea* in Nurragingy Reserve, Doonside. Photo, M. Mo.

REFERENCES

ALA (2015). Atlas of Living Australia. (Atlas of Living Australia: Canberra).

Andrew, D. (2001). 'Post Fire Vertebrate Fauna Survey – Royal and Heathcote National Parks and Garawarra State Recreation Area'. Unpublished report. (NSW National Parks and Wildlife Service, Sydney South Region: Audley).

Anyon-Smith, S. (2006). 'Birdwatching in Royal & Heathcote National Parks'. (Department of Environment and Conservation, Sydney South Region: Audley).

Barratt, D.G. (1998). Predation by house cats, *Felis catus* (L.), in Canberra, Australia. II. Factors affecting the amount of prey caught and estimates of the impact on wildlife. *Wildlife Research* **25**, 475-487.

34

Proc. Linn. Soc. N.S.W., 137, 2015

Barrett, G., Silcocks, A., Barry, S., Cunningham, R. and Poulter, R. (2003). 'The Atlas of Australian Birds'. (Royal Australasian Ornithologists Union: Melbourne).

Bayly, K. (1999). Observations of behaviour of Sulphur-crested Cockatoos *Cacatua galerita* in suburban Sydney. *Corella* **19**, 11-15.

Blakers, M., Davies, S.J.J.F. and Reilly, P.N. (1984). 'The Atlas of Australian Birds'. (Melbourne University Press: Melbourne).

Britton, P.L. and Britton, H.A. (2000). The birds of Charters Towers, north Queensland. *Sunbird* **30**, 61-88.

Burgin, S. and Saunders, T. (2007). Parrots of the Sydney region: population changes over 100 years. In 'Pest or Guest: the Zoology of Overabundance' (Eds. D. Lunney, P. Eby, P. Hutchings and S. Burgin). Pp. 185-194. Royal Zoological Society of New South Wales, Mosman.

Chapman, G.S. (1998). The social life of the apostlebird *Struthidea cinerea*. *Emu* **98**, 178-183.

Corben, D.T. and Munro, U. (2008). The abundance and movements of the Australian white ibis *Threskiornis molucca* in an urban environment. *Corella* **32**, 58-65.

DECCW (2011). 'The Vertebrate Fauna of Royal & Heathcote National Parks and Garawarra State Conservation Area'. Published report. (Department of Environment, Climate Change and Water: Hurstville).

Griffioen, P.A. and Clarke, M.F. (2002). Large-scale bird-movement patterns evident in eastern Australian atlas data. *Emu* **102**, 99-125.

Higgins, P.J., Peter, J.M. and Cowling, S.J. (Eds.) (2006). 'Handbook of Australian, New Zealand and Antarctic Birds. Volume 7: Boatbill to Starlings'. (Oxford University Press: Melbourne).

Hoskin, E.S., Hindwood, K.A. and McGill, A.R. (1991). 'The Birds of Sydney, County of Cumberland, New South Wales, 1770-1989'. (Surrey Beatty and Sons: Chipping Norton).

Keast, A. (1995). Habitat loss and species loss: the birds of Sydney 50 years ago and now. *Australian Zoologist* **30**, 3-25.

Longmore, N.W. (1978). Avifauna of the Rockhampton area, Queensland. *Sunbird* **9**, 25-53.

Mack, K.J. (1967). Apostlebirds in the Murray lands. *South Australian Ornithologist* **24**, 139-145.

Major, R.E. and Parsons, H. (2010). What do museum specimens tell us about the impact of urbanisation? A comparison of the recent and historical bird communities of Sydney. *Emu* **110**, 92-103.

McAllan, I.A.W. and O'Brien, R.M. (2001). The changing distribution of the apostlebird *Struthidea cinerea*. *Australian Bird Watcher* **19**, 14-27.

Morris, A.K. (1983). First breeding of the sacred ibis in the county of Cumberland. *Australian Birds* **17**, 43-44.

OEH (2015). Atlas of NSW Wildlife. (NSW Office of Environment and Heritage: Hurstville).

Roberts, P. (2009). 'Sydney Birds and Where to Find Them'. (Allen and Unwin: Sydney).

Robinson, D. (2000). 'Distribution, Status and Habitat Requirements of the Apostlebird in Victoria and Southern New South Wales'. Unpublished report to Birds Australia, Melbourne.

Schulz, M. and Magarey, E. (2012). Vertebrate fauna: a survey of Australia's oldest national park and adjoining reserves. *Proceedings of the Linnean Society of New South Wales* **134**, B215-B247.

Schulz, M. and Ransom, L. (2010). Rapid fauna habitat assessment of the Sydney metropolitan catchment area. In 'The Natural History of Sydney' (Eds. D. Lunney, P. Hutchings and D. Hochuli). Pp. 371-401. Royal Zoological Society of New South Wales, Mosman.

Smith, J. and Smith, P. (1990). 'Fauna of the Blue Mountains'. (Kangaroo Press: Kenthurst).

Stenhouse, D. (1964). Breeding attempt of *Struthidea* in Brisbane. *Emu* **63**, 283-286.

Woxvold, I.A. and Magarth, M.J.L. (2004). Predation events at an apostlebird nest. *Corella* **28**, 22-23.

Proc. Linn. Soc. N.S.W., 137, 2015

35

A New Species of the Fairy Shrimp *Branchinella* (Crustacea: Anostraca: Thamnocephalidae) from Western New South Wales, Australia.

Brian V Timms

Honorary Research Associate, Australian Museum, 6 College St Sydney, 2000 and Centre for Ecosystem Science, School of Biological, Earth and Environmental Sciences, University of New South Wales, Kensington, 2052, Australia.

Published on 1 September 2015 at http://escholarship.library.usyd.edu.au/journals/index.php/LIN

Timms, B.V. (2015). A new species of the fairy shrimp *Branchinella* (Crustacea: Anostraca: Thamnocephalidae) from western New South Wales, Australia. *Proceedings of the Linnean Society of New South Wales* **137**, 37-43.

Branchinella angelica n.sp. is described from the Wilcannia area in western New South Wales. Its frontal appendage is distinctive and consist of a two branches, each with a central subbranch of a pad on a short peduncle and a large main branch with many lateral and medial digitiform processes of varying complexity. Other male characteristics are unremarkable and the female is like many others in *Branchinella*. So far it has been found only in artificial sites, so that its natural habitat is unknown.

Manuscript received 30 April 2015, accepted for publication 22 July 2015.

Key Words: *Branchinella angelica* n. sp., *Branchinella campbelli*, eggs, frontal appendage, thoracopods.

INTRODUCTION

Australia has three genera of fairy shrimps (*Branchinella, Streptocephalus* and *Australobranchipus*) and two related brine shrimp genera (*Artemia* and *Parartemia*) (Rogers and Timms, 2014). *Branchinella* is by far the most speciose genus, with 39 species presently known with 14 occurring in New South Wales (Geddes, 1981; Timms, 2015, and unpublished data). The only species actually recorded in the Wilcannia area, in the southwest of the state, is *B. lyrifera* (Linder, 1941), though species widespread in Australia are likely to occur there. Such species include *B. affinis* and *B. australiensis* from within 100 km of Wilcannia (author, unpublished data). Years ago I found two individuals of an apparent new *Branchinella* species in a roadside stock dam 19 km SE of Wilcannia, but the diagnostic frontal appendages were immature so they were put aside. Now I have abundant mature specimens of what I believe is the same species from a roadside burrow pit 10 km west of Wilcannia. It is the purpose of this paper to describe this new species.

METHODS

Specimens were examined and drawn under a Wild M3C stereomicroscope with a drawing tube and the 5th male thoracopod was studied under an Olympus BH monocular microscope at mainly 100x. A digital picture of the frontal appendage was taken with a Leica MZ16 Stereo Microscope with a SPOT Flex CCD camera, using Helicon Focus Z stacking software. Eggs were photographed on a Zeiss Evo LS15 SEM using a Robinson Backscatter Detector. Specimens were prepared as detailed in Timms and Lindsay (2011).

SYSTEMATICS

Class Crustacea Brünnich, 1772
Order Anostraca Sars, 1867
Family Thamnocephalidae Packard, 1883
Branchinella Sayce, 1903

Branchinella Sayce, 1903: 233; Linder, 1941: Henry, 1924: 129; Linder, 1941: 244; Geddes, 1981: 255-256; Rogers, 2006: 15-16.

Type species

Branchipus australiensis Richters, 1876 by subsequent designation.

***Branchinella angelica* n. sp.**

Etymology. This species is named for its beautiful angelic frontal appendage which to some look like angel wings.

Type Locality. New South Wales, ca 10 km W of Wilcannia, roadside borrow pit at 31° 22' 12.1"S, 143° 17' 19.8"E.

Type Specimens. *Holotype*. Male, 17.1 mm long, collected BVT from the type locality, 29 January, 2015. AM P97828; *Allotype*. Female 21.1 mm long, same data as hototype, AMP 97829; *Paratypes* 2 males, 19.5 and 17.5 mm long, 2 females, 20.0 and 18.6 mm long, some data as hototype, AM P97830.

Other Material. Six males and 4 females from the type locality, same data as above. AM P97831.

Diagnosis. Male with an elaborate frontal appendage, with two sub-branches each with a central pad on a short peduncle and a lateral elongated structure serially commencing basally with about 20 long digitiform processes laterally, followed by about 8 short digitiform processes medially and subapically with about 7 very short digitiform processes laterally. Each finger terminating in a short spine. Basal antennal segment cylindrical and unadorned. Female unremarkable and typical of many species of *Branchinella*. Egg surface with about 22 deep polygons.

Description. *Male*. Head of typical structure for *Branchinella* (Fig 1A), i.e. with two large compound eyes on short peduncles, ocellus small and insignificant located dorsally between the eyes, first antennae filiform, almost as long as proximal segment of the second antenna, and second antenna with proximal segment robust and fused basally and distal segment consisting of a pair of curved pincers about the same length as the proximal segment. Pincer proximal segment smooth all over and distal segment curved concavely more in shrimp vertical than horizontal plane. Apex blunt and slightly expanded and inner surface with many weak ridges at right angles to pincer axis.

Frontal appendage elaborate (Figs. 1B and C, 2A) forked near base into two branches, each broad proximally but narrowing distally to an acute apex. About 20 long digitiform processes laterally commencing from the fork at about the length of the first finger and gradually shortening at each distal insertion. Each finger terminating in a spine and with pairs of lateral protrusions, the number decreasing distally along the row. After a short gap about 8 short digitiform processes spaced on medial surface, each without lateral protrusions but terminating in a spine. Finally about 7 very short digitiform processes close together on the lateral margin, each with a short terminal spine. About a third way along the medial margin of each branch an oval flat protrusion on a wide peduncle.

Eleven thoracic segments each with a pair of thoracopods. Fifth thoracopod (Fig 3) with endite 1+2 and endite 3 evenly curved, the former about four times the size of the latter. Anterior seta of endite 1 with a single pectin of spines, anterior seta of endite 2 half length of anterior seta 1, more stout and curved and also bearing a single pectin of spines, anterior seta of endites 3-5 similar to that of endite 1. Posterior setae of endites two-segmented and longest of all thoracopod setae (only one shown on Fig 3). They number about 42 on endite 1+2, 15 on endite 3, 3 on endite 4 and 2 each on endites 5 and 6. Endopodite broadly square-shaped but with a shallow notch distally closer to lateral margin than medial margin. Endopodite with about 30 single segmented feathered setae. Exopodite elongated and bearing about 50 single segmented feathered setae. Epipodite bent oval-shaped and without setae. Praeepipodite foliacious, oval and with a scalloped margin; scallops smallest at distolateral margin.

Other thoracopods of similar structure particularly third to eight, with some reduction in size and complexity anterior and posterior to these.

Two genital segments (Fig 1D), the first larger than the second and bearing widely separated gonopod bases. When everted, gonopods reach to about half way along the second abdominal segment; bulbous with many backwardly pointing spines, and with a row of triangular spines medially, larger proximally than those sited distally. No other protrusions on genital segments.

Six abdominal segments and a telson bearing a pair of cercopods, about 1.5 times the length of the last abdominal segment.

Female. Head (Fig 1E) with two large compound eyes on short peduncles, ocellus small and insignificant located centrally just anterior to the eyes, first antennae filiform and a little shorter than second antennae. Second antennae flat, somewhat rectangular, about three times broader than long and terminating in a symmetrically placed narrow sharp projection.

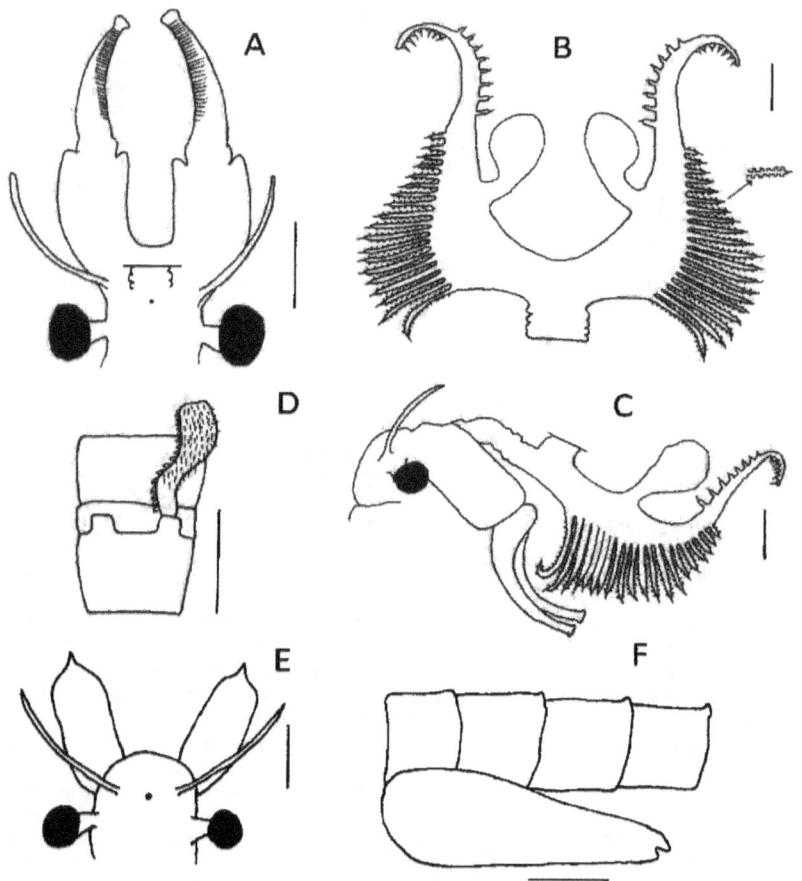

Fig 1. *Branchinella angelica* n. sp. A, male head, dorsal aspect; B, frontal appendage, dorsal aspect; C, male head with frontal appendage, lateral aspect; D, male genital segment with one gonopod expanded, ventral aspect; E, female head, dorsal aspect; F, female genital segments and first two abdominal segments with brood pouch, lateral aspect. Scale bars 1 mm.

Thorax of eleven segments each bearing a pair of thoracopods of similar structure to those of the male. Two genital segments, the first shorter than the second and bearing ventrally a brood pouch expanded proximally and extending to about the second abdominal segment. Six abdominal segments as in the male.

Egg (Fig 2B) spherical 206.8 ± 4.5 μm diameter (n=5) with about 22 polygons with wide rounded ridges and deep (ca 22 μm) flatish floors occupying about a third of the polygons, the remainder being the slopes of the ridges.

DISCUSSION

This species belongs to the genus *Branchinella* because it has gonopods with a single row of larger lateral spines and many smaller spines on the distal half of the everted portion (Brendonck, 1997; Rogers, 2006). Having a frontal organ is also typical, but not absolutely diagnostic (Geddes, 1981; Rogers, 2006).

The thoracopods are like those of other *Branchinella* species for which data are available (Geddes, 1981; Timms, 2001, 2002, 2005, 2008, 2012;

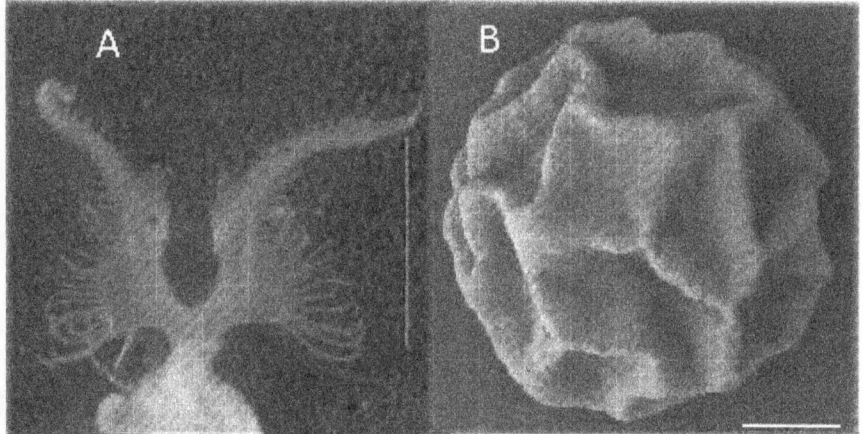

Fig 2. *Branchinella angelica* n. sp. A, image of frontal appendage, scale bar 5 mm; B, egg, scale bar 50 μm.

Timms and Geddes, 2003), with just minor variations in proportions of the endopodite, exopodite, epipodite and praeepipodite, in relative size and spination of

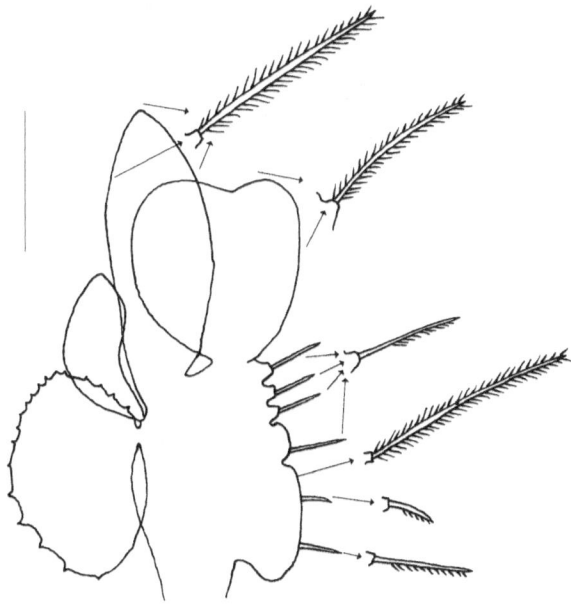

Fig 3. *Branchinella angelica* n. sp. Male fifth thoracopod. Arrows show the seta enlarged or the area of the thoracopod in which that seta occurs. Scale bar 1 mm.

the anterior setae, and in size and numbers of anterior setae (cf. Fig 3 with Figs 1 & 2 in Timms, 2001, Figs 6,7,8,&10 in Timms 2002, Figs, 7,8 & 9 in Timms and Geddes, 2003, Fig 5 in Timms, 2008 and Figs. 3 & 9 in Timms 2012).

It is the frontal appendage of the male that is the most distinctive feature in most *Branchinella* species. The frontal appendage of *Branchinella angelica* is most similar to that of *B. campbelli* Timms (Fig 4A,B). This species too has pads placed centrally on each branch of the frontal appendage and an array of digitiform processes laterally on each branch. However the digitiform processes of *B. campbelli* are of simpler structure than those of *B. angelica* and are all placed laterally whereas in *B. angelica* the basal group are lateral and the middle group of 8 are inserted medially. The second antennae are different in the two species: notably there is a rounded protrusion on the basomedial surface of the proximal segment in *B. campbelli* and not in *B. angelica*. The two halves of the basal segment are angled at about

40

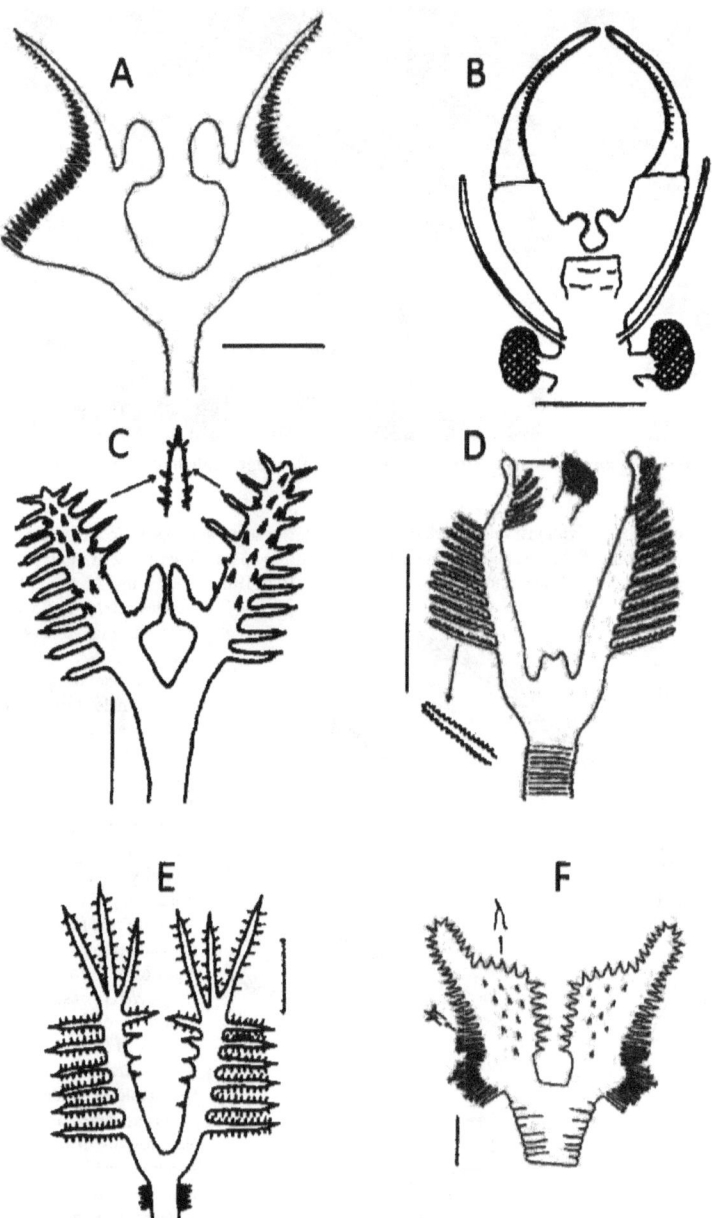

Fig 4. Other similar species of *Branchinella*. A & B, *B. campbelli* from Timms, 2001, A frontal append-age, B, head and antennae; C, *B. herrodi* frontal appendage from Timms, 2012; D, *B. tyleri* frontal ap-pendage from Timms and Geddes 2003; E, *B. multidigitata* frontal appendage from Timms, 2008; F. *B. kadjikadji* frontal appendage from Timms, 2002. Scale bars 1 mm.

60° to the shrimp body axis in *B. campbelli* whereas the two halves are almost parallel (and hence in line with the body axis) in *B. angelica*. Finally the apex of the distal segment is enlarged in *B. angelica*. but not in *B. campbelli*.

The other *Branchinella* species with a central enlargement of the frontal appendage is *B. herrodi* Timms (Fig 4C). However while this sub branch is broadly similar, it is not expanded distally as in *B. angelica* and *B. campbelli*, and the remainder of the frontal appendage is not expanded and the fingers are fewer and similar. The only other *Branchinella* species with digitiform processes on the lateral branches of the frontal appendage on serially alternate sides is *B. tyleri* Timms and Geddes (Fig 4D). However this species lacks the central subbranch of the frontal appendage and its digitiform processes lack the variety and numbers in *B. angelica*. *Branchinella multidigitata* Timms (Fig 4E) and *B. kadjikadji* Timms (Fig 4F) also lack the central subbranch but have numerous digitiform processes laterally and medially. However their arrangement and numbers are quite different from that in *B. angelica*.

The eggs of *B. angelica* are not distinctive, being unseparable from those of *B. affinis* Linder, *B. frondosa* Henry, *B. halsei* Timms and *B. macraeae* Timms, and similar to, but distinguishable with difficulty, from those of *B. basispina* Geddes, *B. campbelli* Timms, *B. erosa* Timms and *B. lamellata* Timms (Timms and Lindsay, 2011). *Branchinella angelica* eggs are easily distinguished from those of the other 32 known species of *Branchinella*.

Branchinella angelica is known only from around Wilcannia on the Darling River in southwestern New South Wales. It almost certainly does not occur further north in the Paroo and Warrego catchments of the Darling basin in western NSW, where extensive collections have not recorded it (Timms and Sanders, 2002); this area has the similar *B. campbelli*. The natural habitat of *B. angelica* is unknown, the present record being from a roadside burrow pit and a past indication from a stock dam.

ACKNOWLEDGEMENTS

I thank Sue Lindsay of the Australian Museum for taking the digital picture of the frontal appendage and SEMs of the eggs, Stephen Keable for facilitating my work at the Australian Museum, and Christopher Rogers for his comments on the manuscript and two anonymous referees for their input too.

REFERENCES

Brendonck, L. (1997). The anostracan genus *Branchinella* (Crustacea: Branchiopoda), in need of a taxonomic revision; evidence from penile morphology. *Zoological Journal of the Linnean Society* 119: 447-455.

Geddes, M.C., (1981). Revision of Australian species of *Branchinella* (Crustacea: Anostraca). *Australian Journal of Marine and Freshwater Research* 32: 253-295.

Linder, F., (1941). Contributions to the morphology and taxonomy of the Branchiopoda Anostraca. *Zoologiska Bidrag Från Uppsala* 20: 101-303.

Rogers, D.C. (2006). A genus level revision of the Thamnocephalidae (Crustacea: Barnchiopoda: Anostraca). *Zootaxa* 1260: 1-25.

Rogers, D.C. and B.V. Timms, (2014). Anostracan (Crustacea: Branchipoda) zoogeography III. Australian bioregions. *Zootaxa* 3881: 453-487.

Sayce, O.A. (1903). The phyllopods of Australia, including descriptions of some new genera and species. *Proceedings of the Royal Society of Victoria* 15: 224-261.

Timms, B.V. (2001). Two new species of *Branchinella* Sayce 1903 (Crustacea: Anostraca: Thamnocephalidae) from the Paroo, inland Australia. *Records of the Australian Museum* 53: 247-254.

Timms, B.V. (2002). The fairy shrimp genus *Branchinella* Sayce (Crustacea: Anostraca: Thamnocephalidae) in Western Australia, including a description of four new species. *Hydrobiologia* 486: 71-89.

Timms, B.V. (2005). Two new species of *Branchinella* (Anostraca: Thamnocephlaidae) and a reappraisal of the *B. nichollsi* group. *Memoirs of the Queensland Museum* 50: 441-452.

Timms, B.V. (2008). Further studies on the fairy shrimp genus *Branchinella* (Crustacea, Anostraca, Thamnocephalidae) in Western Australia, with a description of new species. *Records of the Western Australian Museum* 24: 289-306.

Timms, B.V. (2012). Further studies on the fairy shrimp genus *Branchinella* (Crustacea, Anostraca, Thamnocephalidae) in Australia, with descriptions of five new species. *Zootaxa* 3595: 35-60.

Timms, B.V. (2015). A revised identification guide to the fairy shrimps (Crustacea: Anostraca: Anostracina) of Australia. Museum Victoria Science Reports 19: 1-44.

Timms, B.V. and M.C.Geddes (2003). The fairy shrimp genus *Branchinella* Sayce 1903 (Crustacea: Anostraca: Thamnocephalidae) in South Australia and the Northern Territory, including descriptions of three new species. *Transactions of the Royal Society of South Aust*ralia 127: 53-68.

42

Proc. Linn. Soc. N.S.W., 137, 2015

Timms, B.V. and S. Lindsay (2011). Morphometrics of the resting eggs of the fairy shrimp *Branchinella* in Australia (Anostraca: Thamnocephalidae). *Proceedings of the Linnean Society of New South Wales* **133**: 51-68.

Timms, B.V. and P.R. Sanders (2002). Biogeography and ecology of Anostraca (Crustacea) in middle Paroo catchment of the Australian arid-zone. *Hydrobiologia* **486**: 225-238.

Early Australian Botany Texts for Schools

Presidential Address delivered at the 140th Annual Meeting, March 18th 2015
by Emeritus Professor Robert J. King.

Published on 18 September 2015 at http://escholarship.library.usyd.edu.au/journals/index.php/LIN

King, R.J. (2015). Early Australian botany texts for schools. *Proceedings of the Linnean Society of New South Wales*. 137, 45-55.

In tonight's address I have set myself two basic aims: to introduce some of the early Australian botany textbooks for schools, and to set these in the then prevailing educational environment.

European colonisation of Australia had its beginnings in botany. Australia was to be settled at Botany Bay and entry was to be gained through Capes Banks and Solander. The richness of the flora had led the British to the erroneous conclusion that the Botany Bay environment was especially productive. As Paul Adam has pointed out in his introduction to the plants of the Royal National Park, in the Linnean Society's Field Guide ... 'it was to be almost two centuries before the inverse relationship between fertility and plant species richness was recognised as a general global phenomenon' (Adam, 2013).

In the years immediately following European settlement the biology of Australian plants (and animals) excited the imagination of European natural historians and collectors. At first when explorers, sailors and naturalists paid fleeting visits they returned with their trophies to 'home'. In the next period Australian residents sent specimens back to Europe but it was not until the mid-1800s that Australian botanists themselves observed, collected and described Australian plants (Ducker, 1990). By the mid to late 1800s key Australian botanists recognised the importance of genuinely Australian teaching materials and became involved in their publication.

At this time educational practice paid increasing attention to observation rather than copying and rote learning. Herbert Spencer, writing in 1862 on 'Education: intellectual, moral, and physical', wrote of the importance of the study of nature and fundamentals of science and the need to replace rote learning and rule teaching with object lessons. His strong view was that object lessons should include 'the fields and the hedges, the quarry and the seashore'. Over a century and a half ago he wrote 'We are quite prepared to hear from many that all this is throwing away time and energy; and that children would be much better occupied in writing their copies or learning their pence-tables and so fitting themselves for the business of life' (Spencer, 1890).

The transition, between copy books with the discipline and routine they enforced, and an encouragement to make observations, is beautifully illustrated in Vere Foster's Drawing Copy Books, E1, E2, and E3 'Wild Flowers' (Figs.1&2). These books have no publication date; though on the cover testimonials, dated 1871, appear for other copy books in this extensive series. The series recommend themselves in their introductory remarks with the comment that 'a loving appreciation of nature has in all ages characterised the noblest minds'. The books offer exemplars to be copied, but go on to recommend that observations should be made in the field so that a dull and profitless walk can become an opportunity to find objects of interest and study. 'The ultimate aim is to obtain the power of representing Nature to himself'. The advice was to copy - go carefully through the great majority of the sheets but at the same time if possible observe, having 'a piece of the real plant at his side to refer to'.

In Australia this major change, encouraging the involvement of the pupil in the learning process, coincided with a major change in responsibility for education. In New South Wales this was embodied in the Public Instruction Act of 1880, the first acknowledgement by the State that every child, regardless of class, creed or economic circumstances was entitled to an education – education was to be free, compulsory, and secular. In practice it was none of these, but it was a major advance on the earlier state of play. Similar legislation was to be enacted in other States.

In Victoria in the 1870s a wave of interest in the teaching of science was recorded with the Education Minister in 1879 expressing his wish that teachers be qualified to teach in at least one branch of science

WILD FLOWERS

Fig. 1. Front cover of Vere Foster's Drawing Copy Book E1 'Wildflowers'

(including botany and geology). The first Training Institute was established in Victoria in 1870, though the pupil teacher system remained in practice until the 1950s. In 1900 Henry Tisdall had already been employed as a lecturer on botany at the Victorian Teachers' Training College, the first, perhaps, in a line of well known lecturers in Natural History including Herbert Ward Wilson (a noted ornithologist much involved with the Gould League), Norman Wakefield (natural history writer for the Melbourne Age newspaper, and author of the Field Naturalists' Club of Victoria publication on Ferns of Victoria and Tasmania), Jack Hyett ('Jack of the Bush' on early children's television, author, and more than 60 years ago co-founder with William H. King and J. Marion King of the still flourishing Ringwood Field Naturalists' Club) and John Leach (but more of him later). In order to gain a Trained Teacher's Certificate, botany was acceptable as a science. In New South Wales, Sydney Teachers' College opened in 1906.

Fig. 2. Sample page from Vere Foster's Drawing Copy Book E1 'Wildflowers'

46

Proc. Linn. Soc. N.S.W., 137, 2015

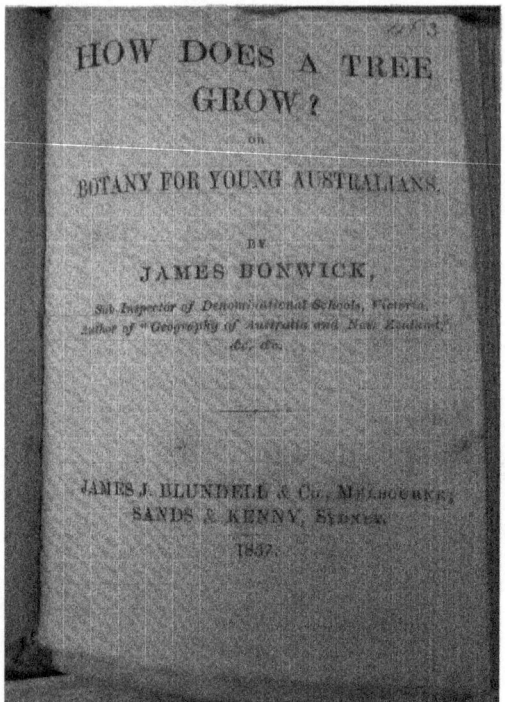

Fig. 3. Frontispiece from Bonwick, J. (1857) 'How does a tree grow? or botany for young Australians'

Prior to this a pupil teacher system appears to have been the major option for teacher training, followed by Hurlstone Residential College for women trainees and Fort Street for men.

The earliest book that one could regard as a botanical text written in Australia is that of James Bonwick, in 1857 (Fig.3). Bonwick was Sub-Inspector of Denominational Schools in Melbourne and published many extended pamphlets or tracts on a variety of subjects: history, early colonisation, natural history and science, and even the history of the Methodist church in South Australia. He had arrived in Australia from Britain in 1841 and ended up in Melbourne after a series of none too successful educational endeavours in Hobart and Adelaide, and with a brief period on the goldfields to try and reclaim some of his losses.

Bonwick's book was entitled 'How does a tree grow? or botany for young Australians'. The preface reads – 'At the request of several Teachers I have commenced a series of school books, chiefly to be confined to subjects of colonial history and popular sciences. The form of a dialogue has been adopted with the 'Botany for young Australians' from a belief that the sympathies of our young friends will be excited on behalf of the juvenile questioner and their interest thus maintained in the study of the sciences'. The book is only 42 pages long and addresses the questions to a primary school child. A companion volume was prepared on astronomy. Interestingly the contents of the book were essentially aspects of physiology: that is, how rather than what. How does a plant grow? How does a plant take in water and nutrients? How does a plant manufacture sugars? Such aspects were largely ignored in subsequent Australian texts written in the 19th Century and the early part of the 20th Century.

Only five years later Thomas Ralph wrote his text 'Elementary botany (Australian edition) for the use of beginners'. This elegant little book is only 72 pages long and contains some beautiful if sketchy coloured plates. The book is set out conventionally and covers seeds, vegetative morphology, and flowers. It is based on an English edition, in the preface of which it is stated that the book is written specifically for the English student. At the time of publication, in 1862, Ralph was living in Melbourne (Leslie Cottage, South Yarra Hill, Melbourne) somewhere near the site of the Royal Botanic Gardens. In the preface to the Australian edition he noted that changes had been made to the English edition to include plants 'carefully selected from such as are either cultivated in the colony or to be met with in the neighbourhood of its towns'. If this is the case it is scarcely noticeable, for example in one plate of flowers there is an illustration of a *Goodenia* (Fig.4), and in another illustrating the flowers of the Liliaceae there is a supposed *Burchardia umbellata* but the illustrations omit any botanical detail. Changes of this nature seem to be the extent of the Australianising, but I haven't had the benefit of seeing the English edition and hence making a detailed comparison of either the text or the plates.

The content in Ralph's text book is that which characterises the first part of a number of subsequent texts by other authors. Plant parts are covered in considerable detail but in later books there then follows detail on different aspects reflecting the aims of the author: for example introducing the Australian

Proc. Linn. Soc. N.S.W., 137, 2015

47

Fig. 4. Illustration of Goodenia from Ralph, T. S. (1862) 'Elementary botany (Australian edition) for the use of beginners'.

flora, or introducing principal plants of economic value, especially those of agricultural significance.

The next two botanical texts published in Australia were written by botanists who, each in their own way, made major contributions as professional full-time scientists. It is interesting to speculate on the fact that these two books appeared within a few years of each other. The authors were Baron Ferdinand von Mueller and William Guilfoyle. Mueller had been appointed Government Botanist in Victoria in 1853, and was Director of the Royal Botanic Gardens Melbourne from 1857 until 1873. He was dismissed because Melburnians (or at least the politicians) wanted a Director of the Gardens with an eye to aesthetic rather than an emphasis on academic botany. Mueller was dismayed but he did retain his role as Government Botanist (Kynaston, 1981). Mueller's position as Director of the Gardens was taken over by Guilfoyle, a move that was not welcomed by the Baron (Pescott, 1974). At an earlier stage Mueller

had described Guilfoyle as a 'distinguished collector' and he even named a genus (*Guilfoylia*) in his honour. When Guilfoyle was appointed Director of the Gardens von Mueller referred to him as 'a nurseryman with no claims to scientific knowledge whatever'. Guilfoyle did however lay out some of the most beautiful gardens in Australia. As it played out Mueller subsequently sunk the genus *Guilfoylia* within *Catellia*. Mueller published 19 papers in the journal of our Society (Proceedings of the Linnean Society of New South Wales): Guilfoyle none.

Given this background one might perceive an element of competition for the hearts and minds of young botanists in the appearance of Guilfoyle's 'Australian botany specially designed for the use of schools' published in 1878, and revised and much enlarged in a second edition in 1884 (Fig.5), and Mueller's 'Introduction to botanic teachings at the schools of Victoria: through references to leading native plants' published in 1877 (Fig.6).

In the first edition of Guilfoyle's text, the preface reads 'In writing this little rudimentary work which has no higher aim than that of familiarising the beginner with the principal parts of plants and their manner of growth, the author has endeavoured throughout to keep in view the suggestion of the great botanist [Dr Lindley] whose words are quoted on the title page.' In summary this advice was 'to avoid the host of strange names, inharmonious, sesquipedalian, and barbarous that found their way into botany. It is full-time indeed that some stop should be put to this torrent of savage sounds and to clothe botany in the English language'.

Subsequent to the publication of the first edition, Guilfoyle also published a small book 'The A.B.C. of botany' (Guilfoyle, 1880) much of which seems to be incorporated in the second edition of his Australian botany text. He noted that this small book (101pp) might usefully be regarded as an introduction to his earlier book.

The second edition of Guilfoyle's textbook (Guilfoyle, 1884) is much expanded and devotes 59 pages to plant parts, 18 pages to systematic botany and the collection and preservation of specimens, a modest

48

Proc. Linn. Soc. N.S.W., 137, 2015

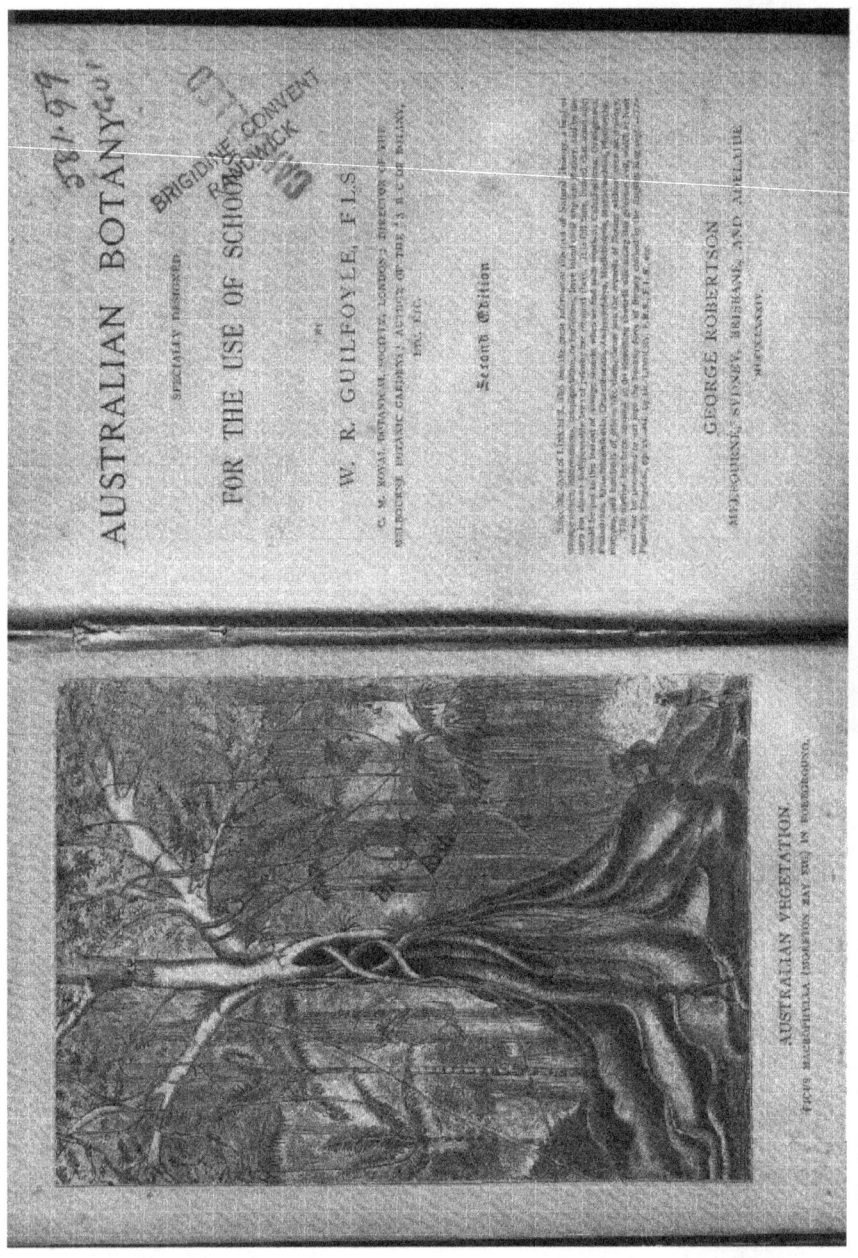

Fig. 5. Frontispiece from Guilfoyle, W. R. (1884) 'Australian botany specially designed for the use of schools', Second Edition.

Fig. 6. Front cover of Mueller, F. Baron von (1877) 'Introduction to botanic teachings at the schools of Victoria: through references to leading native plants'.

15 pages to descriptions of Australian vegetation (a chapter written with the object of pointing out to students of botany and others, some characteristics and the beauty of the Australian vegetation) and an extensive glossary of every plant mentioned in the text (about half of which are Australian plants). This was followed by lists of useful plants, and plants common around Melbourne, though many were noted as being found in other states. He acknowledged input from New South Wales and South Australia in what I would regard as an unsuccessful attempt to justify the title 'Australian Botany'.

Mueller's book (Mueller, 1877) is interesting because it demonstrates a novel plan for teaching botany. He took the view that traditional teaching of botany was 'wearisome alike to the teacher and the children and that the knowledge gained from most elementary works on botany is as quickly lost as gained'. He wished to involve students in observations made on the native plants in their own locality and only afterward to move to the (more difficult) study of anatomy and physiology of plants. In the preface he notes that he had commenced a book to be known as the 'Victorian School Flora' but on ministerial request was required to give precedence to other work, and that even in writing the present book had been asked (or directed?) to 'abandon as much as ever possible scientific terms names and appellations'. Mueller's book was published by the Victorian Government Printer: Guilfoyle's books were commercially published. Mueller noted that those wishing to undertake traditional studies could adopt books published in England, 'all meritorious in their way.' He was anxious that the general population should be introduced to the plants in their environment and had been sending out pressed and dried plants with printed notes in Atlas form under the title of 'Educational Collections'; these being made available to the public through Mechanic Institutes and free libraries. As his book is based on the local flora it is genuinely Australian even if the species chosen are Victorian.

If we regard the books by Guilfoyle and Mueller as competitors how do we assess the outcome? Guilfoyle was clearly more successful, and notes in 1884 that he had much pleasure in saying that, 'owing to the demand for the first edition having exhausted the issue, and from the flattering notices appearing in nearly all sections of the press, it had become necessary to issue a second edition'. The flattering notices in the press included those from the Castlemaine Representative, the Horsham Times, the Geelong Advertiser, the Warrnambool Guardian and Examiner, the Ballarat Star, and even the Sydney Telegraph. As a botanist Mueller's legacy is more significant and the excellent illustrations from his book appear in various guises, often simplified, in a number of later books (Figs.7a,b).

50

Proc. Linn. Soc. N.S.W., 137, 2015

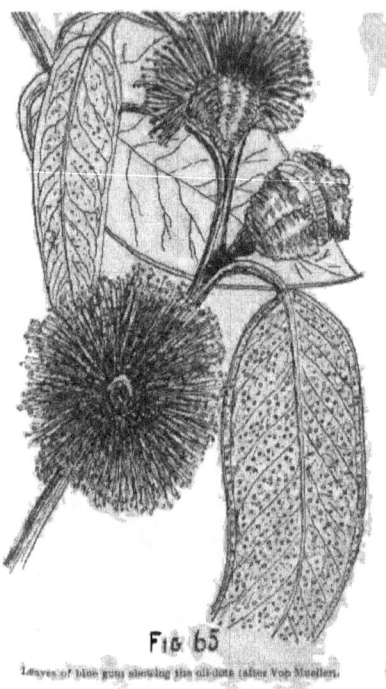

FIG 65

Leaves of blue gum showing the oil-dots (after Von Mueller)

Fig. 7. (a left) Illustration of Eucalyptus globulus from Mueller, F. Baron von (1877). (b right) Illustration of Eucalyptus globulus (after von Mueller), in Gillies, W. (1904) 'First studies in plant life in Australasia'.

1892 saw the publication of Arthur Dendy and Alfred Lucas' 'An Introduction to the study of botany with a special chapter on some Australian natural orders'. The book was dedicated to Baron Sir Ferdinand von Mueller. The first half addressed general botany with considerable emphasis on lower plant groups as well as the algae, the fungi, and bacteria. The second section on flowering plants concluded with a lengthy chapter on the characteristics, distribution and uses of some of the more important Australian flowering plants. Dendy wrote the first section. In 1888 he had moved from Manchester to Melbourne University and was the first zoologist to study Victorian terrestrial invertebrates. He was subsequently Professor at Christchurch, Cape Town and then King's College, London. He published three papers in the Proceedings of the Linnean Society of New South Wales. Lucas was perhaps better known. He had taught at the Leys School in Cambridge but for health reasons migrated to Australia. At the time of publication of this text he was Senior Fellow at Queens College, Melbourne University. He later published 'The Seaweeds of South Australia'. Lucas by no means confined his interests to botany: with William Le Souef, he wrote

'Animals of Australia' in 1909, and later 'Birds of Australia' in 1911. Lucas was a Council member of the Linnean Society of New South Wales for some 42 years, and President from 1907-1909. He published 16 papers in the Proceedings of the Society.

To this point all of the publications I have mentioned emanate from Melbourne. What was happening elsewhere? Not much apparently. In Queensland Frederick Bailey (Colonial Botanist to Queensland) published 'A companion for the Queensland student of plant life' in 1893, and a year later 'Botany abridged, or how to readily distinguish some of our common plants to which are appended a few additions to the companion for the Queensland student of plant life'. These were reissued together in 1897. These two pamphlets, one 108 pages and the other only 24 pages, are scarcely textbooks. The preface to 'Botany abridged' states that 'the only object the writer has in issuing these few pages is that they may be the means of assisting school teachers to readily name some of the more common plants which may be brought to them by students .... and if teachers in their turn point out their distinguishing marks to the young, a habit of observation would

Proc. Linn. Soc. N.S.W., 137, 2015

51

thus be engendered which could not fail to be of service to them in after life'. In these publications Bailey eschews the dictum espoused by Guilfoyle, and dictated to Mueller by his political masters, with regard to terminological obscurantism and exactitude. Primary school teachers were introduced to conivent and connate anthers to solve any confusion between the Apocyanaceae and the Asclepiadae.

We now mark the end of the 19th Century with Henry Tisdall. His book, 'Students' botanical notes' was published in a second edition in 1900 (I've not been able to locate a first edition nor any details). These were notes that contained the substance of a course of 32 lessons in elementary botany delivered during each of the four preceding years. At that time he had held a Lectureship in Botany at the Victorian Teachers' Training College. His emphasis was on plant groups (including the fungi and the algae), plant parts and there was a little on function.

A new century dawned but nothing much changed in terms of botany teaching, at least as far as can be gleaned from the publications available.

In 1904 William Gillies published the first edition of his 'First studies in plant life in Australasia' with numerous questions, directions for outdoor work, and drawing and composition exercises. He suggested that plant physiology could be postponed to a later stage. In his view 'a wise mingling of authoritative and experimental teaching was probably the best method at the early stages'. As he pointed out in his preface telling a child that a snapdragon flower is personate and bilabiate, with didynamous stamens and a two lobed superior pistil may make children tired but if the flower is described in terms of its function (a curious mouth due to visits from bees) they will listen readily.

Gillies and with few exceptions all other authors of botany textbooks up to this time were from Victoria. Why have I bothered to make that point? I do so because I want to draw attention to the key role of the Field Naturalists' Clubs in Victoria in creating public awareness and promoting the study of natural history. Almost all of the texts up to this time acknowledge some sort of input from the Field Naturalists' Club of Victoria, its publications and its members. There was not an equivalent organisation of such influence in New South Wales, though various Field Naturalists' groups have existed and continue to exist. To a certain extent the Linnean Society of New South Wales has fulfilled a similar role although with a greater emphasis on the underlying sciences.

I have already alluded to the key role that lecturers in nature studies at Victorian Teachers' Colleges played, none more so than John Albert Leach,

Supervisor of Nature Study in Victorian Schools and later Assistant Chief Inspector of Schools in Victoria, and co-founder with Jessie McMichael of the Gould League of Bird Lovers in 1909. Leach's contribution was enormous, but here I'll limit myself to comments on his book 'Australian nature studies' which was continuously in press from 1922 until at least 1952. Though not a botany text per se it included significant botanical information, even some plant physiology. At the end of its 500 pages there was a table suggesting a graded series of lessons for pupils in grades 1 to 8 (age 4.5 - 6 up to 13 years) for every week of the school year as the backbone for 'morning talk' or the 'nature table' and where possible the morning walk (Fig.8). As a text it is unsurpassed and its influence was widely felt.

In contrast to the early period most of the textbooks on botany in the early 20th Century originated from New South Wales and the majority is written by women. I'm afraid that there appears to be an element of Linley's 'Ladies botany' resurgent. A friend recalls that in her north coast convent school botany was the only 'science' offered to the girls: it was cheap to teach and seemly. As Eric Ashby commented 'No one doubts that the chemist needs flasks and gas points and sinks. No one questions the need for benches and lenses and galvanometers for physics. But it is still assumed botany can be taught in any classroom with no other aids and a pencil, a south light, and one antiquated microscope' (Ashby in the preface to Carey, 1941).

In 1916 Agnes Brewster and Constance Le Plastrier published their successful textbook 'Botany for Australian students' designed for the NSW Intermediate Certificate. There were at least four editions, with the fourth published in 1930. The 1916 edition covered general descriptive botany and included a detailed section on systematic botany. In the preface the authors expressed a view that the study of botany in Australia had scarcely reached the stage of understanding the ecology. In the expanded second edition there were 63 pages devoted to ecology essentially that of the Sydney region and drawing on research papers and illustrations of R. H. Cambage and A. A. Hamilton, published in the Proceedings of the Linnean Society of New South Wales. Brewster herself was a member of the Society and published one research paper in the Proceedings.

In 1929 Brewster published a companion book 'Botany for Australian secondary schools' to take students on to the NSW Leaving Certificate. This book further developed the ecological aspects citing 16 research papers, 11 from the Proceedings of the Linnean Society of New South Wales. Le

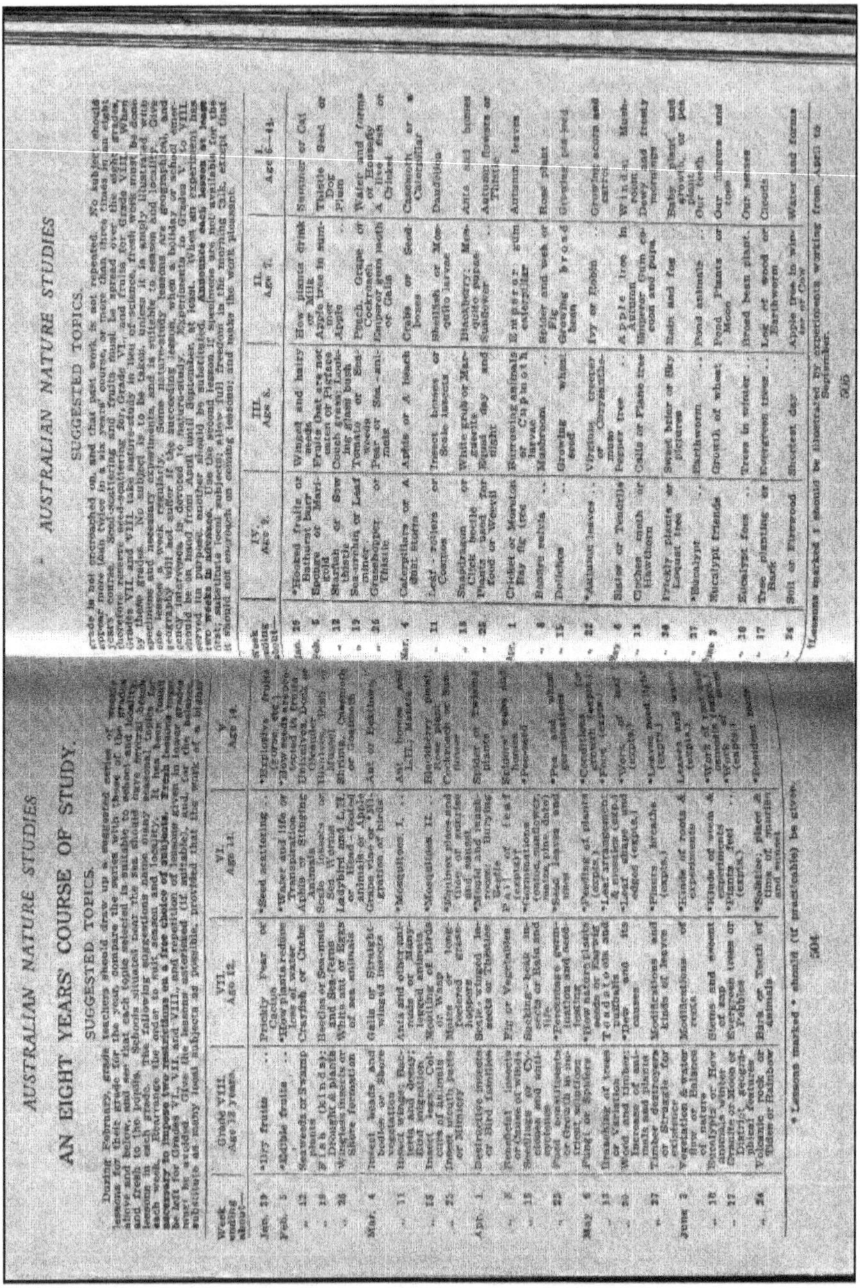

AUSTRALIAN NATURE STUDIES

AN EIGHT YEARS' COURSE OF STUDY.

SUGGESTED TOPICS.

AUSTRALIAN NATURE STUDIES

SUGGESTED TOPICS.

Fig. 8. 'An Eight Years' Course of Study' from Leach, J. A. (1922) 'Australian nature studies;

Plastrier (1933) also wrote another book 'The story of our plants, first steps in Australian botany'. It was described by David Stead (then editor of the Shakespeare Head Australian Nature Series) as a pocket botany, to act as 'a kind of literary footstool on which the general enquirer and the young student might stand, to reach the really excellent library of more advanced Australian botany'.

Other texts in this period included Cooke and Gillham (1932) and Catley (1934). 'A first year Australian botany' by Elsie Cooke and Myrtle Gillham is a short text two thirds of which are devoted to plant parts and the illustrations, mostly of European species. These are followed by a page or two on some major Australian plant families, and a couple of pages on the collection of plants. Allan Catley's 'An intermediate botany' was published two years later and there were revisions and reprints through to 1946. Catley was sometime Lecturer in Nature Study and Agriculture at Armidale Teachers' College. His book presents another more or less standard (perhaps even more old-fashioned) coverage of plant parts and types of plants with a major emphasis on agricultural species. It does present a discussion of subjects with appeal to pupils in rural districts.

A welcome departure was Gladys Carey's 'Botany by observation - a textbook for Australian schools' published in 1941. As Eric Ashby noted in his foreword to that book, textbooks for Australian students were out of date with regard to experimental botany with an emphasis on aspects of plant morphology no longer considered suitable for elementary classes. While recognising there were good modern texts written in England and America he believed the whole purpose of teaching botany at school was defeated if it didn't give children an appreciation and enthusiasm for their own environment; this he considered to be common sense not narrow provincialism. Ashby contended that Carey's book contained up-to-date physiology, promoted observation [a good thing], and was accurate in its statements on ecology and physiology.

I've taken Carey as my arbitrary cut-off date for this survey of early Australian botanical teaching literature, almost a century after the publication of Bonwick. I should add that I have deliberately avoided reference to Newman (1946) and McLuckie and McKee (1954), both written for University studies and neither (but especially the former) likely to enthuse students to take up botanical studies. Ivor Newman, it should be noted, was one-time Linnean Macleay Research Fellow (of the Linnean Society of New South Wales) at the University of Sydney.

From the 1950s the teaching of botany moved from being a central and stand alone pillar of science teaching to being incorporated into a more broad ranging view of biology. The launching of Sputnik by the Russians prompted a dramatic reassessment of science teaching in the United States with the development of new teaching materials in science, with a particular emphasis on biology (Biological Sciences Curriculum Studies) through the National Science Foundation and the American Institute of Biological Sciences. At that time biology was the only science subject studied by more than half of American students. A similar phenomenon occurred in Australia with the production of the landmark 'The web of life' by the Australian Academy of Science, a book that exhibits both the advantages and disadvantages of a book written by a committee. In New South Wales the secondary school syllabus for biology was regularly revised such that by the time I co-authored the textbook 'Senior biology' in 1991 very little of the Higher School Certificate syllabus would have been recognised as botany by the authors of the 19th Century. It had been scaled up with an emphasis on environmental interactions, ecology and conservation, and scaled down with a greater emphasis on microbiology, biochemistry and molecular genetics. Furthermore far greater attention was being paid to ways in which biology affects day-to-day life (human disease, food production, human impacts).

One major consequence of this shift in curriculum has been that aspects of traditional botany appear to have been downgraded, disregarded or dispatched from the curriculum. Whereas once almost every Australian university would have had a separate School of Botany there is now no university where that is the case. The last standing School of Botany, at Melbourne University (a world-class School of Plant Science) has become in 2015 part of the new School of Biosciences. At the University of New South Wales botany is now taught in a School of Biological, Earth and Environmental Sciences – so goodbye to traditional zoology, geology and physical geography as well as botany. Similar changes have been made across Australia. This is perhaps not all bad and I don't want to sound like a grumpy old botanist but having been educated as a traditional zoologist and botanist I do believe we have lost something valuable.

Addressing only one such loss Pat Hutchings and Penny Berents have written, 'We won't know what species we have and what species we're driving to extinction. Taxonomists - those people who name animals and plants and who worry about the relationships between them - are becoming increasingly rare. You might even say that they are becoming an "endangered species". However, the

54

work of taxonomists underpins biological sciences and is fundamental in managing biodiversity'. They point out that the conservation of world biodiversity is a global priority. In 1992, 150 countries (including Australia) signed the United Nations Convention on Biological Diversity in Rio, committing Australia to conserving biodiversity (Australian Museum blogpost, 2015).

REFERENCES

Adam, P. (2013) 'Plants – introduction' in King, R. J. (ed.) 'Field guide to Royal National Park, New South Wales', Linnean Society of New South Wales, Sydney. pp. 51-52.

Bailey, F. M. (1893) 'A companion for the Queensland student of plant life', Government Printer, Brisbane. 108pp.

Bailey, F. M. (1894) 'Botany abridged, or how to readily distinguish some of our common plants to which are appended a few additions to the companion for the Queensland student of plant life', Government Printer, Brisbane. 24pp.

Bonwick, J. (1857) 'How does a tree grow? or botany for young Australians', James J. Blundell & Co., Melbourne: Sands & Kenny, Sydney. 42pp.

Brewster, A. A. and Le Plastrier, C. M. (1916) 'Botany for Australian students', Dymocks, Sydney. 368pp.

Brewster, A. A. (1929) 'Botany for Australian secondary schools', Dymocks, Sydney. 376pp.

Carey, G. (1941) 'Botany by observation: a textbook for Australian schools', Angus and Robertson, Sydney. 356pp.

Catley, A. B. (1934) 'An intermediate botany', Shakespeare Head Press, Sydney. 183pp.

Cooke, E. A. and Gillham, M. (1932) 'A first year Australian botany', Dymocks, Sydney. 77pp.

Dendy, A. and Lucas, A. H. S. (1892) 'An introduction to the study of botany, with special reference to some Australian orders', Melville, Mullen and Slade, Melbourne. 271pp.

Ducker, S. C. (1990) 'History of Australian marine phycology' in Clayton, M. N. and King, R. J. 'Biology of marine plants', Longman Cheshire, Melbourne, pp. 415-430.

Foster, V. (1870s) Vere Foster's Drawing Copy Book E1 'Wildflowers', Marcus Ward & Co., London. 16pp. [there exist scores of such copying books in the series ranging from simple familiar shapes and calligraphy to the complexity shown in 'Wildflowers'. Alongside these there were

writing and water-color drawing books. There is even one titled 'Australian Animals'.

Gillies, W. (1904) 'First studies in plant life in Australasia', Whitcombe and Tombs, Melbourne. 184pp.

Guilfoyle, W. R. (1878) 'Australian botany specially designed for the use of schools', S. Mullen, Melbourne. 99pp.

Guilfoyle, W. R. (1880) 'The A.B.C. of botany', S. Mullen, Melbourne. 101pp.

Guilfoyle, W. R. (1884) 'Australian botany specially designed for the use of schools', Second Edition, George Robertson, Melbourne. 221pp.

King, R. J. and Sullivan, F. M. (1991) 'Senior biology', Longman Cheshire, Melbourne. 392pp.

Kynaston, E. (1981) 'A man on edge: a life of Baron Sir Ferdinand von Mueller', Lane (Penguin), London and Melbourne. 389pp.

Leach, J. A. (1922) 'Australian nature studies; a book of reference for those interested in nature study', Critchley Parker, Melbourne. 501pp.

Le Plastrier, C. M. (1933) 'The story of our plants: first steps in Australian botany', Shakespeare Head Press, Sydney. 94pp.

McLuckie, J. and McKee, H. S. (1954) 'Australian and New Zealand botany', Associated General Publications, Sydney. 758pp.

Mueller, F. Baron von (1877) 'Introduction to botanic teachings at the schools of Victoria: through references to leading native plants', John Ferres, Government Printer, Melbourne. 152pp.

Newman, I. V. (1946) 'The living plant: a laboratory study of its structure, reproduction and general classification', Dymocks, Sydney. 159pp.

Pescott, R. T. M. (1974) 'W. R. Guilfoyle 1840-1912: the master of landscaping', Oxford University Press, Melbourne. 153pp.

Ralph, T. S. (1862) 'Elementary botany (Australian edition) for the use of beginners', Bailliere, Melbourne. 72pp.

Spencer, H. (1890) 'Education: intellectual, moral and physical', Williams and Norgate, London and Edinburgh. 180pp. (the cited work is an unaltered reprinting [twentieth thousand of the cheap edition] of the 1862 edition, itself a compilation of earlier pamphlets).

Tisdall, H. T. (1900) 'Students' botanical notes, second edition', H. Raywood, Melbourne. 75pp.

Proc. Linn. Soc. N.S.W., 137, 2015

55

The Story of Science House and the History of the Linnean Society of New South Wales

HELENE A. MARTIN

School of Biological, Earth and Environmental Sciences, University of New South Wales, Sydney 2052
Australia (h.martin@unsw.edu.au)

Published on 15 December 2015 at http://escholarship.library.usyd.edu.au/journals/index.php/LIN

Martin, H. (2015). The Story of Science House and the history of the Linnean Society of New South
Wales. *Proceedings of the Linnean Society of New South Wales* 137, 57-70.

Science House was built in 1930-31 by its co-owners, the Linnean Society of New South Wales, the Royal Society of New South Wales and the Institute of Engineers Australia, with assistance from the State Government, as "a centre for the Learned Societies". Office space was rented to scientific and professional societies and halls were hired out for meetings. Profits were divided equally between the three co-owners and the venture was successful. In 1968, the State Government gave notice that Science House would be compulsorily acquired for demolition as part of Sydney Cove Redevelopment Authority Scheme. Compensation was paid and the Societies moved out, but the redevelopment did not go ahead. Science House as a physical entity survived, but the Societies had lost ownership. The Linnean Society of New South Wales and the Royal Society of New South Wales attempted a similar venture in a new Science Centre, but this was not successful.

Throughout this time and to the present day, the Linnean Society of New South Wales has successfully maintained its core function of promoting natural history. It publishes a journal of original research papers each year and occasionally, other books. It holds regular members meetings, presents public lectures, sponsors symposia and field trips, and actively supports scientific research. The Society has managed to adapt to the changing circumstances throughout this time.

Manuscript received 18 September 2015, accepted for publication 9 December 2015.

KEYWORDS: Linnean Society of New South Wales, Natural History, Science Centre, Science House.

Note: the original monetary figure is quoted, followed by the value it would be in 2013 (in brackets), when adjusted for inflation.

The Linnean Society of NSW celebrated its Jubilee in 1925 with a publication, *Historical Notes of its First Fifty Years (Jubilee Publication)* by A.B. Walkom (1925). From its inception in 1874, the Society moved around between various rented premises in the city, but as a library was being built up, a permanent home became more attractive. However even at that time, city property prices were high and the Society's "resources were unequal to the strain of the contemplated purchase". Sir William Macleay came to the rescue with an offer of land and a house at Elizabeth Bay and The Linnean Hall was opened in 1885 (see Walkom, 1925). Access to The Hall for monthly meetings was difficult, so when the opportunity arose, the Society purchased 16 College St Sydney, a more accessible location. In 1924, the Society moved in and the building was named Macleay House. Some of the space was rented out to tenants.

Post-Jubilee, Science House and the pre-World War Two Period

In 1925, the Elizabeth Bay property was being subdivided and sold off. By 1927, the premises were entirely evacuated. The library went to the Macleay Museum, University of Sydney and the Herbarium to the Botanic Gardens. The laboratories were removed.

In the late 1920s, publishing the *Proceedings* and exchange of the Society's publications for those of other societies and institutions from around the world was a major activity. The library was built up almost entirely from exchanges. The Society supported up to four Linnean Macleay Fellows to undertake original research, according to the bequest from Sir William Macleay's will (see Walkom, 1925). Conservation was a major interest of the Society. Community groups trying to preserve some local bushland or wildflower reserve would write to the Linnean Society requesting its support.

Ordinary members' meetings were held monthly and members were kept abreast of the Society's affairs. Donations and exchanges received since the previous meeting were tabled. About 1,700 to 1,900 items each year were received for the library, most of them numbers or parts of journals. Notes and exhibits were on display at meetings. There were occasional lectures, such as the Fletcher Memorial Lectures. The President usually chaired both the Council and Members' meetings. A full list of Presidents since 1925 is given in Appendix 1.

Sir William Macleay recognised the importance of new discoveries in bacteriology and was keen to encourage its study in Australia. He left a bequest to Sydney University for a chair or lectureship in bacteriology. Sir William stipulated a number of strict conditions and as they were not met, the money was transferred to the Linnean Society to provide a salary for a Bacteriologist to conduct original research. In 1928, the Society advertised widely for a Bacteriologist, preferably other than a medical pathologist, at a salary of £600 ($44,379) per annum. Mr H.L. Jensen was appointed Macleay Bacteriologist, and arrived in Sydney from Europe in late 1929. Sydney University agreed to house him in the Department of Agriculture until the new Department of Bacteriology was set up.

In 1925 the Institute of Engineers Australia, a tenant on the top floor of Macleay House started discussions with the Royal Society of New South Wales about a proposal for a Professional Societies' House in Sydney. The Institute of Engineers could not finance such a building, so they approached the Linnean Society. The initial proposal was to build an addition to Macleay House but the Linnean Society decided that this proposal was not in its best interests, though future proposals would be considered.

In 1928 the State Government was approached in an attempt to find another site. The Government viewed a Science House favourably and proposed that the Government Architect would sign off on the building, to a value of at least £30,000 ($2,218,949) and there would be an architectural design competition for the new building. The winners of the competition were Messrs Peddle Thorp and Walker who were awarded a prize of £250 ($18,491). There was a second prize of £150 ($11,295) and a third prize of £100 ($7,396). Peddle Thorp and Walker won the Sir John Sulman Medal in 1932 for their design of Science House.

In 1929, the NSW Government granted land at the intersection of Essex and Gloucester Streets (now 157 Gloucester St) to enable the Royal Society of New South Wales, the Linnean Society of New South Wales and the Institute of Engineers Australia to build Science House "as a centre for learned Societies". There were conditions attached to this grant: it could only be used for accommodation of scientific and professional organisations and could not be sold, mortgaged or leased, and the money used for any other purpose, without the consent of the Governor (State Government).

A Joint Management Committee, the Science House Management Committee (SHMC) was set up, with two representatives from each of the three parties to supervise the erection and management of the building, and to let or lease parts of Science House for rent. Each party initially contributed £15,000 (about $1.35 million).

The Director of Public Works proposed to evict the tenants of the Science House site and clear the land as soon as tenders were called. There were fourteen tenders and the lowest of £30,500 ($2,206,940), with £250 ($18,085) for contingencies was accepted. The Linnean Society moved into Science House in January 1931. The College Street property was put up for sale, but when a buyer could not be found, it was leased out.

The SHMC ran the day-to-day affairs of the building and the lettings to scientific and professional societies. The Linnean Society paid rent and received a one third share of the surplus. In 1931, rent was £48-15-6 ($3,528) per quarter. Initially, profits were absorbed by the final building costs, but £8-16-8 ($797) profit was paid for the second half of 1932. There had been a reduction in rents of 20% in late 1931, in accordance with Government's Rent Reduction Act (1931). Rents were adjusted in 1934 since the introduction of the Landlord and Tenants Act (amended) (1932) superseded the rent reduction act. Some reduction of rent was maintained if paid on time. Nevertheless, profits for the second half of 1933 and the first half of 1934 were £640 ($59,338) and £319 ($28,766) respectively.

The Council of the Linnean Society was involved in all of the scientific undertakings carried out in the Society's name. The Linnean Macleay Fellows submitted quarterly reports that had to meet the approval of their supervisory committee. Each Fellow would write and request permission to take annual leave or go on field trips or do anything out of the ordinary. Such requests were rarely if ever refused. A list of Linnean Macleay Fellows since 1925 is given in Appendix 2

An indication of the Council's close involvement is seen in the case of Mr Jensen the Macleay Bacteriologist who was conducting research into the

58

decomposition of cellulose with different organisms. The Bacteriology Committee instructed him to wind up that work and concentrate on nitrification in soils. The Committee was considering further work on legumes and *Azotobacter* and their importance in fallow stubble. Arrangements were made for Mr Jensen to visit agricultural field stations and observe soils from different agricultural systems. In 1938, Mr Jensen requested permission to submit his work as a thesis to the Royal Agricultural and Veterinarian College in Copenhagen.

Funds for the expanded bacteriology research were insufficient and the banks were approached for donations in 1939. The Rural Bank agreed to give £200 ($16,055) for a greenhouse and £100 ($8,028) per annum towards the salary of a chemist to work with the Bacteriologist. Mr Jensen was in demand to give lectures on nitrification in soils to the agricultural students and to review books. Permission was granted for these activities.

World War Two and its effects on the LInnean Society

The challengers of the war years required the Linnean Society to adapt to the circumstances. Late in 1939, the Fisher Library of Sydney University compiled a list of scientific literature it wished to import from enemy countries and sought the Linnean Society's assistance. This list was ultimately submitted to the relevant minister in the Commonwealth Government. The Prime Minister warned about sending publications that might have information useful to the enemy to places other than British and Allied countries.

The Society was concerned about the effects that the "small problems" of the war might have on the Linnean Macleay Fellows. Petrol rationing was in force and extra fuel for field work was initially refused, although relaxed at times. Miss Ilma Pidgeon investigated problems of fruit transport and the physiology of water loss from oranges. Miss Valerie May assisted in the problems associated with the preparation of sphagnum moss surgical dressings. Mr John Dulhunty worked on the coalfields, and this project was supported by BHP. Dr Germaine Joplin was also working on the coalfields and extra petrol was allotted for their field work.

The Bacteriologist was in demand to solve special problems. Dr Jensen investigated the microbiology of retting of flax. Growing flax had been urgently increased since supplies from Europe were cut off. He found certain fungi were active in dew retting of flax and this had commercial possibilities. Dr Jensen and colleagues worked on the prevention of mould

in connection with blood transfusions. Australian made agar had to be tested for bacteria. Dr Jensen was approached to work on rot proofing of paper for wrappings of ammunition and spare parts, and of canvas and electrical parts. The Society gave its permission, on condition that assistance was arranged.

Problems kept on coming. An air raid shelter had to be built in Science House at a cost of £316 ($21,445). Blackout material, a first aid kit and fire fighting equipment in case of incendiary bombs were required and personnel had to be trained for fire fighting. Paper rationing was in force, requiring "rigid economy" in the use of paper. At times, publication of the Proceedings was held up while waiting for a shipment of paper to arrive. Mr N.C. Betty who was assistant to the Bacteriologist was offered a position elsewhere, but had to request release by the Linnean Society under manpower restrictions.

The Halls were in demand for meetings of organisations set up to deal with some aspect of the war and were in use almost every night. This resulted in increased income for Science House that recorded the highest ever profits in 1944 and 1945 of £350 ($23,040) and £450 ($29,623) respectively. Demand for the Halls continued after the war. No action could be taken on rents without the permission of the Fair Rents courts and the Society was advised to make out a case comparing rents in 1949 with those in 1939. As income from rents was satisfactory, no action was taken.

The College Street property was put up for auction again but was passed in at £7,500 ($493,714). It was leased again and the Fair Rents Board determined the rent at £16 ($1,053) per week. The tenant was prepared to pay an extra £2-10-0 ($167) for a three year lease..

By 1945, the ever-expanding libraries of the Royal Society of New South Wales and the Linnean Society were a cause for concern. The possibility of combining the libraries was canvased as there were approximately 160 duplications and storage space was limited. This notion was ultimately rejected. An extension to Science House was proposed and the Government was amenable to granting extra land "after the war". However, the Linnean Society was not in a position to contribute to any extension. Storage cubicles on the roof were built to alleviate the problem.

From time to time, the Government would seek input to scientific matters from the Society. A key to the eucalypts was constructed at Government request (1935). Advice from the Society was sought for the review of the Birds and Animals Protection Act (1940).

The Government invited input from the Society to the Wildflowers and Native Vegetation Protection Act (amended) (1945). The Kosciusko State Park Trust requested the Linnean Society's views about the primitive area (1944). Society members conducted a survey of the Kosciusko area.

The Society also proffered advice unasked. The introduction of the Great Mexican Toad (cane toad) into Queensland to destroy the sugar cane beetle was proposed. The Society wrote to the Council for Scientific and Industrial Research (1935) drawing attention to the experience in Hawaii where the toad has no natural enemies. Similar disastrous results in Australia could be expected since it also had no natural enemies here either. The information was forwarded To Dr J.N.L. Cumpston with whom the final decision to release the toads rested.

The Linnean Society has had interest in conservation issues prior to and continuing as awareness has growing in the community at large. Attempts to prevent summer grazing on the alpine pastures in the Snowy Mountains and the formation of the Kosciusko State Park and the designated primitive area were foremost amongst the issues it supported in 1957. Limestone mining in the Colong region became the conservation issue in 1967.

The immediate post-war period

During the post-war period, the Society became concerned about the low salary offered to the Linnean Macleay Fellows. What had originally been a generous salary in Sir William Macleay's will had been whittled away by inflation. In 1947, the Society went to the Equity Court and requested a variation to Sir William Macleay's will that would allow a salary of £400 ($24,841), for not more than four Fellows. This request was successful, though legal costs to the Society amounted to £123-10-9 ($5,954).

Dr Jensen, Macleay Microbiologist since 1929, resigned in 1947 to take up a position of Chief of the Division of Bacteriology in the State Laboratories of Plant Culture, Denmark and he left Sydney in September. The Bacteriology Account was then only earning £520 ($32,292), insufficient for a salary to attract a first class applicant. Once again, the banks were asked to donate. In 1948, the Rural Bank donated £200 ($11,252) per annum for five years, later to be extended for another three years. In 1949, the Commonwealth Bank made £1,750 ($90,000) available from its Rural Development Fund in instalments of £250 ($12,857) per annum for five years. The Bank of New South Wales and the Commercial Banking Company also forwarded donations to the Bacteriology account (1949). Requests to commercial companies with rural interests for donations were unsuccessful.

A buyer for the College Street property was finally found in 1948. The Society's asking price was £13,000 ($731,428) but Treasury disallowed it and set the price at £11,900 ($669,538). The Society did not accept this and argued with Treasury. Some months later, Treasury relented and allowed the original asking price to stand.

The Society advertised widely for a Bacteriologist to work on topics associated with soil fertility, at a salary of $600 to $900 ($30,119 to $46,285), depending in qualifications. In 1949, the position was offered to Dr Yao-Tseng Tchan, then working in Paris. Being Chinese, entry into Australia was difficult, for the White Australia Policy was in force. Tchan, his wife and child were eventually given permission to reside in Australia for five years and they arrived in Sydney in 1950. His residency permit was renewed at intervals and he eventually stayed for the rest of his life. Dr Tchan soon discovered hitherto unsuspected nitrogen fixing bacteria in Sydney soils.

The library remained an issue with the Society and attention was once again focused it when John Metcalfe of the Library Board of NSW reported on the libraries of the two Societies (19-12-50). Once again, amalgamation of the Royal Society library and that of the Linnean Society's was proposed. At that time, the Linnean Society library had an author catalogue but did not index periodicals. Exchanges and donations accounted for about 90% of library. The report noted that the libraries were not open at night when members were likely to be in Science House and few members used the libraries. Enquiries and loans were considered routine and most could be done elsewhere. It also noted that very little was not duplicated in other libraries in Sydney: older textbooks and travel books had historical values but were little used: the collections did not have any defined scope or purpose and subject indexing would be costly. The principle function of libraries was exchange. The position of the libraries had changed considerably since the foundation of the Society. Members now working in research were mainly in institutions that had their own libraries that were better resourced. Persons trained in librarianship were required to service the libraries and keep them functioning. In spite of the report, amalgamation did not go ahead.

Dr Tchan was in demand to teach bacteriology at the University of Sydney so a joint Linnean Society of New South Wales/University of Sydney lectureship was negotiated with Sydney University. In mid 1953, Dr Tchan was appointed Senior Lecturer/Linnean Macleay Lecturer in Bacteriology in the University of Sydney, pending an expected favourable outcome in the Equity Court that finally approved it in October 1956. This arrangement, with Sydney University part funding the position, alleviated the increasing difficulty of full funding from the Linnean Society.

The Society made a request to the Commissioner of Taxation for tax exemption of donations to the Society. In 1952, the Deputy Commissioner of Taxation approved the Society as a scientific research institution and would allow donations to be exempt from income tax, subject to conditions. A Mr Armstrong of Nyngan saw an article in the journal of the Graziers Association about this tax-deductible fund and made a donation of £10 ($338) to support research. The Commissioner also ruled that there was no income tax on the Fellow's stipend as long as the Fellow did not have a PhD.

By the 1950s, necessary repairs and maintenance of Science House was becoming a costly item and Sydney Council rates were increased substantially. Science House Management Committee (SHMC) went to the Fair Rents Tribunal in 1953 to request an increase. On advice of a valuer, the SHMC believed the Fair Rents Tribunal would approve a 100% increase in rents, taking into account cost increases since 1939. However, SHMC thought this was excessive and not in keeping with the terms of the land grant, and an increase of 60% was requested. The application was made through a Fair Rents Advocate (fee 10%) to the Fair Rents Board that eventually went to a hearing in a Fair Rents Court, and approval was given. Afterwards, applications for increases in rents were made at approximately three-yearly intervals until the early 1960's.

In the late 1960s, extensions to Science House were proposed once again as a possible solution to the library problem. The Institute of Engineers had heard that the State Government was considering development of the area immediately to the north and west of Science House. The Government had indicated (in July 1945) that it was prepared to make the land adjoining Science House available for extensions after the war. The Linnean Society advised SHMC (in 1956) that it did not have the funds available for it to enter into any project to extend Science House and as no action was taken, the problem remained. The library was still expanding at a considerable rate: over a five-year period, from 1953 to 1957, the Society received an average of 1,745 items per year. Ten years later, for the period 1963 to 1967, an average of 2,116 items per year was added to the library, a 17.5% increase.

Again in the post war period, the low attendance at ordinary meetings was a concern to the Council and a committee was set up to look into the matter. The committee recommended that meetings start at 6 pm instead of 7.30 pm and this was adopted, beginning in 1957. The change in starting time seemed to make little difference to the number of members attending the meetings and starting time reverted to 7.30 pm a couple of years later.

Once again, relentless inflation had made the stipend being paid to the Linnean Macleay Fellows quite inadequate. A petition to the Equity court to increase the stipend to £1,600 ($44,908) was granted in December 1959. Henceforth, only one Fellow per year was appointed.

Dr Tchan was appointed Reader in Agricultural Microbiology at the University of Sydney and was still the Linnean Macleay Lecturer in Bacteriology. The Society became concerned that teaching and administration was taking over much of his time. In 1967, he was appointed to the Chair of Microbiology. A joint committee of Sydney University and the Linnean Society selected a replacement and Dr Y.K. Cho was appointed the Linnean Macleay Lecturer in Microbiology in 1969. Dr Cho worked on growing exotic mushrooms commercially and remained the Linnean Macleay Lecturer in Microbiology until his retirement. By that time, the income from the Bacteriology Account could only support a small supplementary research grant.

By the late 1960s, the Linnean Society and its library occupied the third floor of Science House and it maintained its own meeting room and office. Council meetings and lectures were held in its rooms and there was an auditorium on the ground floor for larger meetings. The office and library were open to members during the week. Publication of the Proceedings, members' meetings and public lectures were still the main activities of the society. The Society also organised occasional symposia and field trips. The Society had an honorary secretary and honorary treasurer, and employed an assistant secretary.

A survey of members in the late 1960s early 1970s indicated that they considered the services of the library and scientific publication to be the most valuable functions of the Society. The library was used regularly in those days before photocopiers were common and affordable. The President reported in March 1971 that there were 290 borrowings of books and journals (the only record found) in the preceding year. A report by R. McGreal (29-3-1974) found that the Linnean Society held in its collection some 1,700 serials, 600 of which were still being received. The collection was fully catalogued but services were small scale. The Society published a volume of the Proceedings each year. From 1966 to 1970, 19 to 29 papers per year were published in volumes that had from 252 to 500 pages. There were far fewer journals available for intending authors in those times than there are today

The Science House Management Committee (SHMC) ran the day-to-day affairs of the building and the lettings. The Society paid rent and received a one third share of the surplus. In 1967 and 1968, the Society received $2,724 ($31,689) and $3,859 ($43,628), respectively. But this state of affairs would not remain this way for long.

The 1970s and Science House Pty Ltd
In 1968, the State Government had given control of the Rocks to the Sydney Cove Redevelopment Authority (SCRA) with the intention to demolish the original buildings and replace them with high-rise residential buildings. In June 1970, the Linnean Society of NSW was given notice that SCRA planned to acquire Science House as part of its redevelopment scheme for the Rocks and in November 1970 the Society was given notice of resumption of the site. As work on Science House would not commence for some years, the occupiers would be allowed stay, on much the same terms as had existed but as tenants of the SCRA.

The SHMC sought legal opinion and was advised that if the owner bodies were not prepared to sell voluntarily, they might be forced to sell at a later stage. Each of the owner bodies held an undivided one-third interest in Science House under the terms of the Land Grant. "One of the terms of the Land Grant was that the property shall not be sold except with the consent of the Governor of NSW nor shall the purchase money be applied save as the Governor shall have previously directed. It will therefore be necessary to obtain the Governor's consent not only to the sale, but also to the way to which it is proposed to apply the proceeds of the sale" (letter, Stephen, Jaques and Stephen, Solicitors, 22-6-70).

The solicitors also recommended that a company be set up, with two $1 shares, one for each owner body: the Royal Society of NSW and the Linnean Society of NSW. The Institute of Engineers had indicated that it was not interested in a joint venture. Science House Pty. Ltd (SHPL) was set up and the limited propriety would limit liability of the Societies and their members. SHPL would oversee the reinvestment of the compensation moneys in a Science Centre, as was the legal obligation of the original land grant. Each of the Societies would be entitled to appoint one half of the directors of the Board with the proviso that there shall be not less than two and not more than eight Board Members. A Science Centre Planning

Committee was set up.

A claim for compensation was made to the Crown Solicitor in March 1971. The property was valued at $1,800,000 ($17,956,626) by Property Consultants Jones, Lang and Wooten. With compensation, the one-third claim for the Linnean Society was $637,800 ($6,254,650)

The Linnean Society of NSW sought a new Act of Incorporation to allow wider investment powers, including shares and property, of Sir William Macleay's bequest. The President Prof Neville Stephenson and the Honorary Treasurer Dr Joyce Vickery explained the proposed changes to a Special General Meeting (Nov 1971) and the meeting endorsed the actions of the Council. The solicitors drew up draft legislation in 1972 for approval by the Minister for Cultural Affairs. The Government eventually (in 1974) declined to change the provisions of the Trustee's Act, hence disallowing any wider powers of investment. Dr Vickery reminded the Board of SHPL that the Act stipulated that Trustees (of Macleay's Will) must act with prudence and the Board would have to make the most of its resources, viz. only the compensation money (minutes of the Board of SHPL meeting, 28-6-74)

In 1972, the first instalment of compensation of $15,500 ($145,841) was received from the SCRA. Some of the Linnean Society Council members were taken aback at the changes to the Science Centre planning from a year ago and were concerned that the Society would endanger its own goals by subsidising other societies.

Then followed an intense period of planning and negotiation with the Government for another site in the Rocks. Science Centres elsewhere in the world were studied. When the Government refused to consider a site in the Rocks, there was a search for a suitable site elsewhere. The Government was asked to guarantee a loan, similar to the guarantee it had given to the Labour Council of NSW, a trade union, for purposes connected with a new Trades Hall, but it refused. However, the Government was sympathetic to the cause, and other requests for help were met with limited success.

The company Science House Pty Ltd was registered in 1973 and the directors for the Linnean Society at this time were Prof Derek J. Anderson, Dr Harold G. Cogger, Prof Neville G. Stephenson and Dr Joyce Vickery. There were also four directors nominated by the Royal Society. Prof Stephenson was elected Chairman and Mrs Ruth Inall was the company Secretary

The compensation offered to the Linnean Society was $438,000 ($6,121,181), less than that requested

62

Proc. Linn. Soc. N.S.W., 137, 2015

of $637,800, but the society was advised to take it. As it would take some time, a year or two before the building was required for redevelopment, the Societies could remain there as tenants.

Meantime, in February 1971, a group of local residents felt that the new dwellings would result in increased rents, which would force out the traditional residents of the area and formed the Rocks Residents Group to oppose the plans. The residents' group requested a Green Ban from the Builders Labourers Federation, who had become increasingly active in preventing controversial developments over the previous four years.

By 1973, the Union had imposed the ban, and after discussions with the Sydney Cove Redevelopment Authority, a 'People's Plan' was developed. By October 1973, it appeared that the redevelopment would proceed as originally planned, using non-union labour. For two weeks, demonstrations by local residents and unionists followed, with numerous arrests being made. Liberal Premier Robert Askin was in the midst of an election campaign, and used the protests as a means of conveying his law and order message to voters. However, the green ban stayed in place until 1975, when the state union leadership was overthrown. The bans were ultimately successful, as can be seen in the buildings that survive today. Instead of demolishing The Rocks, they were renovated and Science House was spared the wrecker's ball. But there was no turning back for the Societies as compensation had been paid, they were tenants in Science House and the Science Centre project had commenced.

In August-September of 1973, a suitable site was found at 35-43 Clarence St: the 6-storey F.T. Wimble building, the last building in Clarence St before the approach to the Harbour Bridge. It had been used as a warehouse and was described as "of sound construction, but not pretty". It would need renovation and even required a new roof and lift. SHPL had an option to buy that expired in December. The Commonwealth Bank had notified SHPL that finance was available. In November, the Board was told it was necessary to make a decision, as three other buyers were interested. Only the Secretary of SHPL, Ruth Inall had been inside the building and preliminary plans for its redevelopment had been hastily drawn up.

The Linnean Society director Dr Cogger "expressed grave doubts about the viability of the proposition and his authority to make a decision of such magnitude on behalf of his Society. He suggested asking his Society for guidance. Dr Vickery pointed out that it was the responsibility of the directors to deal with situations rather than expect their Council that was much less informed of the development, to make a decision. Dr Cogger replied that it was a matter of conscience. Prof Anderson (also a Linnean Society Director) agreed with Dr Cogger's sentiment". Mrs Inall reminded the meeting of the conditions of the 1928 Land Grant and an understanding that Science House would continue its function at another location. Prof Stephenson "drew attention to the Council's resolution giving him the necessary authority". The motion to purchase the building was carried, with Dr Cogger's dissent recorded (Minutes of the meeting of the Board of Directors of SHPL, 14 Nov 1973). Both Anderson and Cogger resigned from the Board after this meeting. (Note: This was a time of a property boom with few thoughts that it could end.)

The Wimble Building was bought in January 1974 for $1,248,600 ($9,330,693) and contracts were signed in June: the Commonwealth Bank loan was $1.25 million. Building works were estimated to cost $920,000 ($6,875,090) and by August-September of that year, the Development Application had been approved. F.T. Wimble donated $75,000 ($560,469) to the tax-deductable library funds of each of the Societies. These library funds had been set up to defray the not inconsiderable costs of moving the libraries. The Government also gave a donation of $5,000 ($37,365) to each of the library funds. H.B. Selby Australia donated $4,000 ($29,892) for shelving in the libraries. About a year later, Wimble donated an additional $100,000 ($648,903) to SHPL.

A report on the future of libraries by R. McGreal (29-3-74) recognised that each of the Societies' libraries had a valuable collection, much of it unique. The libraries had a valuable contribution to make to research facilities, but more modern and sophisticated reference and information service techniques were required, particularly the services of a fully professional librarian.

After extensive planning and design, tenders for renovations were called in May 1975 and closed in June 1975. Interest rates were now 11% and building costs had escalated to $1,215,797 ($7,889,341), an increase of 36.9%. A further loan of $300,000 was sought from the Bank to cover the shortfall in building costs. The Bank granted the extra loan and pointed out that it expected half-yearly repayment of $77,925 on the $1.25 m loan and $19, 945 on the $300,000 loan, for twenty years each, making a total repayment of $97,370 ($631,836) per half year.

Science House was leased from the SCRA. SHPL took over the running of Science House from the Science House Management Committee that was disbanded. SHPL had set up a secretarial and editorial service for the scientific societies. A quote given to the Linnean Society in late 1976 for the coming year was rent, $4,445, editorial $4,160 and secretarial service $2,250, making a total of $10,855 ($62,157).

SHPL was treated as a non-profit making charitable organisation and did not have to pay tax on investments and profits, and was exempt from land rates and council rates. They considered a small profit from services was fair, but should not be seen to be profiteering. Ample office space in Sydney was available at this time and attracting tenants was not easy. The State Government gave notice that it was prepared to rent the whole of the fourth floor. A restaurant and other shops on the ground floor were being rented. SHPL hoped to develop Science Centre as a conference centre and the restaurant would do the catering.

Building costs had increased again, the main reason being the more rigid interpretation of the fire safety laws after a disastrous hotel fire. SHPL asked the Bank for an additional $100,000 loan and it was approved, at 12% interest, with half yearly repayments of $6,650. The total of loans was now $1,650,000 ($2,554,600). Repayment of interest on the loans was set down to commence in March 1977, subject to building work being finished.

The Institute of Engineers left Science House in mid 1976 and this made renting Science House from the SCRA unviable. It was planned to move out by the end of the year. Moving the libraries was a major task. Mr Selby of Selby Australia Pty Ltd arranged considerable help. There had been a number of donations to the Library fund and the University of Sydney and University of NSW lent book boxes. The move cost the Linnean Society $4,142 ($23,718) for labour and hire of a truck. The October 1976 Council meeting of the Linnean Society was the first in Science Centre, and in December, the lease on Science House was terminated.

The Governor, Sir Roden Cutler officially opened Science Centre on the 23rd of March 1977. The Premier, Neville Wran opened a fund raising campaign on behalf of Science House Pty. Ltd. There were other distinguished official guests. The Band of the Eastern Australian Area, Royal Australian Navy provided the Vice-Regal salute to the Governor and musical background during the refreshments period after the ceremony (Linnean Society newsletter, April 1977).

Necessary expenses continued unabated. Staff wages were up. The builder submitted his final account of $106,000 ($540,433), but SHPL could not pay the full amount immediately. Unsatisfactory door locks, handles etc. would cost $1,936 ($9,871)

and the law required a lift maintenance contract. An air conditioning maintenance contract would cost $4,584 ($23,372) pa. Changes to the wiring of lights and office partitions were required. Lettings of office space were slow: there was an oversupply at this time. Trade at the restaurant was slow as the foreshadowed conferences had no yet started. A chemist was due to open in a shop on street level. Lettings and the secretariat improved, but SHPL was struggling to pay the day-to-day costs of running the building.

By the end of 1976, Ruth Inall had resigned as part time Secretary of the Linnean Society to become full time Secretary and later General Manager then Company Secretary of Science House Pty Ltd. The Linnean Society had a part time secretary for the first half of 1977 then in July, Mrs Barbara Stoddard was appointed Secretary. There was a part time librarian and the library reopened in September for three days a week.

At that stage, the Linnean Society was struggling to meet the costs of the Science Centre. It could not pay commercial rent of $4,041 ($20,603) per annum for the space the library occupied. Rent for the office was about $443 ($2,259). There was no charge for Council meetings but other meetings, e.g. the Annual General Meeting and a library committee meeting were charged $30 or $40. The quote from the Secretariat was $4,000 for editing the Proceedings and $5,850 for secretarial services, making it a total of $9.850 ($50,220) for an estimated 20 hours a week. The restaurant supplied afternoon tea, at a cost of 35c per cup. The Society was soon looking for ways to reduce expenses. Prof Tom Vallance volunteered to become Honorary Editor of the Proceedings at the end of the year. Mrs Stoddard would take the minutes and the Secretariat would only type a draft for $247 ($1,259) per year (3 hours per meeting) and the Council would arrange its own afternoon tea.

In March 1978, a letter from the loans manager of the Commonwealth Bank to the Society pointed out that the debt was escalating, from $1.65 million of approved loans to $2.16 million ($10.20 million). No payment of interest or repayment of capital had been made. It urged the Societies to do more, for the bank could not allow this situation to continue. This letter alarmed the Council. A joint meeting with the Royal Society in July drew a full revelation of the financial state of SHPL. Income covered expenses with a small surplus. Interest required by the bank on the loans was $19,000 ($89,692) per month but repayments made were $2,000 ($9,441) per month, "constantly under review". After much discussion, a motion to set up a joint committee to examine fund raising options was passed.

64

Proc. Linn. Soc. N.S.W., 137, 2015

An open letter (17 August 1978) by Dr Don Adamson and signed by 12 Council Members explained the situation to members. The letter acknowledged that those involved had worked long and hard to make Science Centre a success. Any moral obligation that the Societies had to use the compensation money for a Science Centre was discharged when it put those monies into Science Centre. Council objected to a role of fund-raiser as a detraction from the core activities of the Society and SHPL was increasingly viewed as a commercial operation. They called for independent financial advice as to whether the company was viable and if it could trade itself out of debt.

A response to the open letter, written by Dr Joyce Vickery and signed by Prof Neville Stephenson (25 August 1978) viewed the concerns raised by the Society as attacks on SHPL. It reiterated the moral and legal obligation of the Societies to Science Centre. It claimed the services of the Science Centre were much needed and the functional operations were a success with income increasingly exceeding expenditure. It acknowledged the problem was paying full interest rate and the capitalisation of the unpaid interest. It exhorted the Society to do more fund raising: the fund-raising effort launched at the opening over a year ago had only realised $43,000 ($202,989). It claimed the Societies would eventually benefit from the surplus, just as it had under the old Science House Management before takeover of the building.

In August, six ordinary members requested a special general meeting so that the membership could discuss the future of the Society. Dr Vickery resigned as Honorary Treasurer of the Society and Dr Don Adamson was elected Honorary Treasurer.

At the Special General Meeting (13 Sept 1978), a full account of the Society's assets was presented. There was some $287,000 ($1,352,823) in four accounts, not in any way involved in the Science Centre project, plus the $400,000 ($1,888,252) compensation that was loaned to SHPL for the Science Centre project. Much discussion centred on the cost of the library to the Society. There were the librarian's wages and the cost of photocopying for interlibrary loans was considerable, and users did not want to pay. The new Treasurer summed it up: the library was a drain on the Society's finances. The meeting voted to relocate the library if rent-free accommodation could be found.

The meeting rejected major fund-raising activities and it reaffirmed its dedication to the promotion of the natural sciences. A motion requesting "full moral support" for the board of SHPL and its efforts to overcome the financial problems was lost but the meeting acknowledged that the Society and SHPL "had different priorities and both should work with mutual support and encouragement as each can afford the other".

Relations between the Linnean Society and SHPL were summed up by Dr L.A.S. Johnson (report to Council, 21 February 1979) thus: the viewpoint of the spokesperson for the Directors of the Board was considerably different to that of the Society and a strong emotional attachment and pressure to keep Science Centre alive had led to optimistic reports of trading. "The Directors, clearly strongly supported and influenced by Mrs Inall, nevertheless pressed the Society to continue with a project, despite frequently, if sporadically, voiced doubts from some of the members of Council, including Directors who have since resigned. The bona fides or probity of the Directors were not questioned, simply the appropriateness of their attitudes in the light of the Council's present and future policies and priorities".

Mr Selby, a businessman and director of SHPL gave a frank appraisal of the situation: "......in his opinion the debt was quite beyond any trading capacity of SHPL. In normal business practice, a bank would be most unlikely to allow a Company to continue its activities with this debt structure, so he could only presume that the nature of the Commonwealth Savings Bank and the character of the two shareholders in the Company allowed the Bank to adopt some special attitude. Mr Selby thought the Company could service a debt of $1,000,000 and he and his co-directors were continually looking for ways and means of reducing the debt to this level. He thought the tolerant attitude of the Bank also resulted from the fact that the Bank could not improve its own position by bringing about a winding-up position: it was therefore better to allow trading to continue in the style of services provided by Science Centre.

"Although there were certainly some shortcomings in the location and appointments of the building as a Science Centre, we have to live with them as a legacy of history and should adopt a positive attitude to the future in spite of them. If as suggested, scientific societies were not using the Centre to any great extent, it was obvious that professional associations were." He pointed out that the Societies had no financial liability arising from the circumstances of SHPL and said the directors, whoever they were, should be given encouragement and freedom to go about solving the problems of the Company for the Societies' benefit. In the commercial world it was neither practicable or usual for shareholders to tell directors what to do. Mr Selby considered the various Directors had put a lot of effort into looking after the

Societies' interests in SHPL. He also urged Council "to avoid taking any action that might have the effect of destroying any equity or interest of the Society in SHPL, or of nullifying the efforts of the Board of Directors to overcome the Company's undoubted problems" (Minutes of the Council meeting 21 March 1979).

The Council greatly appreciated a realistic assessment of SHPL. Mr Selby also reminded Council that the duties and obligations of Directors were as laid down in the Companies Act. Mr Selby found it necessary to resign from the Board because of limitations of his time. In December 1979, the businessman Mr Harry Wallace of F.T. Wimble and Co Ltd replaced Mr Selby as one of the Society's directors on the Board of SHPL

On the 29 May 1979, Dr Joyce Vickery died after a short illness. She had been a Council Member for ten years and was Honorary Treasurer for eight years. During this time, she donated $1,000 anonymously and repeatedly to the Scientific Research Fund, usually giving twice a year. The Scientific Research Fund was re-named the Joyce W. Vickery Scientific Research Fund in honour of her generosity and foresight. Her estate paid almost $34,000 ($140,085) into the research fund.. The first award from the Fund was made in 1980. By 1982, there were twenty applications for funds, requests far exceeding money available for disbursement: nine awards were made.

By 1981, trading of SHPL showed a satisfactory profit, but there was no improvement in the ability to repay the debt on the loans from the bank. Fund raising activities were not successful and donations barely covered expenses. By October 1983, Science House Pty Ltd was in the hands of the Liquidator. This step was taken on the solicitor's advice after a review of the finances of SHPL when an attempt to auction the building failed. The Liquidator advised the Societies that the secretarial services had no goodwill value so it was not possible to sell the business.

The building was put up for auction again. It was valued at $3.7 million, and an approach to the Bank to delay the sale as property values were rising was rejected. The building was sold for $3.775 ($12.162) million. Indebtedness to the Bank was $3.9 ($12.564) million, leaving nothing for the Societies who each lost their compensation of $400,000 for resumption of Science House. When the wind-up was finished (in 1985), the Liquidator declared a dividend of 5 cents in the dollar from the debt in Science House Pty Ltd and sent a cheque for $20,849.50 ($55,013) to the Linnean Society.

Post Science House Pty Ltd

Since the Society had been given notice to vacate Science Centre following the financial collapse of SHPL, a decision had to be made about the library. The library was open for only a few hours a week, was rarely visited by members and had become only a provider of outgoing interlibrary loans. The Society did not have the means of improving its services. Since no one institution could take the library in its entirety, it was decided to disperse the holdings. The Australian Museum and National Herbarium were given first selection, then the universities and then the State Library. If a current title came on exchange, the recipient library would maintain the arrangement. The remainder went to the Department of Agriculture at Wagga Wagga from where they would be distributed to the then Colleges of Advanced Education, later to become Charles Sturt University. Any books of value to collectors and only of marginal scientific value, such as Gould's humming bird books, were sold on the open market.

In November 1983, the Society's office moved to rented premises in Milsons Point. Since then, the office has remained in rented premises, but has at times changed location, as was necessary under the circumstances.

The collapse of SHPL made little difference to the activities of the Society. Thanks to the limited propriety, the Company could not touch the other assets of the Society. The loss was thus the $400,000 compensation for Science House, plus the $1 share. The assets from Sir William Macleay's will were being administered in accordance with the Society's Act of Incorporation that, thankfully, the Government had refused to alter, as had been requested in 1972. The Royal Society did not fare so well, for it had few assets other than the compensation money.

The core activities of the Linnean Society, promoting the Natural Sciences had continued unabated the whole time of the Science House/Science Centre debacle. The Proceedings were published each year, regular lectures were delivered and occasional symposia and field trips were organised throughout. The newsletter was started and the first grants from the Joyce Vickery Scientific Research Fund were awarded during this time. Without the problems of Science Centre, the Council could give its undivided attention to the promotion of the Natural Sciences.

The Proceedings of the Linnean Society of New South Wales has continued to publish original research papers dealing with any topic of the natural sciences. All papers are fully refereed. The number

66

Proc. Linn. Soc. N.S.W., 137, 2015

of original research papers submitted for publication has dwindled somewhat as the number of scientific journals available to authors has increased. Moreover, academics are given more credit for publishing in international journals, a further disincentive to submit papers to the Proceedings. Nonetheless, the Society remains committed to providing an outlet for papers of local and regional interest.

In 2012, the Council agreed to the Honorary Editor, Dr Mike Augee and Mr Bruce Welch adopting electronic publishing of the Proceedings. When papers are accepted for publication, they can be published on line immediately. At the end of the year, the papers are collected together in a volume. Access to papers is available to anyone, free of charge at http://escholarship.library.usyd.edu.au/journals/index.php/LIN Paper copies are available on request, at cost. This change has allowed a more rapid publication, easier access via the internet and has reduced costs considerably.

Papers from symposia are also published and are a collection of the latest research on one topic. The symposia and collection of papers published since 1980 are as follows:

Vol. 136, 2014. Section 1. Papers arising from a symposium held by the Linnean Society of NSW at Jenolan Caves (22-23 May 2013). 6 papers

Vol. 134, 2012. Symposium - Wildlife Conservancy's sanctuary at Scotia, far western New South Wales (13 July 2011). 7 papers

Vol. 134, 2012. Symposium held by the Linnean Society on the Natural History of Royal National Park (October 2011). 16 papers

Vol. 132, 2011. Papers from a symposium held by the Linnean Society on Geodiversity, Geological Heritage and Geotourism (6-10 September 2010). 10 papers.

Vol. 126, 2006. The biology and ecology of Gibraltar National Park. 12 papers

Vol. 125, 2004, A collection of papers on monotremes. 11 papers,

Vol. 117, 1997. Australian Quaternary Vertebrates. 13 papers

Vol. 116, 1996. *Living in a Fire Prone Environment*: Proceedings of a Linnean Society symposium (4 March 1995). 11 papers

Vol. 115, 1995. Papers on Plant Ecology in honour of Dr Peter Myerscough. 12 papers

Vol. 107(3), 1984. Papers from a symposium on the Evolution and Biogeography of Early Vertebrates (February 1983), 14 papers

1984. P. Huchings (ed). *Proceedings of the First International Polychaete Conference*. Linnean Society of New South Wales.

The newsletter, Linn SOC News has been published quarterly since its inception in 1976. It keeps members informed of the Society's current activities.

Some books have been published also: the *Freshwater Crayfishes of New South Wales* by John R. Merrick (1993) and the very popular *Field Guide to the Royal National Park,* edited by Robert J. King (2013)

The Society follows conservation issues and subscribes to the Nature Conservation Council and sends delegates to the annual conference. On occasions, the Society makes submissions regarding the scientific aspects of a conservation issue, but it does not get involved in the politics.

The website was set up in 1998 by Mr Stefan Rose and is currently maintained by Mr Bruce Welch. It contains up to date information on all aspects of the Society's activities.

The awards of research grants continue to be a major activity of the Society. The first award from the Joyce W. Vickery Scientific Research Fund was made in 1980 and grants from it have continued to be awarded every year since. In practically every year, requests for money far exceed that available for disbursement. The value of the Fund has been maintained, thanks to the Treasurer's prudent capitalisation of half the interest earned on the relevant investments.

The Betty Mayne Scientific Research Fund for the Earth Sciences was set up in 1998 with money received by the Society from the closure of the Earth Exchange in 1995. Betty Mayne had been a keen member of the Friends of the Geological and Mining Museum and more recently the Earth Exchange Museum Society (TEEMS). She had left a bequest to TEEMS that was eventually wound up and the TEEMS Council donated the funds to Linnean Society of NSW to assist students in the Earth Sciences. The first award from the Betty Mayne Scientific Research Fund was made in 1998.

Applications for grants from the Research Funds are invited from almost anyone with a demonstrated capability of carrying out the proposed research project. In fact, most grants go to post graduate research students. The grants do more than supplement meagre research funds: they give students practice at the art of applying for research grants, a necessary skill in these modern times and if successful, it is something they can add to their CVs. Recipients of grants and a summary of their projects are published each year in the Newsletter.

Donations to both the Joyce Vickery and Betty Mayne Research Funds are fully tax deductible. Each year, Members make donations to the funds and some

Proc. Linn. Soc. N.S.W., 137, 2015

67

make quite large donations. There have also been some large bequests, as listed below:

2010. From the estate of the late H.J. Hewson, $23, 526. Helen Hewson was a botanist who taught Botany at the Australian National University. She made a major contribution to the Flora of Australia and became Director, Flora at ABRS, and later Director of Botany at the Australian National Botanic Gardens.

2012 From the estate of John Noble, $50,120. John Noble was a mechanical engineer and dedicated conservationist. He was a keen photographer with a special interest in spiders. The best invertebrate project in the applications for the Joyce Vickery Scientific Research Fund is awarded the John Noble Scientific Research Grant.

2013 A gift from Mrs Betty Jacobs in memory of her late husband Dr Surrey Jacobs. Dr Jacobs was a botanist at the National Herbarium of New South Wales and a grass specialist. He took experiments into the field and showed that the behaviour of plants in the field bore little resemblance to their behaviour under controlled laboratory conditions. A Surrey Jacobs Award will be made to the best field work research application.

All donations and bequests are much very much appreciated and are acknowledged in the Newsletter. For more information about the research funds, visit the website, http://linneansocietynsw.org.au

Money from Sir William Macleay's will (1890) set up an account to fund four Linnean Macleay Fellowships to encourage and promote research in the Natural Sciences. Initially, the salary of each Fellow was £400 pa (~$56-57,000). The candidate must reside in New South Wales and have a science degree from the University of Sydney, the only university in New South Wales when Sir William wrote his will. Over the years, inflation has whittled away the value of the Fellowships, and requests to the Supreme Court of New South Wales in Equity allowed an increase in salary with a decrease in the number of Fellowships, eventually to only one grant of $3,200. The Society must adhere to all the other conditions of the will. Inflation has diminished the value of the bequest for Microbiology and is now used to fund amount one or two research grants in Microbiology. Visit the website for further information.

The Society organises lectures on topical subjects in the Natural Sciences. These lectures are free of charge and open to the public. A report of the lecture is published in the Newsletter and posted on the website. Coming lectures are advertised in the Newsletter and on the website.

Through all the changing circumstances of the times, some of them quite tumultuous, the Linnean Society of New South Wales has managed to adapt and continue in its core activities of the promotion of natural history and has made a considerable contribution to Science.

REFERENCES

Minutes of the meetings of the Board of Directors of Science House Pty Ltd, letters and papers (1973-1982)

Minutes of Council Meetings of the Linnean Society of NSW (1925-2015).

Minutes of the Science House Managemant Committee (1928-1975).

Newsletter of the Linnean Society of NSW 'Linn S'O'C News' (1976-2015).

Walkom, A.B. (1925). The Linnean Society of New South Wales: Historical Notes of its First Fifty Years (Jubilee Publication). Australasian Medical Publishing C. Ltd. Sydney.

68

Proc. Linn. Soc. N.S.W., 137, 2015

Appendix 1. Presidents of the Linnean Society of New South Wales, 1925-2015

1925	Mr H.J. Carter	1971	Dr L.A.S. Johnson
1926	Dr E.W. Ferguson	1972	Dr H.G. Coggar
1927	Prof L. Harrison	1973	Dr P.J. Stanbury
1928	Dr W.R. Browne	1974	Prof T.G. Vallance
1929	Dr W.S.R. Wardlow	1975	Mr D.W. Edwards
1930	Mr E. Cheal	1976	Dr Barbara Briggs
1931	Prof T.G.B. Osborne	1977	Prof Barry Webby
1932	Dr C. Anderson	1978	Mr John Waterhouse
1933	Prof A.N. Burkitt	1989	Dr Alex Richie
1934	Prof W.J. Dakin	1980	Dr Frank Rowe
1935	Dr W.L. Waterhouse	1981	Dr Helene Martin
1936	Mr C.A. Sussmilch	1982	Dr Tony Wright
1937	Mr E.C. Andrews	1983	Dr Courtney Smithers
1938	Mr T.C.Roughley	1984	Mr G.R. Phipps
1939	Prof J. MacDonald Holmes	1985	Dr Peter Martin
1940	Mr R.N. Anderson	1986	Dr Peter Martin
1941	Dr A.R. Walkom	1987	Dr Peter Martin
1942	Mr F.N. Taylor	1988	Prof T.G. Vallance
1943	Dr E. Le G. Troughton	1989	Dr Peter Myerscough
1944	Dr L.E. Browne	1990	Dr D.S. Horning
1945	Dr Ida A. Brown	1991	Dr D.S. Horning
1946	Mr A.R. Woodfill	1992	Prof Robert King
1947	Dr G.D. Osborne	1993	Prof Robert King
1948	Dr Lilian Fraser	1994	Mrs Karen Wilson
1949	Dr R.N. Robertson	1995	Mrs Karen Wilson
1950	Mr D.J. Lee	1996	Dr Alex Ritchie
1951	Mr A.N. Colefax	1997	Dr Alex Ritchie
1952	Mr S.J. Copland	1998	Dr R.A .L. Osborne
1953	Mr J.M. Vincent	1999	Dr R.A. L. Osborne
1954	Dr F.V. Mercer	2000	Dr John Barkas
1955	Dr F.V. Mercer	2001	Dr John Barkas
1956	Mr S.J. Copland	2002	Dr Ian Percival
1957	Dr Lilian Fraser	2003	Dr Ian Percival
1958	Dr S. Smith White	2004	Dr M.L. Augee
1959	Dr. T.G. Vallance	2005	Dr M.L. Augee
1960	Dr I.V. Newman	2006	Dr David Murray
1961	Prof J.M. Vincent.	2007	Dr David Murray
1962	Prof B.J.F. Ralph	2008	Ms Michelle Cotton
1963	Mr G.P. Whitley	2009	Ms Michelle Cotton
1964	Miss Elizabeth Pope	2010	Prof David Keith
1965	Dr D.T. Anderson	2011	Prof David Keith
1966	Dr R.C. Carolin	2012	Dr Michael Gray
1967	Mr L.A.S. Johnson	2013	Dr Michael Gray
1968	Prof T.G. Vallance	2014	Prof Robert King
1069	Prof F.V. Mercer	2015	Prof Robert King
1970	Dr N.G. Stephenson		

Proc. Linn. Soc. N.S.W., 137, 2015

69

Appendix 2. Linnean Macleay Fellows since 1925

1924-1926	Murray, Patrick Desmond F.	Zoology
1924-1927	Williams, May Marston	Botany
1925	Osborne, George Davenport	Geology
1925-1927	Mackerras, Ian Murray	Zoology
1927-1932	Brown, Ida	Geology
1927-1929	Weekes, Hazel Claire	Zoology
1930-1934	Craft, Frank Alfred	Geology
1931-1936	Fraser, Lilian	Botany
1932-1934	Weekes, Hazel Claire	Zoology
1933-1936	Newman, Ivor Vickery	Botany
1934	Burges, Norman Alan	Botany
1935-1936	Robertson, Rutherford Ness	Botany
1936-1939	Pope, Elizabeth Carington	Zoology
1937-1938	Voisey, Alan Heywood	Geology
1937-1938	Consett Davis, Harrold Fosbery	Zoology
1937-1941	Pidgeon, Ilma Mary	Botany
1939-1940	May, Valerie Margaret B.	Botany
1939-1940	Cumpston, Dora Margaret	Zoology
1940-1944	Dulhunty, John Allan	Geology
1941-1942	Griffiths, Mervyn Edward	Physiology
1941-1945	Joplin, Germaine Anne	Geology
1942-1946	Hackney, Frances Marie Veda	Plant physiology
1943-1945	Crockford, Joan Marion	Palaeontology
1946-1948	Lascelles, June	Biochemistry
1948-1950	Morris, Muriel Catherine	Zoology
1948	Tindale, Mary Douglas	Botany
1949-1953	Hindmarsh, Mary	Botany
1949-1950	Millerd, Adele	Biochemistry
1949	Bakmain, Judith	Biochemistry
1951	Stevens, N. C.	Geology
1951-1953	Valance, T. G.	Geology
1954-1958	Hannon, Nola	Botany
1954	Simons, Ruth	Botany
1955	Macdonald, Mary B.	Botay
1954	McCusker, Alison	Botany
1961-1962	Peacock, W. J.	Botany
1963-1964	Dart, P. J.	Plant physiology
1965-1968	Wright, Anthony J	Geology
1967-1969	Dandie, Alison K	Botany
1970-1971	Howie, Anne	Geology
1971-1972	Moffatt, Lynnette A.	Biology
1974	McLean, R. A.	Geology
1976-1979	Anderson, Jennifer M.	Entomology
1979-1980	Porter, Barbara D.	Zoology
1984-1986	Johnstone, Ron W.	Zoology
1987-1990	Hush, Julia	Botany
1991-1993	Krauss, Siegfried L.	Botany
2005-2007	Wright, Anthony J.	Palaeontology
2015	Mackay, K. David	Plant ecology

An Allozyme Electrophoretic Study of Populations of Spiders of the Genus *Corasoides* (Araneae: Stiphidiidae) from Australia and Papua New Guinea

MARGARET HUMPHREY

Lot 6 Victor Place, Kuranda, Qld 4881, Australia (margaret.humphrey@yahoo.com.au)

Published on 15 December 2015 at http://escholarship.library.usyd.edu.au/journals/index.php/LIN

Humphrey, M. (2015). An allozyme electrophoretic study of populations of spiders of the Genus *Corasoides* (Araneae: Stiphidiidae) from Australia and Papua New Guinea. *Proceedings of the Linnean Society of New South Wales* **137**, 71-83.

Allozyme electrophoresis was used to delineate the boundaries of the spider genus *Corasoides*, clarify the identity of *C. australis* Butler, 1929, and identify putative new species within the genus. Fixed gene differences, together with similarity and distance trees, showed that *C. australis* was widespread across much of southern Australia while eight new species were differentiated that had comparatively narrow distributions in Australia and Papua New Guinea. Wagner trees were used to show phylogenetic relationships between these species.

Manuscript received 23 February 2015, accepted for publication 23 September 2015.

KEYWORDS: Allozyme, *Corasoides*, electrophoresis

INTRODUCTION

The genus *Corasoides* has only one described species, *C. australis,* Butler, 1929, commonly known as the platform spider. *Corasoides australis* is a medium sized spider which digs a burrow from which it constructs a non-sticky, horizontal sheet web with a tangled maze of threads above. The spider runs on the upper surface of the sheet web (Main 1976). The genus appeared to be widespread and the presence of more than one species of *Corasoides* had been suspected for some time in Queensland (R. Raven, pers. comm.), in the south west of Western Australia (B.Y. Main, pers. comm.) and in Papua New Guinea (Main 1982). Allozyme electrophoresis is used here to clarify the genus and species since it is particularly suitable for systemic studies at the species and intra species levels (Avise 1975; Richardson *et al.* 1986; Quicke 1993), and has been used to delineate spider species by several previous workers (Pennington 1979; Lubin and Crozier 1985; Colgan and Gray 1992).

MATERIALS AND METHODS

Live spiders were collected in the field from populations across Australia and Papua New Guinea (Table 1) and kept in captivity until needed.

Locations consisted of single sites when specimens from those sites were of sufficient number and/or the site was geographically isolated from other sites and/or were distinctly different morphologically or behaviourally.

Populations 1, 2, 3, 4, 5, 6 and 25 were from rainforest habitats. The habitats of the remainder ranged from sclerophyll forest to arid scrubland. Populations 2 and 3 were sympatric but have distinctly different morphology (author's observations).

Electrophoretic methods generally followed those of Richardson, Baverstock and Adams (1986). Mostly muscle tissue from live specimens anaesthetised with carbon dioxide was used and the supernatants obtained were stored at $-80°$ C. Cellulose acetate plates were used to run eighteen enzymes plus general protein giving a total of 21 loci (Table 2). There was

Table 1. Populations sampled (for distribution of material sampled see Fig. 1)

Popn #	Name	Location
1	Kuper	Kuper Ranges, Papua New Guinea
2	Largetown	Tabubil, Papua New Guinea
3	Smalltown	Tabubil, Papua New Guinea
4	Ambua	Tari, Papua New Guinea
5	Windsor	Windsor Tableland, Queensland
6	Terania*	Nightcap and Border Ranges National Parks, NSW
7	Fraser	Fraser Island, Queensland
8	Blackdown	Blackdown Tablelands, Queensland
9	Gibralter	Gibralter National Park, NSW
10	Hornsby	Hornsby, NSW
11	South Coast*	Sydney, NSW to Victorian border
12	Victoria*	Victoria – east coast to Little Desert
13	South Australia*	South Australia, other than Wilpena and Nullarbor
14	Wilpena	Wilpena Pound, South Australia
15	Nullarbor*	Yalata, South Australia to Eucla, Western Australia
16	Kalgoolie	Kalgoolie and Coolgardie areas, Western Australia
17	Stokes	Stokes Inlet and National Park, Western Australia
18	Stirling	Stirling Ranges, Western Australia
19	Yallingup	Yallingup, Western Australia
20	Nannup	Nannup, Western Australia
21	Glenforrest	Glennforrest National Park, Western Australia
22	Cervantes	Cervantes, Western Australia
23	Greenough	Greenough, Western Australia
24	Peron	Peron National Park and Shark Bay, Western Australia
25	Clyde	Clyde Mountain near Monga, NSW

*Pooled sites. Sites were pooled into locations of greater geographical size when specimens were scarce and they did not appear to differ morphologically or behaviourally and/or specimens were widely scattered and not discontinuous.

no variation detected in results between male/female or juvenile/adult.

All locations were tested for Hardy-Weinberg equilibrium for each locus to confirm the absence of multiple species within locations, particularly in locations consisting of pooled sites.

Data were analysed using the computer program "BIOSYS" version 1.7 (Swofford and Selander 1981). Phenograms (trees based on similarity between populations) were derived using the coeficients Nei's (1972) genetic similarity, Nei's

(1972) genetic distance, and Rogers' (1972) genetic similarity. Although overall similarity may be a reflection of phylogenetic distance (Colless 1970), phenetics does not take into account convergence or parallelism so phylogenetic relationships were assessed using Wagner trees. Trees were either rooted at the midpoint of the longest path or by use of outgroup taxa. Since the family affiliation of *Corasoides* is uncertain, four outgroups were selected. The use of *Badumna insignis* Koch, 1872 (Desidae) and *Stiphidion facetum* Simon, 1902 (Stiphidiidae) acknowledge family affiliations put forward by Lethinen (1967) and Forster and Wilton (1973). The two pisaurids, *Inola subtilis* Davies, 1982 and *I. daviesae* Tio and Humphrey, 2010 were also included as outgroup taxa as they share many similarites with *Corasoides*, particularly in behaviour and web structure.

RESULTS AND DISCUSSION

Phengrams derived using Nei's genetic similarity, Nei's genetic distance and Rogers' similarity are given in Figs 2-4. Wagner distance trees are given in Figs 5, 6.

Over 98% of the 525 permutation pairs in the ingroup agree with Hardy-Weinberg equalibrium. None were significant using exact probability and of the few that deviate from Hardy-Weinberg equilibrium, none were from locations where sites were pooled. This confirms the absence of multiple species within the sampling locations.

All three phenograms recognise three major clusters: the Papua New Guinea populations (Kuper, Largetown, Smalltown and Ambua), the Australian rainforest populations (Terania, Windsor and Clyde), and Australian non-rainforest populations (Fraser, Peron, Blackdown, Hornsby, South Coast, Victoria, South Australia, Gibralter, Nullarbor, Wilpena, Kalgoorlie, Greenough, Stokes, Stirling, Yallingup, Cervantes, Nannup and Glen Forrest). Nei's distance and Rogers' similarity grouped the Papua New Guinea

72

Proc. Linn. Soc. N.S.W., 137, 2015

a   n   d

Fig. 1. Map of sampling sites.

Australian rainforest populations together and Nei's genetic similarity grouped all the Australian populations together. Within the Australian rainforest populations Nei's genetic distance placed the Terania and Windsor populations closer genetically to each other than to the Clyde population, while Nei's similarity and Rogers' similarity placed the Windsor and Clyde populations closer together. All phenograms were in agreement with the internal arrangement of the grouped Papua New Guinea populations and the grouped south-western Western Australian populations and also with the separation of these south-western Western Australian populations from the rest of the

Australian dry habitat populations.

Delineation of species boundaries

Within the Australian non-rainforest populations, all phenograms recognised the division between the populations from south-western Western Australia (Stokes, Stirling, Yallingup, Cervantes, Nannup and Glen Forrest) and the rest of the sampled Australian non-rainforest populations previously tentatively regarded as *C. australis* (Fraser, Peron, Blackdown, Hornsby, South Coast, Victoria, South Australia, Gibralter, Nullarbor, Wilpena, Kalgoorlie and Greenough) and agreed with each other in regard to the internal arrangement of these populations except in a few minor areas.

Table 2. Enzymes used in this study.

No.	Enzyme	Abbreviation	Loci
1	fumerate hydratase	FUM	1
2	glucosephosphate isomerase	GPI	1
3	triosephosphate isomerase	TPI	1
4	alkaline phoshatase	AP (ALK*)	1
5	malic enzyme	ME (MEN*)	1
6, 7	malate dehydrogenase	MDH	2
8	mannosephosphate isomerase	MPI	1
9	glyceraldehyde-3-phosphate dehydrogenase	GA-3-PDH (3GP*)	1
10	glucose-6-phoshate dehydrogenase	G-6-PDH (G6P*)	1
11	6-phosphogluconate dehydrogenase	6-PGDH (6PG*)	1
12	glycerol-3-phoshate dehydrogenase	GPD	1
13	isocitrate dehydrogenase	IDH	1
14	esterases	EST	1
15	phosphoglucomutase	PGM	1
16,17	adenylate kinase**	AK (AKI*)	2
18	fructose-1,6-diphosphatase	FDP	1
19	hexokinase	HK (HKI*)	1
20, 21	general proteins	GP (GPR*)	2

* These abbreviations appear in BIOSYS data where a three letter code is needed.
** Adenylate kinase and creatine kinase gave identical multiple bands despite inhibitor used in the latter gels.

Since the type locality of *C. australis* is included in the population of Victoria, I regard the populations of Fraser, Peron, Blackdown, Hornsby, South Coast, Victoria, South Australia, Gibralter, Nullarbor, Wilpena, Kalgoorlie and Greenough as belonging to *C. australis*. These populations were found to have Nei genetic similarities between them ranging from 0.84 -1.00. These figures are in agreement with Avise's (1975) figures (approximately 0.70-1.00 for conspecifics). Similarly, the populations of south-western Western Australia (Stokes, Stirling, Yallingup, Cervantes, Glenforrest and Nannup) have Nei genetic similarities of 0.87 - 0.99 between them so these populations should be considered conspecific. The Nei's genetic similaries between the populations of *C. australis* and those of south-western Western Australia was 0.69 -0.82. (mean 0.75). Although these figures could be said to indicate a genetic similarity compatible with conspecifics, in all cases they are lower than the interpopulation similarities within either group. In addition, the two groups are quite distinct morphologically and biologically (author's observations). Thus, I consider the above pooled south-western Western Australian populations (hereafter referred to as SWWA) to be a sister species to *C. australis*.

The seven remaining populations (Kuper, Largetown, Smalltown, Ambua, Windsor, Terania, Clyde) had 21 permutation pairs between them and had Nei genetic similarity estimates of 0.42-0.85. Sixteen of these similarity estimates indicate separate species status but five are within Avise's (1975) estimates for conspecific species (0.70-1.00) namely Ambua/Smalltown 0.77, Terania/Windsor 0.85, Terania/Clyde 0.83 and Clyde/Windsor 0.83. Kupper/Largetown is borderline. Smalltown/Ambua is a terminal pair on all trees so its borderline conspecific similarity estimate is understandable. The remaining three pairs with high similarity estimates would ordinarily indicate that Terania, Windsor and Clyde are conspecific. However, all three are eastern Australian rainforest inhabitants and although being morphologically distinct in rapidly evolving sexual characters, probably reflect the conservative retention of biochemical attributes in species in similar habitats which have mostly remained unchanged from their ancestral habitat. I thus regard each of the seven populations as having separate species status and they will be referred to here using their population name as a code for their respective species.

Nei's genetic distance measurements were 0-0.17 between conspecific populations (in agreement

74

Proc. Linn. Soc. N.S.W., 137, 2015

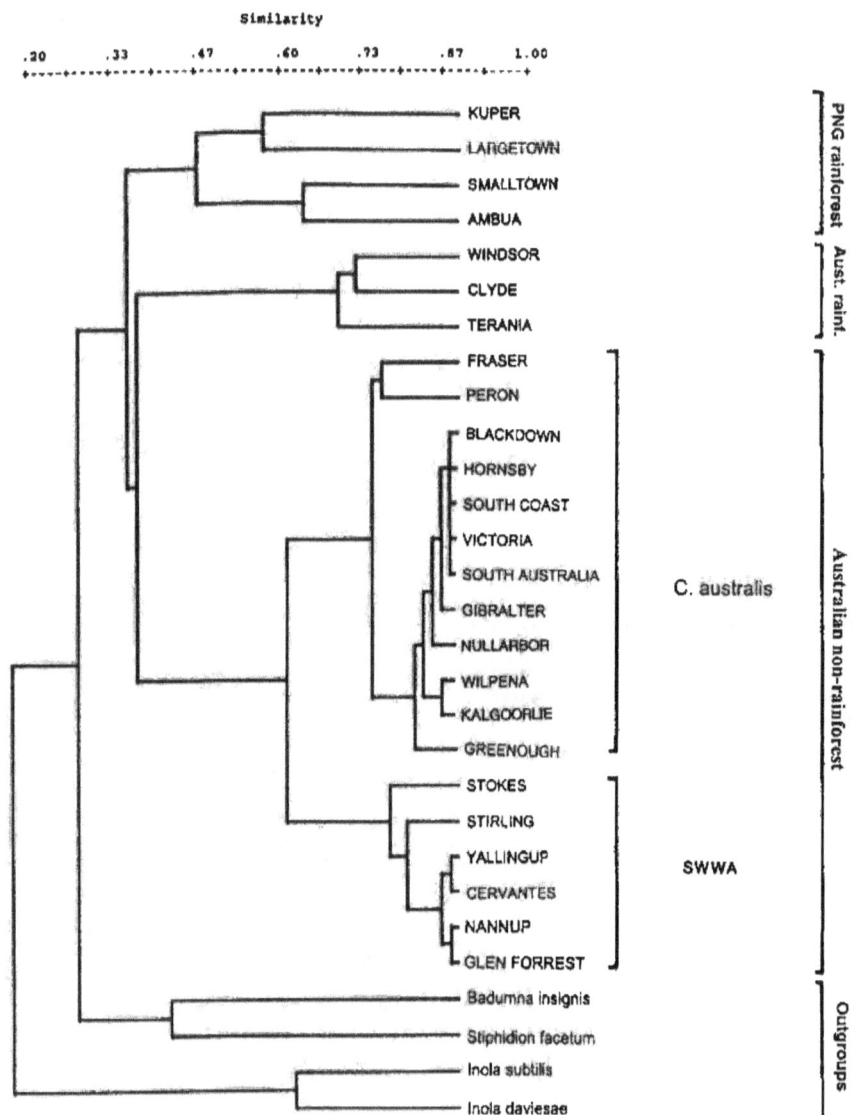

Fig. 2. Phenogram derived using Nei's genetic similarity coefficient of all populations of *Corasoides* sampled and using *Badumna insignis*, *Stiphidion facetum* and *Inola daviesae* as outgroups.

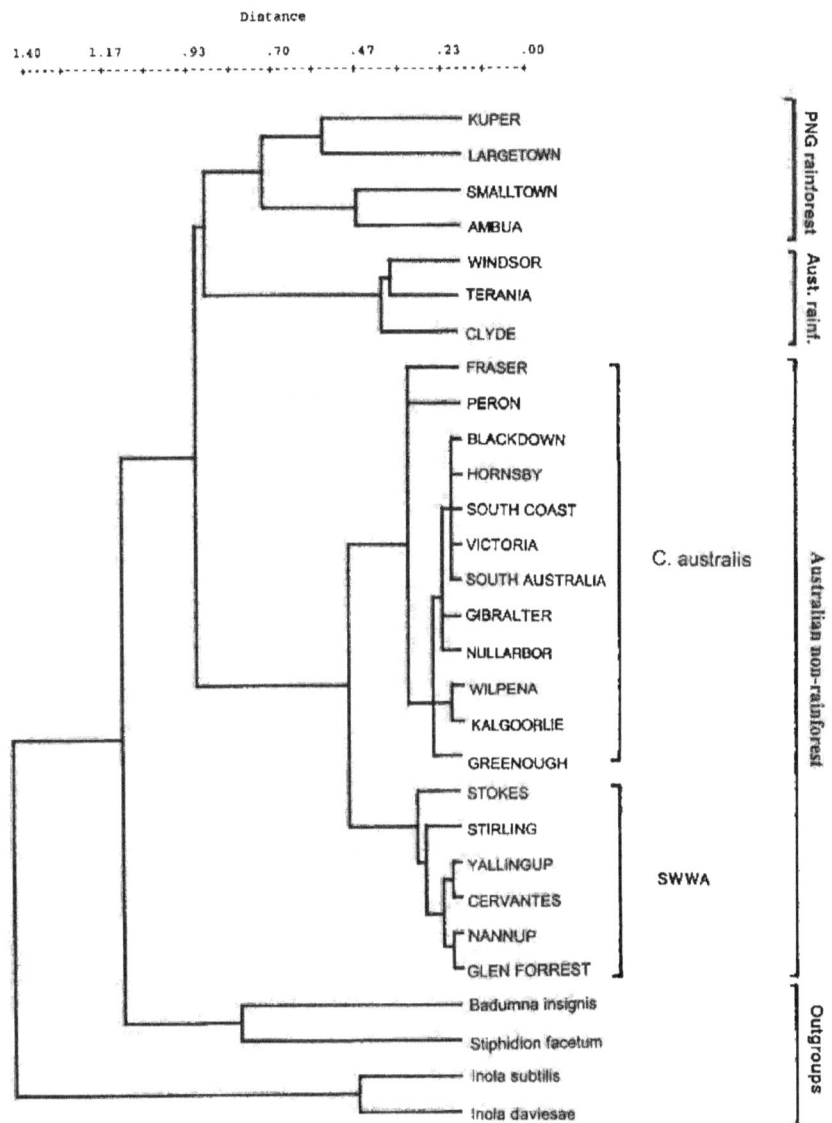

Fig. 3. Phenogram derived using Nei's genetic distance coefficient of all populations of *Corasoides* sampled and using *Badumna insignis*, *Stiphidion facetum*, *Inola subtilis* and *Inola daviesae* as outgroups.

76

Proc. Linn. Soc. N.S.W., 137, 2015

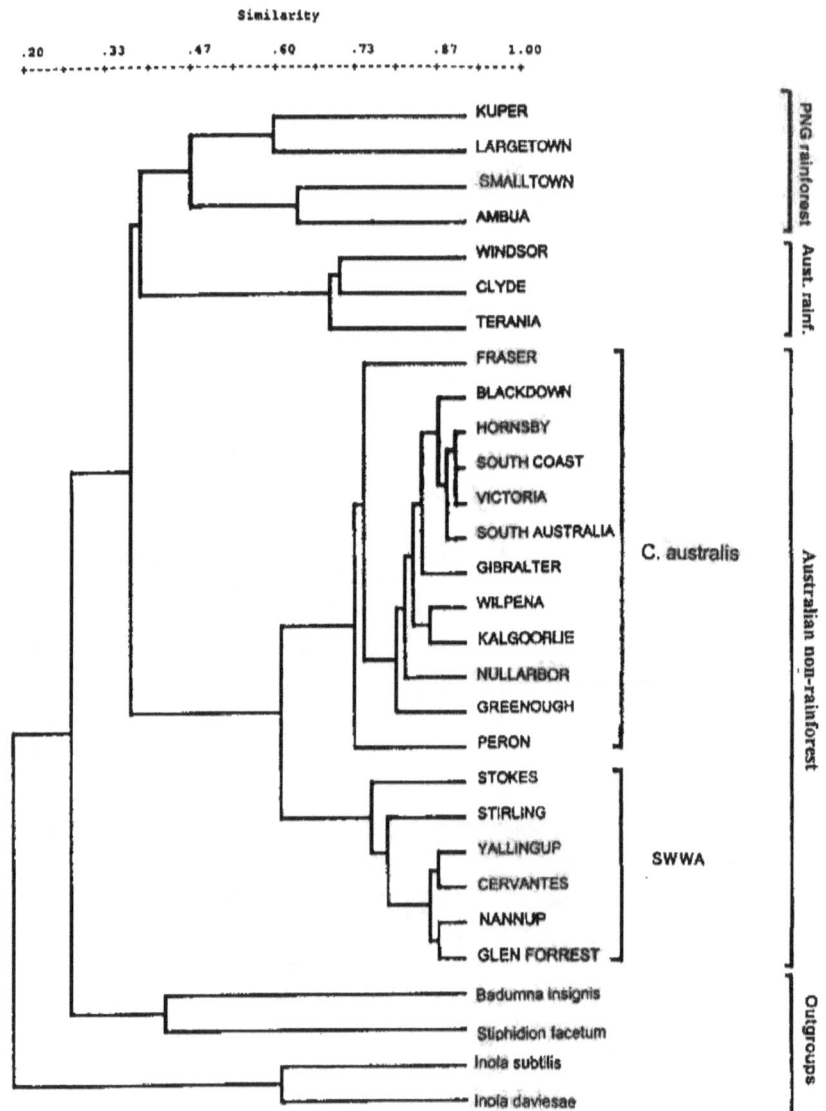

Fig. 4. Phenogram derived using Rogers' similarity coefficient of all populations of *Corasoides* sampled and using *Badumna insignis*, *Stiphidion facetum*, *Inola subtilis* and *Inola daviesae* as outgroups.

Proc. Linn. Soc. N.S.W., 137, 2015

77

Table 3. Fixed differences between species

	Kupper	Large town	Small town	Ambua	Windsor	Terania	Clyde	SWW*A*
Kupper								
Largetown	(6)							
Smalltown	5	(5)						
Ambua	8	(3)	3					
Windsor	9	(10)	9	10				
Terania	7	(6)	8	10	2			
Clyde	9	(9)	8	9	3	3		
SWW*A*	8	(8)	4	6	7	4	3	
australis	5	(7)	4	7	7	5	3	1

Table 4. Percentages of fixed differences between species. Numerals in parentheses are disregarded due to small sample size.

	Kupper	Large town	Small town	Ambua	Windsor	Terania	Clyde	SWWA
Kupper								
Largetown	(29%)							
Smalltown	24%	(24%)						
Ambua	38%	(14%)	14%					
Windsor	43%	(49%)	43%	49%				
Terania	33%	(29%)	38%	49%	10%			
Clyde	43%	(43%)	38%	43%	14%	14%		
SWWA	38%	(23%)	19%	29%	33%	19%	14%	
australis	24%	(33%)	19%	33%	33%	24%	14%	5%

with the figures of Bruce and Ayala (1979) (approximately 0-0.25). Results between sister species within the ingroup were 0.17-0.34, slightly lower than those of Bruce and Ayala (1979) (0.20-0.65). Since Nei's genetic similarity and distance are associated these results are expected and the same explanations follow.

Interspecific fixed genetic differences

The number of fixed differences for all permutations between putative species is given in Table 3 with the percentage of fixed differences over 21 loci in Table 4. Results in parentheses must be considered with caution due to small sample size.

The highest number of fixed differences was ten. The highest numbers of fixed differences (scores of 8, 9 and 10) occurred, with but one exception, were between pairs consisting of an Australian and a Papua New Guinean species. The lowest numbers of fixed differences (scores of 1, 2 and 3), but for two

exceptions, occurred between pairs of Australian species.

Baverstock, Watts and Cole (1977) indicate that 14% of loci with fixed differences are sufficient for consideration as separate species. Only two of these species permutations show fewer than 14% fixed differences.

However, caution is required when drawing conclusions from fixed differences obtained in this study because of the unequal number of sites sampled per species. Although seven populations were sampled for SWWA and eleven for *C. australis*, all other species were represented by only one or two locations. Polymorphism can be expected to rise with an increase in the number of isolated populations sampled and increased polymorphism leads, up to a point, to a lower number of fixed differences recorded. This would explain the low number of fixed differences between pooled populations of *C. australis* and SWWA. If alleles are not pooled

78

for SWWA and *C. australis* and single populations from them compared for fixed differences with other species, then the number of fixed differences increases dramatically so that the 14% level is reached for most permutations.

Intraspecific fixed genetic differences
(i) Within *C. australis*

There are two fixed differences involving Fraser, one (with MPI-1) separating it from all other populations except Blackdown and Peron, and another (with G6P-1) separating it from all other populations except Kalgoorlie, Greenough and Peron. There is one fixed difference for Peron (EST-1) separating it from all other populations except Fraser and Greenough but this must be considered with caution because of small sample size.

Similarly, a fixed difference observed in Wilpena (its single allele in MEN-1 shared only by Kalgoorlie and Blackdown) cannot be substantiated because of the small sample size of two. However, it should be noted that the Wilpena population appeared to be a small, sole, isolated population on the rim of the pound, a rather barren and hostile environment but the only one in the area which apparently had not been affected by cattle grazing. Morphologically the specimens were much smaller than most other members of the species but this could have been environmental, due to the harsh conditions. The habitat and size of specimens was similar for specimens from Kalgoorlie. Blackdown is not as harsh an environment and the area was protected from grazing within a State Forest and the Blackdown specimens were larger, intermediate in size to specimens from sclerophyll forest on the eastern Australian coast. Otherwise all three populations appear morphologically and behaviourally similar to other populations of *C. australis* (author's observations).

The two fixed differences involving Fraser are interesting in that they link Fraser with Greenough and Peron (and to a lesser extent, Kalgoorlie and Blackdown) indicating an apparent east-west link seen also for Peron EST-1.

Fixed differences within *C. australis* could be brought about by their clumped and extensive distributions over thousands of kilometres. This may lead to many locally inbred populations with the potential to become monomorphic for several different alleles. Summing the allelles present for *C. australis* it can be seen that this species is polymorphic for most enzymes, while other species are usually monomorphic. This greater detection of polymorphism is caused also by the imbalance in the sampling numbers; those monomorphic species usually having small sampling numbers so that there is a lower probability of detecting less common localised alleles.

(ii) Within SWWA

There were two fixed differences; one (with MEN-1) between the individuals of the population from Stirling Ranges and all other sampled populations of SWAW and the other (with GPR-2) between the samples from Stokes River National Park and all other sampled populations of SWWA.

The single fixed difference separating the Stirling Ranges population from other populations of SWWA may be just a regional adaptation. The Stirling Ranges, for instance, have a winter far colder than any other region in the distribution of SWWA. It remains to be seen whether populations from further down the slopes or from areas surrounding the Stirling Ranges carry this allozyme in the heterozygous state. (It is interesting that the only other specimens which carry the allozyme allele responsible for this fixed difference are *C. australis* from the Gibralter samples, the only other area sampled with a comparably cold winter). The population from Stokes River National Park is also geographically distant (300km) from the next closest sampled population. Unsampled populations within in this area could well be found to be polymorphic for the locus involved in the fixed difference with alleles common to the rest of the species.

(iii) Within Terania

One fixed difference was detected after calculation of Hardy-Weinberg heterozygote probabilities. In this study there are 88 population pair permutations for polymorphic loci. Of these pairs, twelve had a significant deficit of heterozygotes when calculated using chi-squared probabilities. Of these 12 pairs, five had fewer than five specimens in the sample and of the remainder all but one (Terania/GPD-1) were calculated as insignificant under exact probability. In this last case the sample was pooled, consisting of four specimens from Nightcap National Park and two specimens from Border Ranges National Park. These two locations are over 50 km apart and separated by the Tweed Valley. Since each of the sample sites was monomorphic for a different allele, there would be no deficiency of heterozygotes if the samples had not been pooled. However, there exists instead a single fixed difference between the two sampling sites. Overall, the results from fixed differences between sampled populations within *C. australis* is acceptable for conspecificity.

Delineation of genus

Similarity and distance measurements

There are 300 population pair permutations of *Corasoides* in this study. Of these, all but five (i.e. 2%), have a Nei genetic similarity estimate of at least 0.40. The lowest of these exceptions (0.365) is between Windsor and Wilpena (a small isolated population from which only two individuals were sampled). The other exceptions are between Windsor and four of the eastern Australian populations of *C. australis* (0.384, 0.388, 0.388 and 0.390) and between Largetowns and Kalgoorlie (0.393, another small population of *C. australis* with a sample number of two). With the exception of the above mentioned pairs, the estimates of Nei's gentic similarity are in agreement with the figures cited by Avise (1975) for congeneric species (0.40-0.70).

Distance measurements of populations within the ingroup of this study are often greater than those cited by Bruce and Ayala (1979) (0.20-0.65 for congeneric species). However, with only one exception (between Largetown and Windsor, 0.741), all distance measurements greater than 0.65 involve those populations belonging to the most highly derived species on the twigs of the trees. The figures for both genetic similarity and genetic distance between the two outgroup species of *Inola* are similar to those between species of *Corasoides*.

Therefore, and with the support of morphological data (author's observations), all populations within the ingroup can be regarded as belonging to the one genus, i.e. *Corasoides*.

Phylogenetic analysis – Wagner trees

Both Wagner trees (Farris 1970) from BIOSYSIS (Figs 5, 6) support species status for the nine groups as indicated by the phenetic analysis.

Both Wagner trees, rooted either by midpoint of the longest branch or, by outgroups, also recognised monophyly of both the Papua New Guinea branch and the Australian branch and the further division of the Australian species into those from rainforest habitats and those from non-rainforest habitats. Within the Australian rainforest branch Clyde was the sister group to the other species. There were only minor differences of internal arrangement between the phenograms and the Wagner trees with respect to the Australian non-rainforest populations.

The phenetic trees either grouped together all the rainforest species, as opposed to the non-rainforest species, or failed to resolve them. This could be a reflection of a lack of sensitivity in phenetic methods to convergence and parallelism. Assuming that allozymes are not selectively neutral (Cook 1971, Lewontin 1974, McDonald 1983), natural selection of enzyme variation could be expected to be dependent upon components of habitat such as extremes and variation of temperature. Consequently, non cladistical methods would be expected to group together organisms with like adaptations to the same environment rather than considering the possibility of convergence and parallelism.

Summary of systematic implications

While the pheneticly derived trees are in conflict over the placement of the Australian rainforest group, both the phylogenetic Wagner trees placed it as the sister group to the non-rainforest group, thus dividing *Corasoides* into two monophyletic groups, the Australian species and the Papua New Guinea species. However, the relevant branch distances in all trees are so short that little confidence can be placed in the position of this Australian rainforest branch from the results of these analyses. Nonetheless, all trees supported the existence of three major groups within *Corasoides*; the Papua New Guinea species, the Australian rainforest species and the Australian non-rainforest species.

Phenetic analyses, analysis of fixed differences, Hardy Weinberg equilibria analyses and phylogenetic analyses by Wagner trees of the electrophoretic data supported the recognition of

(1) all members of the ingroup as belonging to the genus *Corasoides*

(2) *C. australis* as a widespread species with a distribution across coastal Australia below 25 degrees South and inland up to 450 kilometres.

(3) eight new species of *Corasoides*. Four of these (represented by the code names Kuper, Largetown, Smalltown and Ambua) are rainforest inhabitants from Papua New Guinea. The other four are from Australia. One, represented here by SWWA, inhabits open woodland and scrub. The other three, represented here by the populations Windsor, Terania and Clyde, inhabit refugial rainforest habitat in eastern Australia.

These conclusions will be developed further in studies of the genus in preparation.

ACKNOWLEDGMENTS

The following people and institutions assisted with loans of material: Museum of Western Australia (M. Harvey), Queensland Museum (R. Raven), Museum of Victoria (C. McPhee), South Australian Museum (D. Hirst), Museum and Art Gallery, Tasmania (E. Turner and A. Green), Australian Museum, (M. Gray and G. Milledge) and Queen Victoria Museum and Art Gallery, Tasmania.

80

Proc. Linn. Soc. N.S.W., 137, 2015

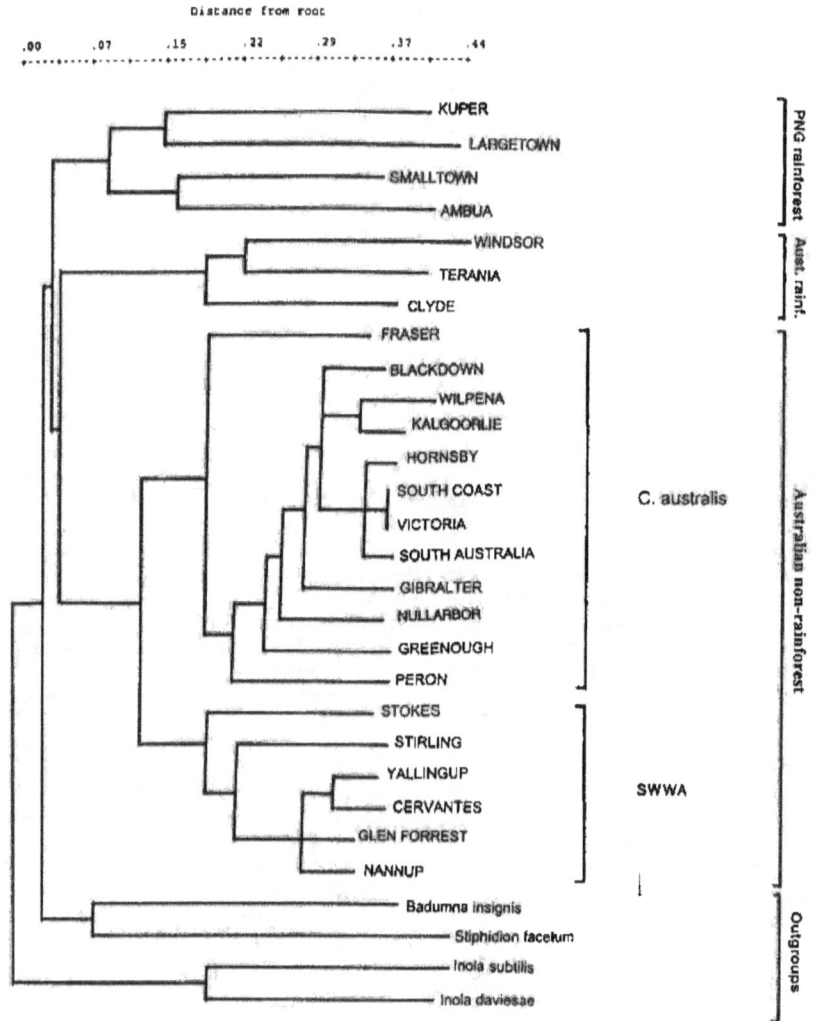

Fig. 5. Wagner tree of all populations of *Corasoides* sampled, *Badumna insignis*, *Stiphidion facetum*, *Inola subtilis* and *Inola daviesae* and rooted at the midpoint of the longest branch.

Proc. Linn. Soc. N.S.W., 137, 2015

81

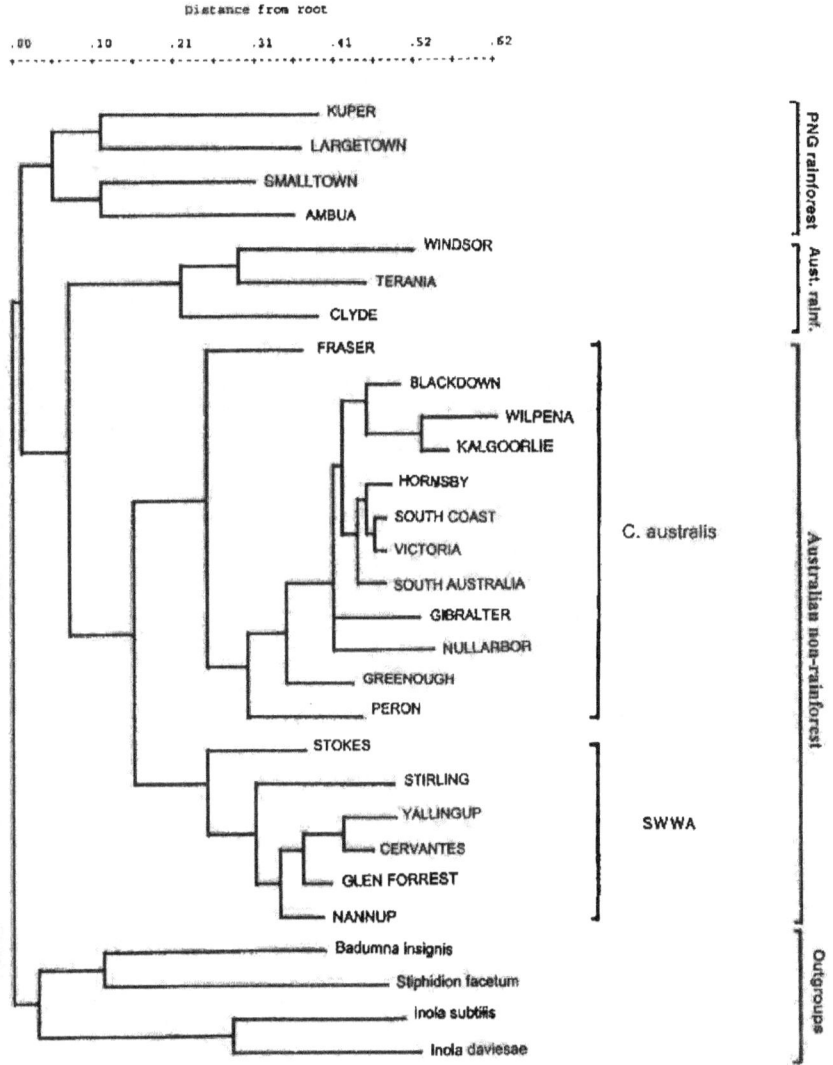

Fig. 6. Wagner tree of all populations of *Corasoides* sampled and rooted by outgroup using *Badumna insignis, Stiphidion facetum, Inola subtilis* and *Inola daviesae*.

82

Proc. Linn. Soc. N.S.W., 137, 2015

The following assisted in field work and/or provided valuable specimens: Warrick Angus, Sally Cowan, Tinal Goh, John Humphrey, Fiona MacKillop, Max Moulds, Helen Smith, John Olive and Judy Thompson. The following provided valuable assistance in Papua New Guinea; OK Tedi Mining Ltd. (especially Marshal Lee) for logistical support including access to remote areas, the Wau Ecology Institute, Wau, and Pru and Murray MacDonald of Ambua Lodge, via Tari.

For collecting permits, I thank National Parks and Wildlife Services and Forestry Departments of Queensland, New South Wales, Victoria, South Australia and CALM, Western Australia.

Financial assistance is gratefully acknowledged from the Faculty of Agriculture, University of Sydney for a Norman Scott Noble Scholarship, the Linnean Society of NSW for a Joyce Vickery Research Award and the Australian Entomological Society for a research award.

Laboratory and other facilities were provided by the Faculty of Agriculture, University of Sydney (Harley Rose) and the Evolutionary Biology Unit of the Australian Museum (Don Colgan).

REFERENCES

Avise, J.C. (1975). Systematic value of electrophoretic data. *Systematic Biology* 23: 465-481.

Baverstock, P.R., Watts, C.H.S. and Cole, S.R. (1977). Electrophoretic comparisons between the allopatric populations of five Australian Pseudomyine rodents (Muridae). *Australian Journal of Biological Sciences* 30(5): 471-485.

Bruce, E.J. and Ayala, F.J. (1979). Phylogenetic relationships between man and the apes: electrophoretic evidence. *Evolution* 33: 1040-1056.

Butler, L.S.G. (1929). Studies in Victorian spiders. *Proceedings of the Royal Society of Victoria* 42: 42-52.

Colgan D.J. and Gray, M.R. (1992). The genetic structure of the *Badumna candida* group of species (Aranae, Amaurobioidae). *Bulletin of the British Arachnological Society* 9: 86-94.

Colless, D.H. (1995). Relative symmetry of cladograms and phenograms: an experimental study. *Systematic Biology* 44: 102-108.

Cook, L.M. (1971). Coefficients of Natural Selection. 207 pp. (Hutchinson: London).

Davies, V.T. (1982). *Inola* nov. gen., a web-building pisaurid (Araneae: Pisauridae) from northern Australia with descriptions of three species. *Memoirs of the Queensland Museum* 20(3): 479-487.

Farris, J.S. (1970). Methods for computing Wagner trees. *Systematic Biology* 18: 374-385.

Forster, R.R. and Wilton. C.L. (1973). The spiders of New Zealand Part IV. 309 pp. *Otago Museum Bulletin* 4: 1-123.

Koch, L. (1872). Die Arachniden Australiens, nach der Natur beschrieben und abgebildet. Nurnberg: Bauer and Raspe. Vol. 1 Pp. 105-338. (330).

Lehtinen, P.T. (1967). Classification of the cribellate spiders and some allied families, with notes on the evolution of the suborder Araneomorpha. *Annales Zoologici Fennici* 4:199-468.

Lewontin, R..C. (1974). The genetic basis of evolutionary change. 346 pp. (Columbia University Press).

Lubin, Y.D. and Crozier, R.H. (1985). Electrophoretic evidence for population differentiation in a social spider Achaearanea wau (Theriiidae). *Insectes Sociaux* 32: 297-304.

Main, B.Y. (1976). Spiders. 296pp. (Collins: Sydney. Reprinted 1984).

Main, B.Y. (1982). Some geographic considerations of families of spiders occurring in New Guinea. Pp. 583-602. In Gressit, J.L. (Ed.), Monographiae Biologicae 42(4). W.Junk: The Hague. 983 pp.

McDonald, J.F. (1983). The molecular basis of adaptation: a critical review of relevant ideas and observations. *Annual Review of Ecological Systematics* 14: 77-102.

Nei, M. (1972). Genetic distance between populations. *The American Naturalist* 106: 283-292.

Pennington, B.J. (1972). Enzyme genetics in taxonomy: diagnostic enzyme loci in the spider genus *Meta*. *Bulletin of the British Arachnological Society* 4: 377-391.

Quicke, D.L.J. (1993). Principles and techniques of contemporary taxonomy. 311 pp. (Chapman and Hall, London and Blackie Academic and Professional: Glasgow).

Richardson, B.J., Baverstock, P.R. and Adams, M. (1986). Allozyme electrophoresis. a handbook for animal systematics and population studies. 410 pp. (Academic Press, Sydney).

Rogers, J.S. (1972). Measures of genetic similarity and genetic distance. In:. Studies in genetics VII, University of Texas publication 7213: 145-153.

Simon, E. (1902). Descriptions de quelque arachides nouveaux de la section de cribellates. *Bulletin de la Societe Entomologique de France* 1902: 240-243.

Swofford, D.L. and Selander, R.B. (1981). BIOSYS-1: a FORTRAN program for the comprehensive analysis of electrophoretic data in population genetics and systematics. *Journal of Heredity* 72: 281-183.

Tio, M. and Humphrey, M. (2010). Description of a new species of *Inola* Davies (Aranae: Pisauridae), the male of *I. subtilis* Davies and notes on their chromosomes. *Proceedings of the Linnean Society of New South Wales* 131: 37-42.

Late Ordovician Conodonts and Brachiopods from near Greenvale in the Broken River Province, North Queensland

YONG YI ZHEN[1], IAN G. PERCIVAL[1] AND PETER D. MOLLOY[2]

[1]Geological Survey of New South Wales, 947-953 Londonderry Road, Londonderry, NSW 2753, Australia (yong-yi.zhen@industry.nsw.gov.au);
[2]Deceased; formerly of School of Earth and Planetary Sciences, Macquarie University, NSW 2109, Australia.

Published on 15 December 2015 at http://escholarship.library.usyd.edu.au/journals/index.php/LIN

Zhen, Yong Yi, Percival, Ian G. and Molloy, Peter D. (2015). Late Ordovician conodonts and brachiopods from near Greenvale in the Broken River Province, north Queensland. *Proceedings of the Linnean Society of New South Wales* 137, 85-133.

Late Ordovician conodonts and brachiopods are described from limestones (previously referred to the Carriers Well Formation) in the Wairuna Formation of the Broken River Province. The conodonts include the new genus and species *Molloydenticulus bicostatus*. *Scabbardella altipes*, *Besselodus fusus* sp. nov. and *Protopanderodus liripipus* dominate the conodont fauna of 24 species, which is typical of the *Protopanderodus* biofacies, with two large, robust species of *Protopanderodus* making up about one-quarter of recovered elements. Associated lingulate brachiopods include species of *Acrosaccus*, *Atansoria*, *Biernatia*, *Conotreta*, *Elliptoglossa*, *Hisingerella*, *Nushbiella*, *Paterula* and *Scaphelasma*, identical with those known from the Malongulli Formation and correlative units of the Macquarie Volcanic Province in central New South Wales. Many of the same conodont species found in allochthonous limestones in the basal Malongulli Formation also occur in the fauna from north Queensland, supporting its assignment to the *Taoqupognathus tumidus–Protopanderodus insculptus* conodont Biozone of late Eastonian age, equivalent to the middle Katian Stage. Subtle palaeoecological differences between the fauna of the deeper water Malongulli Formation limestones and that from the Broken River Province limestones indicate that the latter were likely originally deposited on or near the shelf edge. Recognition of this unstable depositional environment confirms interpretation of these limestones as allochthonous, having been reworked into younger basinal sediments of the Wairuna Formation.

Manuscript received 13 May 2015, accepted for publication 9 December 2015.

KEYWORDS: Biogeography, biostratigraphy, brachiopods, conodonts, Katian, Late Ordovician, North Queensland, palaeoecology

INTRODUCTION

Whereas Late Ordovician conodont and brachiopod faunas from New South Wales are very well known, as the result of more than four decades of detailed systematic studies, those from rocks of equivalent age in Queensland have not had the benefit of such concerted research and hence are relatively poorly documented. The situation in Queensland is compounded by the scarcity of sedimentary rocks of this age, which are limited to the Fork Lagoons beds of the Anakie Inlier in central Queensland (Withnall et al. 1995), and what has previously been referred to in the literature as the Carriers Well Limestone, or more recently, the Carriers Well Formation (Withnall and Lang 1993). The conodont fauna from limestone in the Fork Lagoons beds was monographed by Palmieri (1978), but apart from abstracts listing conodonts from the Carriers Well Limestone (Simpson 1997, 2000) supplemented by illustrations of a few conodont species (Talent et al. 2002, 2003), and descriptions of associated tabulate corals (Dixon and Jell 2012), there has been no detailed study of the Carriers Well fauna. Our contribution will help to remedy that, at least for the conodonts and accompanying microbrachiopods, and in doing so will reveal palaeontological confirmation of the recognition of a strong tectonic and geochemical affinity between the Broken River Province of north Queensland and the Macquarie Volcanic Province of central NSW (Henderson et al. 2011).

REGIONAL GEOLOGIC AND STRATIGRAPHIC SETTING

The Broken River Province is situated approximately 200 km west of Townsville in north Queensland (Fig. 1). It is part of one of several Palaeozoic basins, including the Burdekin River Basin, Clarke River Basin, and Hodgkinson Province (to the north towards Cairns) that together make up the Mossman Orogen (Henderson et al. 2013). These basins occupy the northern Tasmanides of eastern Australia, east of the Gondwana craton and its intracratonic basins; further south into NSW, the Tasmanides includes the New England Orogen and the Lachlan Orogen (Glen 2005, 2013).

Stratigraphy of the Broken River Province is well understood for its Silurian to Carboniferous sequences, largely as a result of detailed mapping by the Geological Survey of Queensland (summarised in Withnall et al. 1993) combined with a tightly constrained biostratigraphic framework based on conodonts that was developed over a decade by John Talent, Ruth Mawson and their students (Talent et al. 2002). The Ordovician sedimentological history of the region is less certain, as it relies on relatively few limestone outcrops to produce age-diagnostic fossils. There is general agreement that much of the Ordovician succession, including clastic and carbonate sedimentary rocks and volcanics, consists of allochthonous blocks. However, whether such blocks have been reworked into younger sediments as a result of erosion and downslope movement (Talent et al. 2002, 2003), or whether they have been incorporated into melanges by accretionary tectonism (Henderson et al. 2011), remains contentious. Increased support for the former scenario has been generated as a result of the present study, but the tectonic model proposed by Henderson et al. (2011), especially its finding of significant geochemical similarity with the volcanic islands forming part of the Macquarie Volcanic Province in NSW, remains relevant to understanding the Late Ordovician development of the Tasmanides.

AGE AND CORRELATION OF THE CONODONT FAUNA

Conodonts recovered from limestones within the Wairuna Formation at the Kaos Gully locality (samples with prefix KCY and KAOS) include 23 identifiable species, including *Aphelognathus* sp., *Belodina confluens* Sweet, 1979, *B.* sp., *Coelocerodontus trigonius* Ethington, 1959, *Besselodus fusus* sp. nov., *Drepanodus arcuatus* Pander, 1856, *Drepanoistodus suberectus* (Branson

and Mehl, 1933), *Molloydenticulus bicostatus* gen. et sp. nov., *Panderodus gracilis* (Branson and Mehl, 1933), *P. nodus* Zhen, Webby and Barnes, 1999, *Panderodus* sp., *Paroistodus?* nowlani Zhen, Webby and Barnes, 1999, *Paroistodus* sp., *Periodon grandis* (Ethington, 1959), *Phragmodus undatus* Branson and Mehl, 1933, *Pseudooneotodus mitratus* (Moskalenko, 1973), *Protopanderodus insculptus* (Branson and Mehl, 1933), *P. liripipus* Kennedy, Barnes and Uyeno, 1979, *Scabbardella altipes* (Henningsmoen, 1948), *Strachanognathus parvus* Rhodes, 1955, *Spinodus spinatus* (Hadding, 1913), *Taoqupognathus tumidus* Trotter and Webby, 1995 and *Yaoxianognathus* sp. (Fig. 2). Although the main limestone body is exposed more or less continuously along Kaos Gully for about 144 m, only 43 samples from the lower part of the section have yielded conodonts (Table 1). The basal part (about 16 m thick) of the limestone succession contains *B. confluens, P. gracilis, Ph. undatus, P. liripipus, S. altipes* and *Yaoxianognathus* sp., and is correlated with the *T. blandus* Biozone (Fig. 2). The remainder of the fauna is interpreted as representing a single zonal assemblage that is referred to herein as the *Taoqupognathus tumidus-Protopanderodus insculptus* Biozone. As *T. tumidus* was only recovered from two samples in the Kaos Gully section (Table 1), this biozone is defined there by the range of *P. insculptus*, which is present from 16.1 m to 59.3 m above the base of the limestone outcrop. In eastern Australia, *P. insculptus* has only been reported as occurring in the *T. tumidus* Biozone in association with *Protopanderodus liripipus* and *T. tumidus*, and is not recorded from the underlying *T. blandus* Biozone.

The fauna from Kaos Gully is identical with that previously documented from allochthonous limestone clasts in the lower part of the Malongulli Formation overlying the Cliefden Caves Limestone Subgroup (Trotter and Webby 1995), which shares 18 species (three-quarters of those occurring in the Wairuna Formation limestones) with the north Queensland fauna. A graptolite assemblage of Ea3 age (the *kirki* Biozone) including *Dicranograptus* cf. *hians kirki, Leptograptus eastonensis, Dicellograptus elegans,* and *Normalograptus tubuliferus,* was reported from the base of the Malongulli Formation, directly underlying the main breccia containing the conodont fauna (Moors 1970; Trotter and Webby 1995, p. 475). Graptolites from the upper part of the Malongulli Formation suggest an early Bolindian age (*uncinatus* Biozone: Percival 1976; Jenkins 1978; Percival et al. 2015). Therefore, age of the conodont fauna from the allochthonous clasts in the lower part of the Malongulli Formation can be constrained by the graptolites occurring immediately below and above as middle Katian (Ea3 and possibly into Ea4, not older than the *kirki* Biozone and not younger than the *gravis* Biozone).

Two spot samples from the two small limestone bodies exposed in Gray Creek near the creek crossing (Gray Creek locality CWZ-1 and Gray Creek bank locality CWZ-2) yielded 29 coniform specimens.

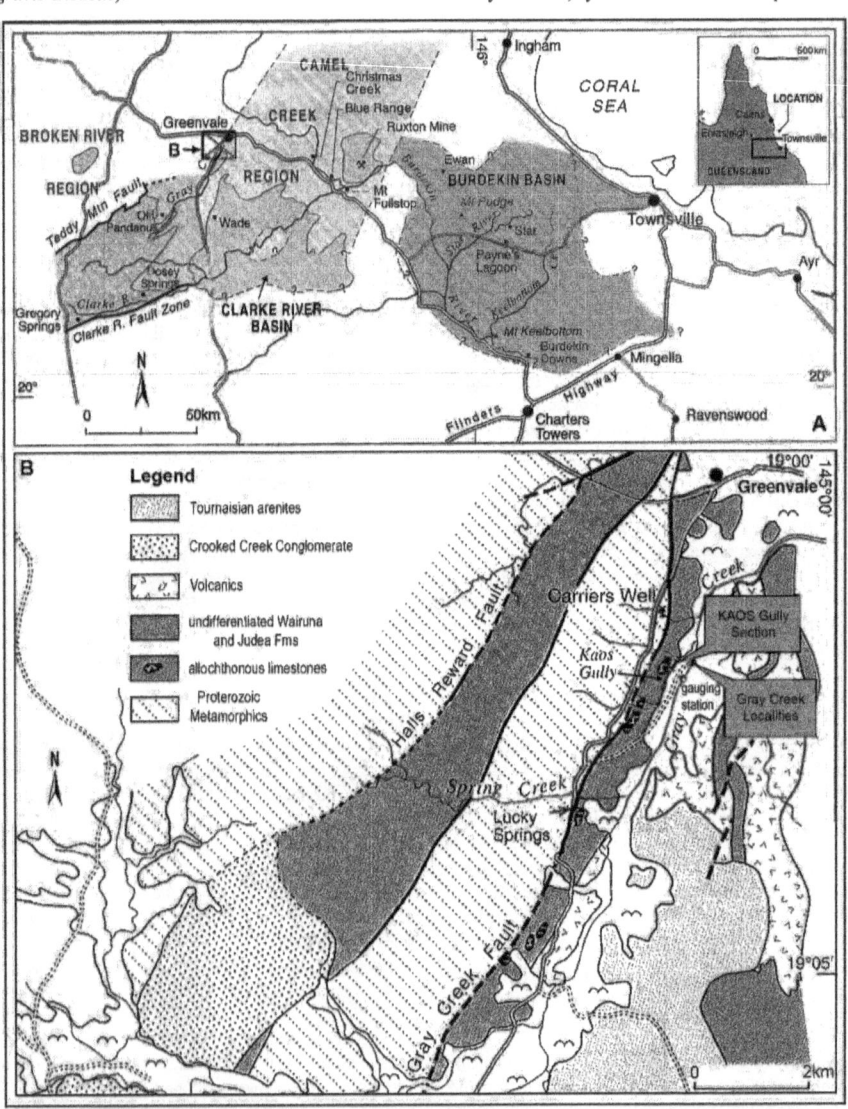

Figure 1. Maps showing the studied area in north Queensland and sample locations. A, Map of Townsville hinterland, north Queensland showing the locations and structural settings of the Gray Creek area, south of Greenvale (modified from Brime et al., 2003); B, Map showing the sample locations of the Kaos Gully section and the two spot samples in Gray Creek near Carriers Well, about 2 km south of Greenvale (modified from Talent et al., 2003).

Table 1. Distribution of conodont species in the samples studied from allochthonous limestones within the Wairuna Formation of north Queensland.

samples	Aphelognathus sp.	Belodina confluens Sweet, 1979	Belodina sp.	Coelocerodontus trigonius Ethington, 1959	Besselodus fusus sp. nov.	Drepanodus arcuatus Pander, 1856	Drepanoistodus suberectus (Branson and Mehl, 1933)	Mollodontichulus biccostatus gen. et sp. nov.	Nordiodus italicus Serpagli, 1967	Parvistriodus? nowlani Zhen, Webby and Barnes, 1999	Parvistriodus sp.	Panderodus gracilis (Branson & Mehl, 1933)	Panderodus nodus Zhen, Webby and Barnes, 1999	Panderodus sp.	Periodon grandis (Ethington, 1959)	Phragmodus undatus Branson and Mehl, 1933	Pseudooneotodus mitratus (Moskalenko, 1973)	Protopanderodus insculptus (Branson & Mehl, 1933)	Protopanderodus liripipus Kennedy, Barnes & Uyeno, 1979	Scabbardella altipes (Henningsmoen, 1948)	Strachanognathus parvus Rhodes, 1955	Spinodus spinatus (Hadding, 1913)	Tasquipognathus tumidus Trotter and Webby, 1995	Tassiangnathus sp.	Total specimens
KAOS-60	1																		1						2
KAOS-59.3																	1	1	1						3
KAOS-59.8				2		1														3					6
KAOS-50.5					2											2		8	18	11	6				47
KAOS-50.4				1		3	3						1					16	25	82					131
KAOS-50.3																		1	3						4
KAOS-50																			1						1
KAOS-49.8																		5	18						23
KAOS-49.6																2		1	4						7
KAOS-48.2		5			1				1	1								25	15	41					89
KAOS-47.8																				3					3
KAOS-47.5																		10	3	5					18
KAOS-47.4																		4		5					9
KAOS-47.2					1										1	1		14	25	10					52
KAOS-46.8																		9	4	3					16
KAOS-46.2																				7					7
KAOS-45.9																				1					1
KAOS-45.6									1									1	5	1		1			9
KAOS-44.8		1	1	1	3	3		6	29									48	2	45					139
KAOS-43.9		9		5	195	3		18	8		1							53	130	442		2			866
KAOS-43.7									1																1
KAOS-43					1																				1
KAOS-42.8					3				1									9	2	8					23
KAOS-42.6					4	2			4	1								10	1	17					39
KAOS-42.2									5									5	1	22		1	1		35
KAOS-41.7																		3		7	5			1	16
KAOS-41.6				4	5	5												43		69	1				127
KAOS-41.4					1				1									2	2	7					13
KAOS-41.3																				1					1
KAOS-39.3				2	1	2												45	4	34					88
KAOS-19.2						3												15	5	29					52
KAOS-19						1			1						1	1				5					9
KAOS-18.2				3											1	2		4	15						25
KAOS-17.5																		1	1	1					3
KAOS-17.2																		1	1	3					5
KAOS-17																		1	1	3					5
KAOS-16.1																			1	2					3
KAOS-14.6					1				1											1					3
KCV-6		3			1				1									4	32	62					103
KCV-5		13		5	181	12		5	41		3	1	8		1	6	1	4	125	130					536
KCV-4b																		5		30					35
KCV-1					5	1			2				1												9
CWZ-2					2														7						9
CWZ-1									2				17	1											20
Total	1	40	1	19	581	19	14	75	249	3	19	3	23	1	4	4	5	91	572	843	20	7	4	1	2594

The Gray Creek samples are dominated by a single species assigned herein to *Nordiodus italicus* Serpagli, 1967, which has not been recorded in any of the samples from the Kaos Gully locality. Based on four other species (*Coelocerodontus trigonius*, *Besselodus fusus* sp. nov., *Periodon grandis?*, and *Scabbardella altipes*) that also occur in the Kaos Gully samples, these two small limestone bodies are regarded as contemporaneous with that at Kaos Gully. Talent et al. (2003) also reported the occurrence of *Amorphognathus ordovicicus* at the Gray Creek locality, which indicates a similar or slightly younger age.

Zhen et al. (1999, fig. 4) and Zhen (2001) established three successive conodont biozones in the Eastonian of central NSW, defined on the

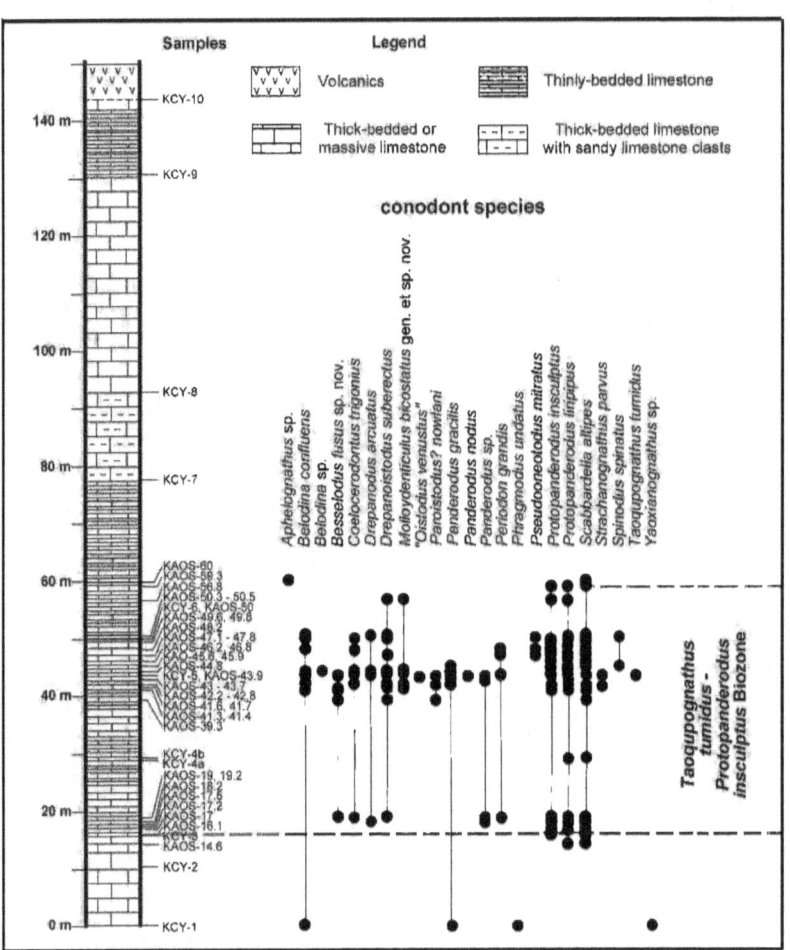

Figure 2. Stratigraphic section showing the sample horizons and ranges of the conodont species in the limestone body exposed along Kaos Gully, south of Greenvale, north Queensland. Samples with prefix KCY were collected by Y.Y. Zhen in 2010 (samples KCY-7 to KCY-10 from the upper part of the section were unproductive), and the remaining 39 productive samples with prefix KAOS were collected previously by John Talent and Ruth Mawson (Macquarie University) from the lower part of the same limestone body. Note that thicknesses shown are apparent, rather than true.

Series	Stage	Conodont zones North American Midcontinent	Conodont zones Baltoscandia	Conodont zones Australia	Conodont zones North China	Conodont zones South China
Late Ordovician	Hirnantian	Aphelognathus shatzeri	O. hassi (lower part) / Noixodontus fauna	?	?	Amorphognathus ordovicicus
	Ka4	Aph. divergens	Amorphognathus ordovicicus		Aph. zuoquensis	
		Aph. grandis			Aph. divergens	
					Aph. grandis	
	Ka3	Oulodus robustus		Tao. tumidus - Pro. insculptus *	Yaoxianognathus yaoxianensis	Protopanderodus insculptus
	Ka2	Ou. velicuspis	Amorphognathus superbus	Taoqupognathus blandus	Yaoxianognathus neimengguensis	Hamarodus brevirameus
	Ka1	Belodina confluens		Tao. philipi	B. confluens	
		Plectodina tenus				
	Sandb.	Ph. undatus	Baltoniodus alobatus	Ph. undatus- Tas. careyi	Ph. undatus	Baltoniodus alobatus

Figure 3. Conodont-based correlation of the allochthonous limestones (indicated by *) within the Wairuna Formation with other Late Ordovician conodont successions established in Australia (*Ph.* - *Phragmodus, Pro. – Protopanderodus, Tao. – Taoqupognathus, Tas. – Tasmanognathus*), North China (An and Zheng, 1990; Mei, 1995; Zhen et al., 2015; *B. - Belodina, Aph. – Aphelognathus*), South China (An, 1987; Wang et al., 2011; *Hamar. – Hamarodus*), Baltoscandia (Webby et al., 2004; Männik and Viira, 2012; Ferretti et al., 2014; *O. – Ozarkodina*) and North American Midcontinent (Webby et al., 2004; Goldman et al., 2007; Saltzman et al., 2014; *Ou. – Oulodus*). Coloured band in blue represents the middle Katian (late Ka2 to early Ka3) defined by the conodont biozones across different parts of the world.

stratigraphical distribution of *Taoqupognathus* species, from oldest (*T. philipi* Biozone) succeeded by the *T. blandus* Biozone followed by the youngest (*T. tumidus* Biozone). Although *T. tumidus* is relatively rare in the material from north Queensland, being represented by only four specimens, it and the associated species definitely support correlation with the *T. tumidus* Biozone, widely recognized in NSW and other parts of eastern Gondwana and peri-Gondwana.

In North China, the *T. blandus* Biozone can be correlated with the upper *Belodina confluens* Biozone (upper part of the Yaoxian Formation, where *Taoqupognathus blandus* makes its first appearance) and the *Y. neimengguensis* Biozone (spanning the lower part of the Taoqupo Formation) of the Ordos Basin in North China. The *T. tumidus* Biozone correlates with the *Y. yaoxianensis* Biozone of North China (Zhen 2001, text-fig. 3), where *T. tumidus* was reported from the top of the Taoqupo Formation (Zhen et al. 2003), and possibly from the Beiguoshan Formation (correlated to the upper part of the Taoqupo Formation) in the Ordos Basin, and with the *Protopanderodus insculptus* Biozone in South China (Fig. 3).

Kaljo et al. (2012) reported *Molloydenticulus bicostatus* gen. et sp. nov. (referred by them to *Nordiodus?* sp.), *Protopanderodus liripipus* and *P. insculptus* from the lower part of the Tirekhtyakh

Formation (sample 115-6/3 from Member 59) in the Mirny Creek section of NE Russia. Co-occurrence of these three species in the faunas documented herein from North Queensland and other parts of eastern Australia (Trotter and Webby 1995) implies a slightly older age (Ka2 to Ka3) for the lower part of the Tirekhtyakh Formation, rather than late Katian (Ka4) as Zhang and Barnes (2007a) and Kaljo et al. (2012) suggested.

CONODONT PALAEOECOLOGY

The conodont fauna from allochthonous limestone in the Kaos Gully section is quantitatively dominated by three species – *Scabbardella altipes* (32.5%), *Besselodus fusus* sp. nov. (22.4%), and *Protopanderodus liripipus* (22.1%) – which constitute over three-quarters of the total number of the specimens recovered (Table 1). *Protopanderodus* and *Spinodus* are widely interpreted to have inhabited relatively deep waters in shelf margin to slope settings (Pohler 1994; Zhang 1998; Löfgren 2003, 2004; Zhen and Percival 2004; Mellgren and Eriksson 2006). Although *Spinodus* is very rare in the material from north Queensland, the two species of *Protopanderodus* that are present make up nearly one-quarter of the total number of specimens, and so this fauna represents a typical *Protopanderodus* biofacies.

The strong taxonomic similarity of this fauna to that in allochthonous limestone clasts from the lower part of the Malongulli Formation in central NSW (Trotter and Webby 1995) has been noted above. However, abundant occurrence of siliceous sponge spicules and radiolarians and the association with argillaceous carbonates suggest that the majority of these Malongulli Formation carbonate clasts represent periplatformal deposits that formed downslope from the island shelf-edge (Webby 1992). Moreover the much higher diversity of the Malongulli limestone clasts fauna with their mixture of typical shallow-water forms, such as *Pseudobelodina* and *Chirognathus*, with characteristic deeper water forms, e.g. *Protopanderodus insculptus* and *P. liripipus* suggested that these clasts might be derived from a variety of sources ranging from the inner platform to slope. In contrast, the fauna from Kaos Gully lacks typical shallow water forms suggesting that the single allochthonous block was likely deposited in a shelf-edge setting. This interpretation is consistent with the common occurrence of corals, stromatoporoids, codiacean algae and bryozoans in these limestone bodies (Dixon and Jell 2012), as well as sedimentological data of these often massive or thick-bedded limestone bodies scattered in the Wairuna Formation.

BRACHIOPOD FAUNA AND PALAEOECOLOGY

Linguliform microbrachiopods recognized in Late Ordovician limestones from the Broken River Province include *Elliptoglossa adela* Percival, 1978, *Paterula malongulliensis* Percival, 1978 and *Hisingerella hetera* (Percival, 1978), in addition to new species of *Acrosaccus*, *Atansoria*, *Biernatia*, *Conotreta*, *Nushbiella* and *Scaphelasma*. Previous discussion of the interpreted palaeoecology of some of these species (Percival 1978) pointed towards a deeper water environment, including both benthic habitats (supported above the sea floor on sponges) and planktic habits, drifting attached to algae. All the new species listed above have been found in limestones (almost exclusively allochthonous) in the Malongulli Formation and correlative units of the Macquarie Volcanic Province in central NSW, and are being described elsewhere on the basis of that more abundant material. There is no doubt, given the identical faunal components, that the depositional environment and palaeoecological setting of the north Queensland limestones was very similar to that of central NSW. But it was not identical, and on the basis of the presence of an abundant and diverse sponge fauna in the Malongulli Formation (and its apparent absence from the Carriers Well limestones) combined with evidence of a shallow-water sedimentological and faunal component in the latter (e.g. Dixon and Jell 2012), we interpret the Carriers Well carbonates as having been deposited at the shelf edge. This would have presumably been unstable and subject to erosion, providing the source of allochthonous blocks to be redeposited into younger sediments. The Malongulli Formation in comparison includes autochthonous graptolitic siltstones and spiculites as matrix to a mixture of spicule-rich limestones interpreted as periplatformal or upper slope in origin (Webby 1992), combined at some horizons with shallower shelfal limestones that have been reworked downslope.

MATERIAL AND SAMPLING LOCALITIES

The conodont fauna documented herein is represented by 2565 discrete identifiable conodont specimens (Table 1) from the lower part of an allochthonous limestone block exposed along Kaos Gully, a tributary of Gray Creek (Fig. 1). The Kaos Gully section extends from the base of the limestone at Lat. 19°02.037' S Long. 144°58.372' E (sample KCY-1) to its top at 19°01.970' S 144°58.405' E (sample KCY-10). Conodonts from these samples are opaque black with a CAI of 5-6, indicating a high level of maturation (Epstein *et al.* 1977). Preservation of the conodont specimens varies from reasonably well-preserved to rather strongly deformed or poorly preserved. The upper part of the section was also intensively sampled for conodonts, but none of the samples collected has yielded conodonts. The main limestone block in the Kaos Gully locality is more or less continuously exposed for about 144 m along the gully, and consists of thick-medium bedded greyish limestone in the lower part, thinly bedded, often laminated sandy limestone in the middle, and thick-bedded to massive limestone at the top, which is overlain by brownish volcanics. Ten samples (only four of which were productive, see Table 1) with prefix KCY were collected by Zhen in 2010, and the remaining 39 productive samples with prefix KAOS were collected previously by John Talent and Ruth Mawson (Macquarie University) from the same limestone body. Two additional samples, yielding 29 conodont specimens (Table 1), were also collected by Zhen from the two minor limestone bodies exposed in Gray Creek, one from a large massive limestone block exposed in the middle of the Gray Creek (CWZ-1: 19°02.080' S, 144°58.564' E), and the other (CWZ2,

Gray Creek bank locality: 19°02.162' S, 144°58.535' E) from massive grey limestone exposed on its east bank, next to the track crossing the creek.

SYSTEMATIC PALAEONTOLOGY

All photographic illustrations shown in Figures 4 to 21 are SEM photomicrographs of conodonts and brachiopods captured digitally (numbers with the prefix IY and PI CWL are the file names of the digital images). Figured specimens bearing the prefix MMMC (4756 to 4954 inclusive; 199 specimens in total) are deposited in the microfossil collection of the Geological Survey of New South Wales, housed at the WB Clarke Geoscience Centre at Londonderry in outer western Sydney. Those conodont taxa that are described herein (by Zhen) are alphabetically listed according to their generic assignment, with family level and higher classification omitted. Authorship of the new taxa of conodonts is attributable solely to Zhen. Conodont species that are either rare in the collection, or those that have been adequately described elsewhere in the literature, are documented only by illustration.

CONODONTS (Zhen)

Genus BELODINA Ethington, 1959

Type species

Belodus compressus Branson and Mehl, 1933 (amended by Bergström and Sweet 1966, and by Leslie 1997).

Belodina confluens Sweet, 1979
Fig. 4b-g

Synonymy

Belodina compressa (Branson and Mehl); Bergström and Sweet, 1966, p. 312-319, pl. 31, figs 12-19 (*cum. syn.*); Barnes, 1967, text-figs 1-2; Palmieri, 1978, *partim* only pl. 3, figs 12-15, 20-21, 23-25, pl. 4, figs 1-17, text-fig. 5.6-5.10, 5.16-5.19 (not fig. 11 = S1 of *Belodina baiyanhuaensis* Qiu in Lin, Qiu and Xu, 1984); Nowlan, 1979, pl. 35.1, text-figs 35.1-35.2.
Belodina grandis (Stauffer); Philip, 1966, fig. 2 (= S2 element).
Belodina wykoffensis (Stauffer); Philip, 1966, fig. 3 (= S1 element).
Eobelodina fornicala (Stauffer); Philip, 1966, figs 4, 8 (= M element).
Belodina dispansa (Glenister); Philip, 1966, fig. 1 (= S3 element).

Belodina monitorensis Ethington and Schumacher; Pickett, 1978, cover photo, figs 7-8.
Belodina sp. A s.f. Palmieri, 1978, pl. 3, figs 1-2, text-fig. 5.1 (= S1 element).
Belodina sp. B s.f. Palmieri, 1978, pl. 3, figs 3-6 (3-4 = S2 element, 5-6 = S1 element), text-fig. 5.2-5.3 (5.2 = S2 element, 5.3 = S1 element).
Belodina sp. D s.f. Palmieri, 1978, *partim* only pl. 3, fig. 18, text-fig. 5.13-5.15 (= S3 element) (not pl. 3, figs 16-17, 19, 22, text-fig. 5.11-5.12 = S1 of *Belodina baiyanhuaensis* Qiu in Lin, Qiu and Xu, 1984).
Belodina confluens Sweet, 1979, p. 59-60, fig. 5.10, 5.17, fig. 6.9; Sweet in Ziegler, 1981, p. 73-77, pl. 2, figs 8-14 (*cum syn.*); Nowlan, 1983, p. 662, pl. 3, figs 3-4; Pei and Cai, 1987, p. 70, pl. 9, figs 9, 14, pl. 14, figs 14-16, text-fig. 3.22-3.23; Nowlan and McCracken, in Nowlan et al., 1988, p. 12, pl. 1, figs 16-21 (*cum syn.*); McCracken and Nowlan, 1989, p. 1888, pl. 1, figs 19-21; pl. 2, figs 1-2; Uyeno, 1990, p. 71, pl. 1, figs 8-9; Pickett and Ingpen, 1990, p. 6, cover photo, K; Savage, 1990, p. 829, fig. 9.1-9.6; Bergström, 1990, pl. 3, figs 8-12; Trotter and Webby, 1995, p. 481, pl. 2, figs 18-20, 24-25, 27-30; Zhen and Webby, 1995, pl. 1, figs 16-21; Bergström and Bergström, 1996, fig. 9P; Nowlan et al., 1997, fig. 1.1-1.2; Wang and Zhou, 1998, pl. 3, fig. 9; Zhen et al., 1999, pl. 1, figs 7-9; Furey-Greig, 1999, p. 309, pl. 1, figs 1-11; Percival, 1999, fig. 3.28-29; Furey-Greig, 2000a, p. 91, fig. 4A-F; Furey-Greig, 2000b, p. 137, fig. 5.1-5.4; Zhao et al., 2000, p. 191, pl. 49, figs 4-13; McCracken, 2000, p. 189, pl. 1, figs 10-11, pl. 2, figs 8-10 (*cum syn.*); Wang and Qi, 2001, pl. 1, figs 15, 26; Nowlan, 2002, pl. 1, figs 7-10; Talent et al., 2002, pl. 1, figs A-B; Zhen et al., 2003, fig. 4E-G; Zhang and Barnes, 2007b, fig. 10.11-10.13; Zhang, 2011, fig. 18.14-18.17; Zhang et al., 2011, fig. 13.29-13.31; Chen et al., 2013, fig. 4d'-f'; Zhang, 2013, fig. 10.19-10.21; Zhang and Pell, 2013, fig. 3C; Dumoulin et al., 2014, pl. 5, fig. f.
Belodina sp. A Trotter and Webby, 1995, p. 481, pl. 2, figs 12-13 (= S2 element).
Belodina sp. B Trotter and Webby, 1995, p. 481, pl. 2, fig. 14 (= S2 element).
Belodina sp. A Furey-Greig, 1999, p. 309, pl. 1, fig. 12 (= S1 element).
Belodina sp. C Furey-Greig, 1999, p. 309, pl. 1, figs 14-15 (14= S1 element, 15= M element).
Eobelodina occidentalis Ethington and Schumacher; Pickett, 1978, cover photo, figs 1-2.

92

Proc. Linn. Soc. N.S.W., 137, 2015

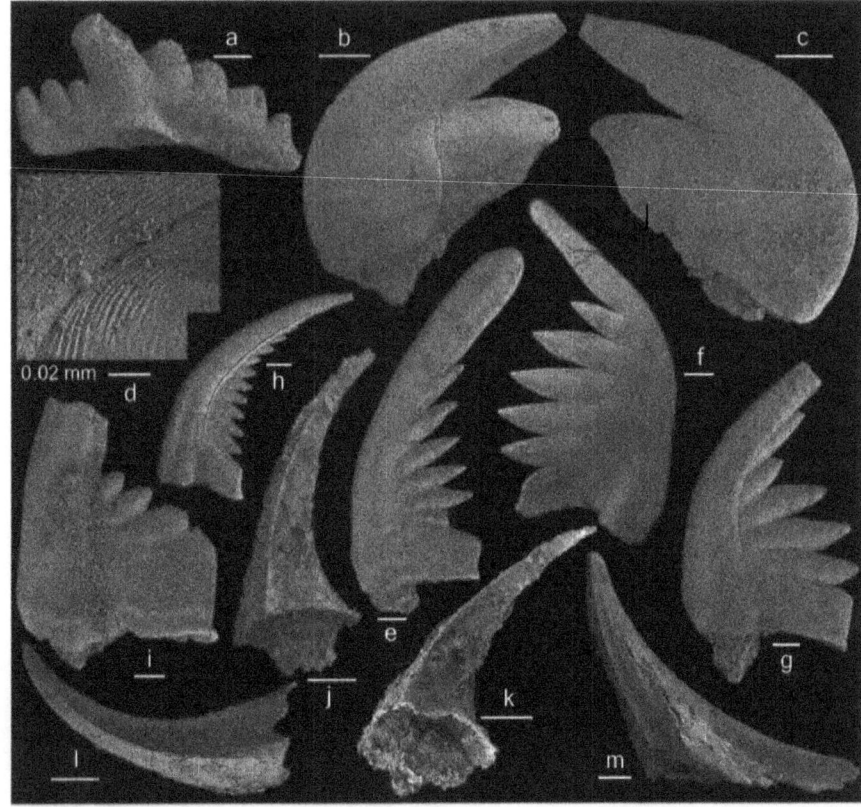

Figure 4. a, *Aphelognathus* sp. Pa element; MMMC4756, KAOS-60, inner-lateral view (IY242-023). b-h, *Belodina confluens* Sweet, 1979. b, d, M (eobelodiniform) element, MMMC4757, KCY-5; b, view of furrowed side (IY233-004), d, view of furrowed side, close-up showing surface striation (IY233-005); c, MMMC4758, KCY-5, view of unfurrowed side (IY233-006); e, S2 (grandiform) element, MMMC4759, KAOS-47.4, view of furrowed side (IY239-007); f-g, S1 (compressiform) element, f, MMMC4760, KCY-5, view of unfurrowed side (IY233-009); g, MMMC4761, KCY-5, view of furrowed side (IY233-009); h, S2 (grandiform) element, MMMC4762, KCY-1, view of furrowed side (IY238-002). i, *Belodina* sp. S2 (grandiform) element, MMMC4763, KAOS-44.8, view of furrowed side (IY243-031). j-m, *Coelocerodontus trigonius* Ethington, 1959. j-k, asymmetrical trigoniform element, MMMC4764, KAOS-42.6, j, outer-lateral view (IY240-016), k, basal-posterior view (IY240-017); l, asymmetrical tetragoniform element, MMMC4765, KAOS-42.6, outer-lateral view (IY240-013); m, long-based, asymmetrical trigoniform element, MMMC4766, KAOS-43.9, outer-lateral view (IY240-016). Scale bars 100 μm.

Material

40 specimens from 10 samples at the Kaos Gully locality (see Table 1).

Discussion

In eastern Australia *B. confluens* had a wide distribution in the Upper Ordovician (Eastonian), reported from the Sofala Volcanics (Pickett 1978; Percival 1999), the Raggatt Volcanics (Pickett and Ingpen 1990), allochthonous limestones in the lower part of the Malongulli Formation (Trotter and Webby 1995), the Cliefden Caves Limestone Subgroup (Savage 1990; Zhen and Webby 1995), the Bowan Park Limestone Subgroup and the basal part of the overlying Malachis Hill Formation (Zhen et al. 1999), and the allochthonous limestones in the Barnby Hills Shale (Zhen et al. 2003) of the Lachlan Orogen in central New South Wales, from the allochthonous

Proc. Linn. Soc. N.S.W., 137, 2015

93

limestones in the Wisemans Arm Formation (Furey-Greig 1999) and in the Drik Drik Formation (Furey-Greig 2000b), formerly the "Trelawney Beds" (Philip 1966), and the "Uralba Beds" (Furey-Greig 2000a) of the New England Orogen in NE New South Wales, from the Fork Lagoons beds of central-east Queensland (Palmieri 1978), and from allochthonous limestones within the Wairuna Formation of the Broken River region, north Queensland (Talent et al. 2002; this study).

Belodina confluens is common in the studied collections from north Queensland, but only M (eobelodiniform), S1 (compressiform), and S2 (grandiform) elements were recovered. The S2 element illustrated herein (Fig. 4e) is identical with that identified by Trotter and Webby (1995, pl. 2, fig. 14) as Belodina sp. B. It is characterized by having a broadly swollen tip of the cusp. A comparable specimen was doubtfully referred by Zhen and Webby (1995, pl. 1, fig. 20) to B. confluens. The illustrated S1 element (Fig. 4f-g) is less compressed with a gently curved anterior margin and is identical with those illustrated by Palmieri (1978, pl. 3, figs 1-2) as Belodina sp. A. We consider that specimen to represent a variant S1 element of B. confluens.

Leslie (1997), studying fused clusters of elements from Missouri and Iowa, revised Belodina compressa as consisting of a quadrimembrate skeletal apparatus, including eobelodiniform (M), compressiform (S1), grandiform (S2) and dispansiform (S3) elements. He also indicated that Belodina confluens was composed of a similar quadrimembrate species apparatus. Morphologically B. confluens closely resembles its likely direct ancestral species, B. compressa, but can be distinguished from the latter mainly by having a regularly curved antero-basal corner of the anterior margin in the S1 element in lateral view, compared to the corresponding element of B. compressa which has a distinctive straight segment (Zhen et al. 2004, pp. 148, 150). Four morphotypes (M, S1, S2 and S3) of elements belonging to B. confluens were first recorded from the "Trelawney Beds" of northern NSW (Philip 1966, figs 1-4, 8), and later reported to be widely distributed in the Upper Ordovician of eastern Australia. Palmieri (1978) documented M, S1 and S2 elements of this species (assigned at the time to Belodina compressa); additionally some of his specimens illustrated as Belodina sp. D s.f. represent the S3 element of B. confluens (Palmieri 1978, pl. 3, fig. 18, text-fig. 5.13-5.15). Specimens he assigned to B. sp. A and B. sp. B are also regarded herein as variants of the S1 and S2 elements of B. confluens. Trotter and Webby (1995) only illustrated the M and S1 elements of B. confluens from limestone breccia in

the lower Malongulli Formation. However, specimens they assigned to Belodina sp. A and Belodina sp. B are considered herein as representatives of the S2 element of B. confluens. In comparison with its rarity in the North American Midcontinent faunas, abundant material of this species (numerically up to 60 percent of the total numbers in some samples – see Zhen and Webby 1995) from eastern Australia shows wider morphological variations in respect to the major characters of the constituent elements. The holotype of B. confluens from the Kope Formation (Edenian) of Ohio (Bergström and Sweet 1966, pl. 31, figs 14-16) is an S1 element bearing a strongly reclined cusp with a smoothly curved anterior margin and six denticles along its posterior margin. The paratype, which came from the same sample of the Kope Formation (Bergström and Sweet 1966, pl. 31, figs 17-19), represents the S2 element with a less reclined cusp bearing seven basally-confluent denticles along its posterior margin. The other specimen figured by Bergström and Sweet (1966, pl. 31, figs 12-13) is the geniculate M element bearing a short and recurved cusp and an extended base (heel) with an arched upper margin. The S3 element of B. confluens, which is more elongate with five or six smaller denticles obliquely arranged along the posterior margin of the cusp, was documented by Bergström (1990, pl. 3, fig. 9), who originally considered it as doubtful juvenile of an S2 element, and by Barnes (1967, text-figs 1-2) and Nowlan (1979, fig. 35.2) in fused clusters, which were originally assigned to B. compressa (see Leslie 1997 p. 924). Among the eastern Australian material referrable to B. confluens, S1 elements typically have four or five denticles, and the anterior margin varies from gently curved (Palmieri 1978, pl. 3, figs 1-2; this study Fig. 4f-g), to moderately curved (comparable to the holotype; Philip 1966, fig. 3; Palmieri 1978, pl. 3, figs 23-24; Savage 1990, fig. 9.3-9.4; Zhen and Webby 1995, pl. 1, figs 16, 19; Furey-Greig 1999, pl. 1, fig. 4), and strongly curved (Palmieri 1978, pl. 3, figs 5-6; Trotter and Webby 1995, pl. 2, figs 23-25). Variation of the M element was well-illustrated by Trotter and Webby (1995, pl. 2, figs 267-30) in respect to the degree of the posterior extension of the base and relative size of the cusp. Apparently those specimens occupying the centre of the variation range (Trotter and Webby 1995, pl. 2, fig. 29; Zhen and Webby 1995, pl. 1, fig. 21) are identical with the type specimen illustrated by Bergström and Sweet (1966, pl. 31, figs 12-13), and occur more often in the Taoqupognathus philipi Biozone (Ea1, early Katian). Specimens of the M element with a more strongly extended base and a reduced cusp (Trotter and Webby 1995, pl. 2, figs 27-28) are only reported

94

from the stratigraphically higher *Taoqupognathus tumidus* Biozone (Ea3-4 = Ka2-3). The S2 element of *B. confluens* from eastern Australia has denticles varying from four to ten (typically four to six) along the posterior margin in comparison with the paratype (seven denticles). Some of the grandiform specimens referrable to the S2 element of *B. confluens* exhibit a swollen distal end of the cusp (Trotter and Webby 1995, pl. 2, fig. 14; Zhen and Webby 1995, pl. 1, fig. 20; McCracken 2000, pl. 2, fig. 9; Fig. 4E). The specimen illustrated by Palmieri (1978, pl. 3, fig. 18) from the Fork Lagoons beds of Queensland and by Philip (1966, fig. 1) from the "Trelawney Beds" of NSW were recovered in association with the other elements of *B. confluens*, and are nearly identical with the S3 element of *B. confluens* documented by Bergström (1990, pl. 3, fig. 9) from Scotland, and by Barnes (1967, text-figs 1-2) and Nowlan (1979, fig. 35.2) from Ottawa in Canada. A single S2 (grandiform) element (Fig. 4i) is assigned herein to *Belodina* sp., characterized by having three denticles rooted more or less on the upper margin of the heel rather than on the posterior margin of the cusp as in the typical species of *Belodina*.

Genus BESSELODUS Aldridge, 1982

Type species
Besselodus arcticus Aldridge, 1982.

Discussion
The genus and its type species, *Besselodus arcticus*, were established by Aldridge (1982) based on a fused cluster consisting of seven elements from the Upper Ordovician of North Greenland. Aldridge (1982, p. 428) noted the most important character of the type species to be the presence of prominent oblique striations in all elements. *Besselodus* can be distinguished from *Dapsilodus* Cooper, 1976 mainly by differences in their skeletal apparatus and appearance of the constituent elements. *Besselodus* consists of geniculate M, and distacodiform S and P elements, whereas *Dapsilodus* has non-geniculate M,

distacodiform and acodiform S elements. Moreover, the oblique striations are only developed in some S elements of *Dapsilodus*, i.e. they have been only recognized in the acodiform Sb and Sc elements of *Dapsilodus viruensis* (Fåhræus, 1966) documented from South China (Zhen et al. 2009, p. 142, fig. 4).

Unfortunately, Aldridge's study was based on only a small number of specimens and an incomplete species apparatus of the type species, resulting in ongoing difficulty in defining *Besselodus*. Nowlan and McCracken (in Nowlan et al. 1988) described the second species *Besselodus borealis*, from the Northwest Territories of Canada, with a quinquimembrate apparatus including an element (originally referred to as the *c* element) without the oblique striations along the anterior margin. Adhering to the original generic concept of *Besselodus*, this distacodiform element is better assigned to a *Dapsilodus* species in the fauna, and should be excluded from the species apparatus of *B. borealis*. More recently, Leslie (2000) expanded the definition of *Besselodus* by accommodating in it several species including distacodiform, acontiodiform and oistodiform elements that apparently lacked oblique striations along the anterior margin, which would be excluded from *Besselodus* if Aldridge's (1982) original concept is maintained. The new species described below includes only elements bearing these oblique striations.

Besselodus fusus sp. nov.
Fig. 5a-p

Synonymy
?*Besselodus* sp. Trotter and Webby, 1995, pp. 481-482, pl. 3, figs 7, 12-18 (figs 7, 12-14, 16-17 = Sb, figs 15, 18 = M).
Besselodus sp. Zhen et al., 1999, p. 86, *partim* only figs 6.1-6.3. 6.5-6.12 (non 6.4) (figs 6.1-6.3 = Sc, figs 6.5-6.6 = Pb, figs 6.7-6.11 = ?Sb, fig. 6.12 = M).
?*Besselodus* sp. Zhen et al., 2003, fig. 4L-O (= Sb).

Figure 5 (next page). *Besselodus fusus* **sp. nov. a-c, M element; a-b, MMMC4767, paratype, KAOS-43.9, a, anterior view (IY240-023), b, enlargement showing striation along inner-lateral margin (IY240-024); c, MMMC4768, paratype, KAOS-43.9, posterior view (IY244-022). d-e, Sa element; d, MMMC4769, paratype, KAOS-43.9, lateral view (IY241-013); e, MMMC4770, paratype, KAOS-43.9, lateral view (IY241-014). f-h, Sb element; f, MMMC4771, paratype, KCY-5, outer-lateral view (IY235-015); g, MMMC4772, paratype, KCY-5, inner-lateral view (IY235-017); h, MMMC4773, paratype, KCY-5, inner-lateral view (IY235-016). i, P element, MMMC4774, paratype, KAOS-41.6, outer-lateral view (IY244-010). j-o, Sc element; j, MMMC4775, holotype, KCY-5, inner-lateral view (IY235-008); k-m, MMMC4776, paratype, KCY-5, k, inner-lateral view (IY235-013), l, posterior view (IY235-010), m, outer-lateral view (IY235-011); n, MMMC4777, paratype, KCY-5, inner-lateral view (IY235-014); o, MMMC4778, paratype, KAOS-43.9, upper view, close-up showing cross section of cusp (IY241-018). p, P element, MMMC4779, paratype, KCY-5, outer-lateral view (IY235-007). Scale bars 100 μm unless otherwise indicated.**

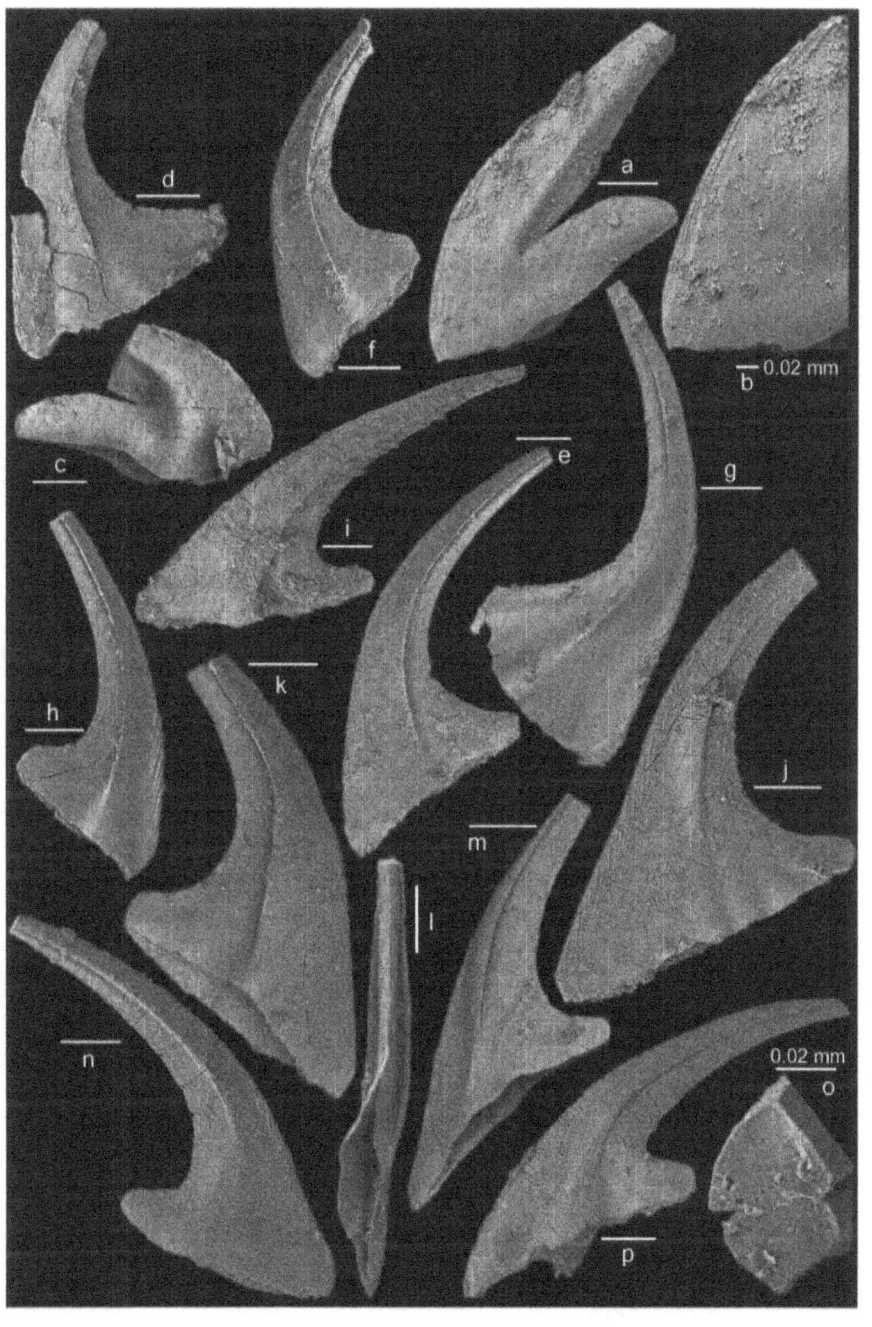

96

Proc. Linn. Soc. N.S.W., 137, 2015

Material

579 specimens from seven samples at Kaos Gully locality, including the holotype (MMMC4775) and 12 figured paratypes (MMMC4767 to MMMC4774, MMMC4776 to MMMC4779) (see Fig. 5), and an additional two specimens from sample CWZ-1 at Gray Creek locality (see Table 1).

Derivation of name

From Latin *fusus*, extended, alluding to the extended base that characterizes the S and P elements of the species.

Diagnosis

A species of *Besselodus* consisting of a coniform-coniform quinquimembrate species apparatus, with all elements ornamented with oblique striations along the anterior margin (S and P elements) or along the inner-lateral margin (M element); geniculate M element makellate with a strongly recurved cusp and an outer-laterally extended base, long-based distacodiform S elements forming a symmetry transition series (symmetrical Sa, asymmetrical Sb and strongly asymmetrical Sc), and short-based distacodiform P element with a strongly antero-posteriorly extended base and a distally recurved cusp.

Description

Geniculate M element is makellate, strongly compressed antero-posteriorly with sharp inner-lateral and outer-lateral margins, and consists of a robust and outer-laterally strongly recurved cusp bearing a sharp costa on broad anterior and posterior faces, and an outer-laterally extended base (Fig. 5a-c); costae are typically in the median position or situated slightly towards outer-lateral margin on the anterior face (Fig. 5a); base is low and extended outer-laterally, with a straight or gently wavy basal margin and a gently arched upper margin on the long outer-lateral extension; inner-lateral corner short and without prominent extension.

Distacodiform S elements are strongly compressed laterally, and consist of a distally reclined cusp and a longer base, which is more or less triangular in lateral view. The cusp has sharp anterior and posterior margins, and bears a sharp median costa bordered with a deep and narrow groove on the posterior side on each lateral face. Lateral costae and the narrow furrows extend distally to the tip of the cusp, but basally vary from extending to the upper portion of the base (Fig. 5j, n) to near the basal margin (Fig. 5h, k). The anterior margin is gently and smoothly curved in lateral view in extending to the antero-basal corner, and the posterior margin merges with the

upper margin of the base through a broadly rounded corner. The Sa element is laterally symmetrical, with a cusp that is basally slightly proclined-suberect and distally reclined, and a posteriorly extended base (Fig. 5d-e). The Sb element is similar to the Sa element, but slightly asymmetrical with anterior margin slightly flexed inner-laterally (Fig. 5g-h) and with a more convex outer-lateral face (Fig. 5f). The Sc element (Fig. 5j-o) is asymmetrical with the base extended posteriorly and also anteriorly to form a prominent basal-anterior corner, which is more or less triangular in outline in lateral view (Fig. 5j).

The distacodiform P element is laterally compressed and asymmetrical with a more strongly developed costa on each lateral side extended to near the basal margin, and displays a distally recurved cusp and a shorter base, which is more open and more strongly extended antero-posteriorly than the S (particularly Sc) elements. Although similar to the Sc element, the P element has a shorter and a more antero-posteriorly extended base (Fig. 5i, p). The posterior margin of the cusp and the upper margin of the base forms an acute angle (Fig. 5i, p), rather than being broadly rounded as in the typical Sc element (Fig. 5j-k).

Discussion

Based on comparison with illustrated specimens representing the M, Sa and Sc elements, *Besselodus* sp. reported from the lower Malongulli Formation of central NSW (Trotter and Webby 1995, pl. 3, figs 7, 12-18) is likely conspecific with *B. fusus* sp. nov. However, the geniculate specimens from the Malongulli Formation display weaker development of the costa (Trotter and Webby 1995, pl. 3, fig. 15), and the Sb and Sc elements are comparable with the Sb element of *B. fusus*, but with a longer base and a more strongly reclined cusp. Trotter and Webby (1995, p. 481) indicated that the symmetrical Sa element was also recognized in the Malongulli fauna, but did not illustrate this.

Elements of *Besselodus* sp. documented from the top part of the Bowan Park Limestone Subgroup of central NSW (Zhen et al. 1999) are closely comparable with the M, Sb, Sc and P elements of the new species and are considered conspecific, although some illustrated specimens with a longer base (Zhen et al. 1999, figs 6.7-6.11) are more similar to some of the type specimens of *Besselodus borealis* (e.g. Nowlan et al. 1988, pl. 2, figs 3-4). Specimens likely representing the Sb element of *B. fusus* were also reported from allochthonous limestones within the Barnby Hills Shale (Zhen et al. 2003).

Proc. Linn. Soc. N.S.W., 137, 2015

97

Both *Besselodus arcticus* Aldridge, 1982 and *Besselodus borealis* Nowlan and McCracken (in Nowlan et al. 1988) are represented only by M and S elements. *B. borealis* differs from the type species mainly by having the costa in the M element situated more towards the outer-lateral margin rather than in the median position in the latter, and by having coarser oblique striations in some S elements that often form a weakly serrated anterior margin. The new species *B. fusus* is readily distinguished from both by having a more antero-posteriorly extended base, particularly its Sc and P elements.

Genus DREPANOISTODUS Lindström, 1971

Type species
Oistodus forceps Lindström, 1955.

Drepanoistodus suberectus (Branson and Mehl, 1933)
Fig. 6a-l

Synonymy
Oistodus suberectus Branson and Mehl, 1933, p. 111, pl. 9, fig. 7.
Drepanoistodus suberectus (Branson and Mehl); Sweet and Bergström, 1966, pp. 330-333, pl. 35, figs 22-27 (*cum syn.*); Nowlan and Barnes, 1981, pp. 12-13, pl. 4, figs 17-19; Nowlan and McCracken *in* Nowlan et al., 1988, p. 16, pl. 3, figs 19-22 (*cum syn.*); Uyeno, 1990, p. 76, pl. 1, figs 13, 16-18; Dzik, 1994, p. 78, pl. 17, figs 2-6, text-fig. 12b; Trotter and Webby, 1995, p. 482, pl. 5, figs 27-31; Zhen and Webby, 1995, p. 282, pl. 3, figs 8-10 (*cum syn.*); Nowlan et al., 1997, pl. 1, figs 7-9; Zhen et al., 1999, p. 88, fig. 6.1-6.7; Furey-Greig, 1999, p. 310, pl. 2, figs 1-3; Furey-Greig, 2000b, p. 137, fig. 5.8; McCracken, 2000, pl. 1, fig. 12, pl. 2, figs 20, 21; Leslie, 2000, fig. 5.16-5.19; Sweet, 2000, fig. 9.23-9.25; Nowlan, 2002, pl. 1, figs 19-21; Talent et al., 2002, pl. 1, figs C-D; Sansom and Smith, 2005, p. 36, pl. 1, figs 1-2, 7-8, 12; Zhang and Barnes, 2007a, fig. 7.15-7.18; Zhang and Barnes, 2007b, fig. 10.7-10.10; Viira, 2008, fig. 3W-X; Zhang, 2013, fig. 9.36-9.38; Ferretti et al., 2014a, fig. 14M-O; Ferretti et al., 2014c, pl. 2, figs 8-10.

Material
75 specimens from 13 samples at Kaos Gully locality (see Table 1).

Discussion
Elements forming the seximembrate species apparatus of this species are recognized, including makellate M element (Fig. 6a-b) bearing an outer-laterally extended base with a strongly recurved basal margin and a robust cusp; drepanodiform S elements that form a symmetry transition series from symmetrical Sa element (Fig. 6c-e) with a base more flared at the postero-median portion of lateral side, asymmetrical Sb element (Fig. 6f-g), to strongly asymmetrical and laterally compressed Sc element (Fig. 6h-i); drepanodiform Pa element (Fig. 6j-k) with an extended antero-basal corner, and Pb element (Fig. 6l) with a suberect cusp and a short base confined by a strongly recurved basal margin. The Kaos Gully material is identical with specimens from NSW, for instance from the limestone breccia in the lower Malongulli Formation (Trotter and Webby 1995), the Cliefden Caves Limestone Subgroup (Zhen and Webby 1995), the Bowan Park Limestone Subgroup and basal Malachis Hill Formation (Zhen et al. 1999), and from allochthonous limestones within the Barnby Hills Shale (Zhen et al. 2003).

Genus MOLLOYDENTICULUS gen. nov.

Derivation of name
In honour of our co-author, Peter Molloy (deceased) who meticulously processed the samples and picked the conodont residues on which much of this paper is based. Peter studied Silurian conodonts for his Ph.D; combined with *denticulus* (Latin): tooth (diminutive).

Type species
Molloydenticulus bicostatus gen. et sp. nov.

Diagnosis
A genus of Protopanderodontidae consisting of a bimembrate apparatus including laterally-compressed, asymmetrical bicostate (distacodiform) Pa and Pb elements bearing a stout cusp with sharp anterior and posterior margins and with a prominent costa on each lateral face, and a short antero-posteriorly extended base; costa more strongly developed basally into a short, blade-like protoprocess and typically with a deep and narrow groove developed on its posterior side.

Discussion
Molloydenticulus is apparently closely related to *Scabbardella*, but consists of a bimembrate species apparatus with only short based distacodiform elements recognized. These differ from distacodiform elements of *Scabbardella altipes* co-occurring in the fauna in having a stouter cusp with a more strongly

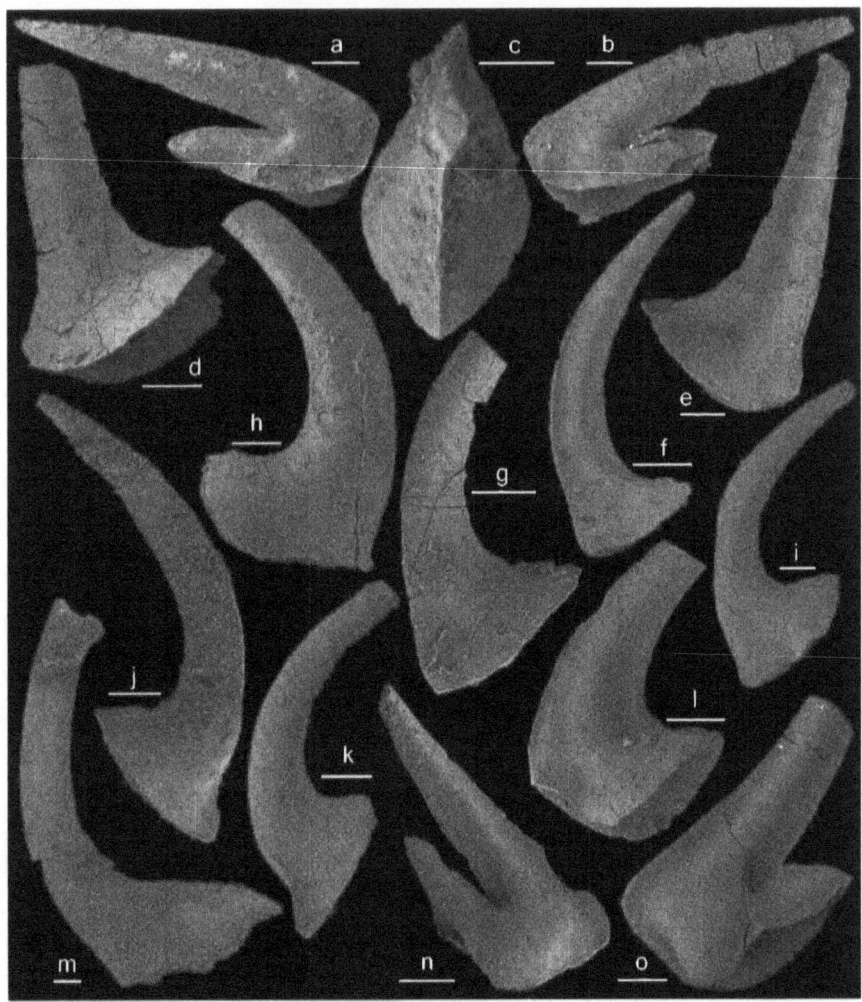

Figure 6. a-l, *Drepanoistodus suberectus* (Branson and Mehl, 1933). a-b, M element; a, MMMC4780, KAOS-42.8, anterior view (IY240-020); b, MMMC4781, KAOS-43.8, anterior view (IY238-018). c-e, Sa element; c, MMMC4782, KAOS-44.8, upper view (IY238-013); d, MMMC4783, KAOS-43.9, lateral view (IY241-004); e, MMMC4784, KAOS-44.8, lateral view (IY238-010). f-g, Sb element, f, MMMC4785, KAOS-42.8, inner-lateral view (IY238-017); g, MMMC4786, KCY-5, inner-lateral view (IY237-023). h-i, Sc element; h, MMMC4787, KAOS-42.6, outer-lateral view (IY240-012); i, MMMC4788, KAOS-42.6, outer-lateral view (IY240-010). j-k, Pa element; j, MMMC4789, KCY-5, outer-lateral view (IY237-021); k, MMMC4790, KAOS-44.8, inner-lateral view (IY238-016). l, Pb element, MMMC4791, KCY-5, inner-lateral view (IY237-016). m, *Drepanodus arcuatus* Pander, 1856. Sa element, MMMC4792, KAOS-44.8, lateral view (IY238-012). n-o, *Paroistodus* sp. M element; n, MMMC4793, KAOS-42.6, posterior view (IY240-011); o, MMMC4794, KAOS-44.8, posterior view (IY238-011). Scale bars 100 μm.

Proc. Linn. Soc. N.S.W., 137, 2015

99

developed costa on the lateral faces and a shorter and more open base. No confirmed P elements comparable with those of the new taxon recognised here were recorded among the abundant material of *S. altipes* from Britain. Therefore the north Queensland specimens are interpreted as representing a new genus (currently monospecific) consisting of a bimembrate species apparatus.

Molloydenticulus bicostatus gen. et sp. nov.

Fig. 7a-m

Synonymy
?*Acodus mutatus* (Branson and Mehl); Palmieri, 1978, *partim* only pp. 6-7, pl. 1, figs 17-18, text-fig. 4a-c (not pl. 2, fig. 19, and text-fig. 5a-c).
Gen. et sp. indet. C Trotter and Webby, 1995, p. 489, pl. 1, figs 16-18.
Nordiodus? sp. Kaljo et al., 2012, figs 5N1, 5N2.

Material
249 specimens from six samples at Kaos Gully locality, including holotype (MMMC4864) and nine figured paratypes (MMMC4858 to MMMC4863, MMMC4865 to MMMC4867) (see Table 1, Fig. 12).

Derivation of name
From Latin *bi*, two, and *cost*-, rib, alluding to the strongly developed costa on each lateral face.

Diagnosis
As for genus.

Description
Two morphotypes of this species are represented (Fig. 7a-m). They are asymmetrical, coniform distacodiform units, more or less triangular in outline in lateral view, and typically with the anterior margin flexed inward (Fig. 7b, i). Both are laterally compressed with sharp anterior and posterior margins. On each lateral face is developed a strong costa, which extends from the tip of cusp to the basal margin, where it is more strongly produced into a blade-like protoprocess. A narrow groove developed on the posterior side of the costa on the lateral faces is deeper and more prominent on the outer-lateral face (Fig. 7f-g, j, l). The base extends antero-posteriorly with a basal cavity of moderate depth (Fig. 7e). The Pa element has a proclined cusp (Fig. 7a-g), while the Pb element has the cusp basally suberect and distally reclined (Fig. 7h-m).

Discussion
Two specimens illustrated by Trotter and Webby (1995, pl. 1, figs 16-18) as Gen. et sp. indet. C, from the lower Malongulli Formation of central NSW, are comparable with the Pa element described herein. A poorly preserved specimen from the Fork Lagoons beds of central Queensland illustrated by Palmieri (1978, pl. 2, figs 17-18) and identified as *Acodus mutatus* (Branson and Mehl) appears to be generally comparable with the Pa element of the new species although it is said to be acodiform (Palmieri 1978, p. 7). Therefore it is only doubtfully assigned to *Molloydenticulus bicostatus*.

The new species also occurs in the lower part of the Tirekhtyakh Formation in the Mirny Creek section of NE Russia, correlated by Kaljo et al. (2012) with the lower part of the *A. ordovicicus* Biozone. However, resolution of the conodont zonation established in NE Russia is still low with the *A. ordovicicus* fauna overlying the long-ranging *Belodina compressa* fauna that spanned the entire Sandbian to middle Katian (Zhang and Barnes 2007a, fig. 2). Recognition of *M. bicostatus* in the Mirny Creek section implies a more precise Ka2-3 age, based on the eastern Australian occurrences.

Genus NORDIODUS Serpagli, 1967

Type species
Nordiodus italicus Serpagli, 1967.

Discussion
Nordiodus was erected based on two form species (*N. italicus* Serpagli, 1967 and *N. proclinatus* Serpagli, 1967) from the Upper Ordovician (Katian) of the Carnic Alps of Italy. In the conodont Treatise (Clark et al. 1981, p. W144), the type species was revised as consisting of a trimembrate apparatus, including a geniculate element (= form species *Oistodus rhodesi* Serpagli, 1967; referred to herein as representing the M element), and two types of nongeniculate elements represented by the form species *N. italicus* Serpagli, 1967 and *N. proclinatus* Serpagli, 1967. The latter are reinterpreted as representing the Pa (=*N. proclinatus*) and Pb (=*N. italicus*) elements. It is likely that the specimens ascribed to *Acodus trigonius* (Schopf, 1966) and *Acodus trigonius aequilateralis* Serpagli, 1967 by Serpagli (1967) may belong to the same species, representing the asymmetrical and symmetrical S elements, respectively, of *N. italicus*.

Nordiodus italicus Serpagli, 1967

Fig. 8a-k

Synonymy
Nordiodus proclinatus Serpagli, 1967, pp. 78-79, pl. 19, figs 1a-6c (= Pa element).
Acodus trigonius (Schopf); Serpagli, 1967, pp. pp.

Figure 7. *Molloydenticulus bicostatus* gen. et. sp. nov. a-g, Pa element; a, MMMC4858, paratype, KAOS-43.9, inner-lateral view (IY240-032); b-c, MMMC4859, paratype, KAOS-43.9, b, upper view (IY240-027), c, inner-lateral view (IY240-026); d-e, MMMC4860, paratype, KAOS-43.9, d, outer-lateral view (IY241-010), e, basal view (IY241-008); f, MMMC4861, paratype, KAOS-43.9, outer-lateral view (IY241-006); g, MMMC4862, paratype, KCY-5, outer-lateral view (IY235-003). h-m, Pb element; h-i, MMMC4863, paratype, KAOS-43.9, h, inner-lateral view (IY241-012), i, upper view (IY241-009); j, MMMC4864, holotype, KCY-5, outer-lateral view (IY234-027); k, MMMC4865, paratype, KCY-5, basal, inner-lateral view (IY234-024); l, MMMC4866, paratype, KCY-5, outer-lateral view (IY235-004); m, MMMC4867, paratype, KCY-5, inner-lateral view (IY235-006). Scale bars 100 μm.

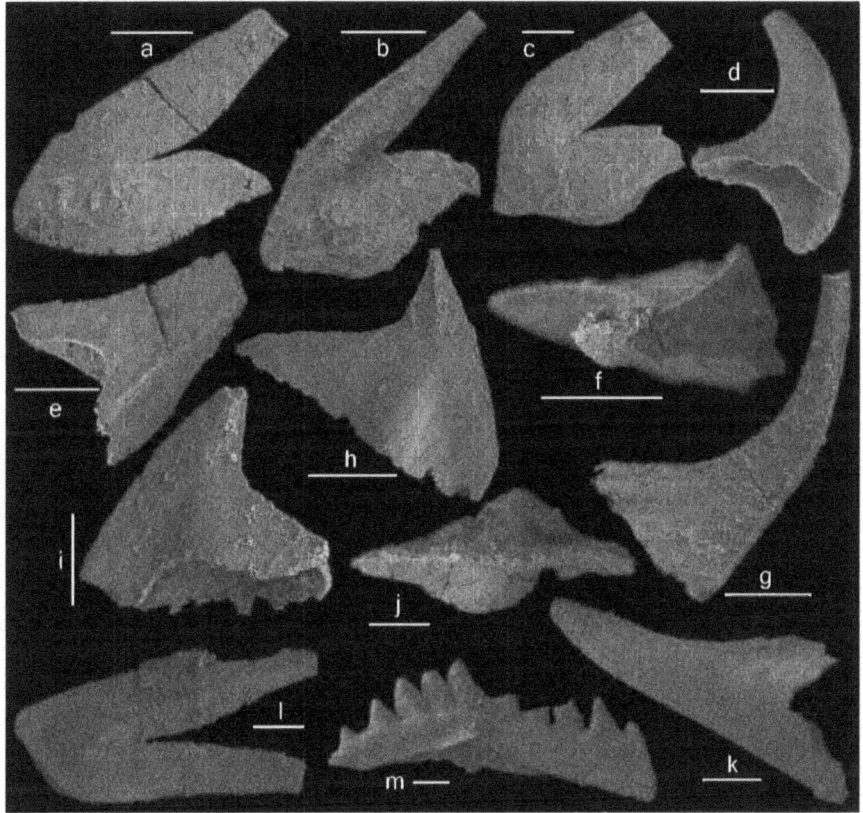

Figure 8. a-k, *Nordiodus italicus* Serpagli, 1967. From sample CWZ-1. a-c, M element; a, MMMC4795, anterior view (IY243-021); b, MMMC4796, posterior view (IY243-022); c, MMMC4797, anterior view (IY243-015). d-g, Sb element; d, MMMC4798, basal-inner-lateral view (IY243-024); e, MMMC4799, outer-lateral view (IY243-026); f, MMMC4800, upper view (IY243-027); g, MMMC4801, inner-lateral view (IY243-025). h-j, P element; h, MMMC4802, outer-lateral view (IY243-016); i, MMMC4803, inner-lateral view (IY243-019); j, MMMC4804, upper view (IY243-014). k, Sc element, MMMC4805, outer-lateral view (IY253-002). l, *Paroistodus? nowlani* Zhen, Webby and Barnes, 1999, M element, MMMC4806, KCY-5, anterior view (IY253-002). m, *Yaoxianognathus* sp., Pa element, MMMC4807, KCY-1, anterior view (IY253-002). Scale bars 100 µm.

44-45, pl. 8, figs 1a-10c (= Sb element).
Acodus trigonius aequilateralis Serpagli, 1967, p. 45, pl. 8, figs 11a-c (= Sa element).
"Oistodus" rhodesi Serpagli 1967, pp. 81-82, pl. 19, figs 13a-18d (= M element).
Nordiodus italicus Serpagli, 1967, pp. 77-78, pl. 19, figs 7a-12c (= Pb element); Clark et al., 1981, p. W144, fig. 92.2a-c; Ferretti, 1998, p. 133, pl. 1, fig. 18a-b.

Material

17 specimens from sample CWZ-1 at Gray Creek locality and two specimens from sample CWZ-2 at Gray Creek bank locality (see Table 1).

Description

Four albid coniform morphotypes, assigned to the M, Sb, Sc and P elements with a deep basal cavity

102

Proc. Linn. Soc. N.S.W., 137, 2015

that likely represent a single species, were recovered from a bulk sample collected from limestone exposed in Gray Creek. The M element is geniculate makellate and strongly compressed antero-posteriorly, bearing a robust cusp and an outer-laterally extended base with a gently arched upper margin and a wavy basal margin in the anterior or posterior view (Fig. 8a-c). The cusp is recurved outer-laterally and also distally slightly bent inward with sharp inner-lateral and outer-lateral margins and smooth anterior and posterior faces. The Sb element is strongly asymmetrical with a proclined cusp and a posteriorly weakly extended base (Fig. 8d-g). The cusp is more or less triangular in cross section (Fig. 8f) with sharp anterior and posterior margins, a flat and smooth inner lateral face and a convex outer-lateral face bearing a sharp blade-like antero-lateral costa (Fig. 8e). The anterior margin is often flexed inward (Fig. 8g). The asymmetrical Sc element is strongly compressed laterally with sharp anterior and posterior margins, and smooth lateral faces, the outer lateral face more convex (Fig. 8k). The P element is asymmetrical and laterally compressed with a small, suberect cusp, and a large, antero-posteriorly extended base with a deep basal cavity (Fig. 8h-j). The cusp is more or less triangular in outline in lateral view (Fig. 8h) with sharp anterior and posterior margins and a broad median carina. The base is flared in the median potion and tapers distally (Fig. 8j) with a posterior extension, which is triangular in outline in lateral view with straight upper and basal margins (Fig. 8h-i).

Discussion

The P and Sb elements in the material from North Queensland are comparable with type material of this species defined herein as representing the Pb (Serpagli, 1967, pp. 77-78, pl. 19, figs 7a-12c), and the Sb (Serpagli 1967, pp. 44-45, pl. 8, figs 1a-10c) elements. The M element of this species in our collection is also comparable with some of the illustrated M elements (Serpagli 1967, pp. 81-82, pl. 19, fig. 13a-d), but other illustrated type specimens show a prominent costa on both anterior and posterior faces (Serpagli 1967, pp. 81-82, pl. 19, figs 14a-18d).

Genus PERIODON Hadding, 1913

Type species
Periodon aculeatus Hadding, 1913.

Periodon grandis (Ethington, 1959)
Fig. 9m-o

Synonymy

Loxognathus grandis Ethington, 1959, p. 281, pl. 40, fig. 6.
Periodon grandis (Ethington); Bergström and Sweet, 1966, pp. 363-365, pl. 30, figs 1-8 (*cum syn.*); Lindström, in Ziegler, 1981, p. 243-244, pl. 1, figs 13-18; ?McCracken and Nowlan, 1989, p. 1889, pl. 3, figs 7-9; Bergström, 1990, p. 11, pl. 3, fig. 7; Zhang and Chen, 1992, pl. 1, figs 13-16; Ding et al. in Wang, 1993, p. 190, pl. 35, figs 18-21; Fowler and Iwata, 1995, *partim* only fig. 2.1, 2.4-2.5; ?Trotter and Webby, 1995, p. 484, pl. 4, figs 13-14, 27-28; Zhen and Webby, 1995, p. 284, pl. 4, figs 3-4; Stouge and Rasmussen, 1996, pp. 62-63, pl. 1, fig. 19; Furey-Greig, 1999, pp. 310-311, pl. 2, figs 1-2; Zhen et al., 1999, pl. 4, figs 19-21; Talent et al., 2002, pl. 1, figs F-G; Zhen et al., 2003, pp. 41-43, fig. 6D-L; ?Nowlan, 2002, p. 195, pl. 1, figs 32-37; ?Tolmacheva and Roberts, 2007, fig. 4G-H; Ortega et al., 2008, fig. 6.14; Tolmacheva et al., 2009, pp. 1506-1509, figs 4, 5a-5o; Wang et al., 2011, pp. 198-199, pl. 84, figs 16-19; Zhang, 2011, fig. 20.10-20.12; Zhang, 2013, fig. 11.1-11.4.

Material

Four specimens from four samples at Kaos Gully locality and one doubtfully assigned specimen from sample CWZ-1 at Gray Creek locality (see Table 1).

Discussion

Periodon grandis is the youngest known species of the genus, whose skeletal species construction has been well-established as consisting of a seximembrate or septimembrate apparatus. According to Bergström and Sweet (1966, p. 365) and Lindström (in Ziegler 1981, p. 243), it can be distinguished from its likely direct ancestor, *P. aculeatus*, mainly by the M element having a large, subtriangular base with an essentially straight basal margin and by developing a greater number of smaller denticles between the cusp and the largest denticle on the posterior process of the S elements. However, Zhang and Chen (1992, fig. 1, table 1) indicated that the shape of the base and basal margin of the M element were variable among specimens referable to *P. grandis*, and suggested that it could be differentiated from *P. aculeatus* using the following criteria: *P. grandis* has more than nine denticles between the cusp and the largest denticle on the posterior process of the S elements, displays five to seven denticles along the inner-lateral margin of the M element, and has four to six denticles on the anterior process of the P elements.

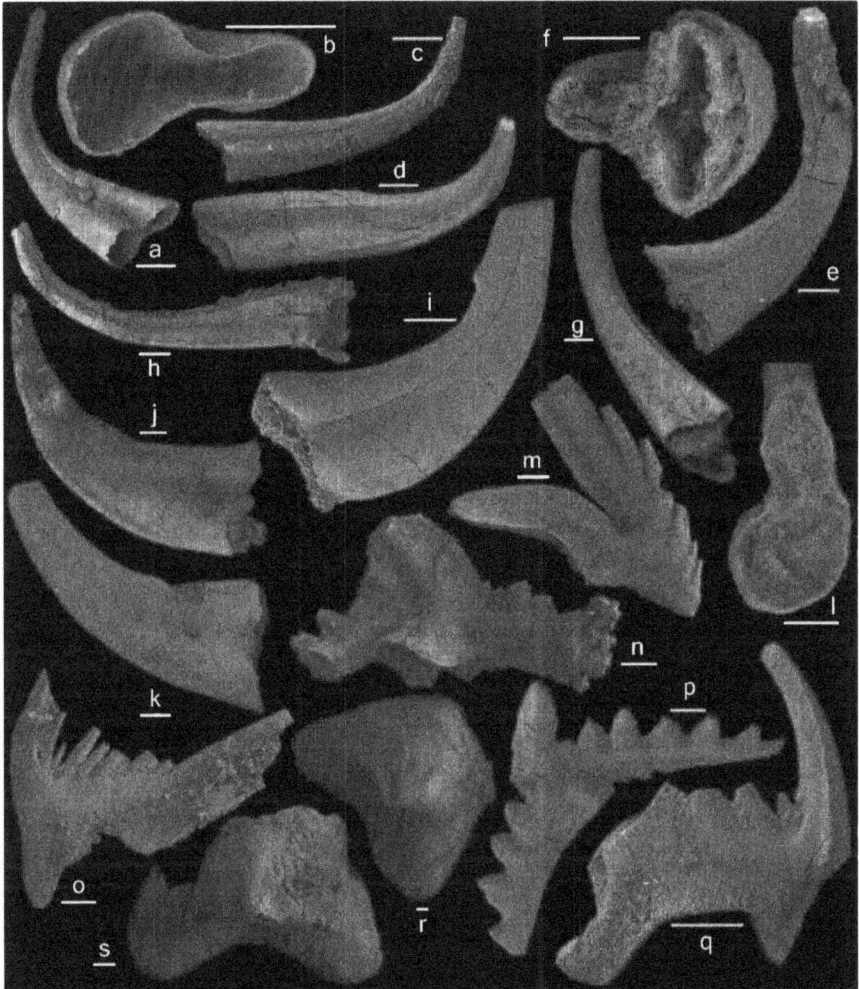

Figure 9. a-h, *Panderodus gracilis* (Branson and Mehl, 1933). a-d, similiform element, a-b, MMMC4808, KAOS-42.2, a, outer-lateral view (IY244-012), b, basal view (IY244-013); c, MMMC4809, KCY-5, outer-lateral view (IY237-015); d, MMMC4810, KCY-5, inner-lateral view (IY237-013). e, falciform element, MMMC4811, KAOS-42.2, outer-lateral view (IY244-011); f-h, symmetrical ae element, f-g, MMMC4812, KCY-5, f, basal view (IY244-007), g, postero-lateral view (IY244-005). h, MMMC4813, KAOS-42.6, postero-lateral view (IY240-014). i, *Panderodus nodus* Zhen, Webby and Barnes, 1999. Long-based element, MMMC4814, KCY-5, outer-lateral view (IY237-011). j-l, *Panderodus* sp. j, MMMC4815, KAOS-18.2, inner-lateral view (IY238-007); k-l, MMMC4816, KAOS-18.2, k, outer-lateral view (IY240-022), l, basal view (IY240-021). m-o, *Periodon grandis* (Ethington, 1959). m, M element, MMMC4817, KCY-5, posterior view (IY233-003); n, Pa element, MMMC4818, KCY-5, inner-lateral view (IY236-019); o, Sc element, MMMC4819, KAOS-47.1, outer-lateral view (IY238-018). p-q, *Phragmodus undatus* Branson and Mehl, 1933. p, Pa element, MMMC4820, KCY-1, posterior view (IY238-009); q, Sb element, MMMC4821, KCY-1, outer-lateral view (IY243-030). r-s, *Pseudooneotodus mitratus* (Moskalenko, 1973). r, MMMC4822, KAOS-48.2, upper view (IY239-011); s, MMMC4823, KAOS-47.1, upper view (IY239-004). Scale bars 100 μm.

104

Proc. Linn. Soc. N.S.W., 137, 2015

Periodon grandis is relatively rare in allochthonous limestones within the Wairuna Formation, and morphology of the M element suggests that it represents an advanced form of the species (see Zhang and Chen 1992, fig. 1).

Genus PROTOPANDERODUS Lindström, 1971

Type species
Acontiodus rectus Lindström, 1955.

Discussion
Under the currently accepted concept of the genus, *Protopanderodus* includes three groups of species, represented by bicostate coniform species (such as the type species, *P. rectus*), multicostate species (such as *P. calceatus* and *P. liripipus*), and denticulate and multicostate species (represented by only one species, *P. insculptus*).

Protopanderodus insculptus (Branson and Mehl, 1933)
Fig. 10a-o

Synonymy
Phragmodus insculptus Branson and Mehl, 1933, *partim* only p. 124, pl. 10, figs 32-33; non fig. 34 = ?Pb element of *Protopanderodus varicostatus* (Sweet and Bergström, 1962).
Protopanderodus insculptus (Branson and Mehl); Palmieri, 1978, p. 25, pl. 2, figs 26, ?27-29, text-fig. 4.10; Harris et al., 1979, pl. 4, fig. 2; An et al., 1981, pl. 1, fig. 26; An, 1981, pl. 3, fig. 28; Lenz and McCracken, 1982, *partim* only pl. 1, figs 15-16; Zeng et al., 1983, pl. 12, fig. 37; Wang and Luo, 1984, pp. 277-278, pl. 8, figs 4-5; Lin et al., 1984, pl. 2, fig. 10; An et al., 1985, pl. 11, fig. 18; An, 1987, p. 172, pl. 11, figs 16, 23, pl. 15, fig. 21; Ni and Li, 1987, p. 431, pl. 60, fig. 54; McCracken, 1989, pp. 16-18, *partim* only text-fig. 3o-p (denticulate); not pl. 3, figs 9-14, 17, 19, text-fig. 3k-n (adenticulate) (*cum syn.*); Trotter and Webby, 1995, p. 485, pl. 4, figs 1, 7-8, 10-11, ?9, ?12; Zhen et al., 1999, pp. 90, 92, fig. 9.6-9.9; Sweet, 2000, fig. 9.21-9.22; Talent et al., 2002, pl. 1, figs L-N; Zhang and Barnes, 2007a, pp. 503-504, fig. 8.11-8.15; ?Kaljo et al., 2008, fig. 8N; Wang et al., 2011, p. 210, pl. 89, figs 13-17, pl. 160, fig. 22.
Protopanderodus aff. *P. insculptus* (Branson and Mehl); Nowlan et al., 1997, *partim*, only fig. 2.10.

Material
91 specimens from 23 samples at Kaos Gully locality (see Table 1).

Diagnosis
Denticulate and multicostate species of *Protopanderodus* consisting of a seximembrate (or possibly septimembrate) ramiform-ramiform apparatus including nongeniculate makellate M1 and M2 elements with a smooth convex anterior face, a costate posterior face and an outer-laterally inclined single denticle on the outer-lateral process, and multicostate S and P elements with two strong costae separated by a deep groove on each lateral side, and with a reclined-recurved single denticle on the posterior process; S elements forming a symmetry transition series from symmetrical Sa and asymmetrical Sb, to strongly asymmetrical and laterally compressed Sc elements; P element similar to S elements, but developing a prominent antero-basal corner, which is triangular in outline in lateral view.

Description
The M elements are nongeniculate and ramiform bearing an outer-laterally reclined cusp with sharp inner-lateral and outer-lateral margins, and an outer-laterally extended base with a wavy basal margin and a non-extended inner-lateral corner; they are antero-posteriorly compressed with an acostate and more convex anterior face, and a multicostate posterior face (Fig. 10a-d). Located near the distal end of the long outer-lateral process is a single denticle, which is variable in size, separated from the cusp by a wide U-shaped gap, and strongly recurved outer-laterally. The M1 element has two weakly developed costae separated by a weak and shallow groove on the posterior face (Fig. 10a-b); the M2 element (fig. 10c-d) has two strongly developed costae separated by a deeper groove and often with short secondary costae developed towards outer-lateral margin (fig. 10c).

The S elements are ramiform bearing a robust multicostate cusp and a long posterior process, which bears a single denticle near the distal end. The cusp and the denticle on the posterior process are laterally compressed with sharp anterior and posterior margins. The cusp is reclined distally with two sharp costae separated by a deep and open groove on each lateral side. The denticle is strongly recurved posteriorly, variable in size, and separated from the cusp by a wide U-shaped gap. Three types of S elements have been recognized, forming a symmetry transition series. The Sa element is symmetrical and biconvex (Fig. 10e-f). The Sb element is similar to the Sa element, but asymmetrical with a more convex outer lateral face (Fig. 10g-j). The Sc element is strongly asymmetrical with anterior margin more antero-basally extended and inner-laterally flexed (Fig. 10k-n).

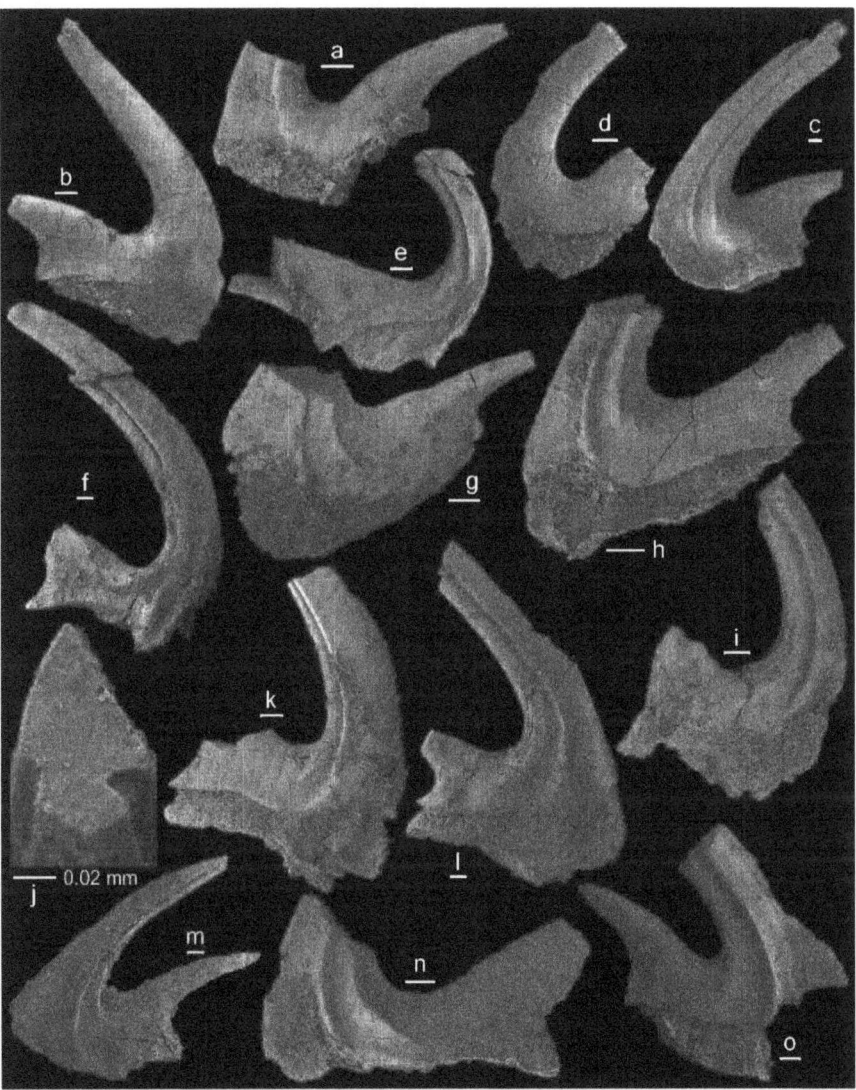

Figure 10. *Protopanderodus insculptus* (Branson and Mehl, 1933). a-b, M1 element; a, MMMC4824, KCY-5, posterior view (IY234-015); b, MMMC4825, KCY-5, anterior view (IY234-014). c-d, M2 element; c, MMMC4826, KAOS-47.1, posterior view (IY238-024); d, MMMC4827, KAOS-47.1, anterior view (IY238-025). e-f, Sa element; e, MMMC4828, KAOS-43.9, lateral view (IY244-018); f, MMMC4829, KAOS-48.2, lateral view (IY239-013). g-j, Sb element; g, MMMC4830, KAOS-48.2, outer-lateral view (IY244-005); h, MMMC4831, KCY-5, inner-lateral view (IY234-016); i, MMMC4832, KCY-5, inner-lateral view (IY234-021); j, MMMC4833, KAOS-44.8, upper view, close-up showing cross section of cusp (IY243-033). k-n, Sc element; k, MMMC4834, KAOS-47.1, outer-lateral view (IY239-003); l, MMMC4835, KAOS-47.1, inner-lateral view (IY239-002); m, MMMC4836, KAOS-48.2, outer-lateral view (IY239-017); n, MMMC4837, KAOS-47.1, inner-lateral view (IY239-001); o, P element, MMMC4838, KAOS-43.9, outer-lateral view (IY242-008). Scale bars 100 μm unless otherwise indicated.

The P element is similar to Sc element, but weakly asymmetrical with a prominent antero-basal corner, which is strongly antero-basally extended and more or less triangular in outline in lateral view (Fig. 10o).

Discussion

Protopanderodus insculptus is characterized by having a single denticle on all the constituent elements, that is on the outer-lateral process of the M element and on the posterior process of the S and P elements. Among the three cotypes illustrated by Branson and Mehl (1933), two (Branson and Mehl 1933, pl. 10, figs 32-33; the specimen figured in pl. 10, fig. 32 is selected herein as the lectotype), although rather poorly preserved, showed the appearance of this distinctive denticle. However, the other cotype exhibits a posteriorly less extended base without the denticle, and has a suberect cusp and short base with strongly recurved basal margin. This specimen most likely represents the Pb element of *Protopanderodus varicostatus* (Sweet and Bergström 1962). This latter species was recently revised as consisting of a septimembrate apparatus, based on the topotype material from the Pratt Ferry Formation of Alabama (Zhen et al. 2011).

McCracken (1989) revised *P. insculptus* according to the multielement concept as consisting of a quinquimembrate species apparatus including both denticulate and adenticulate elements. Although this species definition was subsequently accepted by some authors, An (1987, p. 172) recognized a scandodiform element assignable to the M position of this species (also confirmed from central NSW: Zhen et al. 1999, fig. 9.8-9.9 = M2), and suggested that *P. insculptus* should include only denticulate elements. Relatively abundant material of this species from the allochthonous limestones within the Wairuna Formation, with six denticulate morphotypes recognized representing the M1, M2, Sa, Sb, Sc and P elements, strongly supports this latter view. Therefore, the species definition of *P. insculptus* is revised herein as consisting of a seximembrate (or possibly septimembrate, if the Pa and Pb elements can be differentiated) ramiform-ramiform apparatus including only denticulate elements.

Protopanderodus liripipus Kennedy, Barnes and Uyeno, 1979
Figs 11a-o, 12a-l

Synonymy

Scolopodus insculptus (Branson and Mehl); Bergström and Sweet, 1966, pp. 398-400, pl. 34,

figs 26-27, text-fig. 13B.
Scolopodus? insculptus (Branson and Mehl); Serpagli, 1967, pp. 97-99, pl. 28, figs 1a-6b.
Protopanderodus insculptus (Branson and Mehl); Dzik, 1976, fig. 16h, k.
Protopanderodus liripipus Kennedy, Barnes and Uyeno, 1979, pp. 546-550, pl. 1, figs 9-19; An, 1981, pl. 3, fig. 29; An et al., 1981, pl. 1, figs 16-17; Nowlan, 1981, p. 14, pl. 5, figs 6-8; An and Ding, 1982, pl. 2, figs 4, 13; Zeng et al., 1983, pl. 12, fig. 34; Burrett et al., 1983, p. 184, fig. 9A and B; Chen and Zhang, 1984, p. 129, pl. 2, figs 22-24; Wang and Lou, 1984, p. 278, pl. 8, figs 6-10; An and Xu, 1984, pl. 1, fig. 21; An et al., 1985, pl. 12, figs 5-9; Savage and Bassett, 1985, p. 708, pl. 86, fig. 15; An, 1987, p. 173, pl. 11, figs 4, 11-14; Ding, 1987, pl. 5, fig. 28; Nowlan and McCracken, in Nowlan et al., 1988, p. 29, pl. 11, figs 18, 20 (*cum syn.*); Chen and Zhang, 1989, pl. 4, figs 26, ?27; McCracken, 1989, pp. 18-20, pl. 3, figs 15-16, 18, 20-25, text-fig. 3G-J (*cum syn.*); McCracken and Nowlan, 1989, p. 1890, pl. 4, fig. 1; An and Zheng, 1990, pl. 6, figs ?5, 9-10; Bergström, 1990, pl. 2, figs 7-8, pl. 4, figs 1-4; Duan, 1990, pl. 3, figs 2, 4; Gao, 1991, p. 135, pl. 12, fig. 8; Ding et al. in Wang, 1993, p. 195, pl. 38, fig. 17; Dzik, 1994, pp. 74-75, pl. 14, figs 6-7, text-fig. 11c; Trotter and Webby, 1995, p. 485, pl. 4, figs 2-6; Stouge and Rasmussen, 1996, p. 63, pl. 1, fig. 18; Zhen et al., 1999, p. 92, fig. 9.10-9.13 (*cum syn.*); Leslie, 2000, p. 1125, fig. 6.19-6.24; Zhao et al., 2000, p. 217, pl. 20, figs 1-2, 5, 7, 10-13; McCracken, 2000, pl. 3, fig. 10; Pyle and Barnes, 2001, pl. 2, figs 6-7; Wang, 2001, pl. 1, fig. 12; Wang and Qi, 2001, pl. 1, figs 5, 22; Talent et al., 2002, pl. 1, figs H-J; Agematsu et al., 2007, p. 29, fig. 13.4-13.5, 13.8, 13.10 (*cum syn.*); Zhang and Barnes, 2007a, p. 505, fig. 8.7-8.10; Agematsu et al., 2008, p. 969, fig. 12.23-12.28; Zhen et al., 2011, pp. 243-245, fig. 23C-E; Zhang, 2011, fig. 20.15-20.16; Zhang, 2013, fig. 11.21-11.22; Bergström and Ferretti, 2015, fig. 13A-C.

Material

572 specimens from 32 samples at Kaos Gully locality (see Table 1).

Diagnosis

A multicostate coniform species of *Protopanderodus* consisting of a septimembrate apparatus including nongeniculate makellate M elements bearing a robust suberect cusp with a smooth and more convex anterior face and a costate

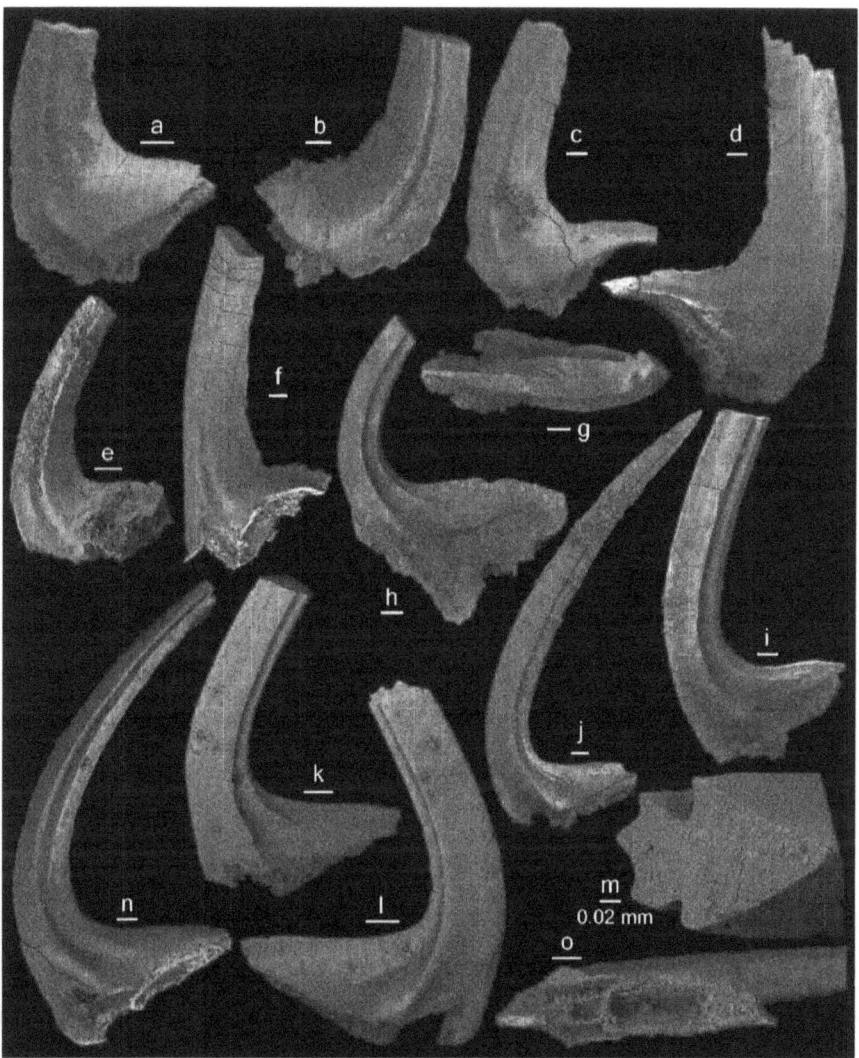

Figure 11. *Protopanderodus liripipus* Kennedy, Barnes and Uyeno, 1979. a-e, M1 element; a, MMMC4839, KCY-5, posterior view (IY233-031); b, MMMC4840, KCY-5, posterior view (IY233-030); c, MMMC4841, KCY-5, posterior view (IY233-028); d, MMMC4842, KAOS-43.9, anterior view (IY244-017); e, MMMC4843, KCY-5, posterior view (IY233-026); f, M2 element; MMMC4844, KAOS-39.3, posterior view (IY244-009). g-j, Sa element; g-h, MMMC4845, KAOS-43.9, g, upper-posterior view (IY242-009), h, lateral view (IY242-010); i, MMMC4846, KAOS-43.9, lateral view (IY242-013); j, MMMC4847, KCY-5, lateral view (IY233-025). k-o, Sb element; k-m, MMMC4848, KCY-5, k, inner-lateral view (IY233-021), l, outer-lateral view (IY233-023), m, upper view, close-up showing cross section of cusp (IY233-019); n-o, MMMC4849, KCY-5, n, outer-lateral view (IY233-024), o, basal view (IY233-020). Scale bars 100 μm unless otherwise indicated.

posterior face, and an outer-laterally extended base; multicostate S and P elements typically bearing two strong costae separated by a deep groove on each lateral side of the cusp and a long and distally tapering posteriorly-extended base; S elements forming a symmetry transition series from symmetrical Sa to asymmetrical Sb and Sc elements; P elements with a strongly developed antero-basal extension, which is triangular in outline in lateral view.

Description

The M elements (Fig. 11a-f) are nongeniculate, bearing a robust, outer-laterally more or less suberect cusp with sharp inner-lateral and outer-lateral margins, and an outer-laterally extended base with a wavy basal margin; they are antero-posteriorly compressed with an acostate and more convex anterior face, and a multicostate posterior face characterized by a prominent median groove between two costae (Fig. 11a-c, e-f). The costae and groove vary from weakly (Fig. 11a, c) to strongly developed (Fig. 11e). The posterior extension of the base varies from short (Fig. 11a) to relatively long and low (Fig. 11c-d, f). The M1 element has a gently rounded antero-basal corner (Fig. 11a-e), while the M2 element (Fig. 11f) has a basally extended, anticusp-like antero-basal extension.

The S elements are multicostate, bearing a robust, distally reclined cusp with two sharp costae separated by a deep groove on each lateral face, and a base with a long, distally tapering posterior extension and a short anticusp-like antero-basal extension. The median groove and its bordering costae on each lateral face are located slightly towards the posterior margin (Fig. 11m). The Sa element is symmetrical and biconvex bearing a basally suberect and distally reclined cusp with sharp anterior and posterior margins (Fig. 11g-j). The Sb element is similar to the Sa element, but asymmetrical with a more convex outer lateral face (Fig. 11k-o). The Sc element (Fig. 12a-e) is strongly asymmetrical with a longer posterior process and with the small anticusp-like antero-basal extension often slightly flexed inward (Fig. 12b).

The P elements are similar to S elements, but with a long anticusp-like antero-basal extension of the base (Fig. 12f-l). The Pa element has a more strongly reclined cusp with the angle of about 50-60⁰ between the posterior margin of the cusp and the upper margin of the posterior extension of the base (Fig. 12f-i). The Pb element (Fig. 12j-l) has a suberect cusp, which is distally bowed inward (Fig. 12k), and a strongly extended antero-basal corner, which is triangular in outline in lateral view (Fig. 12j, l).

Discussion

Kennedy et al. (1979) established *P. liripipus* as consisting of a quadrimembrate apparatus including four elements, which are interpreted herein as representing the M (= scandodiform), Sa (=symmetrical), Sb (= slightly asymmetrical), and Sc (= markedly asymmetrical) elements. Kennedy et al. (1979, p. 547) described the markedly asymmetrical element as having "two costae on one side and one on the other". However, no comparable specimens of the Sc element were present in our collections, and therefore the markedly asymmetrical element described by Kennedy et al. (1979) is interpreted herein as representing an atypical variant. All Sc elements as defined herein from the Wairuna Formation limestones have two sharp costae separated by a deep groove on both lateral faces (Fig. 12a-e). One illustrated paratype (Kennedy et al. 1979, pl. 1, figs 10-11) exhibits a long base and an inwardly flexed antero-basal corner, and is more comparable with the Sc element defined and illustrated herein, but some specimens illustrated by Kennedy et al. (1979) as representing the slightly asymmetrical element (Kennedy et al. 1979, pl. 1, fig. 16) and markedly asymmetrical element (Kennedy et al. 1979, pl. 1, fig. 17) exhibited a shorter base and lacked the anticusp-like antero-basal extension developed in S elements in our collection. Zhen et al. (2011) suggested that material previously ascribed to *P. liripipus* from eastern Gondwana and peri-Gondwana exhibited a prominent anticusp-like antero-basal extension, and might represent a separate species. However, Kennedy et al. (1979) and McCracken (1989) included in the S elements of *P. liripipus* forms showing wider variations in respect to the number and position of the costae (as discussed above), length of the posterior extension of the base, and the development of the anticusp-like antero-basal extension. This wide variation among the type material was illustrated by the holotype and several paratypes (Kennedy et al. 1979, pl. 1, fig. 14, 16, 17) that appear to lack the anticusp-like antero-basal extension, compared to other paratypes (Kennedy et al. 1979, pl. 1, figs 9, 11, 13) that exhibit such an extension. Specimens of *P. liripipus* illustrated by McCracken (1989) from the northern Yukon Territory of Canada also included some with a prominent anticusp-like antero-basal extension (McCracken 1989, pl. 3, fig. 21), but most others display a more or less regularly curved basal margin in lateral view (McCracken1989, pl. 3, figs 15-16, 18, 22-24). Pa and Pb elements from the north Queensland samples are asymmetrical, characterized by having a strongly developed antero-basal extension (Fig. 12f-l), comparable with the P

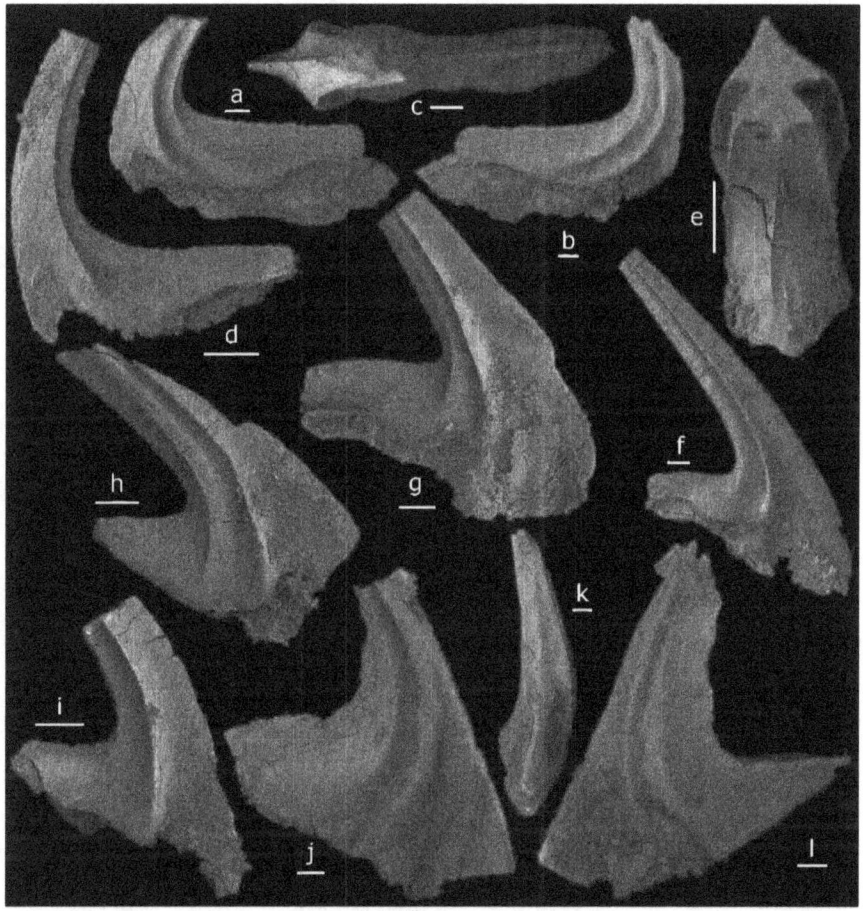

Figure 12. *Protopanderodus liripipus* Kennedy, Barnes and Uyeno, 1979. a-e, Sc element; a-c, MMMC4850, KCY-5, a, outer-lateral view (IY234-011), b, inner-lateral view (IY234-012), c, upper view (IY234-010); d, MMMC4851, KCY-5, outer-lateral view (IY234-009); e, MMMC4852, KCY-5, upper-posterior view (IY233-011). f-i, Pa element; f, MMMC4853, KCY-5, inner-lateral view (IY234-007); g, MMMC4854, KCY-5, outer-lateral view (IY234-006); h, MMMC4855, KCY-5, outer-lateral view (IY233-013); i, MMMC4856, KAOS-47.1, outer-lateral view (IY244-002). j-l, Pb element, MMMC4857, KAOS-45.6, j, inner-lateral view (IY238-019), k, anterior view (IY238-020), l, outer-lateral view (IY238-021). Scale bars 100 μm.

elements recognized in *P. insculptus* (Fig. 10o), and also in the likely ancestor, *P. varicostatus* (see Zhen et al. 2011, fig. 22N-O, referred to as Sd but herein reinterpreted as a Pa element).

P. liripipus differs from *P. insculptus* in lacking a denticle, and is distinguished from *P. varicostatus* by having a longer, distally tapering posterior extension

(S and P elements) and outer-lateral extension of the base (M element).

Genus SCABBARDELLA Orchard, 1980

Type species

Drepanodus altipes Henningsmoen, 1948 (amended by Orchard, 1980).

110

Proc. Linn. Soc. N.S.W., 137, 2015

Scabbardella altipes (Henningsmoen, 1948) amend.
Orchard, 1980
Figs 13-15

Synonymy

Drepanodus altipes Henningsmoen, 1948, p. 420, pl. 25, fig. 14 (drepanodiform = Sc element); Wang and Lou, 1984, p. 257, pl. 2, figs 3-4, 15, 17.
Scabbardella altipes (Henningsmoen); Orchard, 1980, p. 26, pl. 5, figs 2-5, 7-8, 12, 14, 18, 20, 23-24, 28, 30, 33, 35, text-fig. 4C (*cum syn.*); Nowlan, 1983, p. 668, pl. 1, figs 6-7, 11-14; Chen and Zhang, 1984, pl. 2, figs 29-30; Ni and Li, 1987, p. 437, pl. 55, figs 19-20, pl. 59, figs 21-22, 31-32; McCracken, 1987, pl. 2, figs 1-9, 11-13; Nowlan and McCracken, in Nowlan et al., 1988, p. 36, pl. 16, figs 7-20, pl. 17, figs 1-3, 5-6, 8-9 (*cum syn.*); Chen and Zhang, 1989, pl. 5, figs 8-9; non Rasmussen and Stouge, 1989, fig. 3M, P., Q; Bergström, 1990, pl.4, fig. 14; Pohler and Orchard, 1990, pl. 2, fig. 18; Gao, 1991, 137, pl. 12, fig. 18; Ferretti and Serpagli, 1991, pl. 2, figs 12-14; Leone et al., 1991, pl. 1, figs 14-15; Bergström and Massa, 1992, p. 1339, pl. 1, figs 1, 3, 4; Ding et al. in Wang, 1993, 199, pl. 12, figs 26-27; Dzik, 1994, pp. 64-66, pl. 11, figs 36-39, text-fig. 6e; Trotter and Webby, 1995, p. 487, pl. 3, figs 1-6, 8-11; Stouge and Rasmussen, 1996, p. 63, pl. 1, figs 1-6 (*cum syn.*); Wang et al., 1996, pl. 1, fig. 18; Ferretti and Barnes, 1997, p. 34, pl. 1, figs 17-22 (*cum syn.*); Nowlan et al., 1997, fig. 2.21-2.22; Wang and Zhou, 1998, pl. 2, fig. 3; Ferretti and Serpagli, 1999, pl. 2, figs 17-23; Leslie, 2000, fig. 3.36-3.37; Sweet, 2000, fig. 9.14-9.15; Zhao et al., 2000, p. 221-222, pl. 23, figs 10-12; Rasmussen, 2001, p. 130, pl. 17, figs 4-5; Talent et al., 2002, pl. 1, fig. P, ?fig. O; Agematsu et al., 2007, p. 29-30, fig. 11.4, 11.8-11.10, 11.12-11.17 (*cum syn.*); Zhang and Barnes, 2007a, p. 505, fig. 8.16-8.20; Agematsu et al., 2008, p. 969, fig. 10.25-10.34; Tolmacheva et al., 2009, pp. 1509-1510, fig. 6a-6e, 6h; Rodríguez-Cañero et al., 2010, fig. 5.9-5.12; Zhen et al., 2011, p. 252, fig. 9D-O (*cum syn.*); Wang, et al., 2011, p. 225, pl. 95, figs 6-12, pl. 179, figs 1-4; Ferretti et al., 2014a, fig. 13N-P; Ferretti et al., 2014b, fig. 3S-U; Bagnoli and Qi, 2014, pl. 4, figs 13-14; Bergström and Ferretti, 2015, fig. 11-M.
Scabbardella sp. cf. *S. altipes* (Henningsmoen); Zhen et al., 1999, p. 94, figs 9.16-9.19, 10.1-10.9, 10.23.
Dapsilodus similaris (Rhodes); An, 1981, pl. 3, figs 4-5; An and Ding, 1982, pl. 1, figs 17-18; An et al., 1983, p. 91, pl. 15, fig. 22; An and Xu, 1984, pl. 1, figs 8, 15; An et al., 1985, pl. 11, figs 9-10, 13-14; Ding, 1987, pl. 5, fig. 23; Duan, 1990, pl. 3, figs 13-15.
Scabbardella similaris (Rhodes); An, 1987, pp. 179-180, pl. 5, figs 14-17, 19-24, 26-27; Ding et al. in Wang, 1993, p. 199, pl. 17, figs 22-28.

Material

836 specimens from 37 samples at Kaos Gully locality and seven specimens from sample CWZ-2 at Gray Creek bank locality (see Table 1).

Diagnosis

A species of *Scabbardella* consisting of a seximembrate apparatus, including drepanodiform long-based M1 and short-based M2 elements with smooth lateral faces, distacodiform long-based Sa and short-based Sd elements with a broad carina or a prominent costa bordering a deep and narrow groove on each lateral side, and acodiform long-based Sb and short-based Sc elements with a smooth inner-lateral face and a broad carina or a prominent costa bordering a deep and narrow groove on the outer-lateral face; all elements laterally compressed and nongeniculate, bearing a procline to suberect cusp with sharp anterior and posterior margins and a base triangular in outline with a non-flared basal cavity of moderate depth.

Description

The drepanodiform M elements (Fig. 13a-j) are weakly asymmetrical, laterally strongly compressed with sharp anterior and posterior margins, and biconvex, typically with outer-lateral face slightly more convex (Fig. 13h). The lateral faces are smooth and broadly rounded, often more sharply thinning towards posterior margin to form a narrow and thin posterior edge (Fig. 13a-d, f, i-j), and more or less spade-like in cross section (Fig. 13d, h). The surface is ornamented with fine striae (Fig. 13e). The M1 element has a long base that is antero-posteriorly less extended (Fig. 13a-e), while the M2 has a short base that is more extended antero-posteriorly (Fig. 13f-j).

The distacodiform Sa element (Fig. 14g-i) is symmetrical or nearly symmetrical and laterally strongly compressed, bearing a suberect cusp with sharp anterior and posterior margins and a long base. The lateral faces have a deep and narrow groove located more towards the posterior margin and a broadly rounded median carina (Fig. 14h-i).

The distacodiform Sd element (Fig. 14j-m) is slightly asymmetrical and laterally strongly compressed, bearing a suberect cusp with sharp

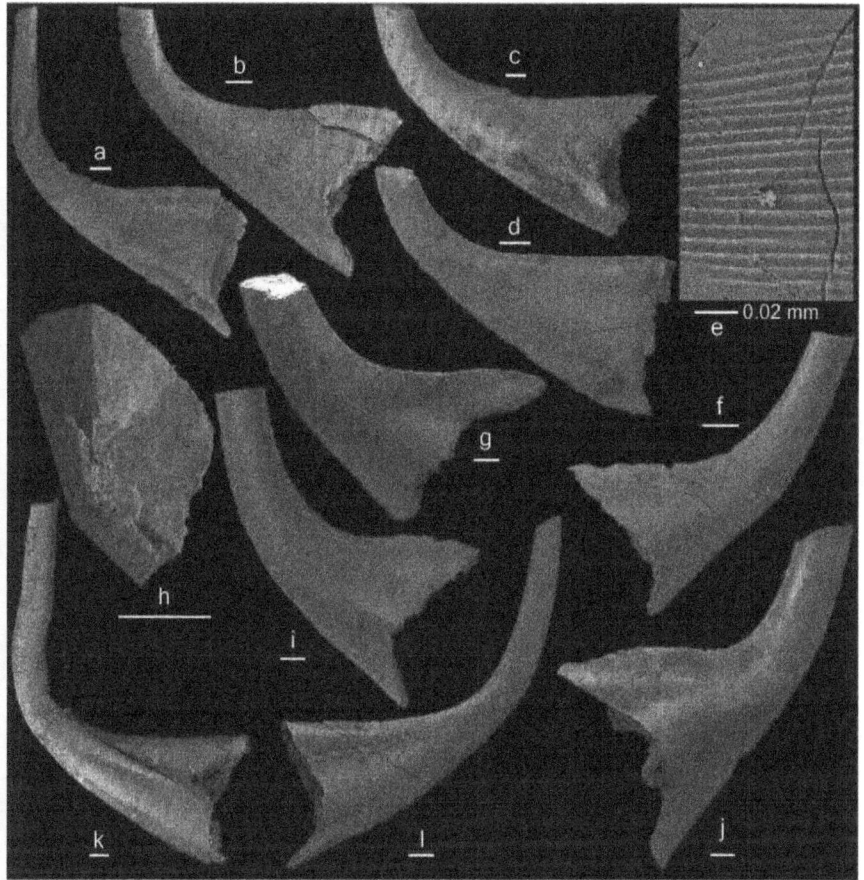

Figure 13. *Scabbardella altipes* (Henningsmoen, 1948). a-e, M1 (long-based drepanodiform) element; a, MMMC4868, KAOS-47.5, inner-lateral view (IY239-006); b, MMMC4869, KAOS-47.5, outer-lateral view (IY239-005); c, MMMC4870, KCY-5, outer-lateral view (IY235-018); d-e, MMMC4871, KCY-5, d, inner-lateral view (IY235-019), e, close up showing surface striation (IY235-020). f-j, M2 (short-based drepanodiform) element; f, MMMC4872, KCY-5, outer-lateral view (IY236-032); g-h, MMMC4873, KCY-5, g, inner-lateral view (IY236-033), h, close-up showing cross section of cusp (IY236-034); i, MMMC4874, KCY-5, inner-lateral view (IY236-010); j, MMMC4875, KCY-5, outer-lateral view (IY236-015). k-l, Sb (long-based acodiform) element; k, MMMC4876, KAOS-41.6, outer-lateral view (IY240-009); l, MMMC4877, KAOS-43.9, outer-lateral view (IY241-005). Scale bars 100 µm unless otherwise indicated.

anterior and posterior margins and a short and antero-posteriorly more extended base. The lateral faces have a sharp costa located more towards the posterior margin (Fig. 14m), and a deep and narrow groove bordering the posterior side of the costa (Fig. 14j). The cusp has a more convex outer-lateral face and

is diamond-shaped in cross section (Fig. 14m). The costa on the lateral faces is more strongly developed around the curvature of the cusp and extends onto the base, but not to the basal margin.

The acodiform Sb element (Figs 13k-l, 15a-f) is asymmetrical and laterally strongly compressed,

112

Proc. Linn. Soc. N.S.W., 137, 2015

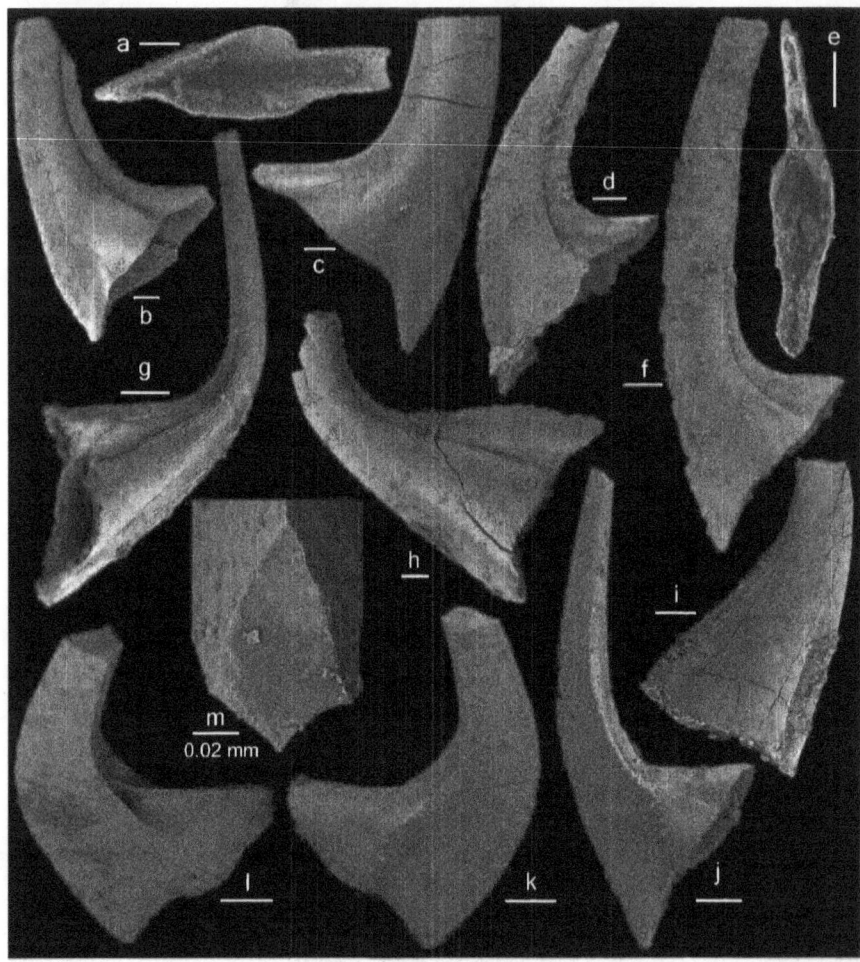

Figure 14. *Scabbardella altipes* (Henningsmoen, 1948). a-f, Sc (short-based acodiform) element; a-b, MMMC4878, KCY-5, a, basal view (IY236-035), b, outer-lateral view (IY236-036); c, MMMC4879, KAOS-41.6, inner-lateral view (IY240-002); d, MMMC4880, KCY-5, outer-lateral view (IY236-020); e, MMMC4881, KAOS-41.6, basal view (IY240-004); f, MMMC4882, KCY-5, outer-lateral view (IY236-019). g-i, Sa (long-based distacodiform) element; g, MMMC4883, KAOS-43.9, lateral view (IY244-015); h, MMMC4884, KAOS-48.2, lateral view (IY239-010); i, MMMC4885, KAOS-48.2, lateral view (IY239-009). j-m, Sd (short-based distacodiform) element; j, MMMC4886, KCY-5, outer-lateral view (IY236-024); k-m, MMMC4887, KCY-5, k, inner-lateral view (IY236-031), l, outer-lateral view (IY236-030), m, upper view, close-up showing cross section of cusp (IY236-029). Scale bars 100 µm unless otherwise indicated.

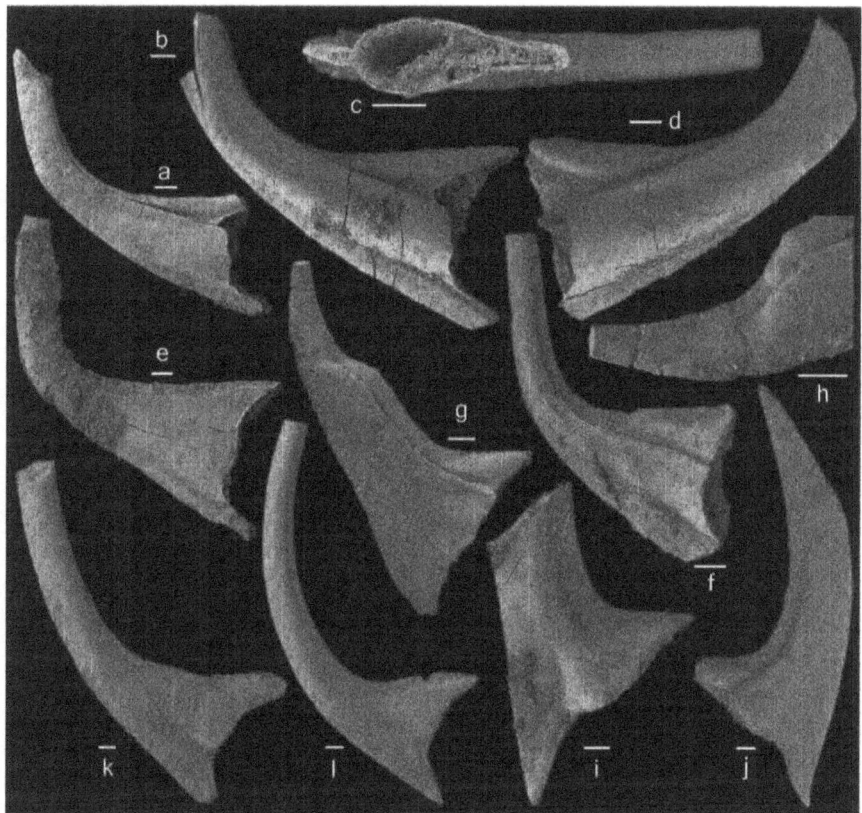

Figure 15. *Scabbardella altipes* (Henningsmoen, 1948). a-f, Sb (long-based acodiform) element; a, MMMC4888, KCY-5, outer-lateral view (IY235-026); b, MMMC4889, KCY-5, outer-lateral view (IY235-024); c, f, MMMC4890, KCY-5, c, basal view (IY235-022), f, outer-lateral view (IY235-021); d, MMMC4891, KCY-5, outer-lateral view (IY235-027); e, MMMC4892, KCY-5, inner-lateral view (IY235-025). g-j, Sc (short-based acodiform) element; g-h, MMMC4893, KAOS-43.9, g, outer-lateral view (IY242-014), h, showing regrowth (pathological repair) of distal part of cusp (IY242-015); i, MMMC4894, KAOS-41.6, inner-lateral view (IY240-008); j, MMMC4895, KAOS-41.6, outer-lateral view (IY240-001). k-l, Sc (medium-based acodiform) element; k, MMMC4896, KCY-5, inner-lateral view (IY236-009); l, MMMC4897, KCY-5, inner-lateral view (IY236-008). Scale bars 100 μm.

bearing a proclined to suberect cusp with sharp anterior and posterior margins and a long base. The inner-lateral face is less convex and smooth (Fig. 15e), and the outer-lateral face is more convex, with a deep, narrow groove located more towards the posterior margin and a broadly rounded median carina to its anterior side (Figs 13k-l, 15f).

The acodiform Sc element (Figs 14a-f, 15k-l) is asymmetrical and laterally strongly compressed,

bearing a suberect or distally reclined cusp with sharp anterior and posterior margins and a short and antero-posteriorly more extended base. The inner-lateral face has a broadly rounded carina (Figs 14c, 15i), and the outer-lateral face is more convex, with a deep and narrow groove located more towards the posterior margin and a broadly rounded median carina to its anterior side (Figs 14b, d, 15j). One specimen (Fig. 15g-h) shows the regrowth of a broken or damaged

114

Proc. Linn. Soc. N.S.W., 137, 2015

distal end of the cusp, demonstrating the capacity of the conodont animal to self-repair damaged parts of the elements.

All elements display well preserved fine surface striae, and also show the gradational change from long-based M1, Sa and Sb elements to short-based M2, Sd and Sc elements respectively (Fig. 15k-l).

Discussion

Scabbardella altipes was originally erected as a form species represented by a drepanodiform element (Henningsmoen 1948, pl. 25, fig. 14) from the Fjacka Shale (*P. linearis* Zone, Katian, Late Ordovician) of Sweden. It was later revised by Orchard (1980) as consisting of six morphotypes including two drepanodiform, two acodiform and two distacodiform elements. Orchard (1980, figs 1, 4) also considered these elements to represent the 'M', 'Sc-Sb' and 'Sa' positions respectively. Following the multielement species concept of Orchard (1980), *S. altipes* is here recognized as consisting of a seximembrate apparatus including long-based drepanodiform (= M1), short-based drepanodiform (= M2), long-based distacodiform (= Sa), short-based distacodiform (= Sd), long-based acodiform (= Sb), and short-based acodiform (= Sc) elements. Although Zhen et al. (2011) acknowledged the existence of a medium-based acodiform element, the abundant material of this species from the Wairuna Formation of north Queensland demonstrates that medium length forms exist in all elements of the species, which vary from long-based to short-based.

Orchard (1980) identified two subspecies representing populations from north England (*S. altipes* subsp. A) and from north Wales (*S. altipes* subsp. B), mainly based on differences of curvature of the cusp and the extension of the base. However, our material shows a wide variation in respect of these two features. Therefore we recognize only a single species *S. altipes* rather than subspecies (e.g. Trotter and Webby 1995) or even two separate species as suggested by some other authors (e.g. Stouge and Rasmussen, 1996).

Distacodiform elements (Sa and Sd) of this species are superficially similar to the S elements of both *Besselodus* (also co-occurring in the Wairuna Formation fauna) and *Dapsilodus*, but can be easily distinguished from those genera. In the collections from Queensland, specimens of *S. altipes* are generally larger in size in comparison with co-occurring *Besselodus fusus* and also *Molloydenticulus bicostatus*. More importantly *S. altipes* differs in having a very different species apparatus, which also

includes drepanodiform M, and acodiform Sb and Sc elements. Furthermore, although specimens of *S. altipes* from the Wairuna Formation exhibit well-developed fine surface striae, apparently no distinctive oblique striations such as those characterizing *Besselodus fusus* were developed along the anterior margins of the S elements of *S. altipes*.

Genus STRACHANOGNATHUS Rhodes, 1955

Type species
Strachanognathus parvus Rhodes, 1955.

Strachanognathus parvus Rhodes, 1955
Fig. 16a-g

Synonymy
Strachanognathus parvus Rhodes, 1955, p. 132, pl. 7, fig. 16, pl. 8, figs 1-4 text-fig. 5; Bergström, 1962, pp. 54-55, pl. 3, figs 1-6, text-figs 2B, 3H-I; Serpagli, 1967, p. 99, pl. 29, figs 4a-5c; Löfgren, 1978, p. 112, pl. 1, fig. 29 (*cum syn.*); Palmieri, 1978, p. 27, pl. 6, figs 27-28, text-fig. 6 (8a-8c); Kennedy, Barnes and Uyeno, 1979, p. 550, pl. 1, fig. 24 (*cum syn.*); Orchard, 1980, p. 26, pl. 14, figs 34-35; Nowlan, 1981, pl. 3, fig. 18, pl. 5, fig. 5; Lenz and McCracken, 1982, p. 1318, pl. 2, fig. 21; Lin et al., 1984, pl. 2, fig. 16; Sarmiento, 1990, pl. 5, fig. 4; Bergström, 1990, pl. 1, fig. 10; Pohler and Orchard, 1990, pl. 1, fig. 6; McCracken, 1991, p. 52, pl. 2, fig. 36 (*cum syn.*); Dzik, 1994, pp. 62-63, pl. 13, figs 1-6, text-fig. 5; Pohler, 1994, pl. 8, fig.3; Trotter and Webby, 1995, p. 487, pl. 4, figs 24-26; Armstrong, 1997, pp. 790-791, pl. 5, figs 1-3, ?4-5; Nowlan et al., 1997, fig. 2.24; Furey-Greig, 1999, p. 311, pl. 3, fig. 16; Armstrong, 2000, pl. 5, figs 6-12, ?13-16; Zhao et al., 2000, p. 226, pl. 26, figs 19, 24 (*cum syn.*); Leslie, 2000, fig. 3.35; McCracken, 2000, pl. 3, fig. 19; Sweet, 2000, fig. 9.11; Talent et al., 2002, pl. 1, figs Q-R; Löfgren, 2000, fig. 4ab; Löfgren, 2003, fig. 8AA; Löfgren, 2004, fig. 7r; Wang et al., 2011, p. 245, pl. 107, figs 18-19; Bergström and Ferretti, 2015, fig. 10AB-AD.

Material
20 specimens from three samples at Kaos Gully locality (see Table 1).

Discussion
Strachanognathus parvus has a distinctive morphology characterized by a strongly laterally compressed robust cusp with sharp anterior and

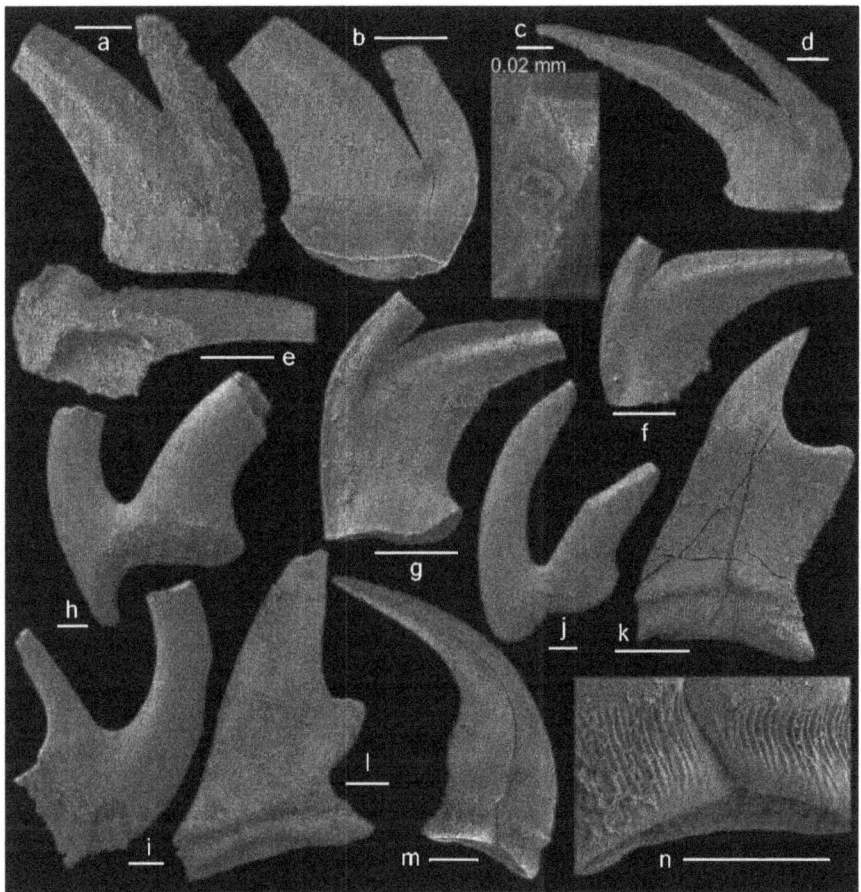

Figure 16.' a-g, *Strachanognathus parvus* Rhodes, 1955. a-e, proclined, short-based element; a, MMMC4898, KAOS-43.9, outer-lateral view (IY241-021); b, MMMC4899, KAOS-43.9, inner-lateral view (IY241-016); c, MMMC4900, KAOS-43.9, upper view, close-up showing cross section of cusp (IY241-025); d, MMMC4901, KAOS-43.9, outer-lateral view (IY242-006); e, MMMC4902, KAOS-43.9, basal view (IY241-029). f, suberect, short-based element, MMMC4903, KAOS-43.9, outer-lateral view (IY241-027); g, suberect, long-based element, MMMC4904, KAOS-43.9, inner-lateral view (IY241-026). h-j, *Spinodus spinatus* (Hadding, 1913). h-i, Sb element; h, MMMC4905, KAOS-50.5, inner-lateral view (IY242-021); i, MMMC4906, KAOS-46.8, inner-lateral view (IY238-022). j, Sc element, MMMC4907, KAOS-50.5, outer-lateral view (IY242-022). k-n, *Taoqupognathus tumidus* Trotter and Webby, 1995. k, Sb3 element, MMMC4908, KAOS-43.9, outer-lateral view (IY242-018); l, Sc3 element, MMMC4909, KAOS-43.9, outer-lateral view (IY242-018); m-n, Sc2 element, MMMC4910, KCY-5, M, outer-lateral view (IY233-001), n, close-up showing coarse striation near basal margin and panderodid furrow (IY233-002). Scale bars 100 μm unless otherwise indicated.

posterior margins, and a short anterior process represented by a single denticle (Fig. 16a-g). It was originally erected as a form species represented by a single element, but the illustrated types from north Wales include short-based (Rhodes 1955, pl. 7, fig. 16, pl. 8, fig.3) to long-based elements (Rhodes 1955, pl. 8, fig.4), and the curvature of the cusp varies from suberect with anterior margin of the cusp more or less normal to the basal margin (Rhodes 1955, text-fig. 5) to procline with the gently curved anterior margin of the cusp smoothly merging into the base (Rhodes 1955, pl. 8, figs 1-2). Therefore at least three (or possibly four) morphotypes can be differentiated among the type material. Based on abundant material of this species from erratic limestone boulders of the Tvären area of southeastern Sweden, Bergström (1962, pp. 54-55) also recognized three morphotypes as illustrated by the types, and indicated that they "only represented stages in a long, continuous series of variations, so that it seemed impossible to draw sharp limits between different types". Specimens representing these three types are also present in our collections from north Queensland, and are referred to herein as a procline, short-based element (Fig. 16a-e), a less common suberect, short-based element (Fig. 16f) and a suberect, long-based element (Fig. 16g).

Armstrong (1997) proposed a quinquimembrate apparatus for *S. parvus* by including two (symmetrical and asymmetrical) coniform elements, which were generally accepted as part of *Parapanderodus* species apparatus. However, these striate coniform elements were not recovered from the allochthonous limestones within the Wairuna Formation of Queensland.

Strachanognathus parvus was pandemic and had a relatively long range extending from the Darriwilian to late Katian. In eastern Australia, it has been only reported from the *T. tumidus* Biozone, such as from allochthonous limestone clasts in the lower part of the Malongulli Formation (Trotter and Webby 1995), from allochthonous limestones in the Wisemans Arm Formation (Furey-Greig 1999) of New South Wales, from the Fork Lagoons beds (Palmieri 1978) and allochthonous limestones within the Wairuna Formation of Queensland (Talent et al. 2002; and this study).

Genus TAOQUPOGNATHUS An, 1985

Type species

Taoqupognathus blandus An, 1985.

Discussion

Three species belonging to this genus are recorded from eastern Gondwana and peri-Gondwana,

including eastern Australia, South China, North China and the Tarim Basin. Zhen (2001) indicated that it had a distribution restricted to the Australasian Superprovince. However, Nowlan (2002, p. 195, p. 2, figs 25-26, 29-31, 36-37) reported a species referred to as *Taoqupognathus* sp. nov. A, represented by 16 specimens from Late Ordovician subsurface core material of Alberta, Canada. As noted by Nowlan (2002), although the slender M element is comparable to the corresponding element of *T. philipi*, this North American species (consisting of slender elements without posterior extension) is significantly different from the three known Australasian species, which have a prominent lobe-like posterior extension. If more detailed study can confirm that this North American species belongs to *Taoqupognathus*, it may represent the morphologically most primitive species among the known representatives of this genus. McCracken (2000, p. 194, pl. 1, fig. 28) also illustrated a single specimen referred to *Taoqupognathus philipi* from the Upper Ordovician of the Foxe Basin of Baffin Island.

Taoqupognathus tumidus Trotter and Webby, 1995
Fig. 16k-n

Synonymy

Drepanodus? altipes? Palmieri, 1978, pl. 2, figs 24, 25.

gen. unident. Pickett, 1978, cover photo, fig. 4.

?*Belodina beiguoshanensis* Yu and Wang, 1986, p. 100, pl. 1, figs 6, 9-11.

Belodina cf. *B. blandus* (An); Duan, 1990, p. 31, pl. 5, fig. 7.

Taoqupognathus tumidus Trotter and Webby, 1995, pp. 487-488, pl. 7, figs 10-24; Zhen et al., 1999, p. 96, fig. 14.1-14.9; Percival, 1999, fig. 3.1-3.2, 3.5; Packham et al., 1999, fig. 3.14-3.16; Furey-Greig, 1999, p. 312, pl. 4, figs 1-9; Zhao et al., 2000, pp. 226-227, pl. 26, figs 1-6, 10-13, 17-18, ?15-16; Furey-Greig, 2000a, p. 94, fig. 6B-H; Talent et al., 2003, pl. 1, fig. 12; Zhen et al., 2003, pp. 43-45, fig. 7K; Wang et al., 2011, p. 247-248, pl. 108, figs 5-11.

Taoqupognathus ani Wang and Zhou, 1998, p. 190, pl. 3, fig. 4.

Material

Four specimens from two samples at Kaos Gully locality (see Table 1).

Discussion

Taoqupognathus tumidus is a morphologically distinctive species, known only from the middle

Katian (Ka2-3; see Fig. 3) in eastern Australia and in the three major Chinese blocks (North China, South China and Tarim plates; see Zhen 2001). In eastern Australia, it is widely reported from allochthonous limestone clasts, such as within the Sofala Volcanics (Pickett 1978; Percival 1999), in the lower part of the Malongulli Formation (Trotter and Webby 1995), in limestone breccias in the basal part of the Malachis Hill Formation overlying the Bowan Park Limestone Subgroup (Zhen et al. 1999), from allochthonous limestones in the Barnby Hills Shale (Zhen et al. 2003), from a limestone body (?allochthonous) within the Forest Reefs Volcanics exposed adjacent to Sheahan-Grants minesite (subsequently destroyed by mining activities; Packham et al. 1999) at Junction Reefs in central NSW, from allochthonous limestones in the Wisemans Arm Formation (Furey-Greig 1999) of the New England Orogen in northeastern NSW, from the Fork Lagoons beds of central-east Queensland (Palmieri 1978), and from allochthonous limestones within the Wairuna Formation of the Broken River region, north Queensland (Talent et al. 2003; this study). *T. tumidus* also occurs in association with *P. insculptus* in the Downderry Limestone Member at the top of the Bowan Park Limestone Subgroup (Zhen et al. 1999), which is autochthonous limestone interpreted as representing shelf edge deposits.

Belodina beiguoshanensis Yu and Wang, 1986 was considered by Wang et al. (2011, p. 247) as a junior synonym of *Taoqupognathus blandus* An, 1985. However, Zhen (2001) suggested that it was morphologically closely related to *Taoqupognathus tumidus*, but with a more stout and short outline in lateral view, and might be either a senior synonym of the latter representing its end member (a subspecies

representing the most advanced forms) or a separate species derived from the latter. It has been treated herein as a doubtful senior synonym of *T. tumidus* pending further detailed study of this species from the upper Beiguoshan Formation (middle Katian) in the Ordos Basin of North China. This designation is also supported by the recognition of several elements assignable to typical *T. tumidus* from a sample at the top of the Taoqupo Formation exposed near Yaoxian in the Ordos Basin of North China (Zhen et al. 2003).

BRACHIOPODS (Percival)

Almost all brachiopod taxa encountered in the fauna from the Kaos Gully section in north Queensland are being described elsewhere from more abundant material obtained from the Malongulli Formation and correlative units in NSW; accordingly the brachiopods are documented herein merely by brief taxonomic notes and illustrations. For brevity, authors of Family/Subfamily level taxonomic hierarchy and above are not cited in the References, as these are readily obtainable from the *Treatise on Invertebrate Paleontology* (Williams et al. 2000).

Subphylum Linguliformea Williams, Carlson, Brunton, Holmer and Popov, 1996
Class Lingulata Goryansky and Popov, 1985
Order Lingulida Waagen, 1885
Superfamily Linguloidea Menke, 1828
Family Obolidae King, 1846
Subfamily Elliptoglossinae Popov and Holmer, 1994

Genus ELLIPTOGLOSSA Cooper, 1956
Elliptoglossa adela Percival, 1978 (Fig. 17a-d)

Figure 17 (next page). a-d, *Elliptoglossa adela* **Percival, 1978. a, interior view of incomplete dorsal? valve, MMMC4911, KAOS-50.4, (PI CWL-3041); b, interior view of incomplete ventral valve, MMMC4912, KAOS-50.4, (PI CWL-3040); c, fragment of posterior end of ventral? valve interior, MMMC4913, KAOS-50.4, (PI CWL-3042); d, interior view of incomplete ventral valve, MMMC4914, KAOS-49.8, (PI CWL-3035). e-g, indeterminate lingulide. e, interior view of incomplete ventral valve, MMMC4915, KAOS-42.8, (PI CWL-3011); f, fragment of ventral valve pseudointerarea showing pedicle groove, MMMC4916, KCY-5, (PI CWL-1012); g, interior view of incomplete dorsal valve, MMMC4917, KCY-5, (PI CWL-1011). h,** *Paterula malongulliensis* **Percival, 1978, interior view of dorsal valve, MMMC4918, KAOS-47.5, (PI CWL-3030); accompanying scale bar is 500 μm. i-k, n,** *Glossella* **sp. i, exterior view of incomplete valve showing smooth post-larval shell flanked by shell ornamented by concentric rows of fine elongate tubercles separated by pits, MMMC4919, KCY-5, (PI CWL-2024). j, fragment of shell exterior, and k, enlargement of lower right side of j to show rows of elongate tubercles, some having the appearance of hollow spines, MMMC4920, KCY-5, (PI CWL-1008, PI CWL-1009 respectively); scale bar for k is 100 μm. n, fragment of shell exterior displaying more widely-separated tubercles, presumably from a more anterior position on the valve, MMMC4921, KAOS-44.8, (PI CWL-3028). l, fragment of shell exterior cf.** *Westonia***, MMMC4922, KCY-5, (PI CWL-1006). m, fragment of shell exterior cf.** *Dictyonina***, MMMC4923, KCY-5, (PI CWL-1010). Unless otherwise indicated, scale bars represent 1 mm; scale bar to right of specimen e relates to specimens a, b, c, d, e, f and g; scale bar beneath specimen i relates to specimens i, j and l; scale bar between specimens m and n relates only to those two specimens.**

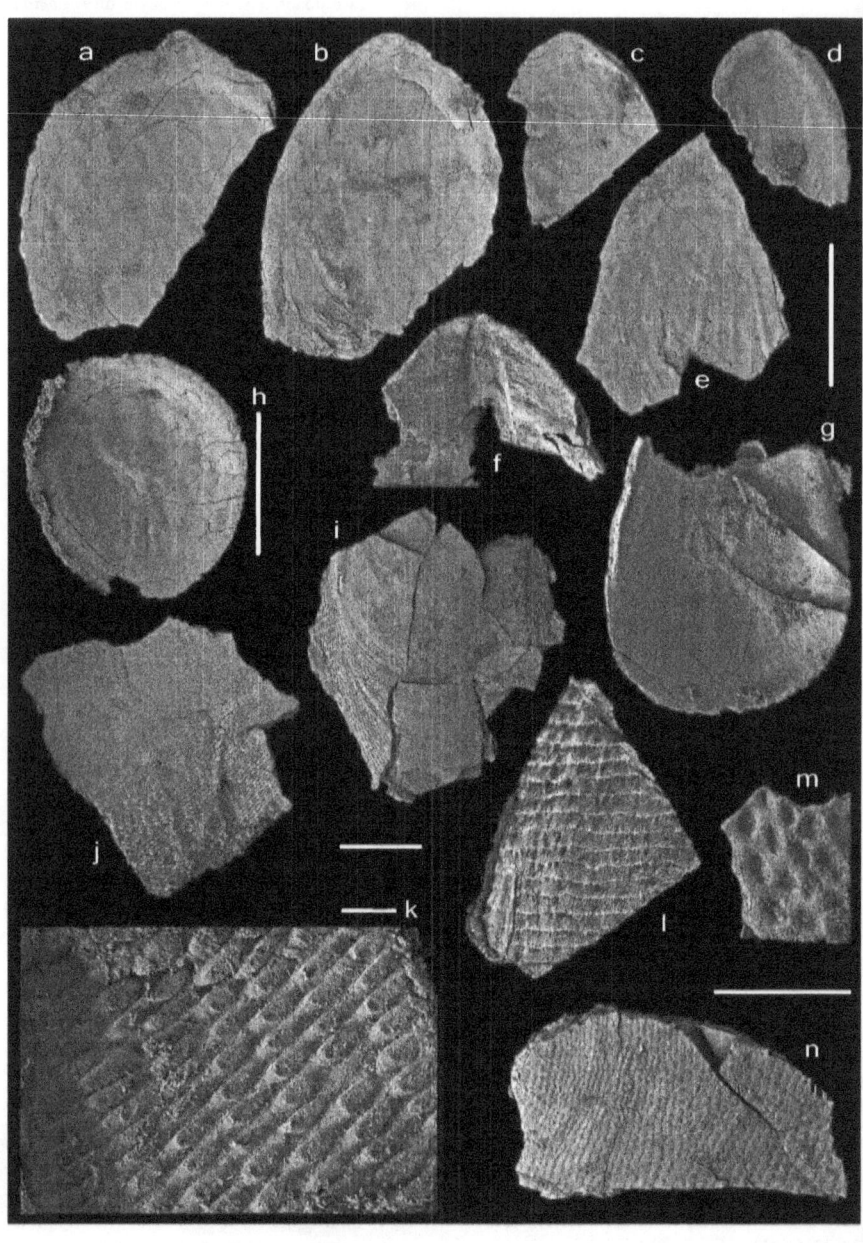

Proc. Linn. Soc. N.S.W., 137, 2015

119

Remarks

The type material of this species was described from internal and external moulds preserved in graptolitic siltstone and spiculite of the Malongulli Formation in central NSW. The isolated valves from the Kaos Gully limestone are at the lower end of the observed range in length and width for *E. adela* measured by Percival (1978). Since the length/width ratio is comparable in both suites and morphological details (or obscurity thereof) are identical, these specimens are confidently identified as *E. adela*.

Distribution

KAOS 49.8, 50.4

Subfamily Obolinae King, 1846

Genus ATANSORIA Popov, 2000 (Fig. 18a-c)

Remarks

Atansoria was first described by Popov (2000) from the Mayatas Formation of Katian age, in the Atansor Lake region of north-central Kazakhstan, solely on the basis of its distinctive dorsal valve. Likewise, no ventral valves were identified in the Carriers Well material, and it is postulated that *Atansoria* was cemented to the substrate by that valve. The dorsal valve is concave, with a large ovoid to diamond-shaped visceral field bounded by strong ridges. *Atansoria* from north Queensland is identical to the new species recognized from the Macquarie Volcanic Province of New South Wales, which differs from the type (and only other known) species *A. concava* Popov, 2000 in exhibiting concentric growth rings, whereas *A. concava* is smooth externally. Furthermore, *A. concava* possesses a far more prominent median septum in the dorsal valve than does the Australian species.

Distribution

KCY-5, KAOS 43.9

Unidentified lingulide

Remarks

Three illustrated fragments (Fig. 17e-g) of comparable size are regarded as conspecific and representative of a lingulide that is restricted in distribution to just two levels in the section. The well-developed pedicle groove is flanked by moderately long propareas (Fig. 17f). Three low divergent ridges extend through the ventral visceral field to about mid length (Fig. 17e). The presumed associated dorsal valve (Fig. 17g) has a suboval visceral field terminating at about mid length and is marked by several indistinct muscle scars and surrounded by low ridges; a faint median ridge extends well into the anterior part of the valve.

Distribution

KCY-5, KAOS 42.8

Genus WESTONIA Walcott, 1901 (Fig. 17l)

Remarks

A fragment tentatively referred to *Westonia*? displays an ornament of terrace lines typical of (but not unique to) this genus. No other material similar to this was found in the residues from the Kaos Gully section.

Distribution

KCY-5

Subfamily Glossellinae Cooper, 1956

Genus GLOSSELLA Cooper, 1956 (Fig. 17i-k, n)

Remarks

Specimens referred to *Glossella* sp. are recognizable by their papillose ornament on the flanks and anterior of the valves. All material is fragmentary, and no useful interior details are known. Thick-shelled fragments with a similar ornament are plentiful in acid-resistant residues from the lower Malongulli Formation of the Macquarie Volcanic Province in central NSW.

Distribution

KCY-5; KAOS 44.8

Family Paterulidae Cooper, 1956

Genus PATERULA Barrande, 1879
Paterula malongulliensis Percival, 1978 (Fig. 17h)

Remarks

The sole dorsal valve was recovered from the limestone at Carriers Well is identical to the type specimens of this species, described from the Malongulli Formation in NSW, in having an undivided umbonal muscle scar.

Distribution

KAOS 47.5

Superfamily Discinoidea Gray, 1840
Family Discinidae Gray, 1840

120

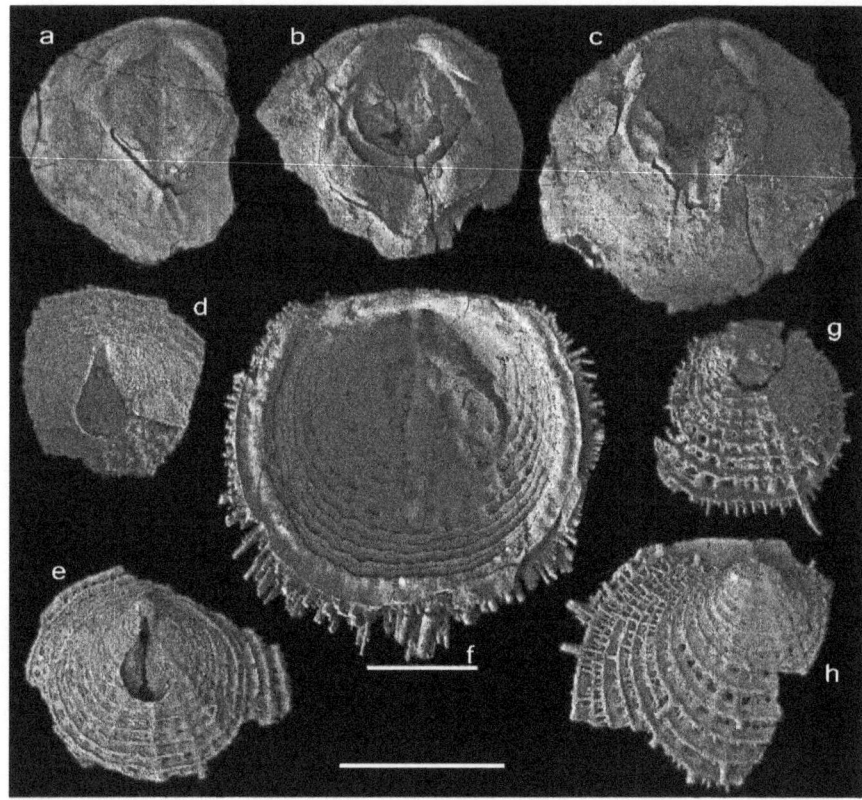

Figure 18. a-c, *Atansoria* sp. nov. a, interior view of incomplete dorsal valve, MMMC4924, KAOS-43.9, (PI CWL-3014); b, interior view of incomplete dorsal valve, MMMC4925, KCY-5, (PI CWL-1002); c, interior view of dorsal valve, MMMC4926, KCY-5, (PI CWL-1001). d-h, *Nushbiella* sp. nov. d, exterior view of incomplete ventral valve, MMMC4927, KCY-5, (PI CWL-1004); e, exterior view of incomplete ventral valve, MMMC4928, KAOS-42.8, (PI CWL-3012); f, interior view of dorsal valve, MMMC4929, KCY-5, (PI CWL-1007); g, exterior view of dorsal valve, MMMC4930, KCY-5, (PI CWL-1003); h, exterior view of incomplete dorsal valve, MMMC4931, KAOS-41.6, (PI CWL-3005). Scale bar (1 mm) beneath f relates only to that specimen; scale bar (1 mm) for all other specimens is at lower centre of figure.

Genus ACROSACCUS Willard, 1928 (Fig. 19a-e)

Remarks

Acrosaccus is the most common linguliformean brachiopod encountered in acid-resistant residues of the limestone from the Kaos Gully section, where it is mostly found as fragments, recognizable by their ornament of strong concentric ridges. Among the more complete specimens, only dorsal valves have been recovered (Fig. 19a-d). One shell (Fig. 19d, e) revealed a previously unrecognised ornament of fine regular micropitting.

These specimens from north Queensland exhibit the same trend as observed in those from central NSW (being described as a new species) where the dorsal apex migrates during ontogeny from a submarginal (e.g. Fig. 19d) to a subcentral position. An intermediate point on this journey is shown in Fig. 19c, illustrating a specimen that is not yet fully grown in comparison to those from the Malongulli Formation and Downderry Limestone Member of the Ballingoole Limestone of the Macquarie Volcanic Province.

Proc. Linn. Soc. N.S.W., 137, 2015

121

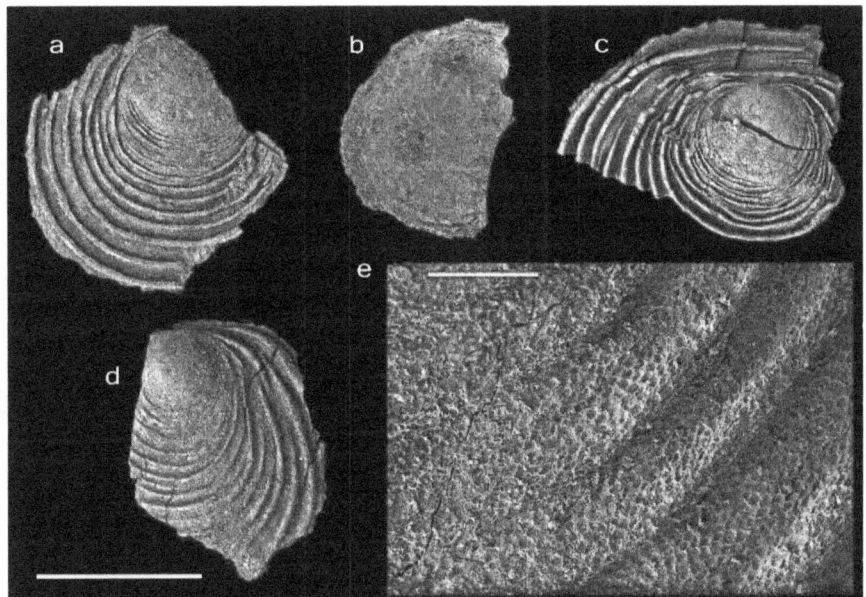

Figure 19. a-e, *Acrosaccus* sp. nov. a, exterior view of incomplete dorsal valve, MMMC4932, KAOS-42.2, (PI CWL-3010); b, interior view of incomplete dorsal valve, MMMC4933, KAOS-43.9, (PI CWL-3018); c, exterior view of incomplete dorsal valve, MMMC4934, KAOS-47.5, (PI CWL-3029); d, exterior view of incomplete dorsal valve, and e, enlargement of micropitting on surface of post-larval shell, MMMC4935, KAOS-43.9, (PI CWL-3016 and PI CWL-3017 respectively). Scale bar (1 mm) beneath in lower left corner relates to specimens a-d; scale bar within e is 100 μm.

Distribution

KAOS 42.2, 43.9, 47.5

Order Siphonotretida Kuhn, 1949
Superfamily Siphonotretoidea Kutorga, 1848
Family Siphonotretidae Kutorga, 1848

Genus NUSHBIELLA Popov in Kolobova and
Popov, 1986 (Fig. 18d-h)

Remarks

Spinose exterior fragments of *Nushbiella* are readily apparent in the acid-resistant residues from Carriers Well, though complete specimens (e.g. Fig. 18f) are rare. Ventral valves are characterised by a large pedicle foramen that may be partly or entirely closed anteriorly by two plates growing inwards from the sides of the aperture (Fig. 18d, e), exactly as is shown by specimens from central NSW. The radial ornament, which in some other species of *Nushbiella* – including the type species *N. dubia* (Popov, 1977) – is relatively prominent on the dorsal valve, is much

more subdued (even absent) in the Carriers Well specimens (Fig. 18g, h).

Distribution

KCY-5; KAOS 41.6, 42.8

Order Acrotretida Kuhn, 1949
Superfamily Acrotretoidea Schuchert, 1893
Family Acrotretidae Schuchert, 1893

Genus CONOTRETA Walcott, 1889 (Fig. 20a-e)

Remarks

Both valves of this species generally resemble those of *Conotreta? mica* described by Holmer (1989) from Västergötland and Dalarna, Sweden, but a conservative approach to the identification is taken in view of the relatively few specimens available from the Kaos Gully section and so this material is referred here to *Conotreta* sp. Dorsal valves of the Swedish specimens have a median septum bearing up to three

122

Proc. Linn. Soc. N.S.W., 137, 2015

anterior spines or denticles, whereas those from the Carriers Well limestone display two (Fig. 20d).

Distribution
KCY-5; KAOS 44.8, 50.4

Genus HISINGERELLA Henningsmoen in Waern et al., 1948
Hisingerella hetera (Percival, 1978) (Fig. 20f-o)

Remarks
Ventral valves of this species (originally described from spiculitic siltstones of the lower Malongulli Formation of central NSW) are common in the Carriers Well residues, dorsal valves much less so. Specimens are smaller and more delicate than those assigned to *Conotreta* sp., but there are other morphological differences confirming that the distinction between the two is not indicative merely of juvenile and gerontic individuals of the one taxon. For example, some ventral valves of *H. hetera* display a weak but distinct interridge crossing the pseudointerarea (Fig. 20h) which is not present in *Conotreta* sp. Similarities in shell construction, such as the presence of twin spines on the anterior edge of the median septum (constructed in both species of concentric layers of bacular lamellae, shown in Fig. 20d for *Conotreta* sp., and Fig. 20j for *H. hetera*) demonstrate the close phylogenetic relationship of these acrotretides.

Distribution
KCY-5; KAOS 43.9, 44.8

Family Scaphelasmatidae Rowell, 1965

Genus SCAPHELASMA Cooper, 1956 (Fig. 21a, b)

Remarks
The species depicted in Fig. 21a-b has a distinctive transversely oval to subquadrate outline and its ventral valve is deeper, more rounded and inflated than is typical for *Scaphelasma*. The presence of a well-developed apical process in front of the internal foramen (Fig. 21b) is reminiscent of *Scaphelasma scutula* Popov, Nõlvak and Holmer, 1994, which has also been recognized in several formations of late Katian age in the Macquarie Volcanic Province of central NSW.

Distribution
KCY-5; KAOS 39.3

Family Biernatidae Holmer, 1989

Genus BIERNATIA Holmer, 1989 (Fig. 21c-e)

Remarks
The species of *Biernatia* in the Carriers Well limestone is characterized by a high, strongly apsacline ventral valve with the intertrough barely visible (Fig. 21c) and two distinct sizes of pitting developed on the larval shell (Fig. 21d) – larger flat-bottomed pits surrounded by multiple micropits. The dorsal valve (Fig. 21e) has a very short, narrow pseudointerarea, prominent cardinal muscle scars, and a relatively short, flat-topped, anteriorly-expanding surmounting plate supported by the median septum. Of the two

Figure 20 (next page). a-e, *Conotreta* sp. a, exterior view of incomplete ventral valve, MMMC4936, KCY-5, (PI CWL-2023); b, interior view of incomplete ventral valve, MMMC4937, KCY-5, (PI CWL-2001); c, fragment of dorsal valve interior, showing pseudointerarea and median septum, and d, enlargement of broken anterior end of median septum displaying concentric layers forming cross sections of two spines, MMMC4938, KAOS-44.8, (PI CWL-3022 and PI CWL-3023 respectively); e, interior view of incomplete dorsal valve, MMMC4939, KAOS-50.4, (PI CWL-3039). f-o, *Hisingerella hetera* (Percival, 1978). f, exterior of ventral valve in plan view with posterior margin uppermost, MMMC4940, KCY-5, (PI CWL-2012); g, oblique interior view of ventral valve, MMMC4941, KCY-5, (PI CWL-2005); h, oblique posterior view of ventral valve pseudointerarea showing weakly defined interridge, MMMC4942, KCY-5, (PI CWL-2007); i, fragment of dorsal valve interior, showing median septum, and j, enlargement of broken anterior end of median septum displaying concentric layers forming cross sections of two spines (lowermost cut off against edge of image), MMMC4943, KAOS-43.9, (PI CWL-3019 and PI CWL-3020 respectively); k, oblique interior view of ventral valve, MMMC4944, KAOS-44.8, (PI CWL-3024); l, exterior of incomplete ventral valve in plan view with posterior margin uppermost, MMMC4945, KCY-5, (PI CWL-2002); m, oblique interior view of ventral valve, MMMC4946, KCY-5, (PI CWL-2006); n, exterior of incomplete ventral valve in plan view with posterior margin at lower right, and o, enlargement of margin of pedicle foramen to show micropitting on larval shell, MMMC4947, KAOS-44.8, (PI CWL-3025 and PI CWL-3027 respectively). Scale bar (1 mm) in lower left corner relates to all specimens except j and o which have their own 10 μm scale bars, and d with a 20 μm scale bar.

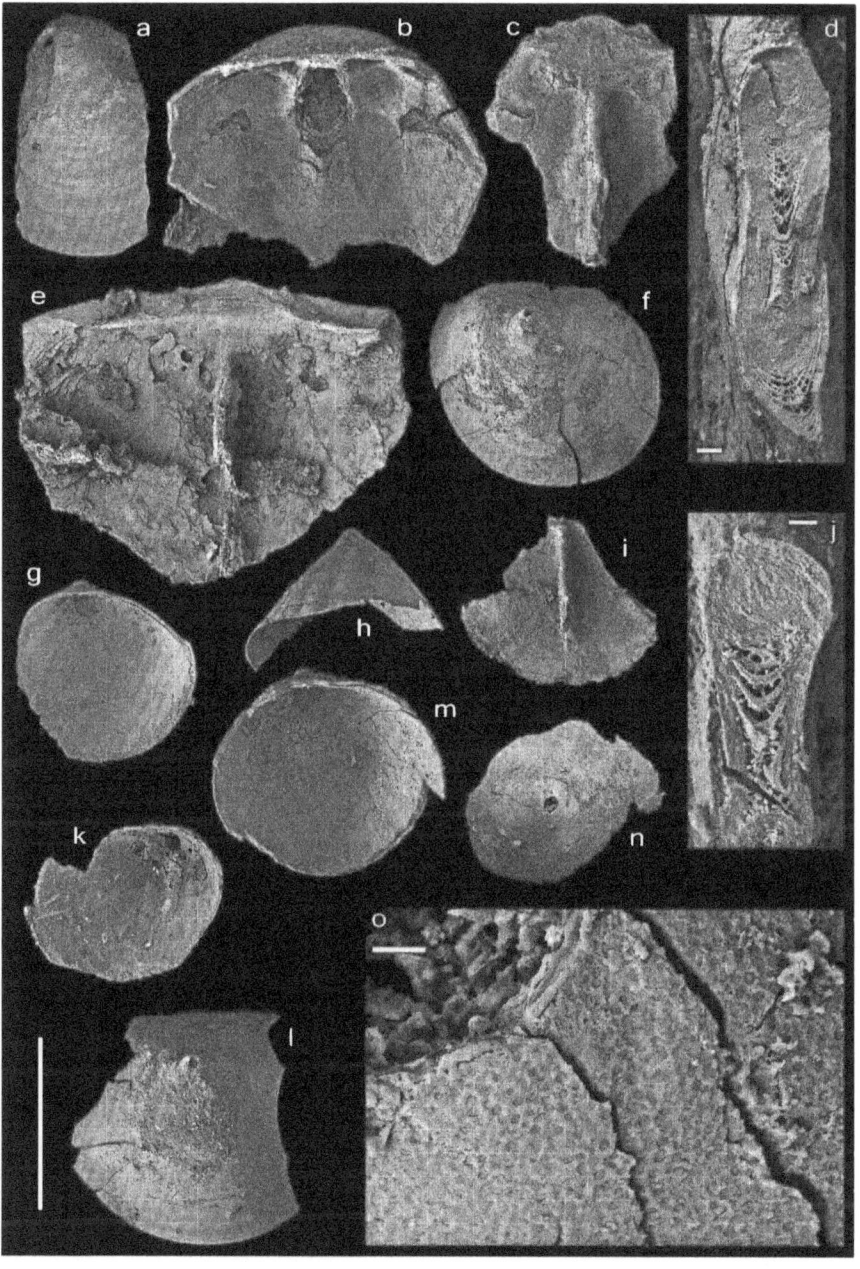

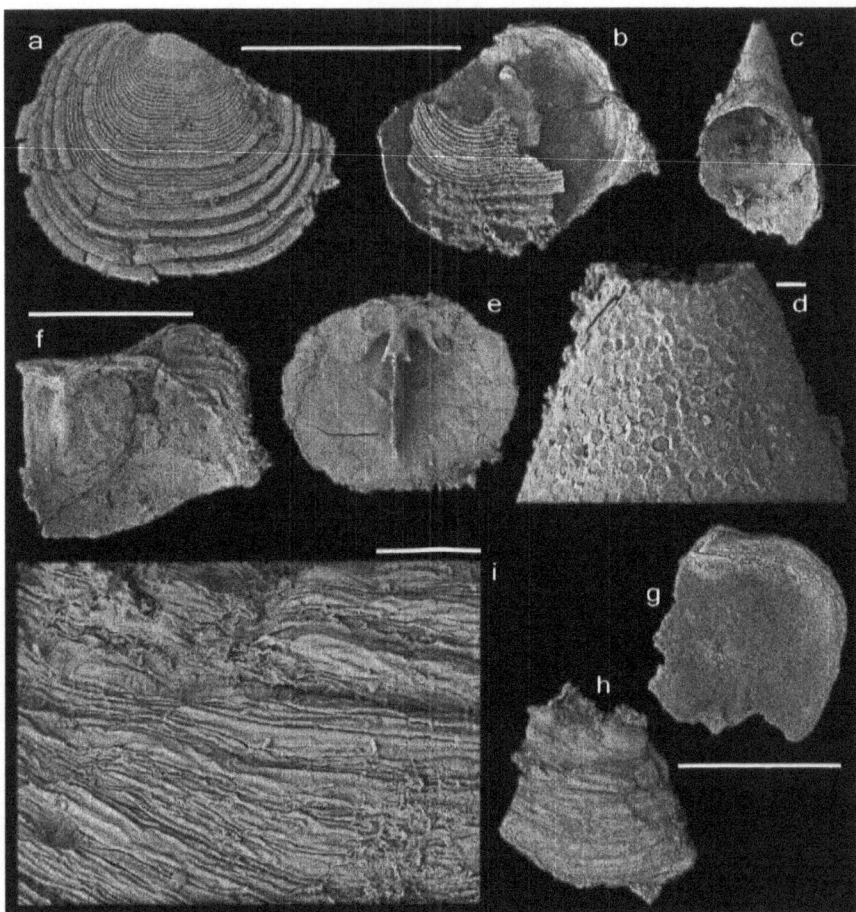

Figure 21. a, b, *Scaphelasma* sp. nov. a, exterior view of incomplete dorsal valve, MMMC4948, KCY-5, (PI CWL-2019); b, view of incomplete conjoined valves from dorsal side, showing apical process in interior of ventral valve, MMMC4949, KAOS-39.3, (PI CWL-3004). c-e, *Biernatia* sp. nov., c, oblique view of ventral valve from dorsal perspective, and d, enlargement of larval shell showing micropitting of two distinct sizes, MMMC4950, KAOS-48.2, (PI CWL 3032 and PI CWL 3033); e, interior view of dorsal valve showing surmounting plate on median septum, MMMC4951, KAOS-48.2, (PI CWL 3031); f-i, *Undiferina* sp. f, interior view of incomplete dorsal valve showing short pseudointerarea and weak median septum, MMMC4952, KAOS-43.9, (PI CWL-3013); g, interior view of incomplete dorsal valve, MMMC4953, KCY-5, (PI CWL-2018); h, fragment of valve exterior, and i, enlargement to show irregular banded ornament, MMMC4954, KAOS-49.8, (PI CWL 3037 and PI CWL 3038 respectively). Scale bar (1 mm) for a, b, c, e is situated at top of figure; scale bar (1 mm) for f is above the latter; scale bar (1 mm) for g and h is in lower right corner of figure; scale bars for enlargements are immediately adjacent to d (10 μm) and i (100 μm).

Proc. Linn. Soc. N.S.W., 137, 2015

125

new species (as yet undescribed) of *Biernatia* that are present in the Malongulli Formation and correlative units of the Macquarie Volcanic Province in NSW, the Carriers Well form is almost certainly conspecific with that having the more suboval outline.

Distribution
KAOS 48.2

Family Eoconulidae Rowell, 1965

Genus UNDIFERINA Cooper, 1956 (Fig. 21f-i)

Remarks
The few available specimens (Fig. 21f-h), although confined to incomplete dorsal valves, display the distinctive ornament of this genus characterised by irregular, wavy distortions (Fig. 21i). They appear to be close to, if not identical with, material from the Malongulli Formation and Downderry Limestone Member at the top of the Ballingoole Limestone in central NSW, that in turn resembles the type species *U. rugosa* Cooper, 1956 from the Pratt Ferry Formation of Alabama, of slightly older latest Middle Ordovician to earliest Late Ordovician age.

Distribution
KCY-5; KAOS 43.9, 49.8

Class Paterinata Williams, Carlson, Brunton, Holmer and Popov, 1996
Order Paterinida Rowell, 1965
Superfamily Paterinoidea Schuchert, 1893
Family Paterinidae Schuchert, 1893

Genus DICTYONINA Cooper, 1942 (Fig. 17m)

Remarks
Identification of this fragment as *Dictyonina*? is necessarily tentative, although the presence of large pits through the shell material suggests this is a reasonable choice.

Distribution
KCY-5

ACKNOWLEDGMENTS

We express our gratitude to John Talent and Ruth Mawson for introducing us to the Broken River region, and for providing samples for us to work on. Field work in Queensland by Zhen in 2010 was supported by a grant from the Betty Mayne Scientific Research Fund of the Linnean Society of New South Wales. B. Webby, A. Cook and R. Jones are thanked for their assistance during the field trip. Paul Meszaros (Geological Survey of New South Wales) assisted with acid leaching and residue separation. Scanning electron microscope photographs were prepared in the Electron Microscope Unit of the Australian Museum. We thank Barry Webby and an anonymous referee for their perceptive and constructive reviews of the manuscript. The study is a contribution to IGCP Project 591: The Early to Middle Paleozoic Revolution. Zhen and Percival publish with permission of the Executive Director, Geological Survey of New South Wales.

REFERENCES

Agematsu, S., Sashida, K. and Ibrahim, B. (2008). Biostratigraphy and Paleobiogeography of Middle and Late Ordovician Conodonts from the Langkawi Islands, Northwestern Peninsular Malaysia. *Journal of Paleontology* **82**, 957-973.

Agematsu, S., Sashida, K., Salyapongse, S. and Sardsud, A. (2007). Ordovician conodonts from the Satun area, southern Peninsular Thailand. *Journal of Paleontology* **81**, 19-37.

Aldridge, R.J. (1982). A fused cluster of coniform conodont elements from the Late Ordovician of Washington Land, western North Greenland. *Palaeontology* **25**, 425-430.

An, T.X. (1981). Recent progress in Cambrian and Ordovician conodont biostratigraphy of China. *Geological Society of America Special Paper* **187**, 209-226.

An, T.X. (1987). 'Early Paleozoic conodonts from South China'. 238 pp. (Peking University Publishing House: Beijing). (in Chinese with English abstract).

An, T.X. and Ding, L.S. (1982). Preliminary studies and correlations on Ordovician conodonts from the Ningzhen Mountains, China. *Acta Petroleum Sinica* **3** (4), 1-11. (in Chinese).

An, T.X., Du, G.Q. and Gao, Q.Q. (1985). 'Ordovician conodonts from Hubei'. 64 pp. (Geological Publishing House: Beijing). (in Chinese with English abstract).

An, T.X., Du, G.Q., Gao, Q.Q., Chen, X.B. and Li, W.T. (1981). Ordovician conodont biostratigraphy of the Huanghuachang area of Yichang, Hubei. In 'Selected Papers of the First Symposium of the Micropalaeontological Society of China' (Ed. Micropalaeontological Society of China), pp. 105-113 (Science Press: Beijing). (in Chinese).

An, T.X. and Xu, B.Z. (1984). Ordovician System and conodonts of Tungshan and Xianning, Hubei. *Acta Scientiarum Naturalium Universitatis Pekinensis* **5**, 73-87. (in Chinese with English abstract).

An, T.X., Zhang, F., Xiang, W.D., Zhang, Y.Q., Xu, W.H., Zhang, H.J., Jiang, D.B., Yang, C.S., Lin, L.D., Cui,

126

Proc. Linn. Soc. N.S.W., 137, 2015

Z.T. and Yang, X.C. (1983). 'The conodonts in North China and adjacent regions'. 223 pp. (Science Press: Beijing). (in Chinese with English abstract).

An, T.X. and Zheng, S.C. (1990). 'The conodonts of the marginal areas around the Ordos Basin, North China'. 199 pp. (Science Press: Beijing). (in Chinese with English abstract).

Armstrong, H.A. (1997). Conodonts from the Ordovician Shinnel Formation, southern Uplands, Scotland. *Palaeontology* **40**, 763-797.

Armstrong, H.A. (2000). Conodont micropalaeontology of mid-Ordovician aged limestone clasts from Lower Old Red Sandstone conglomerates, Lanark and Strathmore basins, Midland Valley, Scotland. *Journal of Micropalaeontology* **19**, 45-59.

Bagnoli, G. and Qi, Y.P. (2014). Ordovician conodonts from the Red Petrified Forest, Hunan Province, China. *Bollettino della Società Paleontologica Italiana* **53** (2), 93-104.

Barrande, J. (1879). 'Système Silurien du Centre de la Bohême. Ière Partie. Recherches Paléontologiques, vol. 5. Classe des Mollusques: Ordre des Brachiopodes'. 226 pp., 153 pls. (Published by the author: Paris).

Barnes, C.R. (1967). A questionable conodont assemblage from Middle Ordovician limestones, Ottawa, Canada. *Journal of Paleontology* **41**, 1557-1560.

Bergström, S.M. (1962). Conodonts from the Ludibundus Limestone (Middle Ordovician) of the Tvären area (S.E. Sweden). *Arkiv för Geologi och Mineralogi* **3** (1), 1-61.

Bergström, S.M. (1990). Biostratigraphic and biogeographic significance of Middle and Upper Ordovician conodonts in the Girvan succession, south-west Scotland. *Courier Forschungsinstitut Senckenberg* **118**, 1-43.

Bergström, S.M. and Bergström, J. (1996). The Ordovician-Silurian boundary successions in Östergötland and Västergötland, S. Sweden. *GFF* **118**, 25-42.

Bergström, S.M. and Massa, D. (1992). Stratigraphic and biogeographic significance of Upper Ordovician conodonts from northwestern Libya. In 'The Geology of Libya' (eds M.J. Salem, O.S. Hammuda and B.A. Eliagoubi) **4**, 1323-1342.

Bergström, S.M., Chen, X., Gutiérrez-Marco, J.C. and Dronov, A. (2009). The new chronostratigraphic classification of the Ordovician System and its relations to major regional series and stages and to δ13C chemostratigraphy. *Lethaia* **42**, 97–107.

Bergström, S.M. and Ferretti, A. (2015). Conodonts in the Upper Ordovician Keisley Limestone of northern England: taxonomy, biostratigraphical significance and biogeographical relationships. *Papers in Palaeontology* **1** (1), 1-32 (published online 2014). http://dx.doi.org /10.1002/spp2.1003.

Bergström, S.M. and Sweet, W.C. (1966). Conodonts from the Lexington Limestone (Middle Ordovician) of Kentucky and its lateral equivalents in Ohio and Indiana. *Bulletin of American Paleontology* **50** (229), 271-441.

Branson, E.B. and Mehl, M.G. (1933). Conodont studies. *University of Missouri Studies* **8**, 1-349.

Brime, C., Talent, J.A. and Mawson, R. (2003). Low-grade metamorphism in the Palaeozoic sequences of the Townsville hinterland, northeastern Australia. *Australian Journal of Earth Sciences* **50** (5), 751-767.

Burrett, C.F., Stait, B.A. and Laurie, J. (1983). Trilobites and microfossils from the Middle Ordovician of Surprise Bay, southern Tasmania, Australia. *Memoir of the Australian Association of Palaeontologists* **1**, 177-193.

Chen, M.J. and Zhang, J.H. (1984). Middle Ordovician conodonts from Tangshan, Nanjing. *Acta Micropalaeontologica Sinica* **1**, 120-137. (in Chinese with English abstract).

Chen, M.J. and Zhang, J.H. (1989). Ordovician conodonts from the Shitai region, Anhui. *Acta Micropalaeontologica Sinica* **6** (3), 213-228. (in Chinese with English abstract).

Chen, X., Bergström, S.M., Zhang, Y.D. and Wang, Z.H. (2013). A regional tectonic event of Katian (Late Ordovician) age across three major blocks of China. *Chinese Science Bulletin* **58** (34), 4292-4299.

Clark, D.L., Sweet, W.C., Bergström, S.M., Klapper, G., Austin, R.L., Rhodes, F.H.T., Müller, K.J., Ziegler, W., Lindström, M., Miller, J.F. and Harris, A.G. (1981). Conodonta. In 'Treatise on Invertebrate Paleontology, part W, Miscellanea, supplement 2'. (Ed. R.A. Robison). 202 pp. (The Geological Society of America: Boulder, and the University of Kansas: Lawrence).

Cooper, G.A. (1942). New genera of North American brachiopods. *Washington Academy of Sciences, Journal* **32** (8), 228-235.

Cooper, G.A. (1956). Chazyan and related brachiopods. *Smithsonian Miscellaneous Collections* **127**, 1-1245.

Cooper, B.J. (1976). Multielement conodonts from the St. Clair Limestone (Silurian) of southern Illinois. *Journal of Paleontology* **50** (2), 205-217.

Ding, L.S. (1987). Preliminary probes into Ordovician conodont biostratigraphy from the Kunshan area, Jiangsu, China. In 'Symposium on petroleum stratigraphy and palaeontology (1987)', pp. 41-53, pp. 375-380. (Geological Publishing House: Beijing). (in Chinese with English abstract).

Dixon, O.A. and Jell, J.S. (2012). Heliolitine tabulate corals from Late Ordovician and possibly early Silurian allochthonous limestones in the Broken River Province, Queensland, Australia. *Alcheringa* **36** (1), 69-98.

Duan, J.Y. (1990). Ordovician conodonts from northern Jiangsu and indices of their colour alteration. *Acta Micropalaeontologica Sinica* **7** (1), 19-41. (in Chinese with English abstract).

Dumoulin, J.A., Harris, A.G. and Repetski, J.E. (2014). Carbonate rocks of the Seward Peninsula, Alaska:

Their correlation and paleogeographic significance. *Geological Society of America, Special Paper* **506**, 59-110.

Dzik, J. (1976). Remarks on the evolution of Ordovician conodonts. *Acta Palaeontologica Polonica* **21**, 395-455.

Dzik, J. (1994). Conodonts of the Mójcza Limestone. In 'Ordovician carbonate platform ecosystem of the Holy Cross Mountains' (eds J. Dzik, E. Olempska, and A. Pisera). *Palaeontologia Polonica* **53**, 43-128.

Epstein, A., Epstein, J.B. and Harris, L.D. (1977). Conodont color alteration: an index to organic metamorphism. *Geological Survey Professional Paper* **995**, 1-27.

Ethington, R.L. (1959). Conodonts of the Ordovician Galena Formation. *Journal of Paleontology* **33**, 257-292.

Fåhræus, L.E. (1966). Lower Viruan (Middle Ordovician) conodonts from the Gullhögen Quarry, Southern Central Sweden. *Sveriges Geologiska Undersökning* C **610**, 1-40.

Ferretti, A. (1998). Late Ordovician conodonts from the Prague Basin, Bohemia. In Proceedings of the Sixth European Conodont Symposium (ECOS VI) (ed. H. Szaniawski), *Palaeontologia Polonica* **58**, 123-139.

Ferretti, A. and Barnes, C.R. (1997). Upper Ordovician conodonts from the Kalkbank Limestone of Thuringia, Germany. *Palaeontology* **40**, 15-42.

Ferretti, A., Bergström, S.M. and Barnes, C.R. (2014a). Katian (Upper Ordovician) conodonts from Wales. *Palaeontology* **57** (4), 801-831.

Ferretti, A., Messori, A. and Bergström, S.M. (2014b). Composition and significance of the Katian (Upper Ordovician) conodont fauna of the Vaux Limestone ('Calcaire des Vaux') in Normandy, France. *Estonian Journal of Earth Sciences* **63** (4), 214-219.

Ferretti A., Bergström S.M. and Sevastopulo, G.D. (2014c). Katian conodonts from the Portrane Limestone: the first Ordovician conodont fauna described from Ireland. *Bollettino della Società Paleontologica Italiana* **53** (2), 1-15.

Ferretti, A. and Serpagli, E. (1991). First record of Ordovician conodonts from southwestern Sardinia. *Revista Italia Paleontologia et Stratigraphia* **97**, 27-34.

Ferretti, A. and Serpagli, E. (1999). Late Ordovician conodont faunas from southern Sardinia, Italy: biostratigraphic and paleogeographic implications. *Bollettino della Società Paleontologia Italiana* **37**, 215-236.

Fowler, T.J. and Iwata, K. (1995). Darriwilian-Gisbornian conodonts from the Triangle Group, Triangle Creek area, New South Wales. *Australian Journal of Earth Sciences* **42** (2), 119-122.

Furey-Greig, T.M. (1999). Late Ordovician conodonts from the olistostromal Wisemans Arm Formation (New England Region, Australia). *Abhandlungen der Geologischen Bundesanstalt* **54**, 303–321.

Furey-Greig, T.M. (2000a). Late Ordovician and Early Silurian conodonts from the "Uralba Beds", northern New South Wales. *Alcheringa* **24**, 83-97.

Furey-Greig, T.M. (2000b). Late Ordovician (Eastonian) conodonts from the Early Devonian Drik Drik Formation, Woolomin area, eastern Australia. *Records of the Western Australian Museum Supplement* **58**, 133-143.

Gao, Q.Q. (1991). Conodonts. In 'Sinian to Permian stratigraphy and Palaeontology of the Tarim Basin II, Keping-Bachu area' (Ed. Xinjiang Petroleum Administration Bureau and the Jianghan Petroleum Administration Bureau), pp. 125-149. (Petroleum Industry Press: Beijing). (in Chinese with English abstract).

Glen, R.A. (2005). The Tasmanides of Eastern Australia. In 'Terrane Processes at the Margins of Gondwana' (Eds A. Vaughan, P. Leat and R. Pankhurst). *Geological Society of London Special Publication* **246**, 23-96.

Glen, R.A. (2013). Refining accretionary orogen models for the Tasmanides of eastern Australia. *Australian Journal of Earth Sciences* **60**, 315-370.

Goldman, D., Leslie, S.A., Nõlvak, J., Young, S., Bergström, S.M. and Huff, W.D. (2007). The Global Stratotype Section and Point (GSSP) for the base of the Katian Stage of the Upper Ordovician Series at Black Knob Ridge, Southeastern Oklahoma, USA. *Episodes* **30** (4), 258-270.

Hadding, A.R. (1913). Undre dicellograptusskiffern i Skåne jämte några dågra därmed ekvivalenta bildningar. *Lunds Universitets Årsskrift, Ny Följd, Afdelning 2* **9** (15), 1-90.

Harris, A.G., Bergström, S.M., Ethington, R.L. and Ross, R.J. jr. (1979). Aspects of Middle and Upper Ordovician conodont biostratigraphy of carbonate facies in Nevada and southeast California and comparison with some Appalachian successions. *Brigham Young University Geology Studies* **2** (3), 7-44.

Henderson, R.A., Innes, B.M., Fergusson, C.L., Crawford, A.J. and Withnall, I.W. (2011). Collisional accretion of a Late Ordovician oceanic island arc, northern Tasman Orogenic Zone, Australia. *Australian Journal of Earth Sciences* **58**, 1-19.

Henderson, R.A., Donchak, P.J.T. and Withnall, I.W. (2013). Chapter 4: Mossman Orogen. In 'Geology of Queensland' (Ed. P.A. Jell), pp. 225-304. (Geological Survey of Queensland: Brisbane).

Henningsmoen, G. (1948). The Tretaspis Series of the Kullatorp Core, pp. 374-432. In Waern, B., Thorslund, P. and Henningsmoen, G. Deep boring through Ordovician and Silurian strata at Kinnekulle, Vastergötland. *Bulletin of the Geological Institutions of the University of Uppsala* **32**, 337-474.

Holmer, L.E. (1989). Middle Ordovician phosphatic inarticulate brachiopods from Västergötland and Dalarna, Sweden. *Fossils and Strata* **26**, 1-172.

Jenkins, C.J. (1978). Llandovery and Wenlock stratigraphy of the Panuara area, central New South Wales. *Proceedings of the Linnean Society of New South Wales* **102**, 109-130.

Kaljo, D., Hints, L., Männik, P. and Nõlvak, J. (2008). The succession of Hirnantian events based on data from Baltica: brachiopods, chitinozoans, conodonts, and carbon isotopes. *Estonian Journal of Earth Sciences* **57** (4), 197-218.

Kaljo, D., Männik, P., Martma, T. and Nõlvak, J. (2012). More about the Ordovician–Silurian transition beds at Mirny Creek, Omulev Mountains, NE Russia: carbon isotopes and conodonts. *Estonian Journal of Earth Sciences* **61** (4), 277-294.

Kennedy, D.J., Barnes, C.R. and Uyeno, T.T. (1979). A middle Ordovician faunule from the Tetagouche Group, Camel Back Mountain, New Brunswick. *Canadian Journal of Earth Sciences* **16**, 540-551.

Kolobova, I.M. and Popov, L.E. (1986). K paleontologitscheskoi kharakteristike anderkenskogo gorizonta srednego ordovika v Chu-Iliyskikh Gorakh (Juzhnyi Kazakhstan). *Ezhegodnik Vsesoyuznogo Paleontologicheskogo Obshchestva* **29**, 246-261. (in Russian).

Lenz, A.C. and McCracken, A.D. (1982). The Ordovician-Silurian boundary, northern Canadian Cordillera: graptolite and conodont correlation. *Canadian Journal of Earth Sciences* **19**, 1308-1322.

Leone, F., Hammann, W., Laske, R., Serpagli, E. and Villas, E. (1991). Lithostratigraphic units and biostratigraphy of the post-sardic Ordovician sequence in south-west Sardinia. *Bollettino della Societa Paleontologica Italiana* **30** (2), 201-235.

Leslie, S.A. (1997). Apparatus architecture of *Belodina* (Conodonta): Interpretations based on fused clusters of *Belodina compressa* (Branson and Mehl, 1933) from the Middle Ordovician (Turinian) Plattin Limestone of Missouri and Iowa. *Journal of Paleontology* **71**, 921-926.

Leslie, S.A. (2000). Mohawkian (Upper Ordovician) conodonts of eastern North America and Baltoscandia. *Journal of Paleontology* **74**, 1122-1147.

Lin, B.Y., Qiu, H.R. and Xu, C.C. (1984). New observations of Ordovician strata in Shetai District of Urad Front Banner, Nei Mongol (Inner Mongolia). *Geological Review* **30**, 95-105. (in Chinese with English abstract).

Lindström, M. (1955). Conodonts from the lowermost Ordovician strata of south-central Sweden. *Geologiska Föreningen i Stockholm Förhandlingar* **76**, 517-604.

Lindström, M. (1971). Lower Ordovician conodonts of Europe. In 'Symposium on conodont biostratigraphy' (Eds W.C. Sweet and S.M. Bergström). *Geological Society of America, Memoir* **127**, 21-61.

Löfgren, A. (1978). Arenigian and Llanvirnian conodonts from Jämtland, northern Sweden. *Fossils and Strata* **13**, 1-129.

Löfgren, A. (2000). Conodont biozonation in the upper Arenig of Sweden. *Geological Magazine* **137** (1), 53-65.

Löfgren, A. (2003). Conodont faunas with *Lenodus variabilis* in the upper Arenigian to lower Llanvirnian of Sweden. *Acta Palaeontologica Polonica* **48**, 417-436.

Löfgren, A. (2004). The conodont fauna in the Middle Ordovician *Eoplacognathus pseudoplanus* Zone of Baltoscandia. *Geological Magazine* **141**, 505-24.

Männik, P. and Viira, V. (2012). Ordovician conodont diversity in the northern Baltic. *Estonian Journal of Earth Sciences* **61** (1), 1-14.

McCracken, A.D. (1987). Description and correlation of Late Ordovician conodonts from the *D. ornatus* and *P. pacificus* graptolite zones, Road River Group, northern Yukon Territory. *Canadian Journal of Earth Sciences* **24**, 1450-1464.

McCracken, A.D. (1989). *Protopanderodus* (Conodontata) from the Ordovician Road River Group, Northern Yukon Territory, and the evolution of the genus. *Geological Survey of Canada Bulletin* **388**, 1-39.

McCracken, A.D. (1991). Middle Ordovician conodonts from the Cordilleran Road River Group, northern Yukon Territory, Canada. In 'Ordovician to Triassic conodont paleontology of the Canadian Cordillera' (Eds M.J. Orchard and A.D. McCracken). *Geological Survey of Canada, Bulletin* **417**, 41-63.

McCracken, A.D. (2000). Middle and Late Ordovician conodonts from the Foxe Lowland of southern Baffin Island, Nunavut. In 'Geology and paleontology of the southeast Arctic Platform and southern Baffin Island' (Eds A.D. McCracken and T.E. Bolton). *Geological Survey of Canada, Bulletin* **557**, 159-216.

McCracken, A.D. and Nowlan, G.S. (1989). Conodont paleontology and biostratigraphy of Ordovician carbonates and petroliferous carbonates on Southampton, Baffin, and Akpatok islands in the eastern Canadian Arctic. *Canadian Journal of Earth Sciences* **26**, 1880-1903.

Mei, S.L. (1995). Biostratigraphy and tectonic implications of Late Ordovician conodonts from Shiyanhe Formation, Neixiang, Henan. *Acta Palaeontologica Sinica* **34** (6), 674-687. (in Chinese with English abstract).

Mellgren, J.S. and Eriksson, M.E. (2006). A model of reconstruction of the oral apparatus of the Ordovician conodont genus *Protopanderodus* Lindström, 1971. *Transactions of the Royal Society of Edinburgh: Earth Sciences* **97**, 97-112.

Moors, H.T. (1970). Ordovician graptolites from the Cliefden Caves area, Mandurama, N.S.W., with a re-appraisal of their stratigraphic significance. *Proceedings of the Royal Society of Victoria* **83**, 253-287.

Moskalenko, T.A. (1973). Conodonts of the Middle and Upper Ordovician on the Siberian Platform. *Akademiy Nauk SSSR, Sibirskoe Otdelenie, Trudy Instituta Geologii i Geofiziki* **137**, 1-143. (in Russian).

Ni, S.Z. and Li, Z.H. (1987). Conodonts. In Wang, X.F., Ni, S.Z., Zeng, Q.L., Xu, G.H., Zhou, T.M., Li, Z.H., Xiang, L.W. and Lai, C.G. 'Biostratigraphy of the Yangtze Gorge area 2: Early Palaeozoic Era' pp. 386-447, 549-555, 619-632 (Geological Publishing House: Beijing). (in Chinese with English abstract).

ORDOVICIAN CONODONTS AND BRACHIOPODS

Nowlan, G.S. (1979). Fused clusters of the conodont genus *Belodina* Ethington from the Thumb Mountain Formation (Ordovician), Ellesmere Island, District of Franklin. *Current Research, Part A, Geological Survey of Canada, Paper* **79-1A**, 213-218.

Nowlan, G.S. (1981). Some Ordovician conodont faunules from the Miramichi Anticlinorium, New Brunswick. *Geological Survey of Canada, Bulletin* **345**, 1-35.

Nowlan, G.S. (1983). Biostratigraphic, paleogeographic, and tectonic implications of Late Ordovician conodonts from the Grog Brook Group, northwestern New Brunswick. *Canadian Journal of Earth Sciences* **20**, 650-670.

Nowlan, G.S. (2002). Stratigraphy and conodont biostratigraphy of Upper Ordovician strata in the subsurface of Alberta, Canada. *Special Papers in Palaeontology* **67**, 185-203.

Nowlan, G.S. and Barnes, C.R. (1981). Late Ordovician conodonts from the Vauréal Formation, Anticosti Island, Québec; Part 1. *Geological Survey of Canada, Bulletin* **329**, 1-49.

Nowlan, G.S., McCracken, A.D. and Chatterton, B.D.E. (1988). Conodonts from Ordovician-Silurian boundary strata, Whittaker Formation, Mackenzie Mountains, Northwest Territories. *Geological Survey of Canada, Bulletin* **373**, 1-99.

Nowlan, G.S., McCracken, A.D. and McLeod, M.J. (1997). Tectonic and paleogeographic significance of Late Ordovician conodonts in the Canadian Appalachians. *Canadian Journal of Earth Sciences* **34**, 1521-1537.

Orchard, M.J. (1980). Upper Ordovician conodonts from England and Wales. *Geologica et Palaeontologica* **14**, 9-44.

Ortega, G., Albanesi, G.L., Banchig, A.L. and Peralta, G.L. (2008). High resolution conodont-graptolite biostratigraphy in the Middle-Upper Ordovician of the Sierra de La Invernada Formation (Central Precordillera, Argentina). *Geologica Acta* **6** (2), 161-180.

Packham, G.H., Percival, I.G. and Bischoff, G.C.O. (1999). Age constraints on strata enclosing the Cadia and Junction Reefs ore deposits of central New South Wales, and tectonic implications. *Geological Survey of New South Wales, Quarterly Notes* **110**, 1-12.

Palmieri, V. (1978). Late Ordovician conodonts from the Fork Lagoons Beds, Emerald area, central Queensland. *Geological Survey of Queensland Publication 369, Palaeontological Paper* **43**, 1-55.

Pander, C.H. (1856). 'Monographie der fossilen Fische des Silurischen Systems der Russisch-Baltischen Gouvernements'. 91 pp. (Akademie der Wissenschaften: St. Petersburg).

Pei, F. and Cai, S.H. (1987). 'Ordovician conodonts from Henan Province'. 128 pp. (Press of the Wuhan College of Geosciences: Wuhan). (in Chinese).

Percival, I.G. (1976). The geology of the Licking Hole Creek area, near Walli, central-western New South

Wales. *Journal and Proceedings of the Royal Society of New South Wales* **109**, 7-23.

Percival, I.G. (1978). Inarticulate brachiopods from the Late Ordovician of New South Wales, and their palaeoecological significance. *Alcheringa* **2**, 117-141.

Percival, I.G. (1999). Late Ordovician biostratigraphy of the northern Rockley-Gulgong Volcanic Belt. *Geological Survey of New South Wales, Quarterly Notes* **108**, 1-7.

Percival, I.G., Kraft, P., Zhang, Y.D. and Sherwin, L. (2015). A long-overdue systematic revision of Ordovician graptolite faunas from New South Wales, Australia. The Ordovician Exposed: Short Papers and Abstracts for the 12th International Symposium on the Ordovician System, Harrisonburg, USA, June 2015. *Stratigraphy* **12** (2), 47-53.

Philip, G.M. (1966). The occurrence and palaeogeographic significance of Ordovician strata in northern New South Wales. *Australian Journal of Science* **29**, 112-113.

Pickett, J.W. (1978). Further evidence for the age of the Sofala Volcanics. *Geological Survey of New South Wales, Quarterly Notes* **31**, 1-4.

Pickett, J.W. and Ingpen, I.A. (1990). Ordovician and Silurian strata south of Trundle, New South Wales. *Geological Survey of New South Wales, Quarterly Notes* **78**, 1-14.

Pohler, S.M.L. (1994). Conodont biofacies of Lower to lower Middle Ordovician megaconglomerates, Cow Head Group, western Newfoundland. *Geological Survey of Canada, Bulletin* **459**, 1-71.

Pohler, S.M.L. and Orchard, M.J. (1990). Ordovician conodont biostratigraphy, western Canadian Cordillera. *Geological Survey of Canada Paper* **90-15**, 1-37.

Popov, L.E. (1977). Novye vidy sredneordovikskikh bezzamkovykh brachiopod krebta Chingiz (Vostochnyy Kazakhstan). *Novye vidy drevnikh rastenii i bespozvonochnykh SSSR* **4**, 102-105. (in Russian).

Popov, L.E. (2000). Late Ordovician linguliformean microbrachiopods from north-central Kazakhstan. *Alcheringa* **24**, 257-275.

Popov, L.E., Nõlvak, J. and Holmer, L.E. (1994). Late Ordovician lingulate brachiopods from Estonia. *Palaeontology* **37**, 627-650.

Pyle, L.J. and Barnes, C.R. (2001). Conodonts from the Kechika Formation and Road River Group (Lower to Upper Ordovician) of the Cassiar Terrane, northern British Columbia. *Canadian Journal of Earth Sciences* **38**, 1387-1401.

Rasmussen, J.A. (2001). Conodont biostratigraphy and taxonomy of the Ordovician shelf margin deposits in the Scandinavian Caledonides. *Fossils and Strata* **48**, 1-180.

Rasmussen, J.A. and Stouge, S. (1989). Middle Ordovician conodonts from allochthonous limestones at Høyberget, southeastern Norwegian Caledonides. *Norsk Geologisk Tidsskrift* **69**, 103-110.

130

Rhodes, F.H.T. (1955). The conodont fauna of the Keisley Limestone. *Quarterly Journal of the Geological Society of London* **11**, 117-142.

Rodríguez-Cañero, R., Martín-Algarra, A., Sarmiento, G.N. and Navas-Parejo, P. (2010). First Late Ordovician conodont fauna in the Beltic Cordillera (South Spain): a palaeobiogeographical contribution. *Terra Nova* **22**, 330-340.

Saltzman, M.R., Edwards, C.T., Leslie, S.A., Dwyer, G.S., Bauer, J.A., Repetski, J.E., Harris, A.G. and Bergström, S.M. (2014). Calibration of a conodont apatite-based Ordovician 87Sr/86Sr curve to biostratigraphy and geochronology: implications for stratigraphic resolution. *Geological Society of America Bulletin* **126** (11-12), 1551-1568.

Sansom, I.J. and Smith, M.P. (2005). Late Ordovician vertebrates from the Bighorn Mountains of Wyoming, USA. *Palaeontology* **48** (1), 31-48.

Sarmiento, G. (1990). Conodontos ordovícicos de Argentina. *Treballs del Museu de Geologia de Barcelona* **1**, 135-161.

Savage, N.M. (1990). Conodonts of Caradocian (Late Ordovician) age from the Cliefden Caves Limestone, southeastern Australia. *Journal of Paleontology* **64**, 821-831.

Savage, N.M. and Bassett, M.G. (1985). Caradoc-Ashgill conodont faunas from Wales and the Welsh Borderland. *Palaeontology* **28**, 679-713.

Schopf, T.J. (1966). Conodonts of the Trenton Group (Ordovician) in New York, southern Ontario, and Quebec. *New York State Museum and Science Service Bulletin* **405**, 1-105.

Serpagli, E. (1967). I conodonti dell'Ordoviciano Superiore (Ashgilliano) delle Alpi Carniche. *Bollettino della Società Paleontologica Italiana* **6**, 30-111.

Simpson, A. (1997). Late Ordovician conodonts from Gray Creek and the headwaters of Stockyard Creek, north Queensland. *Geological Society of Australia Abstracts*, Number **48**, 111.

Simpson, A. (2000). Late Ordovician conodonts from the "Carriers Well Formation", north-eastern Australia. *Geological Society of Australia Abstracts*, Number **61**, 177-178.

Stouge, S. and Rasmussen, J.A. (1996). Upper Ordovician conodonts from Bornholm and possible migration routes in the Palaeotethys Ocean. *Bulletin of the Geological Society of Denmark* **43**, 54-67.

Sweet, W.C. (1979). Late Ordovician conodonts and biostratigraphy of the western Midcontinent Province. *Brigham Young University Geology Studies* **26**, 45-86.

Sweet, W.C. (2000). Conodonts and biostratigraphy of Upper Ordovician strata along a shelf to basin transect in central Nevada. *Journal of Paleontology* **74**, 1148-1160.

Sweet, W.C. and Bergström, S.M. (1962). Conodonts from the Pratt Ferry Formation (Middle Ordovician) of Alabama. *Journal of Paleontology* **36**, 1214-1252.

Talent, J.A., Mawson, R. and Simpson, A. (2003). The "lost" Early Ordovician-Devonian Georgetown Carbonate Platform of northeastern Australia. *Courier Forschungsinstitut Senckenberg* **242**, 71-80.

Talent, J.A., Mawson, R., Simpson, A. and Brock, G.A. (2002). Palaeozoics of NE Queensland: Broken River Region: Ordovician-Carboniferous of the Townsville hinterland: Broken River and Camel Creek regions, Burdekin and Clarke River basins. International Palaeontological Congress Post-5, Field Excursion Guidebook. Special Publication No. 1, Macquarie University Centre for Ecostratigraphy and Palaeobiology. (Macquarie University: Sydney).

Teichert, C. and Glenister, B.F. (1952). Fossil nautiloid faunas from Australia. *Journal of Paleontology* **26**, 730-752.

Tolmacheva, T.Y. and Roberts, D. (2007). New data on Upper Ordovician conodonts from the Trondheim Region, Central Norwegian Caledonides. *Norges geologiske undersøkelse Bulletin* **447**, 5-15.

Tolmacheva, T.Y., Degtyarev, K.E., Ryazantsev, A.V. and Nikitina, O.I. (2009). Conodonts from the Upper Ordovician Siliceous Rocks of Central Kazakhstan. *Paleontological Journal* **43** (11), 1498-1512.

Trotter, J.A. and Webby, B.D. (1995). Upper Ordovician conodonts from the Malongulli Formation, Cliefden Caves area, central New South Wales. *AGSO Journal of Australian Geology and Geophysics* **15** (4), 475-499.

Uyeno, T.T. (1990). Biostratigraphy and conodont faunas of Upper Ordovician through Middle Devonian rocks, eastern Arctic Archipelago. *Geological Survey of Canada, Bulletin* **401**, 1-211.

Viira, V. (2008). Conodont biostratigraphy in the Middle–Upper Ordovician boundary beds of Estonia. *Estonian Journal of Earth Sciences* **57** (1), 23-38.

Walcott, C.D. (1889). Description of a new genus and species of inarticulate brachiopod from the Trenton Limestone. *Proceedings of the United States National Museum* (advance copy) **12**, 365-366.

Walcott, C.D. (1901). Cambrian Brachiopoda: *Obolella*, subgenus *Glyptias*; *Bicia*; *Obolus*, subgenus *Westonia*; with descriptions of new species. *Proceedings of the United States National Museum* **23**, 669-695.

Wang, C.Y. (ed.) (1993). 'Conodonts of the Lower Yangtze Valley - an index to biostratigraphy and organic metamorphic maturity'. 326 pp. (Science Press: Beijing). (in Chinese with English abstract).

Wang, Z.H. (2001). Ordovician conodonts from Kalpin of Xinjiang and Pingliang of Gansu across the base of Upper Ordovician Series. *Acta Micropalaeontologica Sinica* **18** (4), 349-363.

Wang, Z.H., Bergström, S.M. and Lane, H.R. (1996). Conodont provinces and biostratigraphy in Ordovician of China. *Acta Palaeontologica Sinica* **35** (1), 26-59.

Wang, Z.H. and Luo, K.Q. (1984). Late Cambrian and Ordovician conodonts from the marginal areas of the Ordos Platform, China. *Bulletin, Nanjing Institute of Geology and Palaeontology, Academia Sinica* **8**, 237-304. (in Chinese with English abstract).

Wang, Z.H. and Qi, Y.P. (2001). Ordovician conodonts from drillings in the Taklimakan desert, Xinjiang, NW China. *Acta Micropalaeontologica Sinica* **18** (2), 133-148. (in Chinese with English abstract).

Wang, Z.H., Qi, Y.P. and Wu, R.C. (2011). 'Cambrian and Ordovician conodonts in China', 388 pp. (China University of Science and Technology Press: Hefei). (in Chinese with English abstract).

Wang, Z.H. and Zhou, T.R. (1998). Ordovician conodonts from western and northeastern Tarim and their significance. *Acta Palaeontologica Sinica* **37** (2), 173-193.

Webby, B.D. (1992). Ordovician island biotas: New South Wales record and global implications. *Journal and Proceedings of the Royal Society of New South Wales* **125**, 51-77.

Webby, B.D., Cooper, R.A., Bergström, S.M. and Paris, F. (2004). Stratigraphic framework and time slices. In 'The Great Ordovician Biodiversification Event' (Eds B.D. Webby, F. Paris, M.L. Droser and I.G. Percival), pp. 41-47. (Columbia University Press: New York).

Willard, B. (1928). The brachiopods of the Ottosee and Holston formations of Tennessee and Virginia. *Bulletin of the Harvard Museum of Comparative Zoology* **68**, 255-292.

Williams, A., Brunton, C.H.C., Carlson, S.J. et al. (2000). 'Treatise on Invertebrate Paleontology, Part H, Brachiopoda (Revised) Volume 2: Linguliformea, Craniiformea, and Rhynchonelliformea (part)'. (The Geological Society of America: Boulder and The University of Kansas: Lawrence).

Withnall, I.W. and Lang, S.C. (eds) (1993). Geology of the Broken River Province, north Queensland. *Queensland Geology* **4**, 1-289.

Withnall, I.W., Blake, P.R., Crouch, S.B.S., Tenison Woods, K., Grimes, K.G., Hayward, M.A., Lam, J.S., Garrard, P. and Rees, I.D. (1995). Geology of the southern part of the Anakie Inlier, central Queensland. *Queensland Geology* **7**, 1-245.

Yu, F.L. and Wang, Z.H. (1986). Conodonts from Beiguoshan Formation in Long Xian, Shaanxi. *Acta Micropalaeontologica Sinica* **3** (1), 99-105. (in Chinese with English abstract).

Zeng, Q.L., Ni, S.Z., Xu, G.H., Zhou, T.M., Wang, X.F., Li, Z.H., Lai, C.G. and Xiang, L.W. (1983). Subdivision and correlation on the Ordovician in the eastern Yangtze Gorges, China. *Bulletin of the Yichang Institute of Geology and Mineral Resources, Chinese Academy of Geological Sciences* **6**, 1-68.

Zhang, J.H. (1998). Conodonts from the Guniutan Formation (Llanvirnian) in Hubei and Hunan Provinces, south-central China. *Stockholm Contributions in Geology* **46**, 1-161.

Zhang, J.H., Barnes, C.R. and Cooper, B.J. (2004). Early Late Ordovician conodonts from the Stokes Siltstone, Amadeus Basin, central Australia. *Courier Forschungsinstitut Senckenberg* **245**, 1-37.

Zhang, J.H. and Chen, M.J. (1992). Evolutionary trends and stratigraphic significance of *Periodon. Acta Micropalaeontologica Sinica* **9** (4), 391-396. (in Chinese with English abstract).

Zhang, S.X. (2011). Late Ordovician conodont biostratigraphy and redefinition of the age of oil shale intervals on Southampton Island. *Canadian Journal of Earth Sciences* **48** (3), 619-643.

Zhang, S.X. (2013). Ordovician conodont biostratigraphy and redefinition of the age of lithostratigraphic units on northeastern Melville Peninsula, Nunavut. *Canadian Journal of Earth Sciences* **50**, 808-825.

Zhang, S.X. and Barnes, C.R. (2007a). Late Ordovician to Early Silurian conodont faunas from the Kolyma Terrane, Omulev Mountains, northeast Russia, and their paleobiogeographic affinity. *Journal of Paleontology* **81**, 490-512.

Zhang, S.X. and Barnes, C.R. (2007b). Late Ordovician–Early Silurian conodont biostratigraphy and thermal maturity, Hudson Bay Basin. *Bulletin of Canadian Petroleum Geology* **55** (3), 179-216.

Zhang, S.X. and Pell, J. (2013). Study of sedimentary rock xenoliths from kimberlites on Hall Peninsula, Baffin Island, Nunavut. In Summary of Activities 2012, Canada-Nunavut Geoscience Office, pp. 107-112.

Zhang, S.X., Tarrant, G.A. and Barnes, C.R. (2011). Upper Ordovician conodont biostratigraphy and the age of the Collingwood Member, southern Ontario, Canada. *Canadian Journal of Earth Sciences* **48**, 1497-1522.

Zhao, Z.X., Zhang, G.Z. and Xiao, J.N. (2000). 'Paleozoic stratigraphy and conodonts in Xinjiang'. 340 pp. (Petroleum Industry Press: Beijing). (in Chinese with English abstract).

Zhen, Y.Y. (2001). Distribution of the Late Ordovician conodont genus *Taoqupognathus* in eastern Australia and China. *Acta Palaeontologica Sinica* **40** (3), 351-361.

Zhen, Y.Y. and Percival, I.G. (2004). Darriwilian (Middle Ordovician) conodonts from the Weemalla Formation, south of Orange, New South Wales. *Memoir of the Association of Australasian Palaeontologists* **30**, 153-178.

Zhen, Y.Y., Percival, I.G. and Farrell, J.R. (2003). Late Ordovician allochthonous limestones in Late Silurian Barnby Hills Shale, central western New South Wales. *Proceedings of the Linnean Society of New South Wales* **124**, 29-51.

Zhen, Y.Y., Percival, I.G. and Webby, B.D. (2004). Conodont faunas from the Mid to Late Ordovician boundary interval of the Wahringa Limestone Member (Fairbridge Volcanics), central New South Wales. *Proceedings of the Linnean Society of New South Wales* **125**, 141-164.

Zhen, Y.Y., Wang, Z.H., Zhang, Y.D., Bergström, S.M., Percival, I.G. and Cheng, J.F. (2011). Middle to Late Ordovician (Darriwilian-Sandbian) conodonts from the Dawangou section, Kalpin area of the Tarim

132

Proc. Linn. Soc. N.S.W., 137, 2015

Basin, northwestern China. *Records of the Australian Museum* **63**, 203-266.

Zhen, Y.Y. and Webby, B.D. (1995). Upper Ordovician conodonts from the Cliefden Caves Limestone Group, central New South Wales, Australia. *Courier Forschungsinstitut Senckenberg* **182**, 265-305.

Zhen, Y.Y., Webby, B.D. and Barnes, C.R. (1999). Upper Ordovician conodonts from the Bowan Park succession, central New South Wales, Australia. *Geobios* **32**, 73-104.

Zhen, Y.Y., Zhang, Y.D. and Percival, I.G. (2009). Early Sandbian (Late Ordovician) conodonts from the Yenwashan Formation, western Zhejiang, South China. *Alcheringa* **33** (2), 133-161.

Zhen, Y.Y., Zhang, Y.D., Wang, Z.H. and Percival, I.G. (2015). Huaiyuan Epeirogeny – shaping Ordovician stratigraphy and sedimentation on the North China Platform. *Palaeogeography, Palaeoclimatology, Palaeoecology.* http://dx.doi.org/10.1016/ j.palaeo.2015.07.040

Ziegler, W. (ed.) (1981). 'Catalogue of Conodonts, Vol. 4'. 445 pp. (Schweizerbart'sche Verlagsbuchhandlung: Stuttgart).

Proc. Linn. Soc. N.S.W., 137, 2015

133